# COTTER
By

**Peter Glassman**

ISBN-13: 978-1-946229-99-1

This is a novel about a doctor who never existed. The spirit and folklore of such people are indeed real.
–Peter Glassman MD

For Jacob "Jake" Pelletier

# Chapter 1

## July 1868

Cotter always wore the same clothes when confronting his opponents. He wore tan buckskin from head-to-toe. The sweatband on his hat had a single polished silver concho off center to the right but clearly sparkling to the person facing him. His buckskin blouse had bib buttons forming an upside down "L". The buttons on the down stroke of the L on the right side of his chest were also highly polished silver conchos. The horizontal buttons were tan buckskin and almost invisible. His two Colt revolvers were the same models but his right gun was highly polished nickel. It glinted like the hat's concho. His left hand gun had an unobtrusive matte gun-metal finish. Cotter's tan buckskin pants had a row of polished conchos on the outer right leg seam only. His tan buckskin boots gave him almost silent under-footing. He had his photograph taken to help get the outfit just right. To anyone confronting Cotter, the man was off center. The bib buttons and the shiny silver conchos directed an opponent's vision to the right. When Cotter drew his guns he moved slightly to the left. Even if his adversary was faster than he, the bullet usually missed and went off to the right. Usually, on two occasions he was shot superficially, once in the in the right shoulder and once in the right thigh. Every man who drew on him had died.

Cotter adjusted his hat and checked for the weight and balance of his two-gun holster. He went into the saloon.

"Morely." Cotter spoke the name with a penetrating tone. He didn't shout. He didn't have to. Cotter's baritone voice caromed around the saloon and could be heard above the voices at the bar and over the dialogue from the two card game tables. Cotter's back was to the swinging saloon doors and the dirt street.

The suddenness of the silence was a shock to the Saturday night crowd. Within a second of the lack of noise all eyes turned toward Cotter and then focused on Morely.

"Yes, you Morely." Cotter stood with hands on his waist. He reached into his bib top and removed a large sheet of paper and waved it at Morely and the general audience. "I'm taking you to the sheriff's office–'dead or alive'–just like this poster says." Cotter was 6-foot-5-inches of fine-tuned muscle. His two-gun holster rig was three-inches below his beltline. Both buckskin-gloved hands went to his sides after he slid the poster back into his bib shirt.

"I don't know you. Go away and you'll go alive. The last three bounty hunters are under the dirt." Morely pushed his slight beer-bellied form away from the bar to face Cotter. The rest of the men at the bar ran away from the rail, abandoning their positions and drinks. Some ran out the door past Cotter and others took cover behind furniture.

Morely wore one gun. His .44 was tied down two-inches above his right knee. He stroked his scruffy beard and scratched at his left ear. The gunman and murderer was almost as tall as Cotter. Morely's black shirt had a mottled appearance–a result of stains from food and beer. According to the wanted-poster, Morely had killed five men. They were prominent ranchers spread throughout Arizona. The men were anonymous to Morely but he got paid a thousand-dollars for eliminating each one. Cotter had tracked him to the developing town of Cormel by checking with each sheriff from the townships of Morely's victims. They all told the same story. Morely waited for each victim to come to town and provoked a confrontation. Sometimes it was a fraudulent accusation at card-cheating and other times it was outright insulting the person or a member of the person's family. One thing the sheriffs' stories held constant was the style of the showdown. Morely gave the victims to a count of three to draw and then shot them at the count of two.

"'Dead or alive' Morely." The wooden grips of Cotter's guns were black ebony with the bright shiny metal frame of the right .45 reflecting the light from the double chandeliers. Each chandelier held twenty oil lanterns. The hammer and the frame sparkled in the weapon's black leather holster next to his right hand. Cotter opened and closed the fingers of his gloved right hand but did nothing with his left.

"Herman." Morely motioned with his gun hand to the bartender. "Count to three when I tell you. And you, whatever your name is, you have one last chance. Get out of here and never come back or draw your gun and take me on the count of three."

Cotters kept his gaze on Morely's eyes and stood tall and clean in his tan buckskin shirt and pants. He moved slightly to his left to accentuate the reflection of the right side of his glinting conchos. His face was clean-shaven and his appearance was as neat as Morely's was unkempt. "Herman, Morely's asking you to count to three."

The bartender named Herman was trying to maintain his cool by wiping some whiskey glasses. His hands were shaking. He looked from Cotter to Morely.

"Start counting Herman." Morely moved his right hand in an arc from his belt buckle to the side of his .44.

"One." Herman looked from man-to-man.

Morely looked like he was developing a tick in his right eye. His right eyelid twitched twice.

"Two."

The simultaneous explosion from the discharges of one .44 and two .45 caliber rounds made everyone's ears pop and then ring with a high pitched ping. The shock wave brought about a cloud of dust from the saloon's rafters to merge with the smoke from the firing pistols.

Morely stared at Cotter with a look of surprise and shock. The bounty hunter had fired on the count of two just as he did. Morely was thrown back three-feet by the two .45 rounds entering his breastbone. Morely's pistol cleared the holster but didn't reach an aim point. His .44 bullet blew apart a segment from a center pole that extended from floor-to-ceiling to Cotter's right. Fortunately it was only one of eight such supporting structures.

"Five dollars goes to the man who drapes Morely's body over his horse for me." Cotter holstered his guns.

●

"Come in." Sheriff Hanscom Gates sat at his pine log-crafted desk. The assertive three knocks pulled his attention away from a just delivered telegram. The office was only 8-by-12 feet and consisted of two sections partitioned by three-foot-high pine railings. Gates sat to the right. The deputy, who was absent, sat in an identical space to the left.

Cotter entered removing his tan gloves. He reached into his bib top and handed the poster to Gates.

"Morely? You gonna take in Morely? He'll kill you first. He's an outright killer." Gates had a smile on his face.

"Why haven't you collected on this?" Cotter's baritone was friendly but critical.

"He hasn't done anything wrong in Cormel."

"The wanted poster applies to anywhere in Arizona." Cotter would take this track no further. "But I have him draped over his horse outside. You can identify him and telegraph the statute office. They'll wire the five-thousand dollars to my bank in Connecticut. When it's confirmed, I'll leave."

Gates got up and went outside. He came back within a minute. "That's Morely for sure–I can live easier now. Thanks. I'll need identification of who you are."

"Here are my identification papers." Cotter handed Gates a military card and a banker's affidavit attesting to its bearer.

"Have a seat." Gates reviewed the credentials.

"Jake Cotter. I heard a you. Thought you was in Texas." Gates wrote something on the back of the Morely wanted poster and began writing on a telegraph request card. "In my younger days, I woulda got Morely. Criminal like him, I woulda just gone up to him and shot him."

"I was in Texas. Now I'm here and when I get the money I'm going back to Connecticut." Cotter ignored the Sheriff's excuse.

"What's in Connecticut?" Gates rubbed his arthritic right shoulder.

"My family–what's left of them–and school." Cotter stood up and motioned with the signed documents to send the telegraph.

"School? Ain't you kinda old for school?" He walked beside Cotter onto the dusty street.

"I was in school before the war got me and my father. He was killed at Nashville." Cotter didn't want to talk about war or the aging process. He felt ten-years older than twenty-five.

"The war's been over for three years. Why you goin' back now?"

"When my dad died my brother and sister grabbed the family estate and left me out. I needed my own money. With Morely's bounty and what I've accumulated, I can go back to school now."

"Yeah? What school did you say?"

"Medical School–Yale Medical School."

# NEW HAVEN, CON-NECTICUT

# 1868

## TO

# 1870

# CHAPTER 2

## Yale–1868

Train connections were slow but tolerable. In Chicago, Cotter watched as they led his horse from the stable car of the Ohio train which he had picked up in Kansas. The conductor gave instructions to the horse handler to proceed to the Chicago-Erie train for the change. Cotter re-affirmed his ticket for himself and the horse. The horse tender began talking to two men as he led Cotter's horse across the train yard. The two men looked at Cotter's palomino and made some gestures which looked like bartering. Cotter moved fast.

"What's going on here with this horse?" Cotter asked the train horse-tender. He stared at the other two. They were dressed liked cattle drovers.

"Now wait a minute, we saw him first. I offered a firm 50 dollars, he took the money and the horse is mine fare-and-square."

"Do you have a bill of sale for this horse like I do?"

The train horse handler looked uneasy. He gave the reins to the cowhand and started to leave.

"Where do you think you're going?" Cotter grabbed the train man by his back shirt collar. Cotter's travel clothes were heavy black cotton. His black hat was held by a chin cord to counter the evening wind.

"Okay man, back-off. The horse is mine." The man held the reins tight and he and his friend glared threateningly at Cotter.

"I don't think so. Here's one of my 'Bills-of-Sale'." Cotter took the papers from the left coat pocket of his knee-length gray travel duster.

"Well this don't cut nothin' with me. Readin' ain't my strong point and I got a witness to my payment."

"Here's my other Bill-of-Sale." Cotter's gun appeared like magic. For travel he wore only one .45. It was the polished nickel-framed weapon. Cotter held the gun on the duo and released tension on the train horse handler's shirt. "Give the man back his money and take my horse to the Erie train." He extended his gun hand toward the man holding the reins. "And you, take the money and give him the reins." Cotter rested the barrel of his .45 on the man's forehead. With the transaction completed Cotter motioned the duo to leave. "Get out of here. I just saved your asses from being branded horse thieves. Consider yourselves lucky." They left at a quick pace.

The Erie train got him connected to his Hartford destination. After he changed clothes, Cotter bought a sturdy canopied combination buggy-wagon and acceptable age horse for the trip to New Haven. He tied his palomino to the rear and loaded his three bags onto the four-by-five-foot wagon bed. He had a two-hour ride left to the residence hall at Yale.

●

Cotter left his palomino at the livery around the side of the Yale Medical School administration building. It was hot and sunny–typical August. He straightened out his five-button charcoal suit coat, removed his spurs, and walked up the inclined limestone stairs on either side of the large carriage stones. It was measurably cooler inside. Ambient light from the tops of windows was adequate and no lamps were lit for illumination. The foyer of the administration building was spacious with a domed ceiling. Oil portraits of past deans and noted staff physicians were placed at three-foot intervals on the inner walls of the circular foyer. Cotter went to the desk marked 'Reception' and looked down at the woman writing on an unlined notebook. He cleared his throat.

"Jacob Cotter to see Dr. Wainright Randall."

"Just a minute. Let me use my blotter." The 43-year-old woman looked up at him and then looked back at a small ledger-style book. "Yes,. My, you're right on time. Let me check if Dr. Randall is ready to receive you, sir."

Cotter looked around the reception area. There was one comfortable stuffed chair opposite a wooden pew-style bench. The lighting was dim but Cotter saw the portrait of his father to the right of the door marked, Dean of Admissions. He walked up to the portrait and read the brass engraved plate at the center-bottom of the frame. "Edward Cotter MD. Chief Physician and Surgeon. Yale Medical School 1859-1863."

Cotter was aware of the receptionist brushing by him.

"You can go right in, sir."

Cotter didn't look in her direction but moved directly forward, opened the door and walked in.

"Welcome back Jacob." The thickset man behind the desk stood up with his opening remarks and went to greet Cotter.

"Dr. Randall, I've dreamed of this day when we would meet again."

They shook hands vigorously. Randall beckoned him to sit in front of his desk on a brocade parlor chair. The dean had long white mutton-chop sideburns but was otherwise clean shaven. He sat back and folded his hands across the middle of his vested, dark brown suit. His right thumb got caught in his watch chain and he unconsciously readjusted it.

"And I also, although my vision of this meeting was to be with both you and your father. Let me extend my condolences–a few years late to you. I did attend the funeral on behalf of myself and the medical staff."

"Thank you, sir."

"I knew you couldn't break away from the war to come back with his body."

"Dr. Randall, the battle casualties were always overwhelming. Dad and I talked about what we should do in the event one of us was killed. We agreed if we left our duty station for even a week, over a hundred Union soldiers would die from their wounds. They needed surgeons night-and-day Dr. Randall."

"And I understand you worked with Edward side-by-side?"

"Every day until he was killed."

"Jacob, I had the admissions re-instate your status as having three more years left to complete to get your degree, but let me be honest." Randall sat forward and folded his hands on top of his broad dark mahogany desk. "You were at the top of your class and I understand–we all do–why you and Edward heeded President Lincoln's call for physicians. If your performance indicates the two-years spent as an assistant surgeon to your father demonstrates an advanced competence, I will personally advocate those two years to be years spent as training. You could get your diploma in two rather than three years." He sat back for Cotter to ponder his remarks.

Cotter paused only for a few seconds. The aroma of wood oil polish applied to the bulky furniture and looking at the two walls lined with medical texts brought him immediately back to the world of medical academia. "I would gratefully accept such a situation, sir. But only if I truly deserve it."

"We shall see. I have high expectations. Jacob the term will be starting in three-weeks. Do you need help settling in? I understand you've already taken temporary residence in the dormitory?"

"Yes, sir, but I would like to have my own place. I'm looking for an unworked farm, a full-time hand and a part time house maid."

"That's no problem. My secretary can offer you a list to choose from."

Randall shuffled in his chair, obviously uncomfortable at his next question. "You will be seeing your family soon? They're quite anxious about your returning to Connecticut and to New Haven in particular."

"Yes, I'll bet they are but not for domestic affection. You know when dad died they had me disinherited?"

"Yes. I never understood that." Randall sat back and waited for Cotter to elaborate.

"In his will dad signed over his estate to my brother and sister to manage and to legally adjust the inheritance should he die in the war. Unfortunately, he used the word 'family members' and didn't mention my name. Mathew and Nancy defined the family to be just the two of them after his death."

"Are you well with finances? I was told payment for your three years of school is already banked in annual trust by yourself to Yale."

"Yes. I only re-applied to school when I become solvent. I don't need any supplemental income for the next ten-years."

"I see. What is it you did for a living during 1865 to now, Jacob?"

"I assisted law-enforcement officers in apprehending killers and thieves."

"And nothing to do with Medical care?"

"I tended to the wounds of many people along the way."

"One last thing Jacob. We here at admissions were also motivated for your readmission by one of your former classmates who needs help in his practice and has asked for you in particular."

"You must mean Charlie–Doctor–Garrison."

"Yes, Charles Garrison. You two were inseparable in medical school. I was surprised he didn't go with you to the war."

"Charlie needed to finish his training–he was needed in his hometown. There was only one Doctor for a hundred-miles. As for the war itself, Charles was from Texas and his sympathies were for the North rather than the Texas alliance with the Confederacy. It would have been a difficult choice for him."

"Have you two talked recently?"

"Only by letter, sir. It's my intention to set up practice with Charlie–Dr. Garrison–after I finish at Yale."

"That's admirable Jacob. I'm sure that your father would agree. Well, we'll help get your domestic requirements met. In three-weeks, it's back to the books and the midnight oil with you. One more note, Jacob–your new classmates will notice you're a few years older than they are. They may ask questions about what you did after the war. Can you handle that? Yale medical students can be snobby about class affiliations and background."

"I'm sure I can handle any such situation, sir."

"I am always here if you need me." The Dean rose and extended his hand. "Once again, welcome back Jacob Cotter."

"I'm glad I was able to come back Dr. Randall."

Cotter left the office with Randall who spoke with the receptionist about Cotter's request for a dwelling and local labor. He left Cotter with her looking up several folders and writing rapidly on her notepad.

"The man on the top of the list is from the war, Mr. Cotter. He has some disability but is very good with his hands."

"And the house maid?" He leaned over t take the first piece of paper.

"She's trustworthy and a good housewife. She can use the money and will do a good job."

"And the isolated farmhouses?"

"How far away do you want to be, Mr. Cotter?"

"No more than a 30-minute ride."

She wrote rapidly again. "Here you are. These should be suitable for the kind of domicile you want also."

●

Cotter thanked her. He retrieved his palomino and left the buckboard at the livery. He rode slowly from the Yale section of New Haven looking at the list of farmhouses. Each one was a former winery. There were three within a 30-minute commute by the slower wagon. Riding his palomino at a medium gallop, he could shave 10-minutes if the road was in good shape. Two of the unoccupied sites had only been abandoned for less than a year and were far apart from any nearby estates or dwellings. He wanted privacy. Cotter selected the first of the two at random and after ten-minutes on the rutted and rocky road decided against further pursuit. He turned back and took the westerly road.

This road was better maintained and he could push his horse to fast spurts. He reached the farmhouse in 18-minutes by his watch. He looked from his saddled position at the front entrance. It had two doors padlocked together by a chain. The main structure was a two-story colonial house with an extended ranch section. One-half of the building supported a second floor. He moved his horse slowly around the right side and to the back. The top floor looked like it contained two large rooms—one front and one back. The single back door was large with a multi-fenestrated windowed top section but was one piece. He dismounted and tried the door knob. It was locked. Cotter walked his horse completely around the house and then noticed the large barn a good 200-yards to left of the main house. It was surrounded by leafy elms and was not locked. That was good and typical of allowing for the safety of the contained horses for fast egress should an emergency—like a fire—develop. He looked at the two other elongated barn-style buildings. They were remnants of the once active vineyard and then he looked at a small lane leading into the adjacent wooded acreage of the property.

There was a path wide enough for three horses to walk abreast. He mounted the palomino and rode for ten more minutes. According to the plot map, this farm encompassed a 100-acres. He stopped after seeing a spot for his projected purpose. It was far enough from any dwelling to contain any noise. The clearing was about 40 yards wide and 100 yards long and ended in a rise of treeless land the same width. The older trees on the sides of the clearing were dense evergreens. *Perfect.* The space would provide cover year-round. He turned back. He had found his residence for the next two-or-three-years.

Cotter looked at his list of potential caretakers for the house. There were five names. The statistics he had requested were hand printed by the Dean's secretary. He hadn't asked for her name but she signed the list as Mrs. Ruth Roth. The men who were over age 45, he excluded. Three remained for consideration. Like the others from the list, they were unmarried. Two were former domestics. Cotter did not want valets or servants. He really only had the one candidate to consider. He stared at the information written on the square card:

Name: John LaRoque
Age: 31

Unmarried
Height: 6 Foot
Weight: 183 pounds
Past Occupations:
- Blacksmith assistant
- Land clearing
- New Haven Infantry
Address: Coastal Livery, New Haven
Owns horse and saddle

Written in long hand, presumably by Mrs. Roth, was, "Infirmed with Army leg wound." Cotter had asked for the list of occupations to begin with the most recent. He considered John LaRoque's prior jobs. All three were physically taxing. Blacksmithing and land clearing required stamina and muscle. Apparently the leg wound had not restricted Mr. LaRoque. He would ask Mrs. Roth to arrange an interview at the medical school student lounge or the library for tomorrow at noon.

Cotter looked at the second set of cards but like the first set found only one person who conformed to his image of a non-live-in housekeeper. He looked at the documents provided to him from a research lawyer he had hired two-months ago and looked back at the card from Mrs. Roth. He noticed one of her recent positions included housekeeping at the Locke estate three-days-a-week. *Yes, this person will indeed be an asset.*

Name: Mrs. Gertrin Hamer
Age: 40
Married: 3 Children
Height: 5 Foot
Weight: 120 pounds
Past Occupations:
- Lancer Hotel, New Haven
- Ames Hearth Inn and Restaurant, New Haven
- New Haven Women's College, Food and Dormitory Service

Mrs. Roth had written–"no infirmaries and has own transportation".

•

Cotter walked directly to Mrs. Roth.

"Oh. Good morning again. Mr. Cotter." She looked at the packet of cards in his hand. "I see you have already looked through the possibilities." Roth had an assertive alto voice.

"Yes. I would like to interview Mrs. Hamer and Mr. LaRoque. Is there a place I could use?"

"Most certainly, Mr. Cotter, you can use one of the study rooms in the medical library building."

"Is it possible to see both of them today?" Cotter wore the same trim suit of the day before, carrying his duster in his right arm. His pleasant demeanor and clean crisp appearance evoked a smile with Roth's response.

"I'll send our page out right away. He'll set up the appointments. Mrs. Hamer is working at a house down the street but she's due to be through her duties by two this afternoon. Mr. LaRoque is more flexible. He can be summoned from the livery at any time."

"Thank you. I can see Mr. LaRoque in an hour and two o'clock will be fine for Mrs. Hamer." Cotter turned to leave and began putting on his duster.

"Oh, dear, Mr. Cotter you're wearing a gun." Roth placed both palms on her desk blotter. Her look was stern and not fearful.

"Yes. Is there a problem?"

"Yale does not allow firearms on campus. The image of our Doctors and Doctors-to-be, as you may remember, is one of healing and propriety. If you must adorn such a weapon please do so when you are off the medical school and clinic domain."

Cotter looked at his right-holstered shiny pistol and then back at Roth. He smiled, "Mrs. Roth I thank you for saving me embarrassment with the staff and my fellow students. I shall heed your suggestion." He reached under his duster and untied the holster from his right leg. He unbuckled the belt and hostler rig and rolled it up to carry out the front door.

Mrs. Ruth Roth watched him go out the main entrance. She intuitively liked Jacob Cotter.

●

Cotter's nightly dream of his father started as usual.

"We're learning a lot about surgery and medicine in this war, Jacob. We'll pass on our skills when we return to Yale." Dr. Cotter took off his blood-stained operating gown.

"I hope the war ends soon father." Jacob washed up and put on a clean gown.

"The killing and maiming is man's folly. Are you still planning to join Charles Garrison in Texas after you finish your MD degree?"

"Of course."

"Good. The quality of medicine in our developing states and their towns is years behind the times." The elder Cotter donned a new white gown. "Let's get back to work."

A fog-like mist clouded the scene and now a roar of coalesced gunfire punctuated with cannon booms emerged. Cotter could smell the cordite. Several Confederate horsemen mustered the surgical teams outside their operating tents.

"Which ones are the doctors?" A gruff voiced mounted soldier waved his pistol in the air.

The three surgeons moved forward identifying themselves.

"Okay. Shoot them. You kill one of them, you kill a hundred Yankees." The man shot the doctor to the right of Cotter's father and then fired two shots into Dr. Cotter's chest. Cotter ran to his father as the man took aim at him, too.

"No time left for the others. We have to move." The other Confederate assassin motioned the mounted rebels away.

"Father, father. Oh God no." Cotter shouted in his sleep and woke up with a pounding heart.

Cotter looked around his room. It was the dream again. It occurred whenever thoughts of his father were near. Dr. Randall's recollections must have triggered it. He fell back on his sweat-soaked pillow.

# CHAPTER 3

## Gertrin and John

John LaRoque looked at the acne-faced teenager over his red-coaled furnace. He had placed two horseshoes in the glowing embers. The temperature next to the stoking furnace produced such a drenching sweat, he had to stop work every 15-minutes to wipe his face and drink almost a quart of water. He bit into some hardtack to replenish his salt loss. He had learned that in the Army. Dehydration led to confusion and poor judgement.

"At the medical school library, you say?" He put down the small sledge hammer.

"On the next hour." The boy's eye's bulged with admiration and envy as he saw the blacksmith's muscular arms.

"His name is Jacob Cotter, you say?"

"Yes. I must go now." The boy ran out of the open livery stable to the hot August sun feeling relief from the furnace temperature next to the smithy.

LaRoque went over to the horse trough at the entrance to the barn-like livery and blacksmith building. He poured a bucket of water over the right side of his leg. His leg often ached and throbbed because of high temperatures from the forge. Relief was immediate. He massaged his right upper thigh and spoke aloud, "What rotten luck, two-weeks left in the war and I get a minié ball to my leg." It was a recurring thought triggered by the pain. He had bled profusely right after getting shot. Only the quick application of a rope as a tourniquet saved his life. Setting fire to some gunpowder put into the wound finally stopped the bleeding. The wound never seemed to heal. The skin would close over the thumbnail-size opening and then gradually bulge out and ooze brown foul pus. He still walked with a limp and sometimes had to use a cane. He hadn't needed a crutch for over a year now.

The job as blacksmith and livery hand was a godsend. He could not and would not relegate himself to beggar status like so many Civil War returnees. New Haven seemed to have half-a-dozen soldiers missing an arm or a leg begging outside the banks or stores. *Not me, I'm not dead. I just have a bum leg.* No one called John LaRoque "cripple"–to his face anyway. However, he was fearful about what happened to his leg when the temperature soared to high extremes, especially when he was working the anvil. He didn't want to lose his leg. If he had to get another job, who would hire him? This man Cotter, who needed someone to run his estate, might be the opportunity he needed to get away from the hellish temperatures which irritated his leg. He looked out toward the clock tower on the Town Hall building–ten-minutes-to ten. He didn't want to be late. He wiped down his wet pant leg, strapped on his pistol and mounted his horse. He tied his horse to an unoccupied hitch in the alley hitching post area of the main classroom building and walked with a slight limp up the stairs.

"Could you please direct me to the medical school library, please?" LaRoque grabbed the sleeve of a passing student.

The student looked with horror as the sweat-stained large man scrunched his suit coat sleeve. He pointed with his opposite hand to a sign indicating the library's direction.

LaRoque entered the library and approached a gray-haired lady removing books from a recently arrived shipment. She looked up when she smelled his acrid odor.

"Oh dear, are you looking for the clinic?"

"No ma'am, I'm looking for a man named Jacob Cotter."

"Yes. He's here." She pointed to a door marked Study Carrel–3. "No guns can be worn on the Yale campus, sir." Her words waned to inaudibility as LaRoque entered the room ignoring her last statement.

Cotter looked up from LaRoque's card. "You're Mr. John LaRoque?"

"Yes. You are Mr. Cotter, I take it. You have a job offer?"

"Yes. I'm looking for a strong, intelligent man who can manage this estate." Cotter moved the plans to the farmhouse and its large acreage so that LaRoque could read it.

"Eight rooms in the house, three outbuildings and a serviceable barn," LaRoque looked up from the plans on the property. "Over a hundred acres of land–I'm no farmer, Mr. Cotter. I know nothing of the wine business."

"Good. You can read house plans and a real-estate map. I don't want a farmer, Mr. LaRoque." Cotter looked at the way LaRoque was favoring his right leg.

"How did you get shot?"

"Last skirmish in southern North Carolina in '65–two-weeks before the war ended." He slapped his right thigh.

"Sit down, please."

"I'd rather stand."

"Can you still use that gun?" Cotter pointed with the pencil he was using to take notes from a recent surgical text.

"Right now, I use it for visual effects only. People don't take pity on a cripple wearing a gun."

"A cripple is someone who cannot walk, cannot feed himself and needs nursing every day. You are not a cripple Mr. LaRoque." Cotter smiled. "And you're right about the pistol. It prevents derogatory words."

"What kind of work do you offer?" He shifted his weight more to the left side.

"I need someone to get the farmhouse and barn into good repair. Some of the land needs clearing. I also need someone who can keep his mouth shut."

"What do you do to need someone like that?"

"I'm finishing medical school. I need to complete my schooling over the next two-years. I can't tend to many of the daily activities of maintaining a house and I don't wish to live in a hotel or dormitory. I also have plans that need to be kept from certain ears."

"How much does it pay?"

"What do you make now?"

"Ten dollars a month and livery for my horse."

"I'll give your 20 a month plus room and board for you and your horse."

"For how long?"

"At least until I get my MD degree."

"And then?"

"If I stay in New Haven and you work out, the job will still be there."

"When would I start?"

"You start as soon as you get some new clothes, take a bath and shave." Cotter pushed a ten-dollar piece to LaRoque. "Clothes are part of the room and board."

"I could be there tomorrow."

"Excellent. By the way, are you good with that pistol?"

"I stayed alive for five-years in the war. Why?"

"You'll soon find out."

●

"Yes, at 2:00 this afternoon, Mrs. Hamer—in the medical school library." The page gave her the message from Cotter.

"Tell Mr. Cotter I'll be there." Gertrin Hamer watched the teenager leave the lawyer's 12-room house. From the description from Mrs. Roth, the farmstead was only 15-or-so minutes from her home outside of New Haven. It was only for two-or-three-days a week and the house was smaller than the others she usually did housekeeping for. "Certainly we need the money," she rationalized as she re-read the note from Mrs. Roth. She wondered why there was no Mrs. Cotter. His father was the famous Doctor that got killed in the war. Meeting in the library sounded safe enough.

Mrs. Hamer checked herself for appearance before she knocked on the library study room marked "3". Her long beige dress with the dark blue pinstripes was conservative but not totally matronly. The hem was above her ankles showing part of her high-button shoes. She had used the scuffing brush at the library entrance. The street grime flaked off easily. Her black hair reached her shoulders in a tidy fall and was without noticeable gray streaks. A few wrinkles at the corners of her eyes were the only outward taints of reaching age 40. Taking care of her three children, her husband and her own house kept her trim and strong. She knocked three solid raps.

"Please enter."

Hamer moved to center herself in front of Cotter's desk.

"Please sit down Mrs. Hamer. I'm Jacob Cotter." After a brief handshake Cotter picked up the card with her background information. "Mrs. Hamer, Mrs. Roth has already conveyed to you about my need for a housekeeper three-days-a-week, correct?"

"Yes, sir." She sat tall and straight and looked into Cotter's dark brown eyes.

"Let me clarify my needs. I'm about to purchase the old Clark farm north of New Haven. Do you know it?"

"Yes, I do. I mean I have seen it."

"It's been vacant for over one year. It will need to be cleaned first off and I have a man who will make the wells functional and the sanitation workable again." Cotter paused. "His name is John LaRoque, the blacksmith at the livery near the Yale Medical Clinic. Do you know of him?"

"My housekeeping assignments are on the estate section of New Haven, Mr. Cotter. I do not frequent the areas close to the medical school. I'm afraid I'm unfamiliar with…Mr. LaRoque, you say?"

"Mr. LaRoque, yes. Well… it's no matter. He's capable of doing the heavy work around the house and the grounds. He'll also provide your transportation to-and-from my house."

"What? But I have my own transportation. I mean my husband and I have a reliable horse and buggy." Hamer began to stand up.

"Please Mrs. Hamer. You will be safer and it will be more convenient for both of us."

She sat down again. "What days of the week will you need my services? I mean if the job is suitable after I look the place over."

"Any three days of your choosing during the week except Wednesdays."

Hamer was silent and then thought out loud. She pressed the fingers of her right hand with her left with each comment. "Let's see, one of my assignments favors one weekend day and one demands Mondays only. I could move my third housekeeping to Wednesday." She looked up at Cotter. "Yes, I am able to alter my schedule to perform the required domestic chores on Tuesday, Thursday and Friday."

"That will be acceptable to my schedule, Mrs. Hamer. I'll be closing the sale on the property in two-or-three-days. Shall we say on Friday you can be available for inspecting the facility and the grounds with me and Mr. LaRoque?"

"Inspecting, yes, that's good. If conditions are satisfactory then Friday we can reach a decision." She stood up.

"I have a few personal questions, Mrs. Hamer, if I may."

"It depends on how personal."

"They're about your family."

"What about my family?" She began clutching and twisting her gloves.

"Your husband, Mr. Hamer, and your three children, do they not require much of your time? Will you be able to work as much at home with the addition of my three required days?"

"Well, it will cause some stress. My husband you see is a clerk at Holcomb's General Mercantile. He works long hours for not much money. My oldest daughter helps with the two smaller children. I think I can do it, Mr. Cotter."

"Let me add one more thing, Mrs. Hamer. If the position and task is up to your capabilities, I would add the money you make from your other three housekeeping jobs to your proposed salary if you would resign from their services."

"Oh my goodness, Mr. Cotter, I would certainly have more time for my family."

"Come Mrs. Hamer, let me walk you to your wagon. We'll meet on Friday and leave from the main medical school admissions building."

"I am so hopeful this can work out, Mr. Cotter. You have no idea."

●

Cotter walked back into the library carrel and sat down. He had debated to make Hamer the last offer until he was sure the woman had no knowledge of the significance of her other employers' backgrounds. He turned Mrs. Gertrin Hamer's card over and looked again at the three names of her other employers. Two of them were unfamiliar to him. The third was. He said the name aloud. "Mrs. Robert Locke". Cotter took a folded newspaper clipping from his vest pocket. Prior to coming back to New Haven, he had researched the current status of several people known to him. He read the opening sentence of the news item. "Mrs. Robert Locke formerly Miss Nancy Cotter…."

# CHAPTER 4

## Mathew and Nancy

"Thank you, Dr. Randall. I really appreciated your written reference at the property closing." Cotter stood before Randall in the Dean's office.

"Not at all Jacob, I must say, though, I was a little taken aback that your brother and sister didn't come to your aid."

"They have no knowledge of my financial stature. I was obliged to disclose my personal resources to you since you're the Dean at Yale."

"So you didn't approach them for a collateral reference at all?"

"There was no need and I doubt they would have come forward in that capacity, sir."

"Well, I don't understand all this and it's personal business not for my ears." Randall pushed his chair back to rise and escorted Cotter to the door.

"I can only tell you the property I purchased was put out of business by my brother and sister three-years ago. They may fear I might activate the vineyards for competition to their Van Haven Winery." Cotter completed the hand shake and turned to leave.

"There were five vineyards shut down over the last five-years. Was it your brother and sister's doing?"

"The report I possess from my researcher states exactly that."

"Do you intend to re-open the Clark Winery?" Randall raised his bushy gray eyebrows with the question.

"Dr. Randall, I have two or three more years of medical school ahead of me. My chosen career is that of a physician."

"Of course, and will you be meeting with your brother and sister? As I said last week they do want to get together with you. My feeling is there are unresolved grief issues over your father's death to reconcile for all of you."

"I've already arranged such a meeting. Good day Dr. Randall, and thank you again." Cotter left the administrative building and approached the waiting wagon. His palomino was tied to the back.

"John, now that the place is mine, I want to inventory the premises." Cotter glanced into the wagon packed to capacity with supplies. "I see you're ready to move in."

"Yes, sir."

"John, you have to stop calling me sir when we're not in the public eye. In private, my name is Jake to you."

"As you wish–Jake." LaRoque handed Cotter his holstered Colt and signaled the horse to move forward.

There was moderate traffic on the packed dirt and straw road as the sun was moving to a noon-time overhead. No rain had fallen for several days and the morning clearance of horse dung and leveling of ruts by the town's road department made for a better than average ride. The air still had a horse-stable odor to it but it would clear as they left the city.

"Watch it John. Look out for that man." Cotter shouted and pointed to his right.

One of the road maintenance workers was shoveling a pile of horse dung, straw and mud into his single horse-drawn wagon. A thousand flies soared into the air with each plop onto the wagon contents. LaRoque pulled on the reins and pushed the wooden brake lever with his left foot.

"Watch it there, Andy." LaRoque shouted to the man but he didn't respond. LaRoque touched the end of his horsewhip to the man's shoulder.

"Oh, it's you, John. I didn't hear you comin'." Andrew Mashpit gave a salute touching the brim of his Union Army cap. His aged Army clothes were soiled and ragged.

"You know him?" Cotter looked back as the man continued shoveling.

"We were actually in the same unit together. He lost his hearing from the artillery noise. No one would give him a decent job because of his deafness, so he survives as part of the road maintenance crew."

"What did he do in the Army?"

"He was a map writer and logistics sergeant. He's still pretty sharp, 'cept he can't hear worth a damn. He drives people nuts trying to get him to understand what you want."

Cotter was silent for a moment. "What a waste of a good man." He paused and continued. "I want to tell you what my investigator found out about my brother and sister and the New Haven area wine industry of the last few years. Then I want you to answer some questions for me. You're familiar with the wineries north and west of here?" Cotter tied down his gun after cinching the holster buckle.

LaRoque listened without displaying any emotion. When Cotter was through he began with his questions.

"My brother and sister bought out the major wine house right after my father was killed and they inherited the Cotter estate. How did they squeeze out the smaller vineyards to monopolize the entire wine output for this part of southern Connecticut?"

"I got back from the war with my bad leg in late '65. Your father died about that time?"

"Yes."

"Mathew and Nancy Cotter first tried to buy out the small groups and have them supply grapes for their winery. They would all work for them but as low-paid share-croppers after they took a settlement buy-out."

"But obviously it didn't happen to all of them. There are several abandoned vineyards, including the one I bought."

"There was some pressure in the form of violence brought to bear on the small farms. Most of the small vineyards were owned, paid for and without debt or taxes so resistance was effective. Some fires occurred in the vineyards and later two of the vineyards had their main buildings burn down."

"Do you think they were all accidents?" Cotter buttoned his gray duster as dust kicked up from a wagon going the opposite direction.

"No one could prove anything. With the ability to make wine gone and no grapes to grow, several of the wine makers packed up and left after selling their spreads to your brother."

"What about the one I bought?"

"The owner was killed in a hunting accident. At least that was the rumor. His family refused to sell the estate and just abandoned it. They left for California to join another family vineyard just starting up."

"The taxes were in arrears for the past two-years. The realtor told me the former owner was quite successful on the Pacific Coast and let it go for a fair price plus payment of the back taxes. Why couldn't someone else grab it up?"

"I really don't know Jake but it's yours now."

The horse and wagon pulled up to the main farmhouse. LaRoque walked the palomino to the barn. Cotter got down and scanned the area. In addition to the barn, there were several other winery buildings surrounded by abundant weed overgrowth. They held the old vats and presses for winemaking. Cotter went up to the door of the main house and pulled a large white card tacked on its middle. It was an invitation from Mr. and Mrs. Robert Locke. Cotter read it out loud.

"You are cordially invited to dine at the Locke estate at 6 o'clock Friday evening. Mr. and Mrs. Mathew Cotter and an invited guest will also be in attendance. Dress is semi-formal."

●

The Locke estate was ten-miles from the center of New Haven but only five-miles from Cotter's house. The weather was fair and dry as Cotter rode to the entrance on his palomino. A footman met him at the carriage stone to the left of the main door of the house. The man was as tall as Cotter and very thick set. He looked very muscular. His face was clean shaven except for a black mustache which extended around his lips and straight down his chin for a full inch. Cotter dismounted and opened his gray duster. He untied his gun, removed the holster and placed the rolled-up rig into one of his saddlebags.

"I expect you not to touch this saddle bag."

The liveryman said nothing but nodded an assent. Cotter watched the man lead his horse to a barn while he knocked on the solid oak door. He could tell the man wore a pistol underneath his knee-length tunic. In the West, he learned to recognize anyone who did and who did not wear a gun. The door opened slowly and a bald middle-aged servant wearing shiny black shoes, black tidy pants, and a starched white shirt under a vest looked Cotter over.

"You are Mr. Jacob Cotter?"

"Yes."

●

The liveryman looked back at Cotter's large form disappearing into the house. He opened the palomino's saddlebag and took out Cotter's gun. He hefted it for balance and rolled the cylinder. He found four more loaded cylinders in the saddlebag. The pistol was well-oiled. He tested the single-action by cocking the hammer and releasing the trigger slowly so as not to fire the weapon. He looked at the horse and spoke softly to him in the empty barn after he replaced Cotter's gun back in the saddlebag. "This is the gun of a shootist." His smile made an opening in his black hairy mouth and he stroked his mustache. He looked at the horse again. "Just like mine." The man laughed and the palomino jerked back.

●

"Please enter and be so kind as to use the foot scraper," The house valet said.

Cotter moved his boots back-and-forth through the bristled foot scraper which removed road residues of mud, straw and horse droppings. When the domestic was satisfied he beckoned Cotter into the combination open foyer and living room. A fireplace to the left of the airy hall was clean from non-use during the summer months. A 12-lantern chandelier provided adequate lighting.

"You may proceed to the dining area. Please follow me, sir."

Cotter followed looking the place over as he passed dark brown-brocaded parlor furniture. The dining room contained a long rectangular table with seating for twelve but tonight had place settings for only six. Five people were standing with small stemmed crystal glasses half filled with dark red liquid. They turned to face him as the servant announced his presence.

"Mr. Jacob Cotter," He said with a slight bow to his employers. He turned around and left quietly.

After a short period of mutual inspection, a comely woman in her late thirties walked to Cotter and embraced him. She gave him an almost impalpable buss on the cheek. Her dark blue flounced floor-length dress prevented closer contact.

"Welcome back, Jacob dear." She turned to others. "Everyone, I want to introduce my brother."

Nancy Cotter Locke introduced Cotter to her husband Robert and proceeded to facilitate hand shaking between her brother Mathew and his wife Elizabeth Kindle Cotter. Nancy approached the remaining person with a cordial declaration and left them alone.

"Pamela Skyler? I just can't place the name from when I was here last or growing up in New Haven." Cotter looked into her black eyes admiring her pretty face with its slightly upturned nose.

"I'm from Boston. I moved down with my husband in late '63—just before you and your father went into the Army. Otherwise I'm sure we would have met." She sipped her glass of port wine and raised it slightly in silent toast to his presence. A similar glass of wine had been given to Cotter by the domestic upon his arrival.

"And where is Mr. Skyler tonight, may I ask?" He looked at her maroon dress. It was form-fitting in the front with a moderate bodice and the standard-style large bow behind which merged into a waterfall of flowing maroon fabric.

"He was killed in '66 during the 'disputes'."

Cotter noticed the lack of emotion with the statement. *The grief reaction is over. Well, it should be, it's been over two-years.* He sipped his port and swallowed. "Did you say 'disputes'? I don't understand. I've been away."

"We came to join Mathew and Robert in consolidating the vineyards to our company, 'Van Haven Wineries'. Most of the small wineries either joined or sold their places to us but some entered into a 'dispute' over losing their independence and identity of their brand name. A sort of war developed for a short time. Some of the vineyards succumbed to fire and a few owners met with accidents. My husband had an accident during a meeting to coax the residual vineyards to join us."

"What kind of accident happens in New Haven?" Cotter followed her slow walk to the dining room table.

"He was struck down by falling timbers and an anvil during one of the fires. It was really an accident. He'd been meeting with one of the owners when a fire broke out and he ran into one of the buildings to help put it out. His head was struck by the falling roof beams and his head hit an anvil when he fell."

"What a strange thing–falling beams and an anvil?"

"Indeed. It was unexpected and of course I was overcome with shock for a time. I decided to continue my husband Rockland's business and stayed on."

The seating seemed to happen naturally. Mathew sat opposite Nancy and Robert sat opposite Elizabeth. The arrangement left Cotter facing Pamela Skyler. As they became settled at the dining table, Mathew clinked his wine glass to begin an introductory remark for the dinner.

"I would like to formerly welcome you back to New Haven, Jacob. Shall we raise our glasses to reunion and prosperity on Jacob's return and his endeavor to finalize his training as a physician?"

Glasses were raised and met across the table in short tinkling sounds. Mathew continued his monologue. "Jacob, we are indeed glad to have you back. When we heard father was killed and had no word from you we thought you'd been killed also.

Nancy and I invested the family fortune in the land and in some local businesses. As you know from our letters right after the war, we had no money for you to continue your education." Mathew paused and made an eye signal across the table to Nancy.

"We offered you a place in our wine business, Jacob. Why did you not take it?"

"Father and I discussed what I would do if I survived the war. The plan was to continue in medicine. During our travels we both became concerned in seeing the quality of medical care decreasing as towns and villages distanced themselves from the big city medical centers. Our plan was to leave the big city after completion of my training and set up a modern medical practice for the developing outlying communities. The amount of money you offered would not permit finishing my MD training nor see to the future father and I projected."

"So what did you do Jacob Cotter?" Pamela Skyler intertwined her fingers on upright elbows resting on the table.

"I worked in law enforcement and was successful in collecting rewards from criminal apprehension."

"I had no idea being a policeman was so lucrative." Pamela smiled and her pause was a cue for him to continue.

"I wasn't a policeman. My job was to track down criminals and bring them back to the arresting and prosecuting authorities." *There. It's said. The ice is broken and life goes on–I hope.*

"Do you think you'll have difficulty getting back to medicine after an almost 3-year hiatus?" Robert Locke changed direction.

"I'll find out in a few weeks. I resume my third year at Yale next month. In the meantime I've just about been living in the Yale Medical Library catching up. It's coming back fast plus the changes and advances in surgery and medicine seemed to have paralleled what I learned and adapted to during the war when father and I were taking care of the sick and wounded."

"Shall I begin serving, madame?" The interruption by the female domestic was welcomed by Cotter. Her remark was directed to Nancy.

"Yes, please." Nancy looked at the approval nods from her guests.

Bread and cheese appeared very quickly along with a change of wine. Cotter moved the conversation to local politics and business in New Haven as the main course of cured ham and vegetables was served.

"New Haven is still a city full of Democrats, I see." Cotter looked at Mathew for a response.

"The Republicans were okay in war but the Democrats are entrenched in New England," Mathew said. "Small land owners and upper classes are needed for the large labor force. The labor group performs well if we're also allied with the Democratic electorals."

"I want to know where Jacob is living." Pamela Skyler smiled at Cotter.

Cotter put down his fork and looked at the expectant faces. He knew his brother and sister were aware of his probing the purchase of available vacant farms. "I actually just bought one of the old vineyard places."

"Are you going into the wine business? I thought you told us it wouldn't pay." Elizabeth Cotter sipped her wine after her question.

"No. I'm still going to Yale. I wanted a place that wouldn't lose money when I graduated. It's an investment property. I'll clean it up, make it livable and in two-years sell it. In the meantime it offers privacy and solitude–the things required for me to delve back into my medical studies."

"That's good to hear." Nancy also sipped her wine. "We were concerned about you being competition." She looked up. "Oh, here comes dessert."

The young woman set the tea service on a side table and poured for everyone. She came from the kitchen with two large apples pies. Both pies had blackened edges and sunken middles.

There were seeds and parts of the cores still in the body of each pie. No one completed the dessert.

Nancy looked at her cook and server with disdain. She turned to her guests after the woman disappeared back into the kitchen area. "I must apologize. I had to get a new cook and housekeeper at the last minute. The woman I had was the best kitchen domestic and housekeeper I ever employed. She just up and resigned yesterday."

*Too bad, that'll be the least of your problems now that I'm here.* Cotter moved his chair back. The evening was over and everyone stood up. His coat appeared with the male servant as he got to the door. Pamela Skyler stood next to him as he waited for his horse.

"I enjoyed our evening Jacob. I hope we shall see each other again." Pamela Skyler touched his hand.

"Yes, it was a more pleasant evening than I'd anticipated. I think your presence had something to do with the success of the get together."

Cotter received his palomino and removed his holster and gun from the saddlebag. He put a finger into the trigger frame and lifted the pistol out three-inches and spotted the telltale fingerprints of trespass on the oiled gun-frame. He strapped the rig on, tied down the holster around his right thigh and mounted his horse. Cotter looked over to the stable where the liveryman was standing. Their eyes met and Cotter sensed this man was a foe not to turn his back on. He gave Pamela a last farewell nod and rode off.

# CHAPTER 5

## Yale

"Gentlemen, today marks a milestone in surgery and medicine which Yale is pleased to accept and profess in our hallowed halls." Dr. Timothy Hayes, Yale's Medical Director looked down from his podium in the small lecture hall and operating theatre. He panned the body of third-year medical students. They numbered thirty-three of the most gifted members of Yale postgraduates who continued on to enter physician training. There were no females present. "Before I go into detail, I would like to ask the group what they consider to be the latest major milestone in medicine and especially surgery."

The students remained silent and looked around at each other waiting to see which of their number would raise a hand.

"Oh, come now, I know you've all been working on cadavers and have had experience with non-surgical patients. Would anyone offer to guess? " Dr. Hayes placed his hands on the podium gorilla-style and acknowledged the single hand in the air. "Okay, we have someone venturing a response. I know you, sir, from an earlier class, don't I?"

"Yes, Dr. Hayes. I'm Jacob Cotter. My father was a member of your department." Cotter stood up as he spoke. He held both his hands clasped in front of his gray suit coat.

"I remember you, of course. But let me correct you. I was a member of 'his' Medical Director's Board." Hayes relaxed a little. "Okay class, let's welcome Mr. Jacob Cotter back into our fold and hear his answer."

"Dr. Hayes, I practiced surgery during the war with my father and I have to say the biggest advance in surgery was chloroform and ether anesthesia."

"And why do you say that Mr. Cotter?" Hayes looked pleased. This fed into his prepared lecture.

"It enabled us to operate with an immobilized patient. We could perform a more precise dissection and closure–especially in the acute trauma situations."

"Precision and technique are important, indeed, Mr. Cotter. From your battlefield experience can you describe the limitations of the anesthesia?"

"Yes, Dr. Hayes–time. Time was the limitation and training an individual to administer the anesthetic."

"Time?"

"Yes, once the patient was rendered unconscious, the cloth cone saturated with the anesthetic was removed and we had until the patient woke up to perform our surgery. An amputation and closure had to be done within 15-minutes."

"Gentlemen, one of the major advances in medicine today actually departs from the technique described by Mr. Cotter. In 1868 we are experimenting with continuous administration of the ether. This allows more time and less stress. Mr. Cotter your experience is now dated. Any comments or questions from anyone?"

The students looked around again for a courageous volunteer. With no responders Cotter again raised his hand.

"Mr. Cotter once again?"

"During the war we trained a medical orderly to drop the chloroform on the cloth cone. Training was absolutely needed as chloroform can cause some fatal reactions. My question is, who gets the training to deliver the anesthesia?"

"Good question. The answer is simple. You, each of you, learn the technique as part of being a doctor. Remember a physician must be able to set fractures, deliver babies, treat disease and perform surgery. However, you can train a non-physician of your choice in private practice for anesthesia assistance but here at Yale you will be alternating giving anesthesia for a colleague's patient or using one of our trained non-physicians. Gentlemen, when you leave Yale, you will have to train your own people to give the anesthesia, therefore, you must be skilled in this aspect of surgery." Hayes paused. "Mr. Cotter, what was the most common cause of chloroform deaths and why didn't you use ether? Ether seems safer in our experience."

"Dr. Hayes, ether was not readily available and its explosive nature made the field commanders uncomfortable. As a result, chloroform was in abundance and England made chloroform readily available to the Union Medical Corps ever since Dr. Snow's famous administration to Queen Victoria for childbirth. The main problem with chloroform is the breath holding once the anesthesia deepens. If the chloroform continues to drip on the cone when the breath is held then when the patient next takes a breath, a lethal inhalation can occur and complete cardiac collapse ensues. The trick is to hold back the chloroform until normal breathing resumes."

Hayes seemed satisfied with Cotter's remarks. "Students, what Mr. Cotter has imparted is absolutely true. Remember, medicine is changing rapidly, however we learn from the adverse experiences with not only chemicals but with surgical techniques. We have to accept that sometimes death or unhappy outcomes will occur at our hands. This is how medicine advances."

Hayes looked at his notes. "Gentlemen, as much as anesthesia has enabled us to perform more surgical procedures, our outcomes have been limited to subsequent failure and even death from sepsis and putrefaction which comes from cutting into the living human body. And while I agree anesthesia is a surgical milestone, Mr. Cotter, let me say it was a milestone occurring in 1844 with Dr. Horace Wells using nitrous oxide in Hartford Connecticut and in 1846 when Dr. William Morton used ether in Boston. England's Dr. John Snow, in my opinion, led us to further strides with chloroform in the 1850s but more importantly to today's milestone which none of you have yet spoken of." He looked at the puzzlement on his audience's faces.

"John Snow eliminated an epidemic of Cholera by removing the pump handle from the water supply in a town so afflicted. His discovery was timely as in the past two-years Dr. Louis Pasteur demonstrated there are microorganisms which cause the infection and mortality following surgery. Just last year, Dr. Joseph Lister found a solution of carbolic acid applied to the dressings and surgical wounds decreased the incidence and consequence of operative sepsis by at least 50%. Here at Yale, our results are the same. We've also found washing our hands in a dilute solution of soap and carbolic acid further decreased the infection rates. You will all learn this beginning next week in the operating room. Your assignment is to read the original articles by Pasteur and Lister available in the medical library."

Hayes devoted the remainder of the two-hours to descriptions of surgical techniques for treating abscesses and non-healing wounds. At the conclusion of his teaching, he dismissed the class. Cotter was the last to leave the amphitheatre-classroom as he completed his notes.

"Mr. Cotter, may I have a word with you?"

"Certainly, Dr. Hayes."

"In private I will call you Jacob, if I may?"

"Yes, sir."

"Knowing your father and his teaching methods, am I correct in assuming you assisted him in many surgeries?"

"Almost all, sir, except when we were overloaded with casualties. In such situations, I worked solo."

"I imagine such overwhelming surgical workloads were commonplace?"

"Yes, Dr. Hayes."

"I would like you to assist me in the first surgery demonstration for your third-year class, next week. The patient is coming to my office tomorrow. I would like you to be there."

"I am flattered you ask me."

"Not-at-all. Just remember–I am the Professor. Your role is purely as an assistant. The patient is a middle-aged woman and her family is a long-time Yale benefactor. The patient's friend who is accompanying her knew your father."

Cotter thanked Hayes and went to the medical library. He read the details of Pasteur and Lister's work and the strong evidence for the existence of microbes. The data was indisputable about controlling the evils of living organisms, which could not be seen by the human eye. He added the information from the articles to his classroom notes and unfolded a section not a part of the surgical write-up.

Cotter's pulse quickened when he found a reference by Pasteur to a plague on the French wine industry solved by heating wine to 55-degrees centigrade for several minutes. Emperor Napoleon III had asked Pasteur for help with the spoiled wine epidemic and its devastating impact on the French wine industry. The results were amazing. Cotter knew of the troubled winemaking industry in the United States and especially in the New Haven-Hartford vineyards. More than 80% of the wine produced soured if not kept cold in dark, chilly cellars. In the loose folded pages, the process of correcting this fermentation problem was referred to as Pasteurization. Apparently it had not been publicized in America. In fact, the reference was not supposed to be for public record, as France wanted their wine-industry to become paramount in the world market. This document had somehow become incorporated in the medical pages sent to Yale for Dr. Hayes and the Department of Medicine and Surgery. He removed the five-page report.

●

"Why every Wednesday?" LaRoque asked as he finished loading the buckboard. The warm early September day lacked the oppressive humidity of August.

"It's the one day during the week at Yale set aside for study. No classes or clinics are scheduled and it's a free day to catch up on reading or personal activities."

Both LaRoque and Cotter wore gray dusters for traversing the dry roadbed on his property. They were heading to the clearing over two-miles from the main house.

"How does it feel being back to school after what you've been through in the war and after?" LaRoque was fast becoming a friend and confidant.

"It actually feels good. I really think I'm where I'm supposed to be."

They discussed the renovations and restorations taking place at the old vineyard farm.

"I practically had to re-roof all the buildings." LaRoque rubbed his right thigh.

"Just let me know what materials you need. Your leg bothering you much lately?"

"It's all the kneeling on the roof this week. It'll be okay once it begins to drain again."

"I'll have to take a look at it. It might be fixable."

"Not just now. We have too much to do." He slowed the buckboard and they dismounted. The clearing was partially shaded by the hill they would be shooting into. The area was shaped like an "L".

"I'll help hang the gourds on the lines." Cotter grabbed some rope and a bag of acorn squash.

They hung the squash from overhead tree branches and placed them eight-feet apart. A total of eight were suspended at a distance of 30-yards from their firing point. Cotter removed his duster and motioned LaRoque to do the same.

"You always wear those buckskins when you use the two-guns?" It was the first time LaRoque had seen Cotter in his bounty-hunting garb.

Cotter explained the reason for the one silvered-gun, the one matte-finish pistol and the one-sided shiny conchos.

"This theory of yours really works?"

"I'm alive. I think it's helped.

"What do you want me to do?"

"I want you to watch me. After I get through, we do it again but I want you to shoot too."

"You doin' this because of the guy you told me about at your brother's house?"

"Partly. I don't want to get rusty. I have a friend in Texas who may need our expertise with these." Cotter patted the handles of both Colts.

"Our?"

"I'm being premature. I told you outright; when I graduate I'm going out west to practice with a friend. He lives in hostile territory."

"Why not stay here where it's safe."

"It's not going to be safe here."

"What do you mean?"

"If Louis Pasteur is correct, we–you and I–are activating the vineyard. I'll explain later. First things first. I'm going to shoot at the first-and-third gourds. After that I want you to set the others swinging. I want them swinging in forward and sideways motion in a way they won't collide. I'll show you."

Cotter showed his hired man the maneuver and explained.

"Some bad guys will be standing still. Some will be abreast and some moving forward, backward and sideways. You have to be able to pick off any target in a rapidly changing situation." He smiled at LaRoque. "It's a little different than a linear battle line in the war with a bunch of screaming rebels lined up like ducks. The sun will be overhead. Watch what it does to the silver Colt and the conchos.

As the sun moved between 12 o'clock and 1 o'clock Cotter faced the gourds.

"John, get the ones moving like I showed you and then get behind my line of fire."

LaRoque moved behind and to Cotter's left side.

"The gourds–or if they were men are numbered left to right–one through eight. Look at them, give them the numbers in your mind right now." Cotter turned slightly to the left and shouted. "Number one, three and six."

Cotter drew both Colts and destroyed gourds three and six with his right handgun. Simultaneously the designated number-one gourd exploded from his left gun's discharge." The report of the firing Colt .45's was deafening and both men had slight ringing in their ears. Cotter holstered the guns quickly in a reverse twirling motion and turned to LaRoque.

"Good. You had your mouth open. I learned that maneuver in the war too. If you shoot with your mouth closed the pressure wave from the guns increases the ringing and makes you temporarily deaf. Opening the mouth immediately decompresses the ears and you can hear what's going on around you. Another trick I learned is to tell my opponents to shut up and go for their guns. It gives me an advantage in case I missed one or there are others lurking around–I can still hear them."

"Yes, Jake, I learned about it after my first battle. But how can you shoot two with your right hand and another with your left with the same draw?"

"Training. Your brain can be trained. I want to you to learn."

"Why?"

"There may come a time in the months ahead when I will need you to be as good as I am."

# CHAPTER 6

## Mathew and Nancy

Mathew Cotter was seven-years older than Jacob. Mathew inherited his father's stature at 6-foot-2-inches and 183 pounds. Jacob was an inch taller but closer to 190 pounds. The streamline musculature of Jacob's build was a contrast to his brother. Lack of physical activity, opulent dietary habits and daily wine had produced a mid-torso bulge and identifiable second chin with Mathew. Mathew wore tweed jackets and heavy gauge pants daily, except when entertaining which was mostly for business purposes. Today he was to meet with his sister Nancy Locke and Pamela Skyler. The three usually met once a month to discuss business which included finances, vineyard operations and future planning for the Van Haven Winery. Mathew had the housekeeper prepare the dining area for light fare and herald the start of the agenda at noon. Mathew was stoking the low flames of spitting pine logs.

"Elizabeth what was your take on Jacob? I mean do you think he's really going to finish becoming a doctor and then leave the community for another part of the country to practice?"

His wife had a beige crocheted shawl over her shoulders and moved closer to the fireplace. "I'm as concerned as you are about him buying the old Clark place. I'm told he's fixed up the main house and is working on the wine press and vat-aging buildings."

"You didn't answer my question, dear."

"I think Jacob has another agenda. His medical student image is a distraction from what he's really doing." She moved into the dining room with him and sat in one of the side chairs.

"He seemed sincere at our dinner a few weeks ago. What makes you suspicious besides the restoration of the old buildings?"

"Remember Gertrin Hamer, Nancy's former housekeeper?"

"What about her?" Mathew raised his eyebrows.

"She works for Jacob."

"So what. It doesn't mean anything. The only other person on the place is the blacksmith with the lame leg." He remained standing while she poured herself a glass of sherry from the crystal decanter at the center of the table.

"I think it was a deliberate act against us–both buying the Clark place and hiring the Hamer woman."

The door-knocker interrupted further dialogue. The housekeeper announced the arrival of Nancy Locke and Pamela Skyler. Elizabeth rose but stood in place. Nancy and Pamela went directly to the dining room. The housekeeper poured a glass of sherry for them and refilled Elisabeth's glass.

"Please sit down." Mathew motioned to his guests and then to his housekeeper. "Can you begin our lunch as usual, Jenny? Thank you."

"Well, how shall we begin–general comments or right-away financial report?" Nancy Locke always began the meeting and would dominate it.

"I for one would like to finish the conversation Matt and I were having." Elizabeth drained her wine glass. "We were discussing whether or not Jacob has designs on other than being a physician–specifically, activating the Clark winery."

"Good. I wanted to talk about that. I agree. I think Jacob is angry and is definitely capable of providing aggravation to us in the form of opening up the Clark place." As Nancy spoke her left hand waved in the air palm up and her right hand planted a finger in the air without any target. She punctuated her finish with a sip of sherry.

"Maybe and maybe not." Pamela Skyler folded her arms under her pushed-up breasts. The bodice of her green dress was laced from her navel to just beneath her breastbone. "He told us the place was an investment and he would sell it to the highest bidder when he finishes Yale."

"This talk proves one thing—we just don't know. So I suggest we make plans to find out. Any suggestions?" Mathew looked directly at Nancy when he finished speaking.

"Yes. I'm getting suspicious feelings from Kelvin about Jacob." Nancy sat back in her chair. Her gray dress had no lacing and had the effect of flattening her chest.

"Kelvin Danzer? He's a hired ruffian for God's sakes." Elizabeth Cotter poured herself another sherry

"I'm saying, it takes one to know one and I don't mean you Elizabeth. Kelvin told me Jacob may not be the gentle doctor he pretends to become. He can sense Jacob is a vindictive and ruthless person." Nancy looked to Pamela for the next response.

"My feelings are the opposite. I think Jacob has been through a war which has ripped his soul out. He tried to save men's lives but couldn't save them all. He and his father were going to take the practice of medicine to neglected communities. They're idealists. After his father died there was no one else except his medical school friend in Texas to carry out his dream."

"Pamela you're a romantic," Mathew said. "I ask for a plan to determine what direction Jacob is going take."

"I want Kelvin to stalk Jacob and find out about the Clark goings on." Nancy finished another stemmed sherry glass.

"A tender and more subtle approach might be better. I would like to get to know Jacob Cotter as a person." Pamela grinned.

"All right then, let's do both. Nancy, you tell Kelvin to put his nose in Jacobs's business and Pamela if you want a kiss and a hug from Jacob maybe it will release his true feelings and he'll give you his real designs on his future in the Hartford-New Haven Valley."

Pamela did not blush.

"Okay it's settled. Now to business. I have the Van Haven receipts tallied." Nancy opened the ledger and gave her report.

"There were no losses or gains in the past four-months. We still have the same output and have the same overhead. I wish we could cut our losses on the spoiled wine." Mathew frowned.

"I thought we make up for some of the loss during the winter with the cold storage for our dark reds and the sauterne." Elizabeth spoke and poured her third sherry.

"No. As soon as the thaw comes we can't get it to the market fast enough. However, I've heard the Germans are filtering the wine through cloth extending the lifespan and I recommend we look into it. They're having good luck with beer with this technique." Pamela folded her arms on her chest.

"What will it cost us?" Mathew looked at the tally sheets.

"Remember what dad always told us–you have to invest more to get more. We have more to gain than to lose." Nancy paused and looked at the group. "How is our production going? Any problems with the outlying village farms?"

"No, Nancy. Not since Kelvin paid them a visit." Mathew smiled.

"One of the workers almost got killed though. I told Kelvin not to get too rough. I think we almost went too far when we first started. Almost." Nancy drank her wine.

"Well Christmas is almost upon us so let's try to be as cordial as we can. Tell them about the filtering and tell them if profits go up so does their sharecropping return."

"It'll work for most of them–but not all of them." Elizabeth looked at Nancy and sipped her fourth sherry.

"Kelvin will deliver the message. He can reach them all." Nancy closed the ledger.

●

The air was cold and Kelvin Danzer could see his breath. Once a month he went to the perimeter of the Van Haven main vineyard where over a hundred-and-thirty acres of hilly woods provided him with the seclusion needed for practice with his gun and axe. Danzer arrived in the United States from Germany in 1857 at age 32. He was a former soldier with seven-years service in the German Regular Army. Three-years prior to immigrating to America, he was a mercenary hiring out to local land Barons.

Usually he was one of a team of strong-arm hired guns to enforce the mandates of his landowner bosses on the subservient farmers on the Barons' property. Most were vineyards on massive estates along the Rhine River. When Danzer arrived in Connecticut he sought out similar landowners needing muscle or aggressive foremen. His antagonistic personality did not win him many friends other than his employer and this made him more marketable as a supervisor.

Danzer walked from his quarters in the carriage house. He lived there apart from other estate employees. The Van Haven vineyard main farm was five-miles to the southeast of New Haven proper. He enjoyed his relationship to the Cotters especially with Nancy Cotter Locke who had hired him in 1863. Her brother Mathew was assertive enough but Nancy was aggressive and was not above physical expression of enforcing the Winery's business ethics–or lack of ethics–which was perfectly okay with him. He remembered his initial meeting with them and the Skylers.

"Mr. Danzer your references were received last week and we would like to ask you some questions." Mathew Cotter addressed Danzer who remained standing while the others sat around the dining room table.

"As Mr. Cotter wishes." Danzer did not have a thick German accent. His sentences were sometimes short and the grammar not quite correct but no one ever derided him. He stood tall wearing a dark green waistcoat. The coat was unbuttoned and revealed the pistol tied-down at his right thigh. There was a slight bulge beneath the left upper chest pocket but not visible to any observer.

"Your former positions have been supervisory. Did they often involve some distasteful acts of eviction or physical enforcement of policy?"

"If you please Mr. Cotter, any position of authority exercises words first. A firm hand must be shown if words are not working." Danzer scanned his audience. Only the attractive, buxom woman seemed uncomfortable.

Pamela Skyler avoided Danzer's stare.

Nancy Cotter smiled. "Yes Mr. Danzer. You're right. In business we have to do what we have to do." Nancy looked at the rest. "Don't you all agree?"

"Well, within reason." Rockland Skyler looked at his wife. "I mean, we can't kill people or break bones."

Nancy held his gaze. The room was silent. She folded her arms on her tightly wrapped bosom. "Well, Mr. Danzer. How do you feel about that?"

"Without disrespect, accidents happen. Some people do get hurt…" He made eye contact with Rockland Skyler, "…and some people die, sir."

"Business is like war, Mr. Danzer. If we agree to your employ, we would ask that you always discuss with us the nature of any resistance to company policy before we release such sanctions." Nancy received nods of agreement from her partners.

"Whenever such discussion is to be reasonable. Sometimes action must happen immediately without time for consultation." Danzer's tone was gruff and he panned the group with his hands on his hips. The posture made his jacket flare baring the gun more openly and exposing the holster under his left arm.

"Mr. Danzer, is that a gun under your left arm?" Mathew stared at the object.

"No, sir." Danzer reached to the holster with his right hand and pressed a tab on the side of the holster. A metallic "clink" preceded the shiny sawed down axe released to Danzer's hand. The blade faced away from him as the handle slapped quickly into his hand. He allowed a few seconds for his audience to stare at the silvery blade before he replaced it.

"Mr. Danzer may we have a few minutes alone to discuss our offer to you." Mathew got up and walked him to the library in the next room.

Danzer stared at the books and the large dark desk. *They're afraid and they're satisfied. I am what they want.*

Only Rockland Skyler voiced opposition.

"The man is a killer–an axe by God!" Rockland shook his head side-to-side.

"We need someone like him if we are to take over the area's small vineyards. We use kind words first and then send him in when needed."

After five-minutes they were agreed and called him back.

"Mr. Danzer we expect opposition to incorporate some of the New Haven smaller wineries into the Van Haven vineyard company. Would you be interested in becoming our business front man–a sort of foreman for all of our winery operations?"

"I have done this before. I will state my needs for quarters and pay."

The agreement included the Locke carriage house as room-and-board. It also included a horse and any implements of his trade he might need.

That was in 1863. Today he moved briskly in the cold air. Danzer knocked sharply on the main house door.

"Come in Kelvin. We have something we want to discuss with you." Mathew walked with him to the dining room.

"We think we might have a problem with my brother, Jacob Cotter." Nancy Locke motioned him to sit down. "You might have met him a few weeks ago when he came to dinner."

"Yes, Mrs. Locke. You do have a problem."

# CHAPTER 7

## Yale

Cotter walked down the hall to the surgical clinic offices. He knocked on Dr. Hayes's solid oak door and walked in. The female medical assistant and receptionist looked up from her small desk. The waiting room had two seated patients and three being logged in.

"Jacob Cotter? Yes, Dr. Hayes is expecting you."

Cotter knocked and went into the office.

Dr. Hayes sat behind a large maple desk with books and journals in two separate stacks to his left. The window curtains were apart letting the morning sun add heat to the slight chill. Two stuffed chairs with a dark maroon muted floral pattern were in front of the desk. To Cotter's right was a movable curtain with an examining table and stool.

"I'm glad you could come to my office this morning. As I mentioned before I cleared your absence from the service medical clinic for this morning to work with me. Such is the power of being Chief Medical Director." He smiled and beckoned Cotter to sit.

"I appreciate the honor. You mentioned I would be assisting with one patient today. I see your waiting room is starting to fill up."

"The patient we'll be working on later today is coming in shortly. I wanted to talk with you before she gets here." He cleared his throat.

"Does the name Elizabeth Hart Jarvis mean anything to you?" Hayes sat back rubbing his clean-shaven chin.

"It sounds familiar."

"Let me complete the name–Elizabeth Hart Jarvis Colt."

"Sam Colt's wife–of course. I was saddened when he died in '62. He was a patient of my father's and we became good friends."

"That's exactly why I wanted you here today."

"Is she having major surgery?"

"No. She asked about you and remembers how good both of you were to her husband. When I mentioned you were continuing your medical studies she was thrilled and wanted you as part of the team."

"Sam Colt never had any major surgical problems. He had gout, a bad rheumatic heart and finally ended up with pneumonia." Cotter paused. "So who's the patient?"

"A favorite relative has a breast abscess I plan to open and drain under ether anesthesia. Our use of carbolic acid solution should keep re-infection from occurring."

"Do you pour the carbolic into the wound cavity?"

"What I'll show you is now standard at Yale. The instruments, our hands and the patient's skin get treated with the antiseptic. Even prior to this, we wash our hands and immerse them in the dilute carbolic."

Cotter and Hayes continued discussing medical and surgical approaches to the problems of infections. Cotter looked at his pocket watch.

"It's almost 10 o'clock. What about the other patients in the waiting room?"

"They're here for dressing changes. My associate will manage with one of your classmates." Hayes stood up with the knock on the door.

"Mrs. Colt and Mrs. Hunt are here Dr. Hayes." The receptionist peeked into the office.

"Send them in Louise."

A pleasant-looking woman in her early forties preceded a more timid woman who looked much younger. Cotter guessed about age 25.

"Good morning Dr. Hayes and … my, my, my… Jacob Cotter. I was disheartened at the news of your father's death." Cotter received the extended hand and the immediate hug from Mrs. Colt.

"Thank you and you're looking well." Cotter turned to Hayes to resume command.

"Mrs. Ira Hunt let me introduce my assistant today, Jacob Cotter. He's a third-year student at Yale and son of the former Medical Director at Yale."

"Elizabeth has told me so much about Dr. Cotter. I'm sure his son is of the same caliber."

Hayes discussed the breast abscess history with the patient and noted some pertinent aspects for Cotter. She had been breast-feeding her 6-month infant when the infection set in. Post-partum infected breasts were a common malady of the day. They reassured Mrs. Hunt and Hayes asked if she had any questions.

"Mrs. Hunt, please disrobe from the waist up. Louise will assist you and drape this sheet over your top. Louise, please call us when you're ready."

Cotter and Hayes resumed talking with Mrs. Colt while the patient was being prepared for the exam.

"Mrs. Colt, I understand the family is still running the armaments business," Cotter said.

"Yes. It's doing very well. I remember when Sam gave you and your dad a pair of his special .45 Colt-Patterson revolvers. They were from a lot specially made for the Texas Rangers. You were both thrilled."

"Yes, ma'am and I have to tell you they saved our lives more than once." Cotter remembered the day. The guns were a new innovation to firearms in the .45 caliber.

"We continue to make progress in the handgun area, Jacob. In two-years we'll be mass-producing a complete brass cartridge with bullet, powder and primer all in one. The cartridges can be reloaded as well."

"That'll make my Colts obsolete." Cotter smiled. Hayes beckoned him to the examination area. "I'll be back in a minute."

Hayes and Cotter examined the woman's reddened, tender and swollen right breast. Hayes dabbed a toothpick with some blue ink and dabbed a line across the area to be incised. "I want you not to eat until after the surgery Mrs. Hunt. The ether can make you sick. I've written some instructions for the surgical theatre. Your operation is scheduled for noon-time."

Hayes discussed aftercare with Mrs. Colt and Mrs. Hunt and bid them good morning until their noon meeting.

"Meeting with the patient in a friendly atmosphere goes a long way to calming them down and minimizing panic and fear. I'm sure you saw the difference in Mrs. Hunt's face from when she came in the door as compared to when she left."

Cotter acknowledged the importance of a pre-surgical visit and left the office. He would see Hayes in the amphitheater at noon. He walked outside and soon caught up with both women.

"Mind if I walk with you. I'm going in your direction anyway. I'm assisting in a procedure just before yours, Mrs. Hunt." Cotter walked and chatted about pre-war life in New Haven and Hartford. Mrs. Colt stopped when Cotter answered her about where he was living.

"The Clark winery? Is Van Haven finally going to take it over?" Mrs. Colt was clearly upset.

"No. I just live there and I'm fixing up the place."

"Are you going to make wine, Jacob Cotter?"

"Well I wasn't at first but I have second thoughts. There's a new process in France which yields almost 90% non-souring wines."

Mrs. Colt listened to the Pasteur process of stopping residual germ culture from continuing to ferment the wine. As she sat in the waiting area she touched Cotter's sleeve. "Jacob, why don't you do it? Start the vineyard with the French process?"

"Two reasons, ma'am. I won't have the time while finishing medical school and second, my budget won't allow it."

"Jacob you finish your schooling and let's talk sometime soon—next week—about the vineyard. I've partnered several promising ventures over the years."

"I certainly would like to talk further."

"Next week, when we bring Lillith back to Dr. Hayes for her check-up I want you to be there."

"Yes, Mrs. Colt." Cotter felt uplifted.

The ether anesthesia and the surgery went without complication. The use of the carbolic acid solution seemed routine to the staff and it added very little time before and after the procedure. Mrs. Hunt was lethargic from the ether and Cotter offered to provide transportation for them.

"No Jacob. How do you think I got here? My carriage is waiting but thank you for the offer. Remember I want to talk about the wine venture next week." She gave Cotter a goodbye hug and slight kiss on the cheek.

●

"Oh God no. Dad. Dad." Cotter woke up. The dream was back. He got out of bed and paced around the room. Someday, he'd meet the man who killed his father and maybe the other man with him–someday.

# CHAPTER 8

## Mrs. Hamer

Gertrin Hamer loved her new job and most of all she loved the increase in income. There was a component of fun to her job too. Cotter provided the funds for everything she needed to make the house "homey"–new dishes, silverware, furniture and curtains. She had very few items in her own home which were obtained new. In three-months she transformed the place from a dusty abandoned hulk to a serene appearing domestic abode. She wore her winter coat tight around her body with a large trailing scarf and wool kerchief as she swept the first snow of the year from the front steps. Last year it had snowed in late September and she wondered if the first snowfall in mid-November meant a mild or severe winter to come.

It was dark already and John LaRoque would drive her home at 4:30. He was a nice man, she reflected. In the past few months they had exchanged confidences about their family histories. Most of their personal exchanges occurred during the buckboard ride to Hamer's home. Gertrin Hamer had noticed LaRoque often rubbed his right thigh.

"Is there something wrong with your leg, John?"

"Not really ma'am. I mean. Well, I got shot in the war and it still hasn't healed. The bullet's still in there."

"Oh, dear, can't it be fixed?"

"The Army doctors said the bullet might work itself to the surface. It hasn't happened yet. Some days it bothers me and some days it don't. Today it does."

"Your parents must have been glad to see you survived the War."

"My father died of consumption when I was twenty."

"What of the rest of your family? Are they living in Connecticut?"

"My grandfather came from France with my father and my mother. I think it was around 1790 and he was their only child. My mother was French too and I came into the world in May 1837."

"Well what of your mother and did you have brothers and sisters?"

"My only sister and my mother died of the same lung disease as my father about two-years later. I did have an aunt and an uncle on my mother's side and two cousins, but they left to go out west when I was twelve."

"How old were you when they died?"

"I was twenty-five." LaRoque hung his head down as sad memories surfaced.

Gertrin Hamer didn't pursue further because they reached her house.

Over the weeks she learned John had done well in school but had to work and never went beyond the seventh grade. His father ran a livery stable in Hartford where John helped. At age sixteen he was already as tall as his father and getting as muscular. When John LaRoque reached twenty, he was practically running the livery by himself.

"That's how come I came to New Haven. I had to sell the business and use the money for their treatment at Yale." LaRoque continued to offer answers to Hamer's motherly inquisition. Occasionally, he would ask about her but Mrs. Hamer wouldn't offer much until she had obtained his complete history.

"What did you do after they died?"

"I got jobs clearing land and doing livery work. I'm a good blacksmith. Then the war came and I joined up and here I am today.

"What about you, Mrs. Hamer? You always live in New Haven?" He adjusted the reins to deliberately slow the team of horses.

"I was born in New Haven and I'll probably die in New Haven." She smiled. She knew it was her turn to reveal who she was. "I came from a small family too but we were poor. My father was a farm hand at one of the vineyards. When I was younger I worked in the winery and left school early." A hint of regret was in her voice but it quickly changed. "That's where I met Bradley–Mr. Hamer. He was working in the vineyard too. We didn't get married right away. When he got promoted to foreman, he proposed and we settled near the winery. Things were really good, we had three children and then the Van Haven people came along."

"The Cotters." John breathed out the words.

"Well, it was the Locke's at first and then Mr. Skyler. Later Mathew Cotter joined them and they began taking over all the smaller farms. Bradley was forced to leave when the grape vats and the buildings burned up. And then Mr. Snickley, he was the owner–Snickley Vineyard–was killed."

"How was the man killed?"

"They said it was an accident. His leg got caught in the wine press and got cut-up really bad. He bled to death, the poor man."

"Didn't Bradley get work at another winery?"

"He wouldn't even try. He was afraid for us and himself."

"Afraid? Why?"

"He told me a group of men talked to him and some others at Snickley's and warned them not to work for any of the other wineries. It was the night Mr. Snickley died and the vineyard caught fire."

"Caught on fire or set on fire. You said it burned down."

"Oh, dear. Well Bradley and the others thought everything that happened was deliberate. Snickley's wasn't the only farm bad things happened to."

"When was all this going on?" LaRoque was interested and for reasons he couldn't fathom, he was getting angry. He unconsciously sped up the team.

"I think it was three-years into the war."

"And Bradley has been working in a retail store since then?"

"Yes. It's the reason I have to work."

Over three-months of intermittent dialogue was required for both LaRoque and Hamer to ventilate their past history.

The snow was falling lightly and she wondered what she and John would talk about tonight. She saw him hitch up the team and drive them over to her.

"I'm just finishing sweeping the steps for Mr. Cotter."

"Why bother, more snow's comin'." LaRoque got down and put her bag in the buckboard covering it with a weatherproof oilcloth for the trip to the Hamer's small house.

Fifteen-minutes into the journey, the horses began to slow down because of the snow accumulation. LaRoque and Hamer were talking about Cotter and his studies. LaRoque signaled with the reins to get the animals up to speed again. The horses were reluctant. The wind was blowing the snow in a slanting direction away from them.

"What's wrong John?" Hamer was startled at the sudden change in routine.

"I don't know." LaRoque had a bad feeling. He opened the bottom two buttons of his coat. His hand was ready to brandish his six-shooter.

And then he saw it. He pulled hard on the reins.

"Whoa. Whoa there." He pushed down as hard as could on the wooden two-by-four brake for the front wheel. The horses weren't slowing down. The only thing he could do was change direction immediately. He saw the shiny mirror-like flash again and this time he thought he could hear a hacking sound.

The horses were galloping now. He couldn't slow them down. He was off the road but on cleared land. The snow was blowing. He still hadn't turned them enough and then a loud thunderous "crack" pierced the soft wind of the blowing snow.

"Get your head down Gertrin, now." They both ducked as the giant elm with its heavy, and potentially deadly boughs crashed down only a few feet from the buckboard. The horses kept going. After a few minutes he was able to slow the team down and get back onto the road.

"What happened? How did the tree fall? The storm isn't that bad." Mrs. Hamer looked back at the scene.

"I think it was bad enough for that old tree." He calmed her down. "It'll happen to us when we're old too. A little storm will get to us."

"Well it was so sudden. Do you think any more trees will fall?"

"No, I don't think so." LaRoque holstered his gun away from Hamer's vision.

●

Kelvin Danzer put the axe back in its holster. The axe was a trophy from one of his escapades in Germany. Some people called it a hatchet but it was really an axe. The former owner had shortened the handle and honed the edge to a lethal sharpness. It was strong as well as sharp. The metal was polished to a surface creating a mirror finish and Danzer kept it well oiled in a levered holster. The axe blade faced the back of the leather sheath and the unit was released with moderate pressure on a quarter-inch tab at the top. Danzer used his right index finger to depress the lever and the axe handle would spring into his right hand.

The darkness plus the wind and snow provided the concealment he needed. Mrs. Hamer once worked for the Lockes and knew him so he had to keep out of sight. He knew the road Cotter's hired hand always chose to take the housekeeper home. Danzer selected a large elm and hacked a wedge cut which would direct its fall across the road. He only had to give it a few final whacks with his axe when the buckboard was about 100-yards away. But he missed. LaRoque had somehow sensed something–or maybe it was the horses. LaRoque couldn't possibly have seen him. Now Nancy Locke would be madder than hell. She had made her intentions plain enough to him.

"The rumor is Jacob is considering refurbishing the Clark place to start making wine again. Kelvin, Mathew and the rest have decided Jacob needs a message–a warning message. Make it as severe as you want."

*Nancy Locke was a cold-blooded person. Her brother Mathew would agree to anything she said. Pamela Skyler on the other hand, hedged at outright violence. Pamela Skyler was not as bad as her husband, though. Rockland Skyler was a thorn in everyone's side even at the beginning. He took issue at the burning of the small farms and the occasional heads that needed to be bashed. The man had no backbone.* Danzer's thoughts continued reminiscing.

Rockland Skyler had gone with him to the Hanson Farm. The Hansons would not sell and would not become a tenant vineyard to the Van Haven cartel. A confrontation was inevitable. Rockland Skyler insisted on going with Danzer to stay his hand from physically assaulting Hanson. Danzer laughed out loud as he remembered Rockland and the Hansons.

"Kelvin, remember, just raise our offer until he agrees. There's no need to burn anything or injure anyone."

"We'll see what we will see and do what is needed to be done."

"I don't want you on my place. I will not sell at any price. Get off my property or I'll call in the New Haven police." Hanson cradled a shotgun.

"I wouldn't want harm to becoming to you or your family. It would be better for you to sign the agreement tonight." Danzer stepped up to Hanson. Shotgun or not, Danzer was only two-feet away from him. Being this close meant Hanson would not have any room to swing out the shotgun and aim the barrel at his body.

"Please be reasonable here Mr. Hanson. A peaceable solution is best." Rockland Skyler pleaded.

"My family is away and my hired men are at my call. Leave right now." Hanson moved to raise the shotgun to a pointing stance but Danzer was still too close.

Danzer reached into his opened coat and the axe sprung into his right hand. Danzer swung backhanded with the axe in one motion as the weapon made its "clink" sound ejecting from the holster. The back end of the axe smashed into the right side of Hanson's temple crushing the skull on impact. The shotgun and Mr. Hanson fell to the floor.

"You killed him. I told you no more violence. I'm going to the authorities with this. We're not going to jail for your crimes." Rockland was Danzer's height and he pushed Danzer's shoulder to turn him around.

Danzer still had the axe in his right hand at the end of the arc from bashing Hanson's head.

"No. Never will you do that," Danzer's growled. He swung the axe blade into Rockland's face cleaving the left brow, eye and nose. Blood gushed around the axe's penetration as Skyler fell to the floor. His body convulsed as blood spurted from the mouth and left eye socket. The axe blade had penetrated deep into Skyler's skull and Danzer couldn't remove it. He waited for the seizure activity to cease. Danzer looked over to Hanson's limp body with the blood seeping from the nose and ears and wondered why Hanson didn't have convulsions like Skyler. When Skyler was motionless, Danzer put his left boot against the dead man's chest and wiggled back-and-forth with both hands on the axe handle to dislodge it from his head. As soon as the axe was free a combination of opalescent brain substance and blood pushed out like a living fungating mass.

There had been a minimum of noise. There was no sign of any of the winery employees milling about. *The man was bluffing–he had a lot of courage.* Danzer had to admire Hanson for that, as he would admire one of his soldiers fallen in battle. *But not the other one–Rockland Skyler. He was a spineless worm who didn't deserve to be part of the Van Haven Company. I'm going to love telling his bosomy reluctant wife about her husband's fatal accident.* He laughed aloud with the thought.

Danzer set fire to the house and the adjacent barn. He was told not to damage the winemaking structures. He carried Skyler's body to the livery section of the barn and lifted the anvil from the forge and dropped it on Skyler's head. After the fire it would be assumed both Skyler and Hanson succumbed from injuries while fighting the fires. At least, it was how he would tell it.

Danzer stopped reminiscing and turned to the problem at hand–Nancy Cotter. He would try to mellow out the botched ambush. He knocked on the door to the main house.

Nancy Cotter looked at him against the snowy halo background. "Well?"

"I felled a tree to fall within inches of their buckboard. I think they got the message."

"It's too bad you didn't kill the horses or hit the buckboard. I don't like what the Hamer woman did to me. She just up and left me and for Jacob no less."

"Yes, ma'am."

"There may come a time when more direct force is needed. I know you understand. Thank you Kelvin and goodnight."

"Goodnight to you too ma'am."

# CHAPTER 9

## Andrew Mashpit

The air in the house smelled of burning pine logs. It was a pleasant odor lending an attitude of warmth along with the hearth's primary heat radiation. Cotter had turned one of the rooms off the main living room into a study. He had a huge mahogany desk which was part of the original abandoned furniture that Cotter had refinished. It was set against a wall framed with built-in bookshelves. Most of the shelves were bare but by the time he finished Yale, Cotter fathomed them to be full. LaRoque stood to the right of the salvaged desk.

"Why not invite him?" Cotter looked from the page in the latest Massachusetts General Hospital textbook of surgery to LaRoque.

"Well, for one thing, he smells bad."

"Clean him up, get him some decent clothes and make him the offer."

"Andy Mashpit? He scoops up horseshit from the streets, Jake."

"I had a friend from the Army look up his record from the war. The man was a master surveyor and mapmaker. We could use him for confirmation of our boundaries." Cotter pushed his chair back. "And if I'm not mistaken one of your jobs is to shovel horse dung in the stable. We have four horses."

"What if he has other plans?"

"He has no family in the area. He lives in the road maintenance shed. Why are you so resistant? You like the man, remember?"

LaRoque sat in the only other chair in the study. "You're right, Jake. I don't know why I was resistant. I think I kind of accepted him as for what he is now."

"What he is now is a former soldier who can help us here when we open up the vineyard. Can he use a gun?"

"I don't know. He was in artillery and explosives. The noise made him deaf as a door nail."

"I've been looking at him downtown. Mashpit has adapted to his deafness. I think he can read lips. I noticed he responds appropriately when people face him and speak to him."

"Why wait until Thanksgiving, then. Why not talk to him now?" LaRoque stood up and rubbed his leg.

"Great idea. Thanksgiving is a week away. Tell him what we've discussed and then tell him I want to see him at the medical clinic on Tuesday at 4 o'clock." Cotter sat back upright and then bent over his textbook as LaRoque left. Cotter's father had taught him the best way to persuade someone to do something after first resistance was to maneuver the proposal to become their idea. It worked most of the time. It had worked with LaRoque.

●

"Andy. Andy, for God's sakes Andy. I said, before you sack out in the barn you have to clean out the two wagons or the horseshit will rot the wood in the cargo beds." The Road and Maintenance supervisor yelled at Mashpit who had his back turned away from the man.

Mashpit was running his boots through the stiff bristled foot brushes scraping the horse dung, mud and straw from his old Army boots. He hadn't heard a word.

The supervisor tapped Andy on the right shoulder.

"What? Did you want something?" Mashpit had a scraggly beard knotted with unknown debris from his job. The yellowish particles clung to his mustache and the ends of his beard. He had worked out a routine for cleaning the facial hair. At the end of every month he would run the horse mane comb through the beard and when he hit a snarl he would cut the hair at that point. The end result was a beard with irregular chopped-out sections.

"Yes." The supervisor yelled as loud as he could. "Clean out both wagons before you quit for the night."

"Oh, no, sir I don't want to quit, I like my job."

"I said clean out the two wagons."

"I'm leaving right after I clean my wagon, sir."

"No. I said two wagons. Yours and Pauly's wagon."

"My wagon will be spotless, sir."

"You have to clean Pauly's wagon too, I said."

"I'll see you in the morning, sir." Mashpit left and headed for the building, which housed the road maintenance wagons. *Being deaf has one advantage. I'll be damned if I'm going to clean someone else's wagon. The lazy bastard Lance Pauly can clean his own mess.*

Mashpit brought two buckets of water and soap solution and climbed into the open buckboard. He splashed the first bucket and scrubbed the debris clean from the floorboards and side panels. The wagons smelled like a horse barn at best but after working with them for the past three-years his nose had accepted the smell. He knew his own odor was atrocious. At the end of each month he had his clothes cleaned, took a bath and did his defacing beard manicure. His clothes consisted of two uniforms left from his Union Service. It was amazing they still held together. Once navy blue, they were now a non-descript dark gray. The one he had on today had a torn right shoulder seam with some padding extruding from it. The clock at the town hall struck 5 o'clock. His day was done.

Mashpit turned to leave the wagon garage when he saw the silhouette of the large man at the open entrance. The man was wearing a dark duster over a heavy coat. Both garments were open and he could see the tied-down holster. It wasn't that gold-brick Pauly. He approached cautiously and eyed the pitchfork used to layer straw on the roads in the morning. It was his only weapon. The man backed up into the dim light from the street lamp.

"Hello Andy."

"John? John LaRoque?"

LaRoque extended his hand but Mashpit was reluctant. His hands and body reeked of horse crap.

"Come on, shake it. I shovel the same stuff in my job with Jake Cotter." LaRoque smiled and they shook hands.

"I want to talk to you Andy." LaRoque looked around the wagon garage and motioned with his hands. "About this."

"What? The road maintenance shed?"

"No. About you and what you're doing with your life."

"What do you care? You lucked out when we were mustered out of the Army. You got the blacksmith job and I got the only thing left." Mashpit picked up some straw and threw it at a wagon.

"I care. Don't you remember the times we had in the Army? I mean the good as well as the bad."

"Those days are gone. Who needs a dynamiter or a map maker when there are dozens of civilians entrenched in those jobs?"

"We do. Jake Cotter, I mean. He bought the Clark vineyard and is going to make it operational. He needs the land re-documented with an up-to-date mapping and survey of the place. It's over 100-acres according to the deed." LaRoque motioned Mashpit to come outside and they walked slowly to the buckboard. He had just dropped off Mrs. Hamer.

"Say I do the job. I would have to quit this and when I'm finished with your work I'll have nothing."

"There's more to the job than the mapping and survey. We need another hand–someone who has had experience managing men." He paused. "Someone like you. It would be a permanent position."

"What about my handicap? I can't hear worth a shit."

LaRoque laughed. "Look at us. Jake Cotter was right. You read lips. We'll be your ears when your back is turned."

"You're serious?" Mashpit put his hand on LaRoque's right arm.

"Jake Cotter wants to meet with you Tuesday at the Yale Medical Clinic at four o'clock. You're also invited to dine with us on Thanksgiving."

"Oh my god, I can't believe it. But look at me, I'm a mess. My only other clothes are only slightly better than these and they still smell."

"On Tuesday, if you accept Cotter's offer, we go to the General Mercantile for a change of clothes. Consider it an advance on your pay."

"What if I don't measure up to his expectations?"

"You will. I told him all about you–when we were in the Army. He was in the Army too. Just answer his questions and be yourself–not the horseshit, road maintenance man."

LaRoque shook his friend's hand, mounted the buckboard and road off. Mashpit watched him go with glistening eyes.

●

Tuesday morning was busy at the medical clinic. Most of the patients had infections of the head and neck with some chest congestion. One woman with pneumonia had to be taken in to the hospital for fever management and nutrition. With re-hydration she had a 50-50 chance of survival. At 11 o'clock Cotter went to Hayes' office.

"Good morning, Dr. Cotter." Louise smiled with the greeting. "You can go right into Dr. Hayes's office." All Yale Medical students were addressed as "Doctor" in front of patients to put them at ease. The patient's knew, and expected, that a Yale medical student always accompanied the staff physician.

"Good morning to you too, Louise and to you Mrs. Colt and Mrs. Hunt." Cotter smiled and went into the office.

"Ah, Jacob, I'm glad you could come. Mrs. Hunt is doing well and this should be her last visit. Mrs. Colt has been after me to get you two together again. With your clinic duties and classroom commitments this was the only way I could manage it." Hayes stepped from his desk and shook Cotter's hand.

"Thank you, sir. Communications have been difficult."

"I understand you're more than caught up with your classmates. Three years away from medicine hasn't handicapped you at all."

"It's good to hear you say such things Dr. Hayes. I have my nose stuck in the books every night."

"Well let's get to business." Hayes asked Louise to escort Mrs. Hunt into his office.

Hayes and Cotter examined Mrs. Hunt. The abscess was gone and the scarring was minimal.

"As you can see, Drs. Lister and Pasteur have changed medicine forever."

"Washing hands, instruments and the operative field with carbolic solution is certainly effective," Cotter said. "I wished we had this during the war."

Cotter accompanied Mrs. Hunt and Mrs. Colt from the medical office building. Mrs. Colt turned to Cotter outside the steps of the columned façade.

"Jacob, Mrs. Hunt's husband and I have been discussing your venture into the vineyard operation. Mr. Hunt is in the commodity importing business based in Hartford with an office in New York."

Mrs. Hunt and Mrs. Colt stood looking at Cotter.

"I have the documentation indicating the Pasteurization process works. Any vineyard producing a good wine with a long shelf life would be a worthy investment." Cotter looked at them anxiously.

"We agree. I have sponsored ventures before, as you may well know, Jacob." Mrs. Colt gave a nod to Mrs. Hunt and then faced Cotter. "Both my late husband and I are wise in business matters. Failed ventures we called philanthropic adventures. The successful ones made us money. If the Hunts and I back your vineyard it will cost considerable up front. I'm prepared to give you the particulars."

"Please do Mrs. Colt." Cotter folded his arms. He wore a long heavy winter coat. The warming sun was shining and melting some residual snow. He didn't mind the cold temperature and it appeared the two ladies didn't either.

"We propose a tripartite partnership be drawn up–all profits will be shared amongst the three of us–you, the Hunts and my Colt Enterprises. Is that reasonable and agreeable to you Jacob?"

"It is fair and acceptable." Cotter shifted his weight. *This is an interesting place to conduct business.*

"There are a lot of things to do before we see the fruits of our labors. You have to grow grapes, you have to staff your operation and you need to update your vineyard. I've consulted with the several people in the wine industry and Mr. Hunt, it turns out, is a major importer of French wine." Mrs. Colt nodded to Mrs. Hunt. "I'll need to bring a consultant from France. Jacob, you will provide the staffing. The consultant will import the vine cuttings which could give you a crop by next summer."

"I'm in complete agreement with these plans Mrs. Colt."

"Jacob, from this point on, please call me Elizabeth."

"Thank you, Elizabeth."

"What are you doing for the Thanksgiving Holiday?" She cocked one eyebrow and had a slight grin.

"Actually, I'm having friends over to discuss the activation of the vineyard."

"Well, good. I was prepared to invite you to Hartford but your plan is excellent. We should meet again before Christmas and I'll write to you of our progress. Come, Lillith, we're done."

●

The day flew by for Cotter. He had a quick lunch after Mrs. Colt and her friend departed followed by two-hours of Pharmacy class and a boring lecture on childbirth. In January he would be delivering babies where he'd really learn his obstetrics. "The actual 'doing' of medical practice was what really hones the physician", his father had told him many times.

It was almost four o'clock. He had to talk to Andrew Mashpit and then LaRoque would be bringing him two more people. The Medical Clinic would be closed by then so privacy was ensured. All of the clinic offices were locked when they were not being used. He was the only medical student, or medical anything, left on the first floor of the two-story building. Cotter had his door open. He looked at his notes on compounding tablets made from the Foxglove plant. This herb was useful in "dropsy" or heart failure.

Cotter smelled Mashpit before he saw him appear in the doorway. Mashpit knocked just as Cotter lifted his head up when the horse manure aroma hit his face.

"Mr. Jacob Cotter?" Mashpit's bass voice was strong but his tone was reluctant. He was a little nervous. This meeting could be a turning point in his life.

"Yes. You are undoubtedly Andrew Mashpit. Our paths crossed a few weeks ago when John LaRoque was driving my buckboard." Cotter looked at the man. He was about 6-foot tall, muscular and carried himself well. The man stunk to high heaven but was now clean-shaven.

"I remember John but I guess I didn't really concentrate on any other passenger." Mashpit stared at Cotter's lips.

"Please sit down." Cotter motioned with his hands as he spoke. "John explained about your loss of hearing because of blast and gunfire noise from the war."

"I'm afraid it's true. I was in artillery and demolition with the Connecticut Cavalry support division." Mashpit sat only on the edge of the seat. He tried not to touch anything.

"Where did you learn to read lips?"

"In the Army. I wasn't the only one. Most of us in artillery lost all or part of our hearing. We just naturally began looking at each other's faces after using touching maneuver's to get people's attention." He took his Union cap off and kept massaging the visor.

"You do quite well. We're having no difficulty at all."

"As long as we're face-to-face, sir."

"Please call me Jake when we're in private. I understand you were also a surveyor and worked with dynamite for clearing strategic areas." Cotter sat back in his chair but maintained the facial line of sight.

"Yes…Jake." Mashpit replied. "I was also a map maker. There were no detailed maps of any of the battle sites. More often than not, we identified obstacles or had to create obstacles. Occasionally enemy positions were base camps and were filled with supplies–mostly gunpowder, shot and rifle balls. I was part of the team planting the dynamite."

"I see." Cotter paused, took a breath and almost gagged. "John LaRoque told me about his relationship with you in the Army. I want to tell you my story and then I have some business to talk with you."

"Yes…Mr. Cotter…Jake." Mashpit was thrown off guard.

Cotter gave him his story about being unable to get back to Yale. He told of his bounty hunting years making him financially stable. "And so, here we are today. I acquired the old Clark vineyard property and I want to get it up and running. My schoolwork at Yale will consume most of my time and I need a nucleus of two-to-three full time people to run the winery. You'll be the third if you accept the position I have in mind." Cotter proposed Mashpit survey the entire estate and act as second foreman to the wine-making enterprise."

"Who are the others?"

"We're going to be using a new process to prevent the wine from spoiling. Someone from France will be here to set it up. You and he will be responsible for what happens to the grapes and also help with the general layout of the facility. John LaRoque will be overseeing the farm sector. I'll be working with a general manager who I'll be seeing right after you leave today."

"I have no horse–no transportation." Mashpit massaged his hat mercilessly. "My living quarters are in the back of the city horse stables. Look at me…Jake. How can I possibly even look like a supervisor?"

"You'll be living on the estate." Cotter handed Mashpit a small envelope. "Your salary will commence immediately. In this envelope is your first week's pay plus a clothing allowance. Do you want time to consider the offer? I don't want to rush you but people with your qualifications are hard to come by. I'll have to press forward and continue my search tomorrow if you feel you can't do what's expected or you're uncomfortable with the responsibility."

"Mr. Cotter…Jake, I accept your offer." Mashpit hadn't opened the envelope.

"Before you totally commit yourself, I must tell you of a few more requirements. Van Haven Wineries does not look upon competition kindly. I want you to wear a gun. John LaRoque and I will train you. I also want you to begin by buying an ample supply of dynamite."

"The gun is no problem. I can handle a pistol or a rifle." He smiled at Cotter. "Hell, I can even handle cannon. But what's the urgent need for the dynamite?"

"There may be some land needing clearing and a little danger in the job. The gun and the dynamite may be crucial for protection."

"Protection? How?" Mashpit stood up.

"You're expertise in demolition may or may not be needed for offensive purposes but we need immediate defenses set up on the perimeter of my estate. Are you still with me?"

"Yes. You don't have to ask again. When do I start?"

"Right now. Get a change of clothes, burn the ones you have on and scrub that horse stench off."

"Yes, sir…I mean Jake."

There was a knock on the open door. LaRoque's large frame filled the opening.

Cotter looked at his pocket watch. "Four-thirty, right on time." Cotter looked up at LaRoque coming toward him. "Mr. Mashpit will be joining us tonight–permanently."

"Please call me Andy." Mashpit walked to the door and waited while LaRoque and the two others moved into the clinic office.

"Okay…Andy. John will assist you in selecting the correct clothes for the job and direct you about the other tasks we discussed. Gather your necessary belongings. You'll be living with us from now on."

"Yes, sir." Mashpit reverted to formality in the presence of the new arrivals.

"John, I'll see our two guests get safely toward their home. Please get along with Andy."

LaRoque smiled as he got the two people settled in chairs and went out the door with Mashpit.

Cotter turned to the man and the woman.

"Mr. and Mrs. Hamer, I'm glad you both could come." Cotter turned to focus on her husband.

"Mr. Hamer, I have a proposition for you to consider."

# Chapter 10

## Pamela Skyler

Nancy Locke's words rang in Pamela Skyler's ears. "Jacob is going to open the Clark winery. There is no doubt in my mind."

"What evidence do you have?" Skyler spoke in calmative tones

"Kelvin's been spying on them. He and that gimpy blacksmith are fixing up the grape presses and the storage vat buildings. What does that mean to you?" Her face was red with rage.

"Take it easy, dear." Mathew Cotter placed his hand on her shoulder.

There were only the three of them at the meeting. Mathew's wife Elizabeth was in town shopping and Nancy's attorney husband Robert could not break from court. They rarely needed him except for the legalities of the business.

"All right, let's all sit down and look at this." Skyler paused. "Very well, we accept the Clark place is going active. When? They have no grapes. They have no staff. They have no label. They have no market. Jacob is a full-time medical student."

"Yes. There's no immediate threat. So let's talk about the possibilities." Mathew nodded to Pamela Skyler's summary and reality check.

The red engorgement left Nancy Locke's face. She rang the small silver bell on the dining room table summoning the housekeeper.

"Please bring the sherry and pour three glasses." Nancy's voice had lost its bark. She sipped half her stemmed glass and let out a long sigh.

Pamela sipped her sherry and then spoke. "Jacob cannot do anything until next spring and summer. He'll have to get seedlings, till the land, provide irrigation and hire experienced help. We can just let him go ahead and build the place up. He wanted the vineyard as an investment for when he finished school and goes out West. That's what he told us, remember?"

"He told us, yes, but he also said he was not going into the wine-making business. So what are we to believe?" Nancy's neck veins became full again.

"I think we should invite Jacob for Thanksgiving. We should nurture a family attitude. If he was sincere with his plans, then he would sell the Clark estate to the highest bidder." Skyler raised her glass and took another sip. Nancy poured herself another glass.

"Yes. That's a very good idea. We should bring him in closer. Thanksgiving would be good. He's all alone with his hired hand. Let's get him back into family thinking." Nancy drank her sherry. "I think you should foster some friendliness in his direction Pamela. God knows when there last was a woman in his life."

"Honestly Nancy, you don't have to push me on this. I do take a fancy to Jacob and I sense he has a similar interest in me. You must guarantee there will be no more episodes against Jacob and his people like the one Kelvin performed. He must not perceive Van Haven or any of its components as enemies."

"Kelvin's scare didn't work. That's why we should try the opposite–the more friendly, approach." Nancy Locke finished her sherry.

"Very well. I'll drop a letter in his mailbox at Yale." Pamela Skyler smiled.

●

"Mr. Hamer and Gertrin, please relax. I'll open one of the windows an inch-or-two to get the horse smell out. The last man works for the Road Maintenance Department."

Bradley Hamer looked uncomfortable. Neither he nor his wife knew the purpose of this meeting.

"Mr. Hamer, Gertrin has told me of your previous experience in managing a vineyard. I mean, I was told you were a supervisor of the farmhands in the growing and harvesting of the grapes. Is that correct?"

"Yes, Mr. Cotter." Bradley looked at his wife and then back to Cotter with a question mark face.

"May I call you Bradley? And please call me Jake. I'm going to get the old Clark winery back into production. I estimate it will take a year-and-a-half to our first vintage." Cotter allowed a few seconds for the Hamers to exchange glances and then resumed. "I know you have some questions and probably doubts about my involvement. After all, I'm not experienced in this area and I am a full-time medical student."

"But…Jake, what has this to do with us?" Bradley shifted his position in the uncomfortable clinic chair.

"I need a person like you to co-direct the wine-making and assist the supervisor with the planting and harvesting. It will be a full time position and will pay much more than your job at the mercantile."

Bradley seemed brightened and then began to tighten his grip on the cane rails of the wicker chair. "Did Gertrin tell you why I left the wine business?"

"I've been informed of the violence, supposedly from the Van Haven Company."

"There's no supposin'. Several people were killed."

"You do know my brother and sister own the Van Haven winery. Part of my staff's duties will be to deflect, contain and eliminate any such hostile activity." Cotter allowed his gun holster to show through the edge of his opened coat. "For added safety, I would offer one of the carriage houses be converted into a very livable home for you and your family. It would be at no expense to you."

"Mr. Cotter…Jake, I have only recently, and, because of you and your employing Gertrin, realized stability in my home life. There is more to running a vineyard than growing and picking grapes. There are the presses, the storage and bottling."

"You are absolutely correct." Cotter smiled. "I'm going to tell you something which for now is not to be in the public domain. Two Hartford interests in addition to myself will finance my wine operation. They have already sent for a specialist in grape selection and wine processing. We will, in fact, be using a brand new bottling concept called Pasteurization. It will take us up to six-months to install the equipment while the planting is taking place. I need you to identify and hire the appropriate number and kind of hands to work the winemaking. Their jobs would begin in March."

"This is overwhelming Jake." He looked at his wife. "Gertrin and I must consider all the options. We have three children and I have a steady position which may not be available should your farm fail."

"Bradley, we are not planning for failure. We have the financial backing and a winemaking expertise which Van Haven does not. Our wine will not sour in the bottle. Our label will become a New England standard in short order. Life at any level Bradley, is taking risks to establish a secure future. Please consider my offer in such a light. I would like your decision before or right after Thanksgiving. Gertrin do you have any questions?"

"Jacob, I…we are overwhelmed. Bradley and I will have an answer before Thanksgiving I am sure." She smiled and stood up as Cotter rose from behind his desk.

They shook hands and Cotter watched as the Hamers left the clinic.

Outside the Yale Medical Clinic building, Bradley and Gertrin Hamer drove their buckboard at a medium pace as they headed for their home.

The air was crisp and the street lamplights offered shadows in the spaces and small alleys between buildings. Kelvin Danzer stepped out of the alley facing the clinic leading his black horse. Steam from the horse's nose and Danzer's mouth was barely perceptible. He looked at the Hamers disappearing into the night and looked back at the clinic building.

●

"Oh my god, what is that smell?" Samantha Wigglesworth of the General Mercantile and Dry Goods Emporium went to make sure the door hadn't been left open. It was the end of the workday and the accumulation of horse droppings and horse urine on the roads was ripest at sunset.

"Did someone bring their horse in here?" An older lady stopped probing the pile of corsets and sniffed the air.

"I think we should have shopped for the clothes before the bath, shave and haircut." LaRoque had gotten used to the stench of Mashpit's clothes.

"Yeah but Eloise's was the only place taking me and wouldn't do the shave or the haircut until after five o'clock. The barber said flat no, remember?"

"Yeah but the barber's strange. I mean he feels your head all over and starts telling you about who you are or who you should be and what the future holds." LaRoque only went to the barbershop three-times a year but he always went to Mortimer's.

"He calls himself a phrenologist. I bumped into one down in Nashville." Mashpit started to laugh. "I remember he had a weird name like this guy."

"As bad as Mortimer Pignast?"

"No. I forgot his name. I bet he takes me on his barber chair now that Eloise's girl made me over."

"You can bet on it once we destroy those smelly clothes."

The Green Moss saloon provided baths, shaves, and hair-cuts. It also had several rooms upstairs with bedding and dressers. They were for entertainment use only per the sign over the bar. Eloise O'Dhik's saloon and whorehouse was an unspo-ken-of habitat established with the industrial surge in New Eng-land ten-years prior to the Civil War. Eloise's main rule was none of her ladies would be intimate with anyone without proper sani-tation and cleanliness. Husbands who came home from work looking pristine and smelling of non-barbershop cologne were suspect by wives as having frequented Eloise's place.

Wigglesworth kept her distance from Mashpit, as did several other late customers. The store manager motioned her to hurry up and make the sale. She approached Mashpit and LaRoque.

"Gentleman, can I help you?" She held her breath.

"He takes a size like mine." LaRoque patted Mashpit on the shoulder. Mashpit hadn't been facing the saleswoman and turned to look in her direction.

"Yes ma'am, I need a pant-suit, heavy duty work clothes, three shirts, a winter coat and an oiled-canvas duster." He beamed at his new importance. He hadn't been a customer for other than a hot meal in three-years.

Wigglesworth looked down at his worn, stained boots.

"And yes kind lady, a new pair of boots, size 12."

LaRoque ushered Mashpit to the changing area carrying Mashpit's new clothes.  Wigglesworth dropped the new boots outside the closed sliding curtain.

What emerged was truly an amazing transition. Mashpit wore a dark blue six-button vested suit matched with a light blue shirt and bandana. His clean-shaven appearance could now be appreciated without the horse manure impregnated stench to his clothes. The new cologne was refreshing. Mashpit stood as tall as LaRoque in his new black high-heeled boots. He was actually a handsome man without facial scars. His blue attire enhanced his blue eyes. He approached Wigglesworth.

"I would like to pay in cash, Miss...?" Mashpit probed for her name. There was no wedding ring on her finger he noticed.

"Why...it's Miss Wigglesworth, Samantha Wigglesworth." She didn't recognize her customer.

"Andrew Mashpit, or just plain Andy to you Samantha, if I may be so bold as to use your first name." Mashpit put on his best friendly smile.

"Of course, Andy. How come I haven't seen you in here before?" She looked at the cash. "A man of your means should be a regular here."

"I will now as long as you promise to wait on me, Samantha."

"Oh, I certainly will make myself available to you in the store, Andy." She wrapped his other new clothing and gave them to LaRoque relegating him as Mashpit's valet. LaRoque rolled his eyes and looked away.

"One thing Samantha, I always want to be right up front with a proper working lady like yourself. The reason I don't usually shop for myself is I lost my hearing during the war. I'm okay though if we look at each other."

"Oh, I'm sorry, Andy. Such a fine gentleman, and a war hero too." Samantha Wigglesworth was smitten. "You certainly have overcome your handicap."

"Perhaps I can call on you Samantha." Mashpit beamed.

"Well, perhaps. Oh Andy what about a hat, you don't have a hat." Wigglesworth led him to the hat section.

As LaRoque and Mashpit were leaving Wigglesworth shouted after him, "What should I do with your old clothes?"

Mashpit was turned away and didn't hear her. LaRoque answered her. "Burn them."

●

Cotter went to the student's mailroom every morning. So far most of his mail had been from his real estate transactions, his bank and one letter from Elizabeth Colt. The letter from Colt reaffirmed both her's and the Hunt's commitment and gave him a date to expect the French wine expert. His mailroom pigeonhole held two letters today. He looked at the names on the return addresses–Charles Garrison MD and Mrs. Pamela Skyler. *Well, ladies first.* He opened the scented envelope. *It's her scent— lavender.*

Dear Jacob:

I was hoping you would contact me after our delightful first meeting at the Locke's. I certainly do admire how you picked yourself up from imagined isolation after the war ended. Yes, I say imagined because I'm sure we could have worked something out for you to go back to Yale. Not right away, of course, Mathew and Nancy did explain that. You could have worked the winery with us and used the income as you are using your savings now. But it's all in the past. Perceptions, right or wrong, of what might have been or could have been are of no purpose now.

I would very much like to see you again, Jacob. Your brother and sister would also like to see you on a regular basis. But me first. We are very much alike. We are both isolated by circumstance and both of us have goals. It is admirable you will become a physician. As a businesswoman I also admire the way you are investing your money in real estate. You do remember telling us you would be divesting the Clark property when you are an MD. I know this goal is two-to-three years away but you do not have to live in isolation. Please let us talk soon.

Would it be very forward of me to ask to meet at Tabatha's Tea House next Wednesday at two o'clock?

Very much looking for your reply,

Pamela Skyler

Cotter remembered the comely woman. *Could she be as self-centered and devious as my brother and sister? Perhaps it would be good to "know thine enemy" as my father always advised. But not Wednesday. LaRoque, me and now Mashpit have a standing agenda at the shooting range every Wednesday.* He opened the second letter.

Dear Jake:

I sincerely hope the transition back into the world of medicine and surgery was easy for you. I suspect it was. Dr. Randall had told me you might complete Yale in two rather than three years. I really hope this is possible.

Medical practice here in Endura is challenging but every day Dr. Wills and I advance an inch-at-a-time. Wills and I have developed a combination clinic and hospital. We have a woman who helps attend our hospital patients. So far we are the only ones administering ether anesthesia. The town has a population of over 4,000 and typical of this section of east Texas, cattle-raising and farming are the main industries.

Unfortunately lawlessness abounds and I find that 50% of our practice is trauma from gunfights, pugilism or accidents. Most of the accidents are not really accidents, I'm afraid. Our local land baron–his name is Victor Vlack–is trying to control the entire town of Endura. He's dropping hints he wants to be State Congressman. He's using his huge land-holdings and generosity to the town coffers as evidence of his sincerity. He has his strong-arms block any opposition candidate possibilities at this local level. Vlack's appetite for property is abnormal. He pressures the farming community to render their property to him. Does that sound familiar? From what you told me about what your family did to the local wine producing community, I'm sure you can relate to what I'm writing about.

Wills and I really need you down here. If we can develop a full-fledged hospital and establish law enforcement, Endura could become a city with strong political representation. However, first things first. When Jacob Cotter becomes Dr. Cotter you will walk right into a waiting practice begging for modern medical improvements. Wills and I have done wonders and with the three of us we could expand the hospital and the area we serve.

Best of luck and keep writing,

Charles Garrison MD


Cotter folded each letter and put them into his saddlebag. He considered how alike and unalike each person was. *Pamela Skyler–was she really interested in him as a person or was she assigned to keep track of him and his farm? Maybe it was both. They were both alone without mates, although she was married until her husband died during the "disputes".*

Cotter thought about his friend Charlie Garrison. *Garrison had talked about his dream of establishing Yale-quality medicine in his hometown of Endura, Texas even during medical school. He was driven by this ideal and now expressed a responsibility to the community. A strong medical base in a Texas City would have the power to bring about political clout. Both Connecticut and Texas demanded Cotter maintain his Wednesday practice sessions.* He had a strong feeling he had to be honed for both places, especially now that he was going forward with his plans for the vineyard.

# Chapter 11

## Tea

Cotter answered both letters. His reply to Charlie Garrison reaffirmed his intention to join him after graduation. Every letter he sent always included the reaffirmation. Charlie should be receiving Cotter's last letter by Thanksgiving, or the usual two-weeks for it to arrive. The cycle of letters between the two friends was about 18-days. This kind of regularity to their communication seemed necessary for them both to accept the status quo and look forward to a more positive future. Anything more frequent would require the telegraph.

He answered Pamela Skyler immediately, which meant in two-days she would have his response. Wednesday of course was out of the question. He declined but rescheduled for the Monday of Thanksgiving week. Skyler dropped her reply at the New Haven postal service and hired a page to run it to Cotter's Yale mail drop. She had accepted the change of plan and time for four o'clock. As Cotter entered the door of Tabatha's Tea House decorated with yellow and red fallen oak leaves, she waved from one of the eight tables in the small café. Each table was a three-foot circle with four chairs tucked in about a foot each. The only other table occupied had three gray-haired men from the New Haven Port Authority finishing their business. They left as Cotter sat to face Pamela Skyler.

"It's so good to see you again Mrs. Skyler." He touched her offered hand as he sat down.

"And also to see you too, Jacob. Please do not call me Mrs. Skyler. It implies that I'm not available and suggests this meeting is improper, when the exact opposite is true." She gave him a disarming smile.

A matronly lady with an orange trimmed brown apron came to their table and took their order for tea and biscuits.

"I must apologize for not initiating our meeting. Between school and refurbishing my farm, I've lost track of time."

"I understand fully Jacob. Do you find medical school difficult?"

"Not difficult at all. It's just a lot of work with patients during the day. Plus, I have lectures interspersed and study at home at night."

"I selected Wednesday because I understood the students have the day off from the classroom and the clinics. Obviously, I was wrong."

"No, you're correct. I use Wednesdays to work on the farm and catch up on textbook-reading."

"With only one farmhand and a housekeeper, I can understand how you might need the extra day."

"I have two workmen now."

"Jacob Thanksgiving is a family tradition here in New Haven and Nancy and Mathew would like to have both of us to their home this Thursday."

"Why thank you, and them, for the invitation, but I've already made plans at my home."

"Oh dear. I've been presumptuous. I mean, I'm all alone and I thought you might…you know… also be somewhat isolated." Skyler blushed.

"Well my housekeeper and her family will be joining me and my two hands. It's sort of a celebration–it's our first Thanksgiving together."

"I understand, Jacob."  She met his blue eyes with hers. "I've heard you might be fixing up your place for making wine in the near future."

*Good, let's clear the air and then get down to us.* He gave her a small smile and sat back in his chair. "Yes. I have some backers from Hartford who are interested in building up my property as an investment. You may recall my original plan was to restore the farm for sale when I graduate."

"So it's just for speculation?"

"On my investors' part. I'll divest my share of the winery after graduation when I leave Connecticut."

"Are you really going to follow through with that plan? When you told us, I thought it was a tentative idea based on a discussion with your father during the war. The war is over and things change Jacob."

"So far the plan has not changed." He paused and sipped his tea. Cotter waited for her reply.

"Jacob, I see I need to get to know you better. The country is at peace now. We have both experienced life's tragedies and should rethink our future. I propose we meet again and talk about only us." Her voice was mellow. She reached under the table and touched Cotter's hand.

"I would like that very much." *Be careful, she's a beautiful woman.* He looked from her face to her pushed-up bodice. Her light brown hair was silky. It was partly up on the top of her head under a petite brown lacy hat. The rest of her hair fell straight to her shoulders. He felt a slight engorgement in his groin. *Watch out. Be human but watch out.*

"Can we meet at my home next Jacob? It's halfway between your farm and here."

"That would be very nice. I'm looking forward to it." Jacob rose at the same time and left payment for the tea and fare.

"I should be paying for this Jacob. This meeting was my arrangement."

"I actually thought of it first but was late to act. Please let me do the honors." As Cotter stood up to offer Skyler her winter wrap his coat jacket opened revealing his holstered pistol.

"Goodness Jacob, why do you wear the gun?"

"It's just a carryover from the war and my last job. I feel uncomfortable without it. Maybe with time I won't need its security." He walked her to the carriage stone out front with her waiting buggy and helped her up.

"I look forward to our next meeting Jacob." She touched the whip to the horse and went off with the hooves kicking up some straw and detritus from the road.

"What is your agenda my dear Pamela Skyler and how much of it is from my brother and sister?" He spoke to the cool air as he walked to his tethered palomino.

●

Cotter sat in the living room in front of the fireplace with Mashpit and LaRoque. A light snow was settling with barely noticeable accumulation. Cotter commented he always liked snow on both Thanksgiving and Christmas.

"When are the Hamers coming?" LaRoque asked.

"Any minute now. They're due by eight o'clock." Cotter replaced his pocket watch. "Why are you so anxious?"

"I'm getting hungry just thinking about all the food." LaRoque looked at the snow falling outside the window.

"You just ate breakfast for God's sakes." Mashpit was watching their faces.

Cotter faced Mashpit. "Andy, I was impressed with the way you handled the gun yesterday. I thought artillery was your game."

"The problem with artillery, Jake, is the enemy was always trying to overrun our position and I had to use my sidearm more than once to save my hide." Mashpit sat down on the plush couch and looked at the fire. He bent down to pick up a funny-looking log.

"Don't throw that in the fire Andy." Cotter reached over and grabbed it from him in case he didn't hear.

"Why? It's only good for firewood." He looked from Cotter to LaRoque.

"Andy, take a good look at this piece of tree." Cotter held it in a vertical position. It looked like a 12-inch diameter tree trunk segment, bent and fragmented in the middle. It had multiple hack marks. "Did Mother Nature do this?"

Mashpit inspected the bent section. "Hell no and no beaver did either. This was an axe cut but it's at several levels. The cutter must have had poor eyesight."

"Or he chopped it at night."

"Who chopped what? Come on you two what's this all about?" Mashpit put the log down.

LaRoque told the story of the incident three-weeks ago in the snowstorm and of the tree falling. "I saw the glint of shiny steel just before the tree fell. It could have injured Mrs. Hamer, me and the horses."

"Sabotage?" Mashpit looked at Cotter for the response.

"I'm afraid so. It appears we have enemies. I want you to wear your gun at all times." Cotter stared at the expression on Mashpit's face. "What's wrong Andy?"

"The other day when I went into the Green Moss, I got out of the bath while some thick set man got into the next tub. His clothes and gun were draped over the chair in the corner of the room. On top of the gun was another holster. It carried a bright shiny axe."

LaRoque jumped up. "Who was he?"

"I don't know, but he had a mustache shaped like a horse-shoe and extended off both sides of his trimmed chin beard."

"Kelvin Danzer." Cotter breathed.

"Who?" Mashpit looked at his two colleagues.

"Nancy Locke's hired gun." LaRoque rubbed his right thigh as they heard a bustle of activity at the front entrance. He looked out the window. "Great. The Hamers are here. Let's help them in with the rest of the food." The turkeys had already been shot and dressed after they had their Wednesday gunfire exercises.

"I want both of you to keep this Danzer thing to yourselves. I'll inform the Hamers in due time." Cotter was uncomfortable with the task. He'd wait until the Hamers were settled in their new home on the grounds and had a degree of confidence about their safety.

Bradley Hamer was introduced to LaRoque and Mashpit. He spoke to Mashpit who truly looked like a clean-cut businessman with an athletic build.

"You look familiar, Mr. Mashpit. I know Mr. LaRoque from his commuting Mrs. Hamer back-and-forth but I have the feeling we have met before."

Mashpit was silent. He had been looking at the three Hamer children going in and out the door bringing food from their wagon. He hadn't heard a word Bradley had said. LaRoque tapped Mashpit on the shoulder to turn him around.

"Andy, Mr. Hamer was speaking to you."

"Oh, Mr. Hamer, I'm sorry. I'm afraid I'm quite deaf from the war."

Bradley Hamer repeated his remarks.

"Oh no, sir, we've never met. I've just come into the employ of Mr. Cotter."

The four men formed a circle of the living room chairs and discussed the farm and the re-furbishing of the winery. LaRoque and Cotter took Bradley on a tour of the place while Mashpit went into the kitchen after his introduction to Mrs. Hamer.

"Mrs. Hamer one of my talents in the Army was as assistant cook for the artillery battery. May I be of help?"

Hamer was overjoyed, as was her 16-year-old daughter who was helping with the meal preparation and trying to keep her two younger brothers from beating the hell out of each other.

The feast of Thanksgiving was enjoyed by all, even the two younger Hamer boys who especially liked Mashpit and the fact he couldn't hear except when you looked at him. During dessert, Cotter decided to turn to the matter of the expansion of the winery.

"Bradley, have you and Gertrin come to a decision about moving here now that you've seen firsthand what we have and what we have to do?"

"Yes, Jake, we have. The house is more than adequate. It will take about two-months to completely refurbish to our needs. If you give me the okay to begin hiring the people, I would like to start right after Christmas." He looked at his wife for a nod of agreement which was given immediately.

"Wonderful." Cotter raised his wine glass in a toast to his newfound family.

●

"Charles when you were at Yale, did you celebrate Thanksgiving with a turkey or a beef feast?" Dr. Stanley Wills at 56, wearing Benjamin Franklin spectacles and with a slight protuberant belly, looked at the round of beef the cook would rotate over the fire every 2-to-5-minutes. The fireplace was centrally located in the large living room which was also the center room at the first floor of the three-bedroom house. Curtained windows were opened about four-inches in the living room, the kitchen, dining room and the combination study-library. The appetite-stimulating aroma of the roasting meat permeated the house and the immediate perimeter of the ranch-style Texas house.

"Turkey, of course, it's a New England tradition and the damn birds were everywhere." Dr. Charles Garrison looked up from reading the editorial page of Endura's only newspaper–The Endura Clarion. Garrison was trim and muscular compared to his partner. His only real exercise was his "forced" weekly two-mile walk to their combination hospital and clinic. He also assisted the single laborer with carpentry around the house and grounds. Garrison learned construction from his father, who also was a doctor but had nurtured his son in partaking of what he perceived as necessary survival skills. In addition to being able to build a shelter, Garrison's dad taught him how to shoot, hunt and defend himself. The elder Dr. Garrison would take Charlie on house calls when he reached fourteen and praise the boy when he would anticipate his father's diagnosis and treatment. Charles Garrison wanted to be like his dad and he had achieved his goal. Unfortunately his father was no longer alive to see his son as a mirror image of himself. While Charles was at Yale, a highwayman gunned down his father, Dr. Reed Garrison, on his way back to town after delivering a baby at one of the homestead farms. The town marshal had not been able to find his father's killer but the rumor was the killer was Victor Vlack's hired gun.

"What's so interesting you have your nose in the paper on this fine day of Thanksgiving?" Wills was a conservative physician, husband and friend. He had also been a friend and younger colleague of Garrison's father.

"It's Vlack, again. He keeps promoting his anti-city defense about Endura but what really bothers me is his self-justification about assimilating the farmer's land. He actually states 'agriculture and cattle-raising go hand-in-hand but the two should come under one roof'."

"Yes–his roof." Wills looked at his watch and cranked the round of roast. "Jessie is late for turning the beef."

"Vlack wants the whole town of Endura to work for him. Listen to this, 'the burden of taxes and the overhead of seed, fertilizer, crop storage and transportation to market do not have to be shared with the homestead families by the cattlemen.'" Garrison put down the paper. Wills raised his hand to interject a comment.

"You have to admit it's a good sell. He doesn't advertise about wanting to get rid of them. He wants to absorb them–pay them as hired hands."

"At his pay rate. He says in the paper already over five homesteads have come into his fold." Garrison put the paper down.

"And we know how and why. We've had to put together some of their shot up bodies and bury several of the other resisters. Was there anything about us or against the expansion of our clinic and hospital?"

"No, nothing in this issue. Oh, I got a letter from Jake Cotter yesterday." Garrison went into the study and came back unfolding the pieces of paper.

Garrison read the highlights. "It seems Jake has a similar situation developing with a vineyard monopolizer. The group is headed by his brother and sister."

"It's something I could never understand. How does a family cut out a righteous member like Jacob Cotter?"

"They must be from the same mold as our Victor Vlack." Garrison's face changed from severe to hopeful. "Jacob still wants to join us and the good news is Yale is giving him credit for his years helping his father in the War. They knocked off a year of medical school."

"Well, it's good news but we could use him right now." Wills rubbed his chin in contemplation. Some voices from the kitchen brought them back to Thanksgiving Day.

"You men come on in here and help us." It was the voice of Miranda Wills and then joined by Garrison's wife, Deirdre.

"Charles Garrison you get in here. Let Jessie tend to the roast beef. We need your help with the vegetables and clean-up." Deirdre Garrison's voice was musical. "Hurry up before our guests arrive."

"We should be thankful Vlack hasn't tried to attack us yet." Garrison got up and patted his colleague on the shoulder.

"That's right. We have our families and today the good Lord wants us to remember this–and Him of course."

"Of course." Garrison smiled and they both went into the large kitchen.

●

"He's already made plans? That was his reason to deny us his presence?" Nancy Locke clutched her husband's arm, as her face grew red.

Pamela Skyler took a deep breath and brushed imaginary dust from her chest and readjusted the cameo choker at her neck. "He has friends coming to discuss further renovation of the Clark winery."

Pamela had to get this out first and let Nancy ventilate before the festivities of the holiday began. There was only Mathew and Elizabeth Cotter present. Danzer and his friend would arrive soon. Robert had asked a guest to come over but he wasn't due until noon.

Elizabeth Cotter poured a sherry for Nancy and herself. Nancy grabbed it and drank it down at the same time as Elizabeth. Nancy stood upright clutching the edge of the dining room table. She stopped hyperventilating and raised her right arm with the palm up. "All right, all right. We must accept Jacob opening the winery. Your first meeting was good Pamela. It was non-threatening and cordial. Our goal is still to bring Jacob back into the family fold."

"Jacob still maintains his purpose in this venture is realizing his investment in the property, and perhaps gain a small profit. He's still talking about selling out and leaving New Haven when he graduates Yale."

Robert Locke cleared his throat to enter the discourse. "Why don't we just let him build it up and sell it to us? We can outbid anyone in the Hartford-New Haven valley."

"My thoughts exactly," said Mathew Cotter. He walked over to the window and pulled aside the bronze-toned drapery. "Why aggravate ourselves. Let's do as Nancy originally suggested. Get him back into family thinking. Pamela, are you going to see him again?"

"Yes, of course, I am. I've invited Jacob to my place for a more…" she paused and smiled. "…intimate atmosphere to talk about personal things."

"Don't forget to bring up his duty to the family business." Nancy sucked down another sherry. Elizabeth Cotter joined her.

"I don't think it would be appropriate for what I had in mind." Pamela Skyler looked at the group and pulled up her forearm length tan glove. "Let's be practical about this. The next time I see Jacob Cotter I want to be the focus of his attention. It will take a little time but his reorientation to domestic considerations has to be gradual. For him to regain trust in us, we…I mean 'I'…must be non-threatening."

"You're right Pamela. Jacob is still fresh from the war–in his mind, at least. And his two years of bounty-hunting are another layer of insulation which has to be peeled away." Robert Locke turned from Skyler to Nancy. "We must be nice. We must be friendly. And, may I add, he is, after all, a family member."

"His vineyard will not be operational for at least eight-months or more. We have time on our side." Skyler looked at Mathew who was still looking out the window.

"I agree with the soft and gentle approach." Mathew released the drape. "Here come our guests.

Mathew Cotter opened the door for Danzer and the pleasant fortyish woman at his side. The housekeeper took their coats. Danzer surrendered his fur-collared winter coat and kept his buttoned heavy brown tweed jacket in keeping with the semi-formal attire for the holiday. He made an unconscious pat to his left chest and felt the reassuring solid presence of his axe. He hung up his gun on the coat tree. Danzer motioned his lady friend forward.

"I think you all know Miss Eloise. Eloise O'Dhik."

"Happy Thanksgiving," She scanned the room. "Hello Mathew and Robert–it's been a while hasn't it?"

Mathew Cotter and Robert Locke looked at each other and then each, in turn, touched her offered gloved hand.

Elizabeth Cotter poured herself another sherry as she glared at her husband. She chugged down her drink. Eloise and her tavern with its not-so-concealed brothel offerings were known throughout New Haven. It remained a stolid institution over the years because even the Chief of Police occasionally frequented the place.

Attention was diverted from Eloise to the knocking on the door. A tall man, made taller by his formal Dickensonian hat and wrapped in a knee-length fur coat stepped into the room and used the boot brush to scrape off the street debris. His outer garments were taken away and the tall gentleman with the tree-trunk torso and bald head put on a smile when he saw Robert Locke.

"Happy Holiday to all. Hello Robert, I want to thank you for inviting me." They shook hands heartily.

The three women looked at the stranger. He appeared to be well known to Mathew, Robert, Eloise and Danzer.

"It is our pleasure to have you Doctor." Robert stood beside him to perform the introduction. "Let me present Doctor Mortimer Pignast."

Pignast moved around the dining area touching the hands of the female guests in his greeting. Pamela Skyler held on to his fingertips.

"Doctor? Are you from Yale?" Skyler thought she knew all of the more prominent New Haven physicians.

"No, indeed, my dear lady. I am from the school of Dr. Franz Josef Gall–of Vienna. I am a doctor of Phrenology." Pignast smiled at the group and gazed intently at Skyler's head.

# Chapter 12

## LaRoque

"Just watch out, is all I'm saying." LaRoque rubbed his sore leg with his right hand while pointing at Cotter with his left.

"It's just an evening with a young woman. I can afford one night out. I'm doing well in my studies and besides, what should I watch out for? If she's got seduction on her mind, well I'm as horny as she is." Cotter laughed.

"Didn't you tell us she pumped you for stuff about our wine business?"

"Yes and I gave her what is public knowledge and no more."

"Just watch it. A few glasses of wine and a romp on a bed and you'll give them the whole plan along with dates. Your brother and sister could waylay hiring of the laborers or kidnap the Frenchman when he comes."

"Don't be so suspicious. I'll be careful."

Mashpit had been watching the faces of both conversants. He began laughing.

"What is so amusing?" Cotter asked.

"You overlooked the obvious." Mashpit laughed again as he strapped on his .45 revolver. "What if Danzer is hiding behind the drapes waiting to chop your cock off with his axe?"

"I'll be vigilant. You two worry too much." Cotter smiled and looked at LaRoque rubbing his leg again. "Is that wound still draining?"

"No, dammit. Once it does, the pain will go away."

"Drop your pants and let me look at it." Cotter grabbed his treatment satchel.

"Uh-oh. I'm leaving you two at this point. I have some surveying to do while we still have some daylight left. December has short days and Christmas is only two-weeks away." Mashpit donned his winter coat, hat and gloves. A brisk cold breeze infiltrated the fireplace's steady heat as he opened the door.

Cotter examined a purple spot on the outer aspect of LaRoque's upper thigh. It was the size of his little fingernail. He pressed on it.

"Ow, dammit."

"The sinus tract from your bullet wound keeps scarring over." Cotter dabbed a cotton pad soaked with carbolic acid on the purple spot and opened a folded leather pouch revealing his field surgical kit. He removed the shiny scalpel and wiped the carbolic pad on it.

"What the Christ are you going to do with that?"

Almost before he could finish the question, Cotter plunged the blade into the spot and immediately backed away as a stream of brown, foul-smelling pus shot out and hit the wall three-feet away.

"Dammit." LaRoque screamed and then fell into the chair behind him. His forehead was covered with sweat and then he smiled. "The pain is gone. Thanks Jake."

"I've got to take the bullet out and scrape out the sinus tract. If the infection spreads into the blood stream you'll die."

"Now? You're not going to do it now?" He looked up at Cotter with widened eyes.

"No. I'll make arrangements with the clinic. We'll do it just before Christmas. You'll be completely healed by the time the Frenchman comes in January."

"You're sure about this?"

"You'll get ether and sleep through the whole thing. Four days on laudanum for the pain and you'll be back to work. I'll have Andy and Gertrin take care of you. Don't worry." Cotter washed the scalpel and the wall. "I have to go to the Clinic. Sit in a hot tub for an hour and cover it with a carbolic cotton pad. I'll see you guys tonight."

LaRoque watched his boss, Doctor and friend leave. "Don't worry, he says." LaRoque shouted in the empty living room. "Don't worry. Yes, don't worry, it's not your fuckin' leg."

•

The woman screamed so loud Cotter thought his ears would ring.

"Come on Mrs. Franklin, the baby's almost there. One more push just as the next contraction starts." Cotter washed his hands again with the carbolic solution and padded soap and water between the woman's legs.

"This will be your tenth unassisted delivery in three-weeks, Jacob." Hayes stood to Cotter's side as the woman's next contraction began.

"Okay Mrs. Franklin, now push, push, push it out. That's it, I can see the head." Cotter put his hand over the emerging scalp with its sparse black hair speckled with the blood attendant with the normal labor. He eased the head out and turned it sideways facing his left. Keeping the shoulders vertical would prevent any major laceration. This was the woman's third child and her labor had only been slightly over two-hours. "Here he is." Cotter let the uterus push the baby onto his waiting left forearm and he clamped the umbilical cord. The midwife assistant then held the baby boy who promptly cried and urinated four-feet in the air. "A boy, Mrs. Franklin. That makes number two, right. Two boys and a girl."

"Oh, thank you Dr. Cotter. You're wonderful."

"Don't thank me I didn't produce him. Thank yourself and your husband." Cotter delivered the afterbirth and inspected his patient for lacerations. There were none. He tied off the umbilical cord two-inches from the baby and left the continued care and clean up to the midwife.

"That's what I like to see Jacob." Hayes walked with Cotter to the washbasin. "Deliveries without complications. I wish they were all like this."

"Me too. What's the infection rate since Yale has been using the carbolic solution and hand washing?" Cotter washed and dried his hands.

"One-in-ten deliveries still get infected. However, those are the ones that get delivered at home or on a wagon. Using boiled water is adding to our success rate. I'm going to write a paper on this when we reach two-hundred deliveries."

"Thanks for standing by for me Dr. Hayes."

"Jacob you're doing amazingly well and I have to tell you, your study test scores are outstanding. Your academic rating is in the top five percent of your class."

"Thank you Dr. Hayes but I confess it's the teaching here at Yale that makes it easy for me. You'll have to excuse me, I have to go the medical clinic now and I have a late afternoon discussion on heart seizures to prepare for." Cotter removed his once white gown and put his suit coat on. "Oh and sir, I have a patient coming in for a bullet removal–an old war wound. I would like your opinion on the case."

Cotter discussed LaRoque's leg wound and his evaluation.

"See if you can keep it draining until he comes to surgery. It sounds like you've had more experience at infected bullet wounds than I have."

"During the war, I tended to hundreds but the outcomes weren't very good. I have a good feeling about this one though. With the boiled water, soap and carbolic, we should get a good result."

"I'll be glad to see him with you and be your attending surgeon at the operation."

Cotter ran to the medical clinic building. He had ten-minutes to get there. The snow was light but blowing almost horizontally and the wind was extremely cold.

After his presentation on heart attacks and its critique by the staff MD, Cotter went to his mailbox. He extracted the two letters and knew who they were from by the familiar envelopes and the hand-written addresses–Charlie Garrison and Pamela Skyler.

●

Cotter looked at the two envelopes. He opened Skylers first.

Dear Jacob:

I trust that you had a good Thanksgiving. As I said the last time we met, I would very much like to see you again. I want to get to know Jacob Cotter the person and not Jacob Cotter the Doctor or the up-and-coming wine merchant. Public places are not conducive to personal atmosphere and I would very much like to have the pleasure of your company at my home in West Haven. In light of your school schedule can we meet on a Tuesday evening or a Friday evening? I know you have Wednesdays and the weekends off. My instinct tells me you use the weekend for work on your estate just like your Wednesday off.

Please leave a response to this letter with your Yale mail drop as I am in New Haven everyday on business and it's faster than the postal route. I've enclosed a small map with directions to my house.

Warm feelings,
Pamela Skyler


Cotter pondered the letter–short and to the point. *A map and directions–she's either very presumptuous or very hopeful. Well, I need a balance in my life to modulate the stress of school and my business. "Warm feelings?" What the hell does that mean?* Cotter left a short note of agreement to Tuesday evening at the Yale postal mail office for her.

He opened the letter posted from Endura, Texas.


Dear Jake:
With the Christmas Season heading for a conclusion, Stan Wills and I have been soliciting funds for adding another two rooms to our small hospital. Money is coming in mostly from former patients and their families. We had a good response to an ad we placed in the Endura newspaper–the Clarion. I've attached a clipping. The hospital should have its new rooms plus some needed equipment. And–surprise, surprise–Victor Vlack sent a generous donation with the proviso one of the rooms bears his name. Vlack also wanted acknowledgement of his gift in the

newspaper in the "true spirit of Christmas and the well being of the Endura citizenship."

What a crock of horse dung. We initially told him to keep his money. Two-days later a burning wagon was left in front of our clinic and the hospital building. Vlack sent a note–unsigned of course–which said "fire would never demolish any structure endorsed by the Double V". The man is so blatant. "Double V" indeed. Even an illiterate would know it meant Victor Vlack. I went to the town marshal but he was on Vlack's side (and I think his payroll).

Stan Wills and I accepted Vlack's donation and terms against our principals. Stan pointed out to do otherwise would deprive the people of medical care. It is the patient, after all, who is our main concern. But I bit my tongue taking his money.

I understand you're doing well in school and we hope your winery doesn't succumb to any extortion. We wish we had some stand-up muscle to thwart Vlack. We hope we solve our Vlack problem before you arrive.

Merry Christmas from all of us,
Charlie


Cotter noted his friend's signature was not "Charles Garrison MD". *There is a parallel with my New Haven situation and Charlie Garrison's situation in Endura. Well, if I'm going to see Skyler on Tuesday I need to get a haircut.*

●

Cotter looked at the sign on the storefront and smiled. It read, "Haircut, Shave and free Phrenology consultation." The print size of the name of the proprietor was almost as large as the advertisement–DR. MORTIMER PIGNAST. Cotter had been here several times before. The man was a decent barber but his concept of the human mind and the entire sphere of "Phrenology" had no scientific basis. He and the other students liked to taunt the man. One of his fellow students was ahead of him one day.

"What school did you get a 'Doctor' title from, Mortimer?"

"The field of Phrenology my good man, goes back to Germany in 1820 when our founding father Franz Joseph Gall realized one's different aptitudes and character traits are reflected on the bony prominences of our skull."

"Keep it up Mortimer, you're sounding like a Professor. So what school did you go to, besides barber school?" The student watched in the mirror as Pignast probed his fingers in a massaging fashion over his head.

"I have a certificate from Edinburgh and I am validated by the American Phrenological Fowlers as a credentialed phrenologist. I never attended 'barber' school. The art came naturally as I probed my client's cranium."

"Did you learn barbering somewhere else?" The student persisted.

"To trim a person's scalp is necessary to access the protuberances of the skull for proper interpretation. It was part of the Phrenology training my dear 'Doctor-to-be'."

"And a good hair-cutter you are 'Dr. Pignast'. So feel the bumps on my head and tell me if I'm going to pass my exams tomorrow?"

Pignast smiled as others in the shop laughed at the request. He ran his meaty fingers over the student's brow, around the sides of the temples and ended at the occipital prominence at the back of the head. He cleared his throat.

"My dear man, you have the intellect of a seer, the wisdom of a sage and the zeal of a manipulator of human behavior. If you study and apply your energies to acquiring new knowledge you will surely pass the examination tomorrow."

There was more laughter. Everyone liked Mortimer Pignast as a barber and as a witty professor of the vague pseudo-science of Phrenology.

Cotter knew most of the Yale staff frequented Pignast's barbershop and the clientele included his brother Mathew and his wife's husband Robert Locke.

"Ah, the future Dr. Cotter. Please sit in this chair close to the window. It's a little colder but the light is better." Pignast threw a light blue sheet around Cotter's neck and shoulders. "I'm delighted to see you." Pignast began brushing Cotter's hair and kneading his scalp.

"Does anyone actually come in here for your non-hair-cutting expertise Mortimer?" Cotter let Pignast massage his scalp. It actually felt good. The place itself had the aroma of clove and anise herbs.

"To make appointments, most certainly, Mr. Jacob." Pignast brushed Cotter's hair straight down and affected a part on the appropriate side. He began scissor trimming Cotter's hair over the ends of a two-inch amber comb. "I even sometimes go to a client's place of business or to their home."

"What kind of advice do 'clients' seek?"

"Sometimes personal queries take the form of 'would a future marriage work' or sometimes I'm asked about business decisions."

"How can feeling a scalp give you insight about the future of a business deal?" Cotter turned his head to the right yielding to the pressure of Pignast to do so as he focused on cutting the right side of his hair.

"Training, my good man, training. One can determine if the aptitude for the person to succeed exists by noting the size of the skull over the forehead, for example–like yours. You have a prominent brow and…let me just measure." Pignast applied a calibrated caliper to Cotter's forehead and read off some numbers. "Aha, you have a score consistent with confidence, assertiveness and, I have to add, aggression. You will succeed in whatever enterprise you engage."

"I can't believe it. Everyone has prominent brow ridges, Mortimer."

"Not true. Not true. The Fowler's instruments were developed from Dr. Gall's original studies. Why, you take Mr. Kelvin Danzer, his prominent orbital ridges denote a person capable of fierce aggression."

"I didn't know Mr. Danzer was a customer? What makes you so sure he can be a violent man?"

"It's one of the talents of a certified phrenologist. Besides, he always wears a six-gun and carries an axe in a shoulder holster. Those actions fortify and validate my Phrenological impressions."

Cotter became alert and adjusted his position in the chair. "Where do you tend to Mr. Danzer, surely he doesn't wear his gun or his other weapon in town."

"Oh, indeed he does. He even takes them into Eloise's O'Dhik's establishment. I had the pleasure of meeting him at Thanksgiving at your sister's house where he most assuredly was so attired."

"At the Locke's?"

"Oh, yes indeed. He does work for them, after all. They talked a good deal about you, I might add."

"Anything negative?"

"They are most interested in your new enterprise at the old Clark winery."

"That's nothing new. They know everything everyone else knows."

"But not who your backers are. Robert Locke, my good friend and lawyer confidant, is trying to find out who they might be."

"Why?"

"Of course you know the answer to your question. They'll try to buy them out, naturally."

"Naturally."

"Who are your backers, may I be so bold as to ask?" Pignast stopped his scissors.

"You may."

"May what?"

"You may be so bold as to ask but the information is confidential at this point."

"Just between you and I, Jacob Cotter, I am a man of science even if you don't agree about the foundation of my chosen profession. I do not approve of the likes of Kelvin Danzer. Nor do I like the aggression and monopoly by the Van Haven Winery. You do know they asked me to find out from you or others about your financial supporters?"

"I do now."

"Well don't tell me. What I don't know, no one can pull out of me." Pignast was almost finished with Cotter's hair. "Can I ask you a professional question, Jacob?"

"Certainly."

"I am very much interested in anesthetics. I mean, people are rendered unconscious and wake up to their restored sensorium entirely unchanged, correct?"

"Correct."

"What are the qualifications of the person who administers these chemicals for the anesthesia?"

"Well, I…I mean medical students, doctors and dentists learn to do it."

"What about non-medical doctors?"

"During the war, my father and I taught several people to do it. They needed our supervision at first and they became very proficient. "

"Who were these 'people' and can such people still be trained here at Yale?"

Cotter now had an inkling where this conversation was going. "I personally trained two of our Army surgical assistants and one of our cooks."

"A cook?" Pignast let out a sarcastic monosyllabic laugh.

"The Chief of the Medical Staff, Dr. Hayes, informed us that we, as doctors, can train any of our assistants to administer anesthesia." Cotter stared at Pignast via his reflection in the mirror. "You, for example, would be a good candidate. However, you would have to be affiliated with a physician or dentist to do this–someone would have to sponsor you."

"Could you sponsor me?" Pignast lowered his comb and scissors.

"Not until my fourth year–next year–of medical school. Actually, I think you would be an excellent candidate to help the medical profession."

"Would you consider doing this, Jacob? Next year is okay." Pignast evoked a large smile.

"I most certainly will consider it." Cotter paid for his haircut. "I'll see you again after the New Year–for another hair-cut. We can continue discussing both of our futures."

"Yes. Yes. Merry Christmas in case I don't see you again this year."

Cotter left and went to his palomino.

Kelvin Danzer rode his horse slowly from the alley next to the barbershop and halted halfway out into the street. He looked from the fading Cotter and back to Pignast's sign. He turned his horse toward the Green Moss Saloon.

## Chapter 13

### December 1868

"I can do all your chores John." Mashpit walked into the surgical clinic with LaRoque. "Mrs. Hamer and her family are quite used to my deafness."

"They're supposed to be moved in right after the New Year." LaRoque was nervous about his surgery. He was taking the focus from his ailing leg, the impending operation and the convalescence with the alternative conversation but Mashpit's reassurances were not altering his anxiety.

The receptionist directed them into the surgical preparation area. Cotter appeared after LaRoque was appropriately disrobed and covered.

"John, I've done this many times as we've already discussed. I'll be assisting Dr. Hayes who actually invented the operation seven-years ago. The only pain you'll have will be after you wake up from the ether and I've already told you the laudanum will take care of it."

LaRoque looked around the small surgical amphitheater. He felt like the bull in a bullring. The medical students were filing in and taking their seats. Cotter motioned LaRoque to lie down.

"Hello, again, Mr. LaRoque." Dr. Hayes put a reassuring hand on the patient's right shoulder. "We're both going to be here while you breathe the ether. It doesn't smell really bad and the deeper you breathe the faster you go to sleep. When you wake up, your leg will be fixed."

LaRoque nodded assent and the cloth cone was placed over his nose and mouth. A fourth–year medical student was administering the ether. "Please close your eyes and just breathe natural for now Mr. LaRoque."

LaRoque complied and Cotter placed his hand on his friend's right arm. "Everything will be okay. I'm right here." Cotter motioned the anesthesia to begin.

LaRoque began to smell the penetrating chemical fumes. It was unlike anything he had ever smelled before. He took a deep breath and coughed. The student administering the ether reassured him again and Cotter coached his breathing to be rhythmic. LaRoque began to sense a high pitch ringing in his ears, almost like after shooting his pistol without cotton plugs. The ringing was replaced by complete red-to-orange vision, even with his eyes closed. He thought the sensation strange. Even more strange was the red screen being replaced by circles as the student's voice began to fade. The single circles turned into concentric circles and then the circles merged into a single moving cone of concentric rings and then there was darkness.

"This sinus tract probes to five-inches Jacob. Let's deflect the quadriceps muscle and isolate the sinus completely." Hayes dissected the tract while Cotter pulled on the retractor to move the large thigh muscle out of the way. The sinus tract became a firm tube of scar tissue tinged with the blood of the dissection.

"Looks like it ends right at the bullet." Cotter said. "There's no bone or muscle involved."

"Right," Hayes concurred. "There's a large abscess cavity around the minié ball in the patient's sub-quadriceps fascial plane." Hayes and Cotter spoke loud for the medical student observers. "Please come over and look but do not touch anything." Hayes nodded to the have the ether administration to continue.

"In the field, once the patient was unconscious our operating time was limited to when the patient woke up. This is a great advance with continuous anesthesia." Cotter spoke for the benefit of his student fellows. He remembered such a technique was not possible with chloroform because of its lethal toxicity.

"Yes, students, Jacob has a good point. We can literally take more time and perform the best surgery–but we can't take too much time. Let's cut out the abscess, the bullet and the sinus tract as one specimen. It will minimize contamination and infection after the operation." They removed everything "en bloc" and began irrigating out the wound with the carbolic solution.

"Rub the carbolic thoroughly Jacob. We don't want another infection to take the place of the one we removed." Hayes and Cotter were vigorous in their dousing the operative field and tissues with the germ-killing fluid. Hayes then left a wick of cotton gauze soaked with carbolic beneath the tissues and sewed the wound with only the wick protruding. "Never close an infected wound completely." He told the students. "If you do, it's a guarantee the infection will recur and could be worse than the original." Hayes motioned to have the ether stop.

Cotter accompanied LaRoque to a "wake-up" room curtained off the main amphitheater operating room.

"Well it was uncomplicated, thank God." Hayes wrote some notes in the chart for the attendant. "Don't give him any laudanum until it's certain the ether is not going to make him vomit."

The two young women nodded agreement. They knew their job and they knew about the nausea and emesis sometimes occurring with emergence from the ether.

"Jacob, let's keep him in the hospital for three-days. If the drain stops oozing and there's no bleeding you can take him home and take the drain out after three more days." Hayes smiled at Cotter. "How did I do, Jacob? I know you've done more of this kind of surgery than I have."

Cotter smiled. "You did fine, sir. Thank you."

●

Cotter finished the day with two more deliveries. He was careful to wash his hands thoroughly and was generous with the carbolic solution. He certainly was loathe to have any of the germs from LaRoque's surgery contaminate anyone else. He looked at his pocket watch. It was four o'clock and he was due at Pamela Skyler's at five-fifteen. There was enough time to see LaRoque.

Cotter heard him before he saw him. He also smelled him before he saw him. The sound of retching and unproductive vomiting slowed Cotter's approach. The smell of the ether was still strong. It takes almost thirty-six hours for all the ether to leave a patient's body. He waited for LaRoque to appear to have a respite from his ether nausea.

"John we got the bullet and infection tract out intact. It was all soft tissue without any bone or muscle destruction."

LaRoque looked at him with glassy eyes. "Why am I so sick?"

"It's the ether, I'm afraid. Do you have much pain?"

"No. My leg doesn't really hurt unless I move it and then it's not so bad. When do I stop heaving like this?"

"It varies from patient-to-patient. The fat ones throw up for two-days. Muscular people like you are okay by the evening of the surgery." Cotter thought a moment and asked, "John are you sure the pain is not bothersome?"

"I hardly notice it why?"

"I delivered two babies this afternoon and each lady told me I smelled awful. When you got your ether, all of us in the room were also breathing it, but only the fumes from above your cloth mask."

"So what does it mean?" LaRoque gave a slight retch.

"Well, these women in labor were screaming with pain until after 30-minutes of my return. I'm thinking maybe low dose ether can produce pain relief."

"So what does that have to do with me?"

"After the ether wears completely off, I think you'll need the laudanum for pain relief. This may be important, John. I want you to note the time you ask for your laudanum." Cotter had thoughts of using low dose ether for pain relief during labor. He'd talk to the attending physician supervising the obstetrics unit on Thursday.

"Okay. When do I get out of this place?"

"In two more days if the drains produce only minimal seepage."

LaRoque gagged some more and Cotter excused himself.

"I'll see you tomorrow John."

"What about my package? Where did you put it?"

Cotter went to the bag under the only chair in the room next to LaRoque's bed. He opened the carpetbag suitcase and removed the .45 caliber pistol.

"I don't think you'll have unfriendly visitors. Keep it under your pillow. See you tomorrow."

"Thanks Jake. Oh God..." LaRoque had a paroxysm of dry heaves as Cotter left the room.

Outside, the air was crisp with cold and a slight breeze made it colder blowing a wisp of light snow over the older snow banks. Cotter rode his horse in the direction of West Haven according to Skyler's map.

●

Pamela Skyler was pacing around the living room and going from the dining room to the kitchen and back again. She stopped at the fireplace and rubbed her hands even though they weren't cold–just sweaty.

"For goodness sake Mrs. Skyler, he'll be coming for sure. It's not even time for him to be here yet..." Skyler's matronly 51 year-old housekeeper placed a palm on each of the two pots cooking the evening meal. "...and everything will be ready and warm when he gets here."

"I feel so foolish–being nervous I mean." Skyler touched her right hand to her hair without altering anything. "Don't forget, once the dishes are washed you can go."

"Privacy is guaranteed Mrs. Skyler. You won't even know I'll have left." She laughed.

Skyler gave her housekeeper a reproaching look but the smile stuck.

Both women looked at each other at the sound of a horse snorting and trotting to the carriage stone and hitching post.

"Oh dear, see if it's him, Nester." Skyler wanted to look out the window but didn't want Cotter to see how anticipatory she was.

"Of course it's him. I'll have Jules take his horse to the barn." Mrs. Nester Smood went to the door.

Nester watched through the small pane as Cotter tied his horse to the rail and walked on the cleared path to the doorway. The snow was a little higher here than in the center of New Haven. The door opened just as he was about to elevate the iron knocker.

"Good evening, sir. You must be Jacob Cotter. I'm Nester, please come in."

"Yes. Good evening." Cotter used the boot brush and mat to remove the snow and debris.

"Your horse will be tended to. I must go back to the kitchen."

Cotter stood in the small foyer and continued to dry the soles of his boots on the mat while looking around for his hostess.

"Hello Jacob. I'm so glad you could come for dinner." Pamela Skyler entered from the living room to Cotter's right.

"Come let's sit next to the fire while you warm up." She touched his cold hand and led him into the room.

The fire provided most of the light which was enhanced by a large central candelabrum off to the left in the open dining room and an overhead oil chandelier with the flames on low. A combination of melting paraffin and burning oil provided a base-line atmosphere, which was immediately overlaid by whatever perfume Skyler had chosen for the evening. Cotter gazed at Skyler as she sat down on a sofa cushion still touching, but not holding, his hand. Cotter sat next to her and looked at the fire-place and back to her.

"You're hair is most attractive the way you have it up tonight, Pamela." Cotter smiled. She had minimal face powder and the perfectly placed single drop ruby earrings enhanced the symmetry of her features. She smelled of some kind of flower Cotter couldn't identify.

She returned the smile. "Honestly, I never know whether men even look at a woman's hairstyle. I thought only other women did."

Cotter continued to absorb Skyler's physical appearance. Her green velvet dress clung to her body revealing the shape of her legs. She wore no petticoats and no stays or corset to artificially enhance her bosom. Her neckline was a squared bareness revealing a natural cleavage.

"Since my entry into the medical profession, I'm afraid I've lost my normal powers of observation for femininity–until tonight. Maybe it's the setting and you did tell me there would be no business-talk." Cotter felt his face get warm and feel slightly flushed. He couldn't remember the last time the sensation had occurred.

"Goodness Jacob, I'm glad you qualified that statement." She smiled at his blush. "Wasn't there ever a love-of-your life in your recent past? Oh, excuse me Jacob, I wanted to lead up to such talk. Can I start over?"

"Certainly." Cotter sat back allowing Skyler's fingertips to fall to her lap. It was history-taking time. Nestor appeared with a tea service and left as quietly and as rapidly as she appeared. Skyler poured tea for both of them.

"Well now, you're the youngest in your family. Did Mathew and Nancy treat you like a baby brother? Did they protect you and bring you into their games and circle of friends?"

"This is going to be reciprocal, you know. I'll tell you what it was like being little brother and you tell me what they told you. Agreed?"

"Agreed." She cocked her head in a listening and absorbing pose.

"Nancy came first and then Mathew. It was all the family my mother wanted. When I came along, my mother distanced herself from dad. I mean she then had her own bedroom and locked the door at night. She shunned me and my father had a nanny do the nursing. Mother always referred to me as 'him' or 'your son'. She favored and doted on Nancy and Mathew. Nancy and Mathew joined forces to further alienate me as a member of the family or 'their brother.' As I grew up, I tried to tag along with Mathew but Nancy would always hit me or push me down and grab Mathew's hand and run from me. The nanny left when I was about five and mother would send me to my room crying and sometimes lock the door. Dad would find me later in the evening and he tried to console me. He ended up, more often, than not, taking me to his clinic where he set up a small play area where the children of some of the female patients would be. I got to be a regular fixture in his office." Cotter saw the look of disbelief on Skyler's face. "I can see this is not what you expected."

"Jacob, Nancy never spoke of this." Her brow was furrowed.

"School became a blessing. I had friends at last; even though mother never let me have any at our house. School also was a haven for me and the bonding with dad solidified even more. He'd help me with my studies and took me out hunting and fishing when he could. Mostly, I went with him on house calls."

"What about Nancy and Mathew as you grew older? Didn't they get jealous of your father favoring you over them?"

"On the contrary, our relationship fed into mother's ongoing poison about dad and me. She would slap me on the top of my head and tell Nancy and Mathew the only real family was she and them–not me and dad. Nancy and Mathew were always together. They had few friends. Mother played down my relationship with dad. She told them our hunting, shooting guns and fishing was crude and was for people of low breeding. She took my brother and sister to tea parties with some of her remaining society friends. She was always telling Nancy power belonged to the 'takers' and she and Mathew should aspire to take things of value from others. She taught them about having money and owning property was the same as power. Mother would use me as an example. She had Mathew take away my fishing pole and my Dickens novels. She showed him he could use these things to get me to do his chores. And I succumbed to this. I would wash down Nancy's horse and buggy if Mathew would let me use my own fishing pole or Nancy would let me read my Dickens. They did the same thing to children in school. Nancy got Mathew to have one of his schoolmates come to the coatroom where Nancy was dressing. She deliberately exposed herself to the boy and then both she and Mathew threatened to tell the headmaster about the lecherous peeking unless he did some of their home assignments for them."

"Come now Jacob, How did you know of such things?" Skyler was open-mouthed.

"I overheard them plotting the scheme at home. They laughed and derided me as I labored in my studies. They didn't know I actually enjoyed the assimilation of knowledge. The intimidation and extortion went on through the rest of my school days and into college. Nancy and Mathew went to college in Boston and I stayed here at Yale. With both of them gone, mother began to stay at home and sit idly most of the day. Dad had to get a full-time housekeeper for her. She even needed help to wash and dress herself. When Mathew and Nancy would come home for the holidays or at school breaks she would come out of her depression but with time even these lucid periods became less frequent. Dad and I became closer. I saw him almost every day at Yale, with the Medical College being on the same grounds as the main campus. I lived at the dorm both during college and medical school. I couldn't stand to see my mother wither away even though she had relegated me to an almost non-existence when I was growing up." Cotter looked at the change in Pamela Skyler's appearance. She seemed pensive. "I can stop now or finish with the war."

"Please, please, Jacob, please continue."

"In medical school, I became more of a sponge in absorbing every bit of what was taught and what was in the textbooks. Dad, as usual, was right there for me when I had questions or problems with either an academic or a practical situation. Dad had become Chief of Medical Staff at Yale. Since Yale focuses on surgery, I was swept up with my father's up-to-date skills. We would go over a surgical procedure long after it was completed. Even if it was done extremely well, he would reflect on how we might have improved not only the technique but the management of the patient's stress and anxiety. When the war came he received letters from fellow surgeons begging him or anyone else to enlist. I was caught up in the plea."

"But you weren't a doctor then. You hadn't finished medical school."

"I read the letters to dad. They were heart wrenching. Union soldiers were dying because there was a shortage of doctors. Some of my classmates dropped out and enlisted as surgeon's assistants. It was happening all over the North. I talked my father into letting me go with him. The deciding factor was when mother died. It was right after Christmas of '61. She'd been more reclusive than usual and when Mathew and Nancy came for the holiday she didn't really snap out of it like she usually did. When we all left to go back to classes, she took off by herself in the middle of a blinding snowstorm. It was days before dad and I found her along with a large searching party. She died of exposure. We found her almost five-miles from home in the woods far from the road. The snow was so deep we had trouble even finding the road. It was after her funeral that dad became pre-occupied with the war."

"How did your mother's death affect Nancy and Mathew?" Skyler readjusted her sitting position and crossed her knees. The long dress clung to her thighs accentuating her curves. She draped an arm over the sofa parallel to, but not touching Cotter's shoulders.

"Nancy and Mathew approached dad. Nancy was done with college and Mathew had one semester to go. She'd been buying up land and had purchased a large winery with dad's blessing and Mother's instigation. I was too involved with my medical studies to see how obsessive the wine business had and would become."

"Didn't they ask you to be a part of it?"

"Nancy and Mathew didn't consider me in any of their endeavors from when I was a child to when I was becoming a doctor."

"Didn't they write to you during the war–to tell you of the plans and what they were doing?"

"No. Father and I were perpetually busy. You have no idea how hellish the war was. Every day when we weren't in the field operating rooms we were in the field hospitals tending the wounded soldiers. We worked sometimes a full twenty-four hours. When we slept, people died. In our unit, we were one of nine surgical teams and it wasn't enough. The Southerners had it worse. They had at most only four surgical teams. Sometimes they lost more men to inadequate and unavailable medical care than to outright deaths in battle. Dad and I discussed our plans for after the war. He and I would go back to Yale. I would finish my MD degree and go out west with my friend Charlie Garrison. Dad would resume his academic career and establish a specialty on trauma surgery. We never considered one or both of us dying. At Nashville, our field hospital was overrun and a group of rebels deliberately shot into the hospital tents and then they rounded us all up outside. One of them shot dad point blank in the chest. I'll never forget it. Our forces drove them back. If they had come earlier dad would still be alive. If they had come later I'd be dead also. I wrote back to Mathew and Nancy but never received any mail."

"But they said they offered you a position in the Van Haven Winery when and if you came back." She sat upright and her right arm now touched Cotter's upper back as it leaned on the sofa.

"I never came back. Robert Locke, their lawyer and then Nancy's husband, sent me a letter saying Nancy had become the power of attorney for the family. Dad's will left almost everything to them as I was not considered a survivor of the war."

"You said you wrote to them about your father's death. Didn't the letters convey you were alive?"

"They never answered any of my letters until the war ended. I wrote I was coming home and needed money to complete Yale. I also sent a telegram. I had no idea they considered me dead."

"When my husband and I joined Van Haven, Nancy told us both you and your dad were killed in the war."

"Did they show you a telegram or letter from the War Department stating that?"

"No. We assumed it was true."

"As I said, I wrote to them before the War Department contacted them. Casualty lists of the dead lagged behind sometimes for a month."

"Jacob, are you implying…."

"Yes. They lied. They knew I was alive. Once they legally had the estate to themselves, they wrote back about all the inheritance being tied up in the Van Haven business. They said I could come into the business but there was no money for me to finish Yale."

Skyler moved closer to Cotter. Her arm reached around to touch his right shoulder. "Oh, Jacob, I had no idea."

Cotter raised his right hand. "Now it's' your turn. Who are you, Mrs. Pamela Skyler?"

●

The Green Moss Saloon had a façade painted a flat green with its name in yellow-gold. To the right and below the foot-high print in smaller yellow-gold lettering was "Eloise O'Dhik, proprietor". In still smaller letters on a separate one-foot-square sign read, "Phrenology readings free on Saturday evenings with escort service."

Mortimer Pignast had talked Eloise into supplying his professional services by qualifying the "free" phrenological surveys to her clients.

"My dear Miss Eloise," Pignast began, "If you see an increase of clientele due to my professional presence, I would expect a gratuity of say, one-dollar per person."

"Dr. Pignast, we have a deal only if the clients come more often." Eloise smiled at the bald, pleasant man.

"I can almost guarantee it, madam."

"And remember, two of my girls are barbers, so please, no soliciting for your barbershop."

"Of course not." Pignast had a brisk haircut and shave business without the Green Moss attendees.

Pignast, as "Doctor of Phrenology", provided a service actually desired by the men seeking women for biological release. The ladies of the Green Moss always extolled superlative adjectives on their "escorts-pro-temps" as Eloise liked to call them.

"Oh Mr. Campbell, you are one of the best sexual partners a woman could wish for." This was a common flattery which not only kept the men coming on a regular basis but set them up for Pignast's readings of the natural bumps on their heads.

Pignast used a red-brocade upholstered parlor chair to seat the recently satisfied male. As in the barbershop, he would run his fingers through their hair pressing down on the front, the sides and the backs of their heads. He would announce the anatomically correct names of the skull–"frontal, temporal and occipital protuberances my dear sir."

A typical reading would stimulate the patron to return. One of Mortimer Pignast's favorites was, "Sir, the pulsating sensation on your left temporal reflects an increase in your life span as a result of your recent satisfaction." Another one getting the man coming back was, "It must have been a truly successful and mutual biological release. It is well known by the Fowlers society of such happenings favoring your marital (if married) harmony or (if single) your attracting a correct mate." This latter was always from meditative palpation of the occipital bone with the fingers of his skilled phrenologist hands.

On this Saturday evening, as most others, Eloise greeted her patron, business partner and friend with a hug and a light buss on the cheek.

"Welcome, Dr. Pignast." Eloise voiced the greeting to reassure the men at the bar and the tables were aware of his presence. The women would increase their integration with the men and whisk them up to one of the upstairs rooms.

"Greetings my dear Eloise." He surrendered his winter coat, hat and gloves to a young woman in an evening dress. She wore the typical Green Moss attire–full-length gloves and petticoat-free floor-length clinging dress with either bared shoulders or the top strap or sleeve just falling from the shoulder. The atmosphere was not yet visible. It would be later with smoke from cigars and cigarettes floating like a cloud just above the hurricane lantern chandeliers. Right now Pignast inhaled the essence of beer and pine. Most of the pine scent was from a floor cleaner with a second more biting pine component coming from a large central fireplace.

"Fern is waiting for you upstairs. You are very punctual as usual, Mortimer." Eloise used his first name after the louder public announcement of the phrenology reader being present.

"Thank you, my dear. I shall proceed post-haste and then be available for our 'escorts-pro-temps'."

"Take your time Mortimer. They always wait for you no matter what the time."

Pignast was in good physical form. He was clean-shaven as was his head. At 45 years he had remained unmarried by choice. Biological needs were always tended to by places like Eloise's. However, at this point in his life his emotions had connected with one of the older women of the Green Moss–one Fern Ferndock.

"Fern dearest, I so looked forward to the end of this day when we would meet." The scent of pine left after his ascent to rooms above the courtyard-like saloon. The waft of lilac essence was in the room and would be strongest on Fern. Pignast always used cologne sold by the Phrenology Society regional office in Boston, which arrived by train mail every six months. His was the odor of sweet citrus.

"Mortie, you are truly a wonder." They hugged and kissed like true lovers. "Did you talk with Jacob Cotter?" Fern held his hand as then sat on the love-seat side-by-side.

"Yes I did."

"And...? Come on, don't keep me in suspense." Fern snuggled closer. Her 130 pounds appeared diminutive next to his 180. But both were at their ideal weight for their heights. Fern was 5-foot-7-inches and Pignast was at an even 6-feet.

"Jacob Cotter agreed to enter me in training to administer ether when he enters his last year at Yale which is only six-months away."

"That's wonderful." Fern put her arms around him and they kissed.

"Once I become trained, my income from my shop and the surgery will be more than adequate for our plan."

"Oh, yes, Mortie. I truly love you. We can marry and I can move from this place." Fern's glassy emotional eyes suddenly became serious. "Remember, Eloise mustn't know. If she knew, she might throw me out on the street and bring in someone more long term. She is a creature of business, you know."

"That part is easy, Fern." Pignast and Fern were still in an embrace. "There is a harder part. We must keep Jacob Cotter alive."

"Alive! What on earth do you mean?" Fern pushed herself away to look into his eyes.

"I have been taken into the confidence of the Lockes and Mathew Cotter. If Jacob presents a threat to their winery empire, they will see to his elimination. They have asked me to spy for them. I'm to keep my eyes and ears open to any rumor or fact about Jacob's activation of the old Clark place. They want to know who his partners are. They plan to buy him out when he finishes Yale."

"So. We have a year-and-a-half. They won't do anything until then."

"I don't know. If he has plans to remain independent and the information reaches the Van Haven group, they might eliminate the competition as they have in the past.

"You're leading up to something." Fern stood up placing her hands on her hips.

"I've found out the person enforcing Van Haven's terror tactics and executions is Kelvin Danzer."

"Danzer. God, I knew the man was evil–but a killer. Are you sure?"

"Nancy and Robert Locke have made implications in my presence. At Thanksgiving, Danzer was there with Eloise. Did you know Danzer always carries his pistol? That's why we must be careful about us. I need you to listen up when Danzer is here and to keep an ear about rumors concerning Jacob."

"He also wears a hatchet inside his jacket. One of the girls who had him once told me." Fern shuddered. "Okay. Robert Locke and Mathew still come here. Their wives must not be romantic enough in the bedroom. I'll be alert to the other girls too."

Pignast beckoned her back into his arms. "We'll be all right." The hug and kiss became prolonged and progressed to gentle groping. Within minutes their tensions achieved release on the bed.

●

"You remember I told you I come from Boston. My family, the Prescotts of Beacon Hill, were notables in Boston society since the establishment of the first thirteen states." Pamela Skyler ran her hands down her dress to straighten imaginary wrinkles. She sat straight and directed her blue eyes into Cotter's. Her hands ended up folded on her lap.

"I remember."

"I was an only child. My mother and father told me I was a difficult childbirth and damage to mother meant no brothers or sisters were ever to be." She took a deep breath. "They told me this often–mostly when I complained my friends had siblings or sometimes when they were upset with me. I never knew whether they were directing blame in my direction or just trying to justify to me why I was an only child." She became silent for a moment and looked down at her hands.

"What about school friends? I told you my situation at home sent me to schoolmates and a strong relationship with my father." Cotter allowed her offered hand to rest in his.

"Both my parents were supportive. They sent me to private schools to be with kids of equal station. I met several girls who were also without brothers or sisters. What amazed me was the commonality of active imaginations we shared. I mean, I had imaginary friends in dolls and my closest friend, Agnes, told me she used to talk to a scarecrow in their field whenever she got lonely. Her parents rarely talked with her. I actually considered my situation rather good. Maybe that's why I liked Agnes so much." Skyler picked up her teacup. "My mouth is dry from talking and I haven't said much."

"You're doing fine." Cotter drained his teacup and poured more for the two of them.

"Well, I went on to Vassar College. They taught a liberal arts program which centered on how to be a good society girl and husband to a proper man. A proper husband was defined as an extremely good provider who was Protestant and a graduate of Harvard or other basic society-endowed college–like Yale." She squeezed Cotter's hand and smiled. "I met my husband when I was in my senior year. He was a senior in Harvard.

"Rockland Skyler was one of a dozen men in my debutante dance book. His parents were second generation founders of the Boston Business Association and Security Bank." She blushed at this. "It must seem strange to define him by where he came from but it's how I grew up. I mean, I was introduced to him as Pamela Prescott of 'Prescott Imports'. He immediately began talking about college and then about after college. Neither of us had made any social plans but Rockland's father had directed him to go into the wine business. 'This great new country of ours needs its own labeled wines,' his father told him. We became friends and after college he invited me to several of his trips to vineyards he was considering buying. They were mostly in New York and Connecticut. In between his winery research for a promising acquisition, he worked for his father's import business–mostly with imported wines. We married in 1860 and in 1861 we met Nancy Locke and Mathew Cotter. They seemed to have everything we needed but still wanted another capital investor and partner. At first Rockland thought that Van Haven's business practices were too aggressive but his father advised him an aggressive posture was a sign of good business potential. We moved down here at the end of '63. We just missed your disappearance into the Army."

"We probably never would have met. Nancy and Mathew still cut me out of their activities and interests. Dad never mentioned any of this either–of course there was mother's death and the war at the time." Cotter sipped more tea.

"And I was married."

Cotter raised his teacup acknowledging her statement. "And you were married."

"But I'm not, now." She stared into his eyes again.

"No children?"

"No. We tried but it just never happened and we did nothing about it. I mean I never saw any doctor."

"I know this has nothing to do with you but I don't consider I'm in any position to ask my brother and sister about their personal lives. Why aren't there any children with either of them? Nancy and Elizabeth must have talked about this. I know the topics women discuss behind men's backs."

"Oh, Jacob Cotter, the soon-to-be doctor of great wisdom." She chuckled. "What do women talk about when the men aren't around?"

"They talk about food, clothes, sex and family problems."

"Well, sometimes we do and sometimes we don't." Skyler wrinkled her brow. "Nancy mentioned once she didn't want to bear children. She's afraid she'll die in childbirth. Elizabeth, on the other hand, hasn't been able to consummate her marriage. She told me Mathew cannot…gain access. Why do you want to know about this?"

"Dad always talked about values and why people worked hard. He always told us parents always work to provide for the betterment of their children–the next generation. And what I see, or at least my perception, is Nancy and Mathew are selfish people. They seem to be aggressive for personal gain only."

"And what of me? I'm a business partner."

"What are your personal goals? I wanted to work up to the question–to justify it. I mean personal and not Van Haven Winery goals."

"My background dictates I shall be capable of self sufficiency and not want for life's necessities. It's a Beacon Hill-Boston ethic, I think. At least it's what mother and father always told me. I must excel in business and have a soul mate of similar if not better prospects."

"Rockland fulfilled those ideals, I take it." Cotter stood up as Nestor Smood came into the room.

"Dinner is served, madame. I set the desert and coffee at the hutch. I shall be leaving after you're seated." She was pleasant and motioned them to the dining room while she picked up the tea set.

Cotter and Skyler sat opposite each other as Nestor explained what was in the covered dishes.

"Pheasant, green beans, boiled potatoes and cheese sauce. The wine is claret as you selected, madam. Pie and coffee are on the hutch. Have a good dinner. Good evening, Mr. Jacob Cotter."

"I'm really hungry and this looks and smells wonderful," Cotter said.

Halfway through their meal and only making eye contact, Skyler put her fork down and sipped her wine.

"This is our wine, you know–Van Haven."

"It's very adequate."

"Just 'adequate'?"

"It has a slightly tart or acidic flavor. The cellar temperature must not be correct."

"Well, it's just wine. You asked about Rockland and I take it to mean did I find my suitable mate?"

Cotter smiled and nodded.

"Yes and no. I mean, we fell in love and tried to produce a family but the barrenness put our focus into the business side of living. That's when I became disappointed in Rockland. He was too compromising and not assertive enough in his dealings with

Nancy or Mathew and especially with the tenant farmers. He tried being friendly when being forward and unyielding was what was really called for."

"I'm sure Nancy was aggressive enough for all."

"She certainly is the 'boss' when it comes to decision making. What I'm really saying is when slight force had to be exercised on our competition and our tenants, Rockland was shy and non-confrontational."

"If he voiced an antagonistic opinion, it certainly isn't being shy." Cotter held his knife and fork against the edges of his plate.

"I guess not, but he didn't like to go out in the field with our foreman."

"By foreman, you mean Danzer?"

"Yes. Kelvin Danzer was once a military man and his overbearing no-compromise attitude was at odds with Rockland's principles."

"It's unfortunate about his accident and death. I would have liked to meet him. I met people like Danzer in the Army and there are ways to alter their character." Cotter patted his mouth with a napkin. "Excuse me, Pamela, I have no right to offer any judgment here."

"We're through with the main meal. Let me pour the coffee and put the pie and cheese on the table." She offered no further comment.

He watched her serving the desert. "Pamela, forgive me for being so intrusive." He stood up.

"No. No. I actually feel good about talking about what's in my past. And remember, Jacob, I was speaking of my past." She put a hand on his left shoulder to prompt to sit back down.

They sat on the sofa again after he helped clear the table and get rid of the debris from their meal. The dishes would await Nestor in the morning for cleaning, she told him.

"Jacob, will you be joining your family for Christmas?"

"No. My current commitment is to my small staff and our new vineyard supervisor for this Christmas."

She feigned a pout. "Not even if I give you my Christmas present in advance?" She placed her hands on his.

"Pamela, we don't really know each other intimately enough to share presents."

"Jacob, I can know who and what people are like after the first visit. This is our third." Skyler stood up as Cotter rose–still holding his hands.

"I should go. It's late."

"Tomorrow's Wednesday, it's your day off."

"Only from school. I have the place to tend to. My chief man was operated on today. There's double the work."

"When will I see you like this again, Jacob?" She brought her arms up to his shoulders and stared in his eyes.

He stared down to avoid her face but only got as far as her cleavage.

"I should be settled again after the New Year."

"Can we meet like this again, Jacob? Please." She cupped her hands around his neck and brought her lips to his. "Merry Christmas, Jacob Cotter–almost a Doctor." Skyler held the embrace and her lips compressed to his.

Cotter held his hands at her waist. This was partly to prevent any progression of her romantic efforts and partly to hide his growing erection. She let him go and stood back.

"That was only half a Christmas present because you weren't there, Jacob Cotter. You owe me the other half." Her voice was soft like velvet. "When will I see you here again Jacob?"

"We'll talk after the holidays. Thank you for a lovely evening." He squeezed her hands and went to the door. "I mean it, I had a wonderful evening."

Pamela Skyler watched him ride his palomino from the barn.

Cotter rode at a brisk trot. He reviewed the evening conversations. *Fear of pregnancy and "inability" to have intercourse. No wonder Robert Locke and his brother Mathew were frequent guests at the Green Moss.*

•

Cotter paced the room. The dream about his father had recurred again. This time the sequence had been reversed. He was lying over his father's bleeding body and the fog came. His father was alive and he was talking about both of them going back to Yale.

"Yes, Jacob, going out west and practicing with Charles Garrison would be a wise and noble next step after the war. Medicine is outdated there, as your friend writes to you. You'll be needed more there than in the east." Dr. Edward Cotter's image faded into the foggy mist.

Cotter woke and looked around the room. He went to his desk and read some of the earlier letters from Charles Garrison. "Yes, father, my plan is still in place." He replaced the letters and went back to bed.

# Chapter 14

## The Range

Christmas passed very much like Thanksgiving except for the exchange of presents amongst the same celebrants. The Hamers proclaimed this was their best Christmas not only because they had more money but also because their future was brighter and John LaRoque survived his surgery. LaRoque's leg healed rapidly. Cotter advanced the cotton drain an inch every day after LaRoque came home and although the scar was significant, recovery was complete. Within three-weeks LaRoque's limp was gone as was any pain. His thigh muscles developed to equal size and he was able to work longer and harder without much fatigue. Bradley Hamer, Mashpit, LaRoque and Cotter, when he could, help finish the carriage house to the complete habitability of Gertrin and her family. Everyone was busy.

January at Yale was intense for Cotter. His clinics now were longer than classroom lectures. From this point on his schooling would be almost 90% hands-on medicine. Textbooks augmented the knowledge gained from doing surgery, treating the medical patients and delivering babies. Cotter did get Yale, via Dr. Hayes, to try the low ether concentration inhalation to ease labor pain. His results with three patients so far showed mother and baby did extremely well during labor and delivery. Feeding the baby, however, was a problem. The infant would not take breast milk flavored with the ether being eliminated from mother's body. His notes showed sucking became successful after four-days. The baby took cow's milk up to that point. According to Dr. Hayes and the other staff they would have to collect data on at least 100-deliveries, which would take them to April before the first results could be really assessed.

Cotter's only anxiety came from Pamela Skyler. She kept leaving notes for him at Yale asking for another Tuesday evening meeting. He left friendly replies indicating he didn't have time and would let her know when they could meet. Skyler wanted a solid date which she didn't receive. To Skyler, this sounded like deliberate avoidance. Cotter hadn't planned it that way. He really wouldn't mind continuing their relationship. He would gain more knowledge about Van Haven and what his brother and sister were scheming in the background. He was very suspicious about Nancy and Matthew's Christmas present of 100 grape seedlings from their best vines as a token of good faith. *If it was such good faith then why did they have Kelvin Danzer deliver them?*

February was cold for the first three-weeks of the month and it had snowed each Monday. The total accumulation was between 8-and-12-inches per snowfall. The snow didn't impede the task on the agenda for the new winery.  The work was all indoors. Bradley Hamer received the delivered heating pots for the wine's first pressings. Setting up the winery became his primary job. Only secondarily would he help LaRoque with hiring and managing the new hands. The rest of the equipment inside was left over from the Clark's operation and did not have to be replaced. They did have to wait for the Frenchman to come from Europe to help them complete the set-up. Fabian Rosicot was due to arrive in the next few weeks according to Mrs. Colt. Today was Wednesday and LaRoque, Mashpit and Cotter finished breakfast and adjourned to the living room in front of the fireplace. Bradley Hamer left to drive his children to school–a 15-minute journey.

"When should we bring Bradley to the range?" Mashpit checked the cylinders for his pistol he had loaded yesterday. He and LaRoque had two extra loads per gun and per Cotter's tutelage they wore two-gun rigs like his.

"I think we should get him settled down a little more." Cotter strapped on his double holster and adjusted the fit of his buckskin outfit. He put on his heavy winter coat.

"About spring, I would say." Mashpit was now dressed and ready to go out the door. "It's too cold for him to start learning how to hold and shoot a gun accurately."

"And from what you told us, he needs a high level of confidence that violence not only can be prevented but can be warded off." LaRoque motioned for them to leave.

LaRoque hitched the team to the buckboard and they began their short trip to what now had become the "range". Cotter spoke as they entered the wooded road.

"These fir trees keep the road from having much snow accumulation." Cotter brought out a bag from the back of the buckboard.

"Yeah, I don't think we'd get any shooting practice otherwise." Mashpit looked at their faces as he spoke.

Cotter opened the bag. "These gloves arrived at my mail drop at school yesterday. They're tight fitting and lined with rabbit fur. My friend Dr. Garrison in Endura Texas sent them for us."

"Why. We have these?" LaRoque brought up his hands showing the heavy buffalo gloves.

"It gets cold in Texas just as bad as here. Guns are made of iron and cold iron sticks to your hands. It'll ruin your aim and recovery for second shots. They use these gloves down there. We're going to use them today. Put them on now and get them all heated up. We're almost there."

Target practice took the usual two-hours. Reloading the cylinders accounted for most of the time. They loaded their two guns a final time before they headed home.

"Andy you're getting pretty good with both guns. John you're getting your aim point back too."

"My aim crapped out when I started to stand up straight from the surgery. I'll be better than before." LaRoque smiled and then frowned as they approached the house.

"Whoa, what have we got here?" Mashpit was the buckboard driver for the return trip. He stopped the team and the three men looked at the five wagons in front of the wine-pressing building.

"Leave our wagon here. John you move wide to my right and Andy go wide to my left but make sure you can see my face.

Only draw your gun on my command unless someone draws down on you."

Eight able-looking men emerged from the barn to remove more boxes from their respective buckboards. A ninth person came out reading from a stack of papers. Jake looked toward the main house and saw a covered carriage at the front door.

Cotter considered the worst case. Danzer and a bunch of hired thugs were sabotaging their farm.

"I'll cover the middle three wagons and you two watch the ones on the ends." Cotter looked again at the main house. Danzer was nowhere in sight. He would have to turn toward the house right after he cut down the men on the middle wagons.

They unbuttoned their coats pushing the hems back so they hung at the pistol grip level of each of their two guns. The man with the papers looked up at them. He was just under six-feet. He looked a little startled as he saw Cotter and his two friends.

The man moved toward the third wagon and placed his stack of attached papers on the buckboard seat. He unbuttoned his two topcoat buttons and reached inside with his right hand.

Cotter reacted immediately. "Now." He yelled. "Cover them. If they reach for any gun, shoot their arms."

With lightening speed Mashpit had his two guns out and pointing. LaRoque and Cotter drew in unison.

The men froze in their tracks. The ninth man still had his right hand reaching into his coat.

Cotter gave a quick glance toward the main house. Nothing happening there. "You. Raise your hands in the air. All of you."

The ninth man removed his hand from his coat and raised his other. The hand contained another sheet of paper and not a pistol.

The other eight looked like they were going to soil themselves. "All right," Cotter used his penetrating bounty hunter timbre. "Who speaks for you?"

"I do Monsieur. I am Fabian Rosicot."

●

The ship had arrived on Monday. Elizabeth Colt met with Fabian Rosicot right after he disembarked.

"Welcome to America, Fabian. It's been a long time since we last met."

Rosicot gave Colt a slight hug and a kiss on both cheeks. "Oui, Madame. I trust all is in order. Being on the ship meant I missed any change in plan happening for a few months, non?"

"Nothing has changed Fabian. Come. I have a room for you in a warm hotel. After you get settled we can dine and then pack the wagons for the trip to the vineyard on Wednesday. I hired the five wagons and the necessary men to get the crates into the buildings at the vineyard. How was the voyage?"

They walked away discussing the trials and tribulations of stormy winter seas and climbed into her covered carriage. In town, five heavy-duty covered buckboards used to haul freight from the shipyard were getting their harnesses connected.

Kelvin Danzer walked into the livery and spoke to the assistant blacksmith. "I understand you're looking for help at the shipyard? Heavy work? I do heavy work."

"I'm sorry. You're too late. We have all we need and it's only for three days." The smithy looked at Danzer's large bulk. "Can I take your name in case they need one more or someone cancels out?"

Danzer ignored the question. "Where are the wagons going?"

"The old Clark place. I guess it's goin' to be back in business. A shipment of wine processing vats and some other stuff is goin' out there on Wednesday."

"Wednesday? No I cannot work on Wednesday." Danzer left the man staring after him.

Danzer hit the iron knocker hard.

"Kelvin? What's the matter? You knocked so loud the housekeeper hid, for God's sake." Nancy Locke beckoned him inside.

Danzer told her what he had overheard in town. "There's a hiring of people needed to move and help install some heavy wine-making machinery. It's going to Jacob Cotter's place."

"Well now, we knew it was going to happen didn't we. He shouldn't need too much equipment. I remember the Clark place was pretty well stocked with recent presses and storage vats. What are you so hot about this for?"

"They hired eight men and five freight wagons."

"What? Are they going to replace the equipment already there? No, Jacob's partners, whoever they are, wouldn't do that. Something's going on. Find out." Nancy dismissed Danzer. She went to the dining room table and poured herself a tumbler of port. She had to talk with Pamela Skyler and wait for Danzer's report.

Danzer didn't really know what he was looking for. He'd follow the wagons to Jacob Cotter's place and spy on them.

The wagons moved slowly through the rutted streets. The small troughs were made of ice and mud. In the coldest part of winter the road maintenance crews couldn't even-out the surface with their rakes. They added more gravel from the storage barns for the extreme holes. Another thing they couldn't do as well was remove the horse droppings. The urine froze and together with the horse dung, the city odor of wintertime smelled like a horse barn behind in its sanitation schedule.

Danzer had to follow far behind but it was of no concern. He knew where they were going. He just didn't want to be seen. Ahead of the first wagon was an expensive-looking carriage. He didn't see who went into it and couldn't see anything now.

At Cotter's farm the wagon hands halted at the grape processing building. They kept the horses hitched and under the direction of a man in a fur-collared coat, they began taking large crates from the wagons. He still couldn't see anything in detail. Halfway through the unloading, Jacob Cotter and his two hired hands road up. He was astonished. They drew down on the people. *What the hell did they point their guns at them for? Weren't they working for him?* This was confusing to Danzer. His heart was pounding and he was sweating and getting a chill. Danzer was suddenly afraid. His fear was not at the nine men who came with the wagons. Danzer had never seen any man draw their guns as fast as any of Jacob Cotter's men had done. And Cotter himself was lightning fast with his two pistols. He'd have to come back when the crates were unpacked to find out what they had contained. He skulked back to his horse in the woods and rode to town. He was cold and worried. He needed a plan requiring a few more gun hands on his side. Nancy would back him on this. She always did.

# Chapter 15

## Elizabeth Colt

Cotter holstered his guns and signaled the others to do the same. "Lower your hands. I'm sorry. I didn't know who you were." He dismounted and went to Rosicot who looked as relieved as the other men. "Please, I beg your pardon, I'm Jacob Cotter and I mistook you for trespassers."

Rosicot still held the paper he had withdrawn from his inside coat pocket. "Surely Monsieur Cotter, did not Madame Colt announce our visit?"

"Not specifically for today, I'm afraid." Cotter looked at Mashpit and LaRoque. "John and Andy, join me in the house after the horses are tended to."

They nodded and rode to the stable with Cotter's horse in tow. Mashpit threw Cotter a few glances before he went into the livery.

"Monsieur Cotter, I am having all crates placed into the building for the apparatus to be assembled. The wagons will remain to take the empty crates back to the port."

"Please call me Jake." Cotter shook Rosicot's hand.

"I have checked this list and everything has been received. These men will uncrate the equipment now but must check with me before they go away."

"Good. Please come with me to the house. I'm sure Mrs. Colt will want to talk to us together."

"Oui...Jake." Rosicot smiled and walked beside him.

Inside Cotter removed his hat. Gertrin Hamer beckoned him into the living room where Elizabeth Colt and she were having tea. Colt stood up to greet the two men.

"I'm sorry if my communications were not timely Jacob." She was a foot shorter than Cotter and looked up to speak. "Please take off your coat. We have a few things to discuss."

"Well, Mrs. Colt, I should change my clothes. I've been working in the field all morning."

"Nonsense, sit down and later I want Fabian to look at your seedlings from Van Haven."

Cotter sat down across from Colt. Rosicot removed his coat and hat and sat next to Cotter. The fireplace crackled and filled the room with a pleasant pine scent. Mrs. Hamer took Rosicot's coat and went to Cotter.

"Mr. Cotter, your coat please."

Cotter didn't want to bare his shooting clothes to Colt. No one other than his immediate workers ever saw him this way. Mashpit and LaRoque came through the door.

"I'll take your coats too." Hamer took Cotter's coat and then the others to a storage closet off the entryway.

"My word Jacob Cotter. You still have those old guns Sam and I gave you and your father." She looked at LaRoque and Mashpit as they came into the room. "Is this some sort of uniform? You're all dressed the same."

LaRoque and Mashpit looked to Cotter for direction.

"This is our shooting outfit. We practice on Wednesday mornings."

"May I see your guns Jacob? Why do you have one nickel plated and one blued? Why aren't they paired?"

"Just my...er...our preference Mrs. Colt."

"And what have you done to the hammers?"

"It's just a modification to get them out of the holster faster."

Elizabeth Colt pointed the nickel-plated revolver toward the ceiling and cocked the gun with a sharp click. She released the trigger slowly and then spun the cylinder." You did something here too. The cylinder spins very freely."

"That's for rapid fire...I mean ...in case we need rapid fire."

"Jacob, Colt Firearms is developing a new line of pistols and I want your modifications looked at by one of my engineers. Will you speak to him if he calls on you?"

"Of course."

"I presume you two gentlemen have pistols identical to Jacob's?"

They nodded yes.

"I will have Carlton Strom call on you on Wednesday, since he'd want to test fire your guns."

"That would be acceptable." Cotter looked at Mashpit and LaRoque to back up his agreement with affirmative nods. He hadn't a clue as to what Colt was talking about.

"But that's not why I'm here, of course. Please, everyone sit down."

Mrs. Hamer brought a pot of coffee and another tea setting and left the room.

"Before I let Fabian speak, I must tell all of you, and please pass this on to the rest of your help, that the process being set up is most secretive. No one must know what it is other than just another part of the wine press. Is that understood?"

They all nodded in agreement. Fabian sipped his coffee cup and then stood up.

"Monsieurs, Dr. Pasteur's process is not to be revealed to anyone. Only because of Madame Colt's sponsorship to Pasteur has this gift to you been possible." He looked at Mashpit and LaRoque. "Which gentleman will I be working with to make the wine?"

"That would be Bradley Hamer, Mr. Rosicot. He's in town getting some supplies. He'll be here by four o'clock."

"Very well, Jake. I will wait until he is here. All of us must be in conference when I talk of the Pasteur effect."

"Is there a great rush to get everything ready? It's still winter–February. We won't even be planting until late April Fabian."

"It is trés importante Jake, and …Monsieurs. We must have all hands hired and ready to work by the middle of April."

"John and Andy…" Cotter pointed respectively. " … Andy is deaf and you must let him see your lips."

"Ah, oui…yes Andy." Rosicot was very animated. He spoke with his hands waving in the air and jerked his head from person-to-person. "No later than April must we have all of the people we need. Wine will be made in May."

"May?" Cotter stood up. "How? We don't have any grapes."

"You will Jacob." Mrs. Colt beckoned him to be seated again. "I'm having a cargo of grapes shipped from several vine-yards from down South. They're a quality vintage, I might add."

"I suppose we'll also have bottles and corks. What about labels?"

"Ah, Jake the three of us must work on the labels in the coming weeks. What do we call ourselves and what should our label look like?"

There was a knock on the door and Mrs. Hamer let in Colt's carriage driver. He whispered he would like to talk to Cotter.

Cotter excused himself and walked to the door. The windows were steamed to opacity from the fireplace heat and the humidity within the house.

"Mr. Cotter, I walked around the area and found footprints at the edge of the wood facing your winery buildings. Someone was watching you."

"Did you follow the footprints backwards?" Cotter looked in the direction of the tree line.

"Yes, sir. They led to a single horse. I have no more information, but I thought you should know." The man was about to excuse himself to ready the carriage for Colt and her trip back to town. He turned back to Cotter. "There was one thing–the horseshoe tracks. They were strange. The front horseshoe prints left an imprint of a five-cornered star. The rear prints were flat."

Cotter returned to the group.

"Well, people, we've begun. There's hard work ahead. I must go. I'll be staying in town for the night and returning to Hartford in the morning." Elizabeth Colt donned her cold weather garb.

"You could stay here Mrs. Colt."

"No thank you Jacob and stop calling me Mrs. Colt. It's Elizabeth. I'll come back later only long enough to talk to Bradley Hamer." She turned to say goodbye after buttoning her full-length coat. "It was nice meeting you gentlemen and …" She paused. "… my, my you all look like brothers wearing those same clothes and same holster rigs."

Cotter watched her carriage disappear down the road. The sky was now gray with clouds but it didn't look like it was going to snow.

"Fabian, let's all go to the wine building and see the progress." Cotter led the way.

Rosicot matched his paper drawings to each item of un-crated equipment which had been placed in a proper sequence for assembly later in the week.

"We will need a chimney located here for the fire to heat the water jacket around the newly-made wine." Rosicot walked to one of the last crates to be opened. "Here is the stove and the collecting cover and pipe to go into a chimney. The chimney can just be a hole cut in the roof for now." Rosicot and the others watched the wagon drivers pack all the empty crates for the return trip.

"Fabian you'll be staying at the main house. We've made a special room for you which I trust will be acceptable."

"Merci, thank you very much, Jake."

After Rosicot was in his room, Cotter told them of their spy.

"Any ideas who it might be?" Mashpit removed his holster rig and placed it in a large oilcloth bag. His shooting clothes would go into the same bag after washing.

"No." Cotter then turned to LaRoque. "Wait a minute, Colt's driver said the front shoes had five-cornered stars on them–they left imprints in the snow. John you were a blacksmith for a long time before I came. Does that ring a bell?"

LaRoque didn't have to think long. "Yes–Kelvin Danzer's horse."

•

Thursday, Cotter had to purge his thoughts of the previous day. He was to rotate through the home-visit service. Every Thursday for the next two-months he would go with one of the staff doctors to people's homes. Many patients lived in districts accessible to the Yale clinics but most were indigent families without transportation. The mail coach would pick up notes from the homes and bring them to the central medical clinic. Cotter's mentor for this rotation was to be Dr. Winthrop Noseworthy. Later, as a senior medical student, after the first eight visits with Noseworthy, he would go unaccompanied and have his visits reviewed.

Cotter found three letters in his Yale students' mail drop. They were from Dr. Noseworthy's office, Charles Garrison and Pamela Skyler. He opened Noseworthy's envelope.

Jacob Cotter.

Please report to Dr. Noseworthy's office promptly at 1100AM Thursday. Bring your stethoscope only. Everything else will be supplied by the clinic.
Home visit office

Cotter rarely came into Yale on Wednesdays. "A day off is a day off", he was told by the Dean. Mail addressed to his home used to be picked up at his box in New Haven by LaRoque when he dropped Mrs. Hamer off. However, since the Hamers now lived at his farm, Cotter had to drop by the Post Office himself, which he did on the way home. The only mail he received at the main New Haven box was usually from Mrs. Colt or from winemaking suppliers. Everything else came through Yale. He looked at Garrison's letter and then at Skyler's. Pamela Skyler's seemed to be reaching out for him.

Dear Jacob:

You haven't accepted any of my last two invitations to dinner again. I know you are busy at school and at setting up your wine operation but you should make time for yourself. I extend again my sincere wish to have you return for a relaxing evening. February is almost over. Could you find time next Tuesday evening? Please leave the answer with your Yale mailroom attendant. I will check it on Friday.

You owe me the other half of my Christmas present.

Best wishes,

Pamela

Cotter folded the letter and put it in his leather bag. The brown-scarred bag looked like a single saddlebag. Cotter used it to carry at least one textbook, his stethoscope and only one of his two Colts. He opened the last letter.

Jake

Thanks for sending the Pasteur and Lister publications. I know how long it takes to get these things from the publishers. Also, thanks for the five gallons of carbolic solution. We can't buy that stuff down here. Stanley Wills and I tried to make it up from straight phenolic acid but it burned skin and eroded our instruments. I'm really impressed with Yale's low infection rate with this stuff. But that's what I would expect from Yale.

We're getting more people to use our clinic and are getting across the concept of what a hospital is for. Our patients want to go right back to work after a snakebite is cut open or an abscess is lanced. The concept of "rest" as part of treatment is tough out here and I'm sure it's still troublesome in New Haven. Most of our severe injuries needing a hospital bed are gunshot wounds. The majority of these are from Vlack's hired guns intimidating innocent citizens. I really hate him. When one of his gunslingers needs the hospital and the beds are full, he reminds us he paid for one of the hospital rooms–the one with his name on it as benefactor. I knew I shouldn't have accepted the money. I really had no alternative though, as you remember. He would have burned the place down.

Well, half a year has gone by for you at Yale. I hope you still have a mind to head out here. I always write about the dark side but the good side prevails. We're slowly but definitely getting our hospital and clinic moving forward.

Best,

Charlie

Cotter smiled. Well, Charlie had Vlack and Vlack's gunslinger and he had his sister and brother along with Kelvin Danzer. He looked at his father's old pocket watch. He had two-hours to go before he took off with Noseworthy. Cotter went to the surgical building. The obstetrics service was located on the first floor in the back of the two-story building. There was always someone in labor and whenever he had free time, he would get another patient to sniff some ether and contribute to his cumulative evidence for pain management during labor being better than no pain management. If only he could find a way to eliminate the three-days of ether coming out in the breast milk.

He could hear the woman screaming as he went into the labor room. The room was set up like a regular domestic bedroom except most of the furniture had metal frames which were easy to wipe down with the carbolic. Adding the sodium bicarbonate to the carbolic stock solution did eliminate the irritation to the skin and stopped oxidizing the metal instruments; however, it still did a job on the wooden bed frames and chairs. Cotter made a mental note to tell Charlie about the bicarbonate. Cotter acknowledged the midwife who was trying to console the sweaty woman grimacing in pain at the start of another contraction.

"Oh, you bastard. You animal. Oh God no." She screamed and gripped the edges of the bed frame.

"Hello Anne. Is this patient early enough for me to try the ether?"

The midwife named Anne wrinkled up her nose at the mention of ether. "I suppose."

Cotter removed the ether bottle and the funnel with the fresh cotton filter serving as the dripping chamber for the ether. He introduced himself and asked the patient if he could help her with her pain by placing some medicine over her face in the cotton plugged cone.

"Oh God, yes. Anything. Please hurry."

This was the usual response. He had tried to solicit agreement to women in early labor when the pain wasn't too severe and they almost universally turned him down once they smelled the ether.

The midwife cracked one of the windows open a little to let out the excess fumes. Cotter washed his hands in carbolic solution and started the slow ether administration. He placed is left hand over the woman's umbilicus. It was the thinnest part of the abdomen and the best place to tell when a contraction was beginning and ending. The trick was to give the ether during a contraction. The breathing was deeper and the effect to the baby was lessened, he had learned.

The patient slept between contractions and sniffed the ether during her labor pain. The discomfort was still there but her reaction to it was blunted. She now moaned very audibly but did not thrash around on the narrow labor bed. Within the hour Cotter delivered a yowling baby boy. Cotter asked the midwife his standard questions.

"Anne, please answer honestly as in the past, do you think the patient was more comfortable with or without the ether?"

"Honestly, I hate the smell and it's going to be with me overnight and my family is going to smell it too."

Cotter stared at her and pointed to the paper he was recording her answer on.

"Okay. It's pretty obvious it helps. Let's see what she says."

Cotter asked the patient if the ether had helped her labor.

"Oh, yes, Doctor. It was much better. I wish I had had it for my last two babies."

Cotter completed the forms and placed them in the "ether-obstetrics" cubbyhole above the large shelves holding each patient's labor-and-delivery chart. The document on top of the pile listed the names of all patients to-date who had been administered ether. There were now 69 names. He looked at his pocket watch again. He had 30-minutes to get to the home visit service office.

•

Dr. Winthrop Noseworthy was about 50-years-old. He was just under 5-foot-6 with slightly stooped shoulders. The square-framed glasses were worn on the end of his nose and always looked like they would fall off with even a slight sneeze. Noseworthy had begun the home visit service at Yale 11-years ago. Several of the staff doctors met with the Board of Trustees with their concerns of men, women and children dying from inability to get earlier administered medical care because they lacked the means of transportation to get to the Yale clinics. A few women died in childbirth or later because of "childbirth fever" or infection. Noseworthy had now incorporated a midwife to travel a circuit once a week to homes of expectant parents. Posters and newspapers announced the home-service existence and word of mouth bolstered its growth and acceptance.

"Good morning, Dr. Noseworthy."

Noseworthy was inspecting his large heavy-gauge navy-blue cotton bag for completeness of supplies. He was mumbling to himself as he checked off an inventory list.

"Oh, yes, Cotter. I think we're ready. Let's go over my list."

Cotter tried to memorize the tools needed for tending to patients in their homes. He smiled as Noseworthy's list included several toys for boys and girls. Among the medications was carbolic solution, laudanum for pain, several poultices for wound application and digitalis elixir for heart failure. A small and a large surgical kit was for treating abscesses, removal of foreign bodies like large splinters and two bottles of ether.

"Jacob, you are going to find most of your unsupervised student practice will be house calls." They rode on the iced bumpy road in the one-horse canopied carriage.

"I plan to help start-up a hospital in Texas after I graduate." Cotter said.

"Outstanding Jacob. I've been preaching this kind of thing for ten or more years. Yale trains its doctors to bring state-of-the-art medical care to states and territories where there isn't any. The home-service is going to be a very important part of your last year-and-a-half of medical school. You'll be making a house call at least once every week from today on."

"I'm looking forward to it Dr. Noseworthy."

Their first stop was at a rundown house with peeling paint. A small stable with its door half hanging from its upper hinge housed a horse and wagon and was not big enough to accommodate Noseworthy's small carriage and horse.

"I know the three people who live here–the Thompsons. Edgar and Joanna live here with Joanna's mother. Edgar is always looking for work and does anything available. The old lady tends to get overweight and swell up with fluid. One of these days dropsy's going to kill her.

The Thompsons were middle aged and childless. Mrs. Thompson was concerned with her mother as usual.

"Dr. Noseworthy, she can't lay flat again and when she tries she chokes and bubbles of water come out of her mouth. It's her heart again, isn't it?"

"It always is."

They went to the old woman's small bedroom. She was bundled with winter clothes and two or more blankets on top. She was reclining at a 60 degree angle and was having obvious breathing difficulties.

"This is another one of my students Florence." Noseworthy beckoned for Cotter to get his stethoscope as he reached into his bag for his. "It sounds like a gurgling brook in there again. You've gained too much weight and I bet you're still eating a lot of salt."

"Just…give…me…some…more…of… the…awful-tasting …medicine…Doctor." The old woman used one breath per word. Her skin was sweaty and the room and her coverings smelled like soiled, rancid laundry.

Cotter looked at the old woman. Her lower eyelids were puffy. He uncovered her ankles and looked at the swollen trunks. "I'm just going to listen to your heart and lungs." Cotter listened just as Noseworthy had done. He had his finger on her pulse. He looked at his mentor as he pulled the stethoscope earpieces down to rest on his neck.

"The rhythm of the pulse doesn't match what you hear, does it."

"Classical dropsy," Cotter said.

Florence continued her gasping respirations. She was now sitting at a 45-degree angle.

"We have to get you to a full 90 degrees Florence. We've done this before but this time we have to get you sitting on the commode. We'll need everyone's help."

The chamber pot was located beneath the armed wooden chair next to the bed. Cotter, Noseworthy, Edgar and Joanna Thompson positioned Florence on the chair.

"I'm giving you two medicines. If they don't work, you'll need Cyril's services before the day is done. Your heart can't take much more of this punishment Florence."

Noseworthy gave her the teaspoon of the Foxglove solution and a tablespoon of a green-colored cloudy preparation. "You know the digitalis medicine my dear. The second one is something new for your dropsy–it comes from Padua, in Italy. It'll help get the congestive fluid out of your body faster than the digitalis."

"I read about the mercury elixir last week." Cotter commented while he read the bottle's label.

Noseworthy turned to the family. "This will work if anything will. Remember, no salt in her food and she has to lose about 60 pounds. We'll swing back by here tonight on our return to the clinic. Joanna, you can expect to empty the chamber pot about four times over the next three-hours."

On board the buggy Cotter commented further on the new mercurial preparation. "How does the mercury work? The paper I read in the Italian Medical Journal just said that only one dose a day would have her urine output filling a bucket in two-hours."

"We don't know Jacob, but believe me it works. I've been using it on patients swollen up like her for the past six-months now. If it doesn't work that means we're too late and the heart has failed irreversibly."

"That reminds me Dr. Noseworthy, wasn't it too much of a scare to tell her and the family to call Cyril." Cyril Bumpkiss was the New Haven County undertaker.

"No, Jacob. You have to tell patients the worst-case scenario to get their attention. You've probably already realized one of the biggest frustrations in medicine is getting the patients to follow your instructions. They cling to us in an emergency but immediately forget what we tell them as soon as they feel better."

"Oh, oh," Cotter looked up from the list of patients on today's route. "Jonas Carney's house. Jonas is the bouncer at the Green Moss. He sends our emergency clinic half-a-dozen patients a week. Is he going to be trouble?"

"I don't know. The note we have says his jaw is swollen shut and he's out-of-his head with fever."

The Carney's had a small one level cottage at the end of Frost Street. The street ended at their home with the wilderness becoming their backyard.

Mrs. Carney was waiting at the door and immediately let them in. She was in her late twenties and was six-months pregnant. Cotter had seen her in the obstetrics clinic twice for routine care.

"He's lying down. He's sick and sweaty and the lower part of his jaw is swollen shut."

"Jacob take a look and tell me you're findings." Noseworthy held the lantern to get maximal light in the dim room.

The bedroom had a window but the trees just outside impeded any direct sunlight.

Cotter had seen abscessed jaws many times in the Army. "Right submandibular abscess." Jonas Carney jumped upright at Cotter's tender touch and mumbled something unintelligible but obviously threatening.

"Correct, and how are we going to treat it?" Noseworthy was opening his bag as he spoke.

"We have to cut it open–as soon as possible."

"Have you done this before, Jacob?"

"Many times, sir."

"Okay, I'll pour the ether and you open it up."

"No ether, Dr. Noseworthy. We used chloroform and it made the patients puke but since they couldn't move their jaws, the vomitus went into their lungs and they died."

"MMbbllggggg." The phrase or words that merged from Jonas Carney showed he understood what Cotter had said.

"I agree." Noseworthy looked at Jonas. "You have a new baby on the way. If you want to be alive to see it, you have to let us help you."

Jonas's eyes bulged and reached under his mattress and came up with his .44 caliber pistol.

Cotter immediately went to his saddlebag valise to get his .45 but Noseworthy interrupted.

"Give me that Jonas. Do you want me to tell them at the Green Moss you're a coward? You can dish it out but you can't take it."

Jonas Carney let Noseworthy take the gun.

"Jonas. This will hurt for about two-seconds. As soon as I lance the abscess it will decompress and your pain will go right away."

Cotter splashed some carbolic solution over the swollen bulbous mass. He blocked Jonas's view of the scalpel blade and looked into his patient's eyes. "Jonas, take a deep breath in and hold it." Cotter opened the abscess up with his last word and a bloody-yellow splatter of pus hit the cotton pad waiting for it.

Jonas Carney's eyes shut tight as his exhalation of garbled probable profanity filled the room. Noseworthy held on to Mrs. Carney who looked a little ashen.

"Okay, Jonas, it's done. I have to put in a small piece of cloth for a drain. The swelling will go down overnight. Mrs. Carney you have to put fresh hot water soaked pads on this every three-hours." Cotter looked at Noseworthy for further instructions.

"Jonas, I'm leaving some laudanum for pain but only enough for four-days. That should be all you need. I'll stop by tomorrow to check on you."

Jonas Carney nodded grateful agreement. The intense pain of the expanding abscess was gone and replaced with the more tolerable incision pain.

"Well done Jacob. We have ten more calls to make and then we'll swing by the Thompson's. The old lady will either be better or dead."

Cotter, like all physicians in training or not, couldn't help wonder if infection was a true blight on humanity. They saw two cases of pneumonia, an infected hand, children in three different families with tonsillitis and two children with ear infections. One housewife had a fractured wrist and another was in a depression for which they could do nothing. The family was advised to get her to the clinic for admission since she had stopped taking care of herself and hadn't eaten in five-days.

●

At night Cotter wrote back to Charlie Garrison and reaffirmed his commitment to relocate to Endura after graduation. He wondered how many times he would write such a statement. One thing was sure, he felt, his letters of reassurance were sparks of hope for Charlie Garrison and Stanley Wills. He turned next to compose his note to Pamela Skyler. It was shorter than hers.

Dear Pamela:
I'm really busy at the farm and with school. I do not foresee my workload easing up. However, you are right about my

needing a break. I can meet you at your home next Tuesday evening.

       Sincere wishes,
       Jacob

*I hope it doesn't sound like I'm making the date. After all, she's the one pushing for another soiree. As long as we keep away from business, I'll be all right.* In the back of his mind, however, he could hear her voice–"You owe me the other half of my Christmas present."

# Chapter 16

## Andrew Mashpit

Mashpit had his doubts but with newfound confidence he felt there was a good possibility she would remember him. He wore the blue suit of their first meeting. A smile crossed his face as he remembered Samantha putting his old shit-kicker boots outside the store entrance. To ensure no malodorous aura surrounded his presence today, he had used some of Fabian Rosicot's French cologne. He put his hat on and looked in the mirror. Mashpit frowned. He needed a haircut. Well, this time the barbershop wouldn't refuse him. He wouldn't go to the Green Moss where the whores cut his hair last time after the bath. It wouldn't do for his new image to be seen frequenting the place.

It was 10 AM and plenty of time for the haircut. Mashpit wrote on his now ever-present notepad. He would show this page to the barber as a reminder of his verbal message.

"Greetings, sir. Welcome to my establishment and please go to the chair on your left." Mortimer Pignast waved his right palm for Mashpit to proceed.

"Thank you. I must tell you that I am deaf but can read lips. If you talk to the back of my head, I won't hear you." He gave Pignast the written page reminding its reader to face him when speaking.

"Well, Mr. Andrew Mashpit," Pignast read from the page, "this gives me a worse handicap. As a barber and practicing phrenologist the spoken word is part of my livelihood. However, I think we can converse if I move you to the other chair with the large mirror in front of it."

"That should do very well." Mashpit was wary with his first experience with a mirror. He thought lip movement would be reversed in the mirror just as the right and left sides of the body were and be confusing for speech interpretation. It was not.

"And where is it you work Andrew? I haven't seen you here before."

"I don't believe we've met. I recently came under the employ of Jacob Cotter at the old Clark vineyard."

"Jacob Cotter, you say." The news startled Pignast. "I know Jacob very well. He's a regular customer. And what is it you do for Mr. Cotter?"

"I'm a surveyor and map maker by profession."

"I've heard Jacob Cotter is going to reopen the winery?"

"It's common knowledge, I'm sure."

"When will we good citizens of New Haven be able to see a finished product?"

"I don't know yet."

"I met some wagon drivers who were taking heavy equipment out to the place. The machinery was imported I understand."

"Yes."

"Well, pray tell, imported from where?"

"It will be public knowledge after the first bottle of wine is labeled."

"I'm almost done my good man. Andrew, as you may know I am also a certified phrenologist. At no extra charge I would like to scan your cranium with my fingertips. My skillful eyes and hands can detect your deportment and aptitudes for your most productive contributions to society and yourself." Pignast massaged Mashpit's scalp and then carefully brushed the hair in place.

"The haircut is very acceptable Mortimer." Mashpit made motions under the sheet indicating he was going to get up.

"Thank you, very much." Pignast received his payment and brushed any hairs from Mashpit's blue suit.

"You certainly don't dress like a wine maker Andrew. You look more like my interpretation of your skull refinements which tell me you are an intellect and a man of assertion. I can tell from your temporal eminences you tend to be successful in romance. What brings you to town, sir?"

"You're entirely correct in your estimations Mortimer. I am in town to assert myself to a particular situation." Mashpit put on his hat and coat and left.

"A man of many meaningless words," Pignast mumbled. Another customer entered the shop.

•

*I hope he's right about success in romance.* Mashpit felt slightly more confident but still unsure. Before the war he had a girlfriend but she was married by the time he got released from the Army. *I hope Samantha Wigglesworth is still working there. Why shouldn't she? Would she remember me? It's almost March and I haven't been to the Emporium since the first time back in November.* He was becoming a little nervous.

The General Mercantile and Dry Goods Emporium was known as the Emporium to all it customers. This distinguished it from two other smaller General Stores also advertised as "Dry Goods". The Emporium was fairly new and was the largest store in New Haven. Mashpit made some meaningless last minute adjustments to his hat and coat. His single shiny Colt strapped to his right hip was concealed underneath his blue suit jacket. *The barber, Pignast, had not commented on the gun. So what. Jake had advised he and LaRoque to wear it at all times.* He walked down one aisle of work clothes hanging very orderly on wooden framed racks. The store smelled of pine soap tainted with burning fireplace logs. The floors were clean and adequate lighting came from the glass panes set at regular intervals in the ceiling. The windows were peaked to allow water and snow to slide off. Several chandeliers with four lanterns each were only lit where there was no rooftop illumination. A man dressed in a striped brown shirt with a black tie and creased black pants came over to him.

"May I help you, sir?"

"Yes, I hope so. I'm looking for the young lady who sold me this suit I'm wearing." Mashpit opened his coat to expose the dark blue jacket and pants.

"We only have one female clerk. Shall I get her for you, sir?"

"It will be good if you could direct me to where she's working."

The man pointed to an aisle and went to greet another customer arrival.

Samantha Wigglesworth was opening a large box in the aisle labeled "work clothes". She was having difficulty opening the box. The box was bulky, heavy and the lid was sealed with some tenacious adhesive. Her straining efforts succeeded only in having a few locks of her dark brown hair fall over her right brow. She stood up frustrated and emitted a curse Mashpit didn't comment because her head was pointed down.

"Excuse me. Perhaps I could help."

She looked up at him and then straightened up. "Oh, no. I mean I can call on Titus, he's our stock man. He can do this. Customers shouldn't be involved in this kind of thing." As she spoke, her face and eyes suddenly glowed with recognition. "Andrew. Andrew Mashpit. Oh, my."

"Yes, and it's Andy remember?"

"Of course I do…Andy." She stared at him.

"Samantha I think I should explain some things."

"What things?"

"Things about me. I mean, I'm sort of late calling on you like I said I would."

"The Emporium isn't exactly a place to call on someone Andy, but I knew you didn't know where I lived. I should have said something except the store manager gets very angry if we socialize with customers." She looked around to see if she was under scrutiny. Mashpit's eyes followed her gaze. There was no one glancing their way.

"Let me give you my address Andy. Oh dear. I'm so presumptuous. You haven't even asked to call on me. I'm so embarrassed. Did you just come in to buy some more clothes?" She reddened and then recovered when she saw Mashpit's smile.

"Of course I'm here to ask permission to see you on a personal basis. But there are things you have to know about me."

"Okay, Andy, tell me those 'things'." Samantha had her head turned away form him.

He didn't respond. She asked again while not looking into his face. The awkward silence that followed caused her to turn and make eye contact.

"Well, how many times do I have to ask, Andy? What do I have to know?"

"Were you talking to me when you were looking into that box?"

"Yes, you know I was."

"No, I didn't hear you. I'm deaf, Samantha. It was the war. I lost my hearing from the artillery shells being fired. Unless you look at me, I can't read your lips."

"I forgot. I never would have guessed. You've adapted so well. Is there anything more? Do you have missing body parts I should know about?" She reddened again and laughed when she saw Mashpit laugh.

"I have all my body parts." He laughed again.

The laughter brought the Emporium manager to the scene. He was a balding man in his 50's with a sneer on his face and dark brown eyes darting from Mashpit to Wigglesworth. He tucked his thumbs into his black vest pockets and rocked on his heels.

"Is there something amusing about one of our products?" He glared at Wigglesworth. He turned to Mashpit.

"No, there's nothing wrong. I just wanted to know if you have a darker vest to go with the suit the young lady sold me a few months ago." Mashpit removed his coat revealing his dark suit with the light blue vest. "I require a darker vest for solemn occasions and the lady assured me you do carry them."

"Miss Wigglesworth please take care of this customer. I thought I heard laughing over here. This is a place of business. We do not laugh." He walked rapidly away taking short steps with a turned out gait and jutting buttocks which made him look like a waddling duck. They both suppressed laughing by turning toward each other covering their mouths with their hands.

"Do you really want the vest?"

"Yes."

Wigglesworth completed the fitting and the transaction. She wrapped the vest in a paper bundle and tied it with twine. She pressed a square of white paper into his palm with his change. Mashpit looked at her address and smiled.

"There's an art exhibit at Yale this Saturday at one-thirty. I shall pick you up at ten so we can have lunch near the arts building."

"It sounds delightful. I look forward to it Andy."

As Mashpit turned away to exit the store his outer and inner coats parted simultaneously. He put the package down and buttoned up to go out into the still frigid February air.

Samantha Wigglesworth called after him. She wanted to ask him about the gun he wore tied down on his right leg. He didn't respond. She would easily adapt to his hearing handicap.

●

Tuesday arrived fast for Cotter. Fabian Rosicot had everyone working in the grape pressing building, even Bradley Hamer. They had the warming apparatus in place just next to the metal tubing coming from the wine press. A flat-topped stove fueled by coal provided the high temperatures required to change the boiling water to steam. The steam circulated around the first tank receiving the wine.

"Monsieurs, the heat kills the germs we know causes the wine to spoil. The stove is fired exactly one week after the wine is sitting in the vat. Such hotness will stop the fermentation also but that is what we want. We will have consistent wine of good taste, character and alcohol content."

Cotter and the others helped get everything put together.

"We can make wine by April. The grapes they have to come first, Monsieur Hamer?"

"Oui, Monsieur Rosicot." Bradley Hamer replied. Everyone smiled at the returned French response.

It was Tuesday, and with the Monday surgical cases behind him and the maternity deliveries and after care done, Cotter found he was really looking forward to meeting with Pamela Skyler. The thought of not having to think about medicine or making wine was initiating a calmative and serene feeling. Cotter bade farewell to his friends and rode to Skyler's home.

The liveryman at Skyler's house appeared immediately upon his arrival at five o'clock and took his palomino into the stable. The door opened just as his gloved fist met the door. As Cotter entered the small foyer, Nestor Smood, Skyler's housekeeper greeted him hello and goodbye.

"Welcome, Mr. Cotter, everything is ready for your evening. The Madame will tend to service tonight. Have a pleasant time."

The door closed behind him and a hand immediately clutched his shoulder.

"Right on time Jacob. I like that. Let me take your coat and hat." Skyler grabbed his coat from the back collar as Cotter removed his gloves, unbuttoned the front, and took off his hat. She turned around from hanging his things on the wall coat and hat dowels. "Please unbuckle that too. I'll hang it with the rest of your things."

Cotter untied and unbuckled his holster.

"I'm impressed you think you needed a weapon to protect yourself from me tonight Jacob." She smiled.

Cotter felt like he was caught up in a whirlwind. Everything was happening so fast. Skyler grabbed his hand and practically pulled him into the living room in front of the comfortable fire. Two glasses of Port were ready on the tea table. There was no tea, he noted.

"Pamela, I…you…everything is so efficient tonight."

Skyler was wearing a clinging blue velvet full-length dress with a square-cut front exposing cleavage plus the tops of ample breasts. Blue sapphire drop earrings, a touch of rouge on her cheeks, bright red lip paint and the essence of roses made her the focal point of his vision and thoughts.

"Jacob, sit next to me." Skyler led him down to the sofa and kept her hand on his in her lap. "Efficient is actually a good choice of words. For over two-months now time has been the barrier between us. In your last letters you used those exact words–'no time'. Well, we're here tonight. I don't want to hear about winemaking or medicine. I want to talk about life and having a balance in life." She lifted her glass of Port to her lips and beckoned him to do the same.

Cotter sipped the sweet alcoholic smoothness. It felt warm as it went to his central core. "You're about the fifth person who's told me to do that, Pamela." He smiled and began to relax. "So it must be true." He sipped more Port.

"Oh, and who were the others?" She raised her right eyebrow with a playful expression. Her red lips were redder from the wine.

"Dr. Randall and Dr. Hayes at Yale for two." He paused feigning thought. "My housekeeper Mrs. Hamer and my two hired hands for three more.

"Jacob, people work to have things for the ones they care about. It doesn't matter what the job is, the ultimate concern is something beyond work. Haven't you ever considered that people need companions and mates to add more meaning to their lives?"

The Port glasses were empty. Skyler didn't wait for Cotter's response to her question. "Come to the dining room. Dinner is ready. We can talk while we eat."

"The soup is wild mushroom and pheasant. The rest of the pheasant is our main course." They sat across from each other. "So feel free to answer my questions between bites." She flashed her combination serious and mischievous look.

"Actually, I agree with you…about needing others to provide a fuller meaning to one's existence."

"I didn't mean 'one's' existence, Jacob. I was talking about 'your' existence."

"I have a timetable Pamela. I must complete medical school by next year. Then I'll plant my roots and be open to a domestic situation and relationships." Cotter found he was comfortable saying this. The words justified his long days of work and study.

"Life's just not like that, Jacob. You can't just pigeonhole and plan certain experiences. Things happen." They were finished their main meal and she uncovered the cinnamon custard desert.

"Yes, things happen. I agree. But they can happen in a programmed way." Cotter finished his desert and sat back in his chair.

"Oh, balderdash. Why are you so stubborn about this?" Skyler stood up. "Help me put the dishes in the soaking tub."

Cotter walked obediently behind her to the kitchen and placed the dishes in the cleaning tub next to the pump at the sink. They dried their hands and went back into the living room. Before they sat down Skyler faced him and held both of his hands by his fingertips. She looked into his azure eyes.

"I want the other half of my Christmas present now Jacob Cotter." Pamela Skyler's voice was velvety smooth and soft. She let go of Cotter's hands and placed her arms under his, reaching back to his shoulder blades. She stood on her toes but could only get to within an inch of his lips. "Now, Jacob, please." She closed her eyes.

Cotter felt warmth develop from his abdomen which spread upward and downward. He knew his face had reddened but she had her eyes closed. He wanted to do this. He bent his head forward obliterating the small space and stopped just touching her still red moist lips. "Merry Christmas, Pamela."

It was the longest kiss Cotter could remember. He hadn't kissed a woman in passion since early medical school and he had trouble remembering who she was. Skyler moved in closer pressing hard on Cotter's shoulder blades. Cotter responded and wrapped his arms around her. They continued breathing while still connected at the lips. Finally, she moved her face back a tiny bit.

"Merry Christmas, indeed, Jacob Cotter," Skyler whispered. "It was worth waiting for–you are worth waiting for." She moved back to his lips and Cotter responded in kind.

They had both reached a point of no return and needed more than an oral declaration of feeling. Skyler gently moved back from her toes and stared at Cotter with moist glassy eyes. "Come with me Jacob." She led him to her bedroom on the other side of the central fireplace and closed the door. She removed her earrings and the matching sapphire drop on the silver chain around her neck. Skyler turned around with her back facing him.

"Unlace me please, Jacob."

Cotter complied and then removed his jacket and shirt. He had left his boots at the door and now removed his knee-length stockings. Cotter was fascinated at the slow motion pace seeming to be taking place. Skyler was now totally nude with her back still toward him. Cotter removed the rest of his clothes. She looked perfectly formed and he felt a little embarrassed as his maleness began to rise. Skyler turned around to face him and looked directly into his eyes again.

Skyler's firm globular breasts heaved up and down with her deep breathing. She draped her arms around his neck and they kissed. Skyler giggled and moved her pelvis backward as it touched his erection.

"My goodness." She looked down at him. "Our emotions are preventing us from getting closer." She led him to bed and lay facing him. "Now we can get as close as two people can ever get."

"You're beautiful, Pamela." Cotter was breathing heavy. He eased himself on top of her and let her hand hold him next to her pelvis. She moved upward slightly and their bodies merged.

They exchanged passionate moans for what Cotter perceived as a very long time. She climaxed two or maybe three times before he could hold back no longer. They both finished in a simultaneous convulsive verbal and physical union. Cotter kept his position until both their breathing resumed to normalcy and then slowly withdrew from her.

They lay side-by-side, smelling the burnt pine air. Cotter reached over and wiped the sweat from above Skyler's upper lip. He moved over and grabbed her left shoulder pulling her to face him sideways. They kissed again.

"Oh Jacob, that was most wonderful.   It's been a long time for me."

"Yes Pamela, too long for us. I was foolish to push aside our personal time."

After they made love again, Cotter felt a wave of fatigue enveloping him. His eyelids became heavy and he fell asleep.

Cotter awoke with a start and sat up in bed causing the down comforter to fall from his shoulders. Skyler was already awake.

"Relax Jacob. You're not dreaming. You really are here with me."

"What time is it?"

"The clock chimed two in the morning about a half-hour ago."

"I have to go home." He began to sit up and throw his legs over the side of the mattress.

"Why. It's Tuesday, remember, and tomorrow's your day off. Wait until after breakfast."

Cotter fell back to his pillow. He looked at Skyler. Her dark hair was splayed behind her head. She smiled. He didn't know how to interpret his feelings. He felt fluttery in his belly, almost like the feeling he had when an important school examination was about to take place. *No, this was different. I need to define my feelings–and hers. She could still be the enemy. No, that was a stupid thought.* He kissed her and pulled the covers up over them.

"Okay. I'll stay until breakfast."

# Chapter 17

## The Wine Machine

"You know all about our wine-making equipment Kelvin. What the God's sakes came out of those crates?" Nancy Locke looked at Danzer. "We have to know what they're up to."

"Damned if I know. I couldn't get any closer than four barn distances away." Danzer hated working with women and having one for a boss was extremely difficult.

"We need to know what's going on at Jacob's place. Have they started hiring for the vineyards yet?"

"Yes. They plan to start planting at the end of April, praying for no frost. They have posters all around town and out on the main roads asking for hands."

"Get someone on our payroll to go to work for Jacob. Do they have a name for their wine yet?"

"The posters call the place 'Serenity Vineyard'."

"Serenity…bullshit. I wonder who thought that up–certainly not Jacob." She paced around the foyer. "Go. Go out there and get one of our people to work for 'Serenity... whatever'. Who's doing the hiring?"

"His chief foreman for the farming–a man named John LaRoque. He used to be a blacksmith five streets down from Yale. "

"Hah. This is getting more stupid by the minute." Nancy went to the carafe on the tea table and poured a large sherry into a teacup. She drank half and glared at Danzer. "Who's making the wine for him?" She punctuated her question with a burp.

"A Frenchman named Fabian Rosicot." Danzer read the name from a torn piece of envelope.

"Frenchman? Does this Frenchman know what he's doing?" She finished the cup and poured another. "Jacob couldn't possibly have had time to do all this or even think it out."

"It must be his partners. All I could find out about them was they're from Hartford." Danzer folded his arms and adjusted his stance. He was tired of standing.

"I want to know who they are, damn it." She filled another teacup with sherry.

Danzer was weary of listening to her demands. He watched her suck down the sherry in a single gulp. He had not yet heard about his request to his Van Haven bosses with his hiring needs.

"What about my hired guns. If a physical confrontation ever happens it's going to take at least two other people to help me. I told you about his two hired hands. They handle a gun like lightning and that goes for Jacob too."

"First things first. Calm down. Once we know who we're confronting, then we'll get you appropriately trained assistants."

Danzer could accept this. The translation for "assistants" was "gunslinger" but the Van Haven prima-donnas used alternative language.

"Very well ma'am. I'll take my leave and get one of our best men into the Serenity operation." He left and just as the door closed he heard Nancy Locke shouting and the crash of a smashing teacup.

"Serenity Winery–bullshit. It's all bullshit."

●

Danzer walked directly to the Green Moss. It was Saturday night and he needed a stiff drink, food, conversation and companionship. He looked for Eloise as soon as he closed the doors behind him. It had started to snow lightly and he brushed the flakes from his coat, and then stamped the snow, ice and crud from his boots. The background noise of the weekend patrons smothered his stamping feet. A piano player was banging out some unrecognizable tune and either singing or shouting to one of the suggestively gowned ladies oozing cleavage.

"Kelvin, over here." Eloise O'Dhik shouted and waved her arms. He saw the arms and did not hear the shout.

They met and kissed and went up the staircase on the far right wall opposite to the one with the piano player. Inside the room the noise from the saloon was muted. They kissed again and hugged.

"Kelvin!" She pushed him away. "I like to hug but not with the goddamn axe. How many times do I have to tell you about that?" Eloise rubbed her right shoulder and then smiled. She went to her private liquor cabinet and poured them both two large brandies. "This will take the serious look off your face."

Danzer sipped the brandy and removed his winter outer garments followed by his axe and pistol in their respective holsters. "I need information about what's going on at Jacob Cotter's place. They're hiring a crew for planting and harvesting grapes and another crew for working in the winery itself. You know who, has given me orders to find out everything about that place."

"And you want my girls to get the information during their playtime?" She untied her tight bodice string and pulled apart the laced sides. She took a few deep breaths of relief as her grapefruit-size breasts were released. "God this thing is so tight. I'm so glad to loosen it and get out of the damn thing." She removed the rest of the dress and stood there topless in lacy pantaloons.

"Looks like your tits are glad too." They both laughed and kissed. "Yes I need your ladies to loosen the tongues of any of Jacob Cotter's men who come in here. See if you can get Pignast in on it too."

"Mortimer? What can he possibly do?" Eloise helped Danzer out of his clothes.

"Are you kidding? He can tell them they have a great aptitude–that's his favorite word–at their job. And then he can ask them what they do at Cotter's place. By the way, it's now called Serenity Vineyard."

They lay side-by-side on the bed.

"Yes," Eloise said, "That'll work." She looked down at his groin. "I see something else is working too." She blew out the remaining lit candle at the bedside as Danzer moved on top.

●

Cotter was upset because Pamela Skyler now occupied his thoughts at least once every day. Most often it was when he arrived home and asked for a report of the day's activities which came from Rosicot, LaRoque and Bradley Hamer. Mashpit offered comments but usually only when asked about geographical or logistical things. Skyler and Cotter had two more soirees and now it was April. The only one who questioned him after the first all-nighter was Mrs. Hamer.

"Mr. Cotter, I was worried sick when you didn't come home last night."

"As I go into my last year at the Medical School I will be away some nights." His tone was polite. "I promise you and the others though, I'll let you know in advance." He passed on the same comment to the rest. Only Fabian Rosicot queried him further when they were in private.

"Monsieur Jake, it is good to have a woman in your life. I hope I may find someone in the two-years of my stay in America."

"I didn't mention a lady. I have to spend more time in the hospital or if the weather is too bad, it wouldn't make sense to take hours to come home and then more hours to go back."

"I understand fully Monsieur Jake and it is good you will tell us in advance."

Cotter dropped further conversation about this. It must be really obvious and soon everyone will know about him and Pamela.

Tonight the ritual report began with LaRoque.

"I have all the men we need to till the land, set up the vines and plant the seedlings." LaRoque had a list in his hand. "Half of them are from New Haven and the rest from outlying villages which are closer than the city. The ones in the country are all married and only one of the other seven lives in New Haven."

"I trust we have no criminals or allies to my brother or sister." Cotter looked from LaRoque to Bradley Hamer.

"I helped John with the recruitment. Most of the men were refugees from previous jobs because of the Van Haven violence. They're good workers and glad to be doing vineyard work again." Bradley Hamer nodded to LaRoque.

"Very good. What about the inside workers, Fabian? How are you coming with getting your complement ready? The grapes are coming in a week or two are they not?"

"I have been in good fortune to find some people who have worked grape presses before and some who have worked with heating machines not so much different than ours." Rosicot looked around at his audience. The occasional snap in the fireplace lent a feeling of security. "They are all from the City of New Haven."

"Do we need someone to spend the night at the wine press building when we're in production in case of a problem with the heating?"

"Oui, it will be important to keep the heating stoves fired up at all times during grape pressings. This will only be for several weeks every quarter year. Our production plan is not only centered on our own grape harvest but we will import grapes from across the country."

Cotter noticed the concerned expressions from the others. He looked at Mashpit who moved his head around to focus on everyone's lips. Mashpit spoke first.

"I didn't realize Serenity will be producing wine during every season." Mashpit looked to Cotter for explanation but Cotter beckoned Fabian to speak.

"Monsieurs, Serenity Vineyard wines will have a very long shelf life because of the Pasteur process. Our business should realize profits after only the first year."

LaRoque looked at Cotter. "Jake, if we're successful outright, you know damn well Van Haven isn't going to just sit around. Five-years ago they destroyed their competition if they couldn't annex them."

LaRoque's comment jarred Bradley Hamer to stand up. "I saw many good men killed or lose their jobs when it happened. Jake, you never mentioned anything about violence when you offered me this job."

"Calm down Bradley. Nothing has happened yet. For re-assurance, I would like to have both you and Fabian join us every Wednesday morning. We have a training session with firearms."

"But I know nothing about such things." Hamer stammered a little and stared at Rosicot.

"Monsieurs, I do know of such things. In my country similar business terror happens. It is a part of life to stand up and protect what is ours, is it not? America is built on such ideals, is it not?"

"It certainly is," Mashpit said. There were nods from all but Hamer.

"I have a family and we are living right here."

"And right here is what we protect." Cotter looked at his assemblage and continued. "Next Wednesday we all go to the range. We'll also have one of our sponsor's advisors with us. He's from the Colt firearms company in Hartford."

"Why is he coming out with us?" Mashpit asked.

"Elizabeth Colt, who is one of Serenity's partners and benefactors, is developing a new line of firearms. She wants her chief engineer to see the modifications I made to our own Colt pistols."

"You mean, he just wants to see us shoot?" LaRoque looked perplexed.

"I think there's more to it than that. Last year she told me about a new line of handguns with brass cartridges replacing the paper cap-and-ball ammunition we load our cylinders with. We might be the kind of field testing they're looking for."

"I really am afraid about this. My main concern is about my family. We could all get hurt or even killed." Bradley Hamer's fear was not shared by the others.

"Bradley, when I offered you the job you accepted without hesitation. You knew we would be competition for Van Haven. You didn't flinch then. You thought of a better life for you and your family. Aren't you willing to stand up and fight for that better life? Even Fabian here talked about us as Americans standing up for what's right."

"I need to talk to Mrs. Hamer about this."

The meeting adjourned with words of reassurance passed to Bradley Hamer by the others as they filed off to their rooms. As Bradley Hamer opened the door to go back to his new home, Cotter stopped him at the door.

"I want you to look at what you see when you open the door, Bradley." Cotter opened the door and pointed to the Hamer home. "See. That home is yours. It will always be yours. You are a part of this organization. You don't just work for it. Have a good night Bradley."

In bed Bradley Hamer explained what had taken place at their meeting.

# Chapter 18

## Colt Firearms

Saturday through Tuesday kept the newly titled Serenity foremen busy orientating and training their new hires. April's weather was pleasant and sunny with an occasional bountiful but short-lived rainstorm. The buds of future leaves were returning to the trees. Very little snow was left on the ground. LaRoque, Mashpit, Rosicot and Bradley Hamer were together in the living room of the main house.

"Jake wants both of you to be familiar with firing a pistol and a rifle." LaRoque had the weapons spread out on an oilcloth covering the dining room table.

Bradley and Rosicot picked up a pistol. There were two rifles and two shotguns left on the table.

"I tried shooting a pistol several times, John. I can't hit what I'm aiming at." Bradley Hamer put the Colt back on the oilcloth.

"What we do is called point shooting. We don't really aim. We pull out the guns and fire at what we're looking at." LaRoque had his two-pistol holster rig on and drew both guns in demonstration. "You'll just have the one handgun, but you should be able to use the rifle. You do have to aim it and it has accuracy for long distances. The Colts aren't much good beyond 50 yards–for accuracy I mean."

"Monsieur, I can use the pistol but I prefer this to the rifle." Rosicot picked up a shotgun. "In my country, a shotgun is very useful for hunting birds and for causing fear in aggressors."

"It'll do that all right." Mashpit hefted the other shotgun and handed it to Bradley.

"I think you're right Andy." Hamer lifted it to his shoulder. "The shotgun is my kind of weapon. I'm bound to hit something with buckshot peppering the area I'm pointing at."

They all laughed. Bradley Hamer put the gun down and assumed a serious expression. He looked directly at Mashpit to make sure his words were understood.

"Have you all considered what Mrs. Hamer and I proposed? It is the only way we could stay in good conscience with the prospect of violence."

"But of course," Rosicot brightened, "Going to church is trés magnifique. In France, we have God in our lives and going to le Church is good."

"I think I know what your French words mean, Fabian, and I agree it's okay for us to become Church-goers. In fact, it seems like a logical thing to do, after the war and all. Don't you think so John?" Mashpit looked at his friend's face.

"As long as I'm becoming humanized again–why not?" LaRoque looked around the room and focused on Bradley. "What about Jake?"

"Jake talked to me this morning about this." He paused. "Well, he talked to Mrs. Hamer more than me. He feels religion, or God, is an active player in our lives. He sees it help his patients. He feels it his good fortune to be back in medical school and have a new circle of trusting friends. We all 'make church appropriate'. Those were his words."

"Monsieurs let us not forget that another of Jake's friends is his amour. All of these things are good, non?"

"Yes and that's why Jake isn't here tonight." LaRoque raised his glass of wine to a toast with the others. "Here's to tomorrow and all other tomorrows. May our shooting tomorrow never have to be tested."

Mashpit added, "May tomorrow's training be effective if it ever is tested."

"May God be with us if we ever have to use these weapons," Bradley Hamer clinked his glass to the others.

In unison they said, "Amen."

●

Cotter used the bristled boot scraper to remove the mud and street debris and then used the horseshoe shaped bootjack to remove the boots.

"You're easy to train Jacob Cotter." Pamela Skyler hugged him before he had a chance to get his coat off.

Cotter removed his coat and unbuckled his gun and holster. He let her hold his hand and lead him into the dining room. The table was set with all courses laid out in an orderly sequence. Cotter looked at the table and smiled. "You're pretty well trained yourself. I assume Nestor is gone for the night?"

"It has now become a Tuesday evening ritual. I don't even have to ask her to set up anything." She sat opposite him and separated the two single candleholders to eliminate any visual obstruction.

"You know, I've never told her what a good cook she is."

"I'll tell her in the morning."

"I can do that–on my way out."

They both laughed.

"Jacob, do you really have to leave. It's your one-day off. Can't you cancel that Wednesday schedule of yours?"

"No. I can't."

"Can't you tell me where you go or what you do? And why haven't you invited me to your place yet?"

"Wow, three questions in one breath. Okay, I'll tell you where I go. I go home and meet with my staff every Wednesday– about the business." He sipped his wine. "I'll invite you to my place when it's ready. Right now we have hired hands coming in to work the fields and another group to learn the wine-pressing routine. You'll have to wait until things settle down."

"I don't care about the crowding or the mess. Honestly, Jacob Cotter I won't feel a part of your life until I see the rest of it."

"You will, Pamela. Be patient. It's my way of life right now and it's chaotically busy. When it stabilizes I will be proud to display you to my friends."

"You haven't invited your brother and sister to your home either."

Cotter froze his fork in mid-air. "Why should I do that?" He put his utensil down.

"Oh, I'm sorry Jacob. I should know better. Brother and sister seems like a meaningful relationship to me."

"I don't understand. You're an only child."

"I am, but a single child fantasizes what it would be like to have a brother or a sister."

"My brother and sister would just as soon I had gotten killed in the war."

"I shouldn't have said anything. Let's change the subject."

"Gladly.  What do we do after this desert?"

They laughed. "Help me clear the table and scrape the plates."

Cotter dried his hands completing the kitchen chore. He turned to Skyler with his hands around her trim waist. "I hope that's not the end of the evening?"

"Since when has that ever been the end of our evenings?" She threw her arms around his neck and snuggled into a tight embrace. They kissed for several breaths. Cotter's hands roamed her back. Skyler dug her fingers into his shoulders and backed her pelvis away from his growing groin. As she moved apart from his face she glanced down. "I think we should move to another room."

"I'll meet you there." Cotter smiled and went to the foyer to get his gun.

"Why do you have to bring the pistol into the bedroom, Jacob?"

"It must be a left over habit from the war and my last job. I can't go to sleep without it being close by."

"Well I'm close by."

"I know." Their kissing again triggered removal of clothing and renewed embraces under the blankets and sheets.

Cotter awoke refreshed. He washed and shaved after running in from the commode outside.

"You know you can use the chamber pot? You don't have to use the outbuilding."

"I'm embarrassed about things like that."

After breakfast, which Nester Smood served with only a cordial "Good morning" to each of them, Cotter strapped on his gun and donned his outdoors coat and boots. As Nester was taking the dishes to the kitchen, he stopped her. "Nestor, you're one of the best cooks in Connecticut." He kissed her on her cheek with her arms full of dishes and cloth napkins.

"Oh really, Mr. Cotter." She reddened then smiled and disappeared into the kitchen.

Cotter turned to Skyler as his hand touched the doorknob. "And as for you Pamela Skyler." He took her into his arms and planted a long kiss. He opened the door and mounted his waiting horse.

Skyler stood looking at him move away on his palomino. She held the inside of the door with her left hand on the knob and her right hand on an outside pane. As Cotter trotted away she spoke to his wake, "Oh really, Mr. Cotter."

●

"So we're all going to church on Sunday. Good. Who's that?" Cotter pointed to a tall man at the dining table sipping coffee.

The man stood up and extended his hand. "Carlton Strom, Mr. Cotter. Mrs. Colt may have told you my name."

"Oh, yes. That's your wagon out front?" Cotter looked around the room. "Where's your driver, Mr. Strom."

"I drove it down from Hartford myself. May I speak freely Mr. Cotter?"

"Go right ahead." Cotter sat down with the others.

"Mr. LaRoque and Mr. Mashpit have allowed me to inspect their pistols. I assume yours are identical?"

"Yes. I only have one on right now but for Wednesday practice I wear the two-gun rig just like theirs."

"Very good. Mr. Cotter I have seen guns altered like yours before. Several western law enforcement officers and civilians have asked us to perform such hammer and cylinder adjustments. You also have the triggers widened. Who did this for you?"

"My own guns were altered by our gunsmith in the Army but John LaRoque is also a blacksmith and he reworked the metal for us for the other guns."

"And you two gentlemen. What will you be shooting today?"

Rosicot and Bradley showed him their pistols and the rifles. Hamer also handed him the shotgun.

Strom looked the weapons over. "They're in fine shape. The two pistols for these gentlemen have the same modifications as the others. That's good. When will we be going to the shooting site, Mr. Cotter?"

"Right away. I just have to change clothes and get my holsters."

Strom followed their buckboard in his shorter wagon that contained a heavy gauge wooden crate reinforced with leather straps.

At the clearing, Mashpit and LaRoque attached the gourds to the ropes and set up stationary targets.

"Please stand behind us, Mr. Strom. Bradley, Fabian, John, Andy and I'll be going through our regular routine. Use the cotton for your ears."

The horses jerked at their tethers at the gun blasts. When the smoke cleared they inspected the targets. All of the gourds and melons had disintegrated. Cotter and LaRoque instructed Fabian and Bradley with their guns.

"Fabian you're a good shot with both the pistol and the rifle." Cotter raised his eyebrows.

"Oui, Monsieur, but not so fast as you and them."

"Bradley, I'm surprised at you." Cotter smiled. "I thought you couldn't shoot a gun. You did better than Fabian."

"Jake, I detest violence. My father taught us how to shoot at the same time we learned to walk. My concern has always been that one man cannot make a difference against a group of aggressors. I must say after what I just saw my confidence is up. As a group we are indeed a force to be reckoned with."

"Yes indeed. I go along with such an assessment gentleman. Please, Mr. Mashpit and Mr. LaRoque can you help me with the box in my wagon please?"

Strom removed several smaller boxes and two large oiled canvas wrapped packages. He opened a box and pulled out a handful of shiny brass objects. He gave one to each of the men.

"Mrs. Colt told me she already made you aware of Colt Firearms next milestone Mr. Cotter."

Cotter held the inch-and-a-half brass tube capped with a lead bullet. "I forget what she called it. My name is Jake..." Cotter pointed to the others. "...and Fabian, Bradley, John and Andy."

"Very well, and you can call me Carlton." Strom held up one of the brass objects. "It's a metal pistol cartridge, Mr. Cotter...Jake. The first metallic cartridges were introduced for the Henry rifle in 1860. The brass shell has the primer cap contained in its base. The powder charge is inside the casing with the bullet mounted on top. We have dies to perform the loading of these shells in several stages." Strom opened another box. He showed the group how the sequence of primer, gunpowder and the pre-formed bullet was seated by the tubular die device. "In less than a minute, gentlemen, these cartridges can be reloaded. Colt Firearms will be selling cartridges in boxes of twenty-four. All the brass is reloadable and the components will be available at any sales location."

"But, Monsieur, what gun does this bullet go into. We have but our paper cartridges in our cylinders."

"They go into this." Strom opened the oiled canvas bag and removed a nickel-plated Colt revolver. Its barrel was seven-and-a-half inches long just like the Colt-Patterson style guns they were using. He handed the pistol to Jake.

"My god. This is beautiful. How is it loaded?" He handed it back to Strom.

"Just like this." Strom swung the side cylinder cover open and inserted six cartridges as he rotated the cylinder in crisp clicks. He put the gun in his empty holster and moved forward ahead of the group. In a rapid draw, Strom fired all six cartridges at one of the stationary targets. Cotter and the others stared in amazement.

"I want each of you to fire this gun and tell me what you think." Strom was smiling at their awestruck faces.

Cotter and the others took turns firing the pistol. "We have to carry several cylinders for fast reloads after we insert the paper cartridges on our Colt-Pattersons. They're very bulky. What about these brass bullets?"

"Look at my holster, gentlemen." Strom opened his coat to reveal the row of cartridges strung along the entire length of his belt. He held up a box of cartridges. "And you can refill the belt loops with these."

●

Mrs. Hamer served a hearty lunch of soup, beef and corn muffins. Strom had brought the gun and a box of cartridges into the house and summarized what he had seen and what they had seen.

"Gentlemen you truly amaze me. You've made the most out of a now out-dated weapon. The reason I'm here is to have you test out these new Colts. They won't be ready for the public for another few years. The Army wants the guns for field-testing by 1872 and our target for civilians is 1873. Colt Firearms needs them to be evaluated by people like you. Our contract with the Army is totally dependent on the success of our field demonstration in June 1871."

"I speak for my group. We'll be glad to participate in this testing. When can we expect the new Colts?"

"I'm going to make modifications on our prototypes to make them as refined as your old ones. The trigger adjustment is easy but I'll have to adjust the cylinder ratchet to get the same or better speed–about two-months. Are there any questions?"

Cotter spoke up. "Yes. Is it possible to have one with the nickel finish and one with the matte gray?"

"Of course. Can I ask you why all of you wear one of each rather than a matched set?"

"It's personal and I'd rather not let the reason be known." Cotter rested his hands on each of his holstered guns.

"Very well. Your reasons are your reasons and don't affect the manufacture of the gun itself. I bid you good day gentlemen."

After some discussion about the morning's events with Carlton Strom, Cotter focused on Bradley Hamer. "You look like a ton of stress has been lifted from your arms Bradley."

"It has, Jake. Carlton Strom is a messenger from heaven. The Lord helps those who help themselves. This is a sign from God. He is with us and will help us protect ourselves if the need occurs."

Mrs. Hamer came in to collect the dishes and the utensils. She heard her husband's words and added, "Don't forget church on Sunday, boys."

# Chapter 19

## Summer and Wine

"Do something, dammit Kelvin. I told you to get someone in there for us." Nancy Locke paced the floor. "They've been making wine for three-months now. It'll be ready for bottling any day now."

"I tried my best. The people I could get for job interviews by them fell down on their face when they talked to that damned Frenchman."

"Why?"

"He could tell after just five-minutes they didn't know anything about pressing grapes or any of the steps in making wine."

Locke stopped pacing, swilled down some port and pointed a finger at Danzer. "Kelvin, I have an idea. I should've thought of it three-months ago. Sit down." She wrote a note on a piece of paper and handed it to Danzer.

"What's this?"

"Send it out by telegraph. I know someone at one of the Hartford mills who owes me a favor. He knows about wine and he'll be our spy."

"They don't need any more hires at Serenity." Kelvin frowned.

"Kelvin you're going to create a need." She paused and raised her right eyebrow. "Understand?"

"Yes, ma'am." Danzer smiled. He left the Locke estate and headed straight for Cotter's place.

Nancy Locke informed Danzer the next day that her man was on the way. Danzer arrived at Cotter's woods early in the morning and took cover. Most of the winemaking people hadn't arrived. According to his previous surveillance there were always two people on duty at the presses and vats overnight. He would waylay one of them.

Two men came out upon the arrival of three daytime hires. They exchanged greetings and the night shift men went to the barn for their horses.

Danzer followed as far back as he could where he could still see without being seen. The region was hilly and he was not far from his quarry. At a fork in the road each man went in opposite directions. Danzer chose the one to the right. There was a falls with a precipice three miles away on that road. He speeded up his horse and passed the rider and stopped about a mile ahead of him.

Danzer was in the middle of the small rutted road when the wine worker caught up to him. Danzer was stroking his horses left forefoot. The wine man stopped.

"He spooked when he heard the waterfall and turned on his leg." Danzer looked up at the mounted man with a look of sympathy or helplessness.

"Let me take a look. I do a lot of work with horses." The man got down, pushed his stained hat back on his head and knelt beside Danzer. "Easy boy," he said to the horse as he stroked the leg and then picked up the forefoot. He inspected the horseshoe and then looked at Danzer who was now standing.

"What do you think?" Danzer wore a leather waist jacket and had his right hand inside touching the axe release button.

"Let's walk him a bit. The leg actually looks okay." The wine man moved away from Danzer leading the horse by the reins.

The wine man turned when he heard the "thuck" sound of the axe slapping Danzer's palm. By the time he turned Danzer had the axe high in the air. The morning sun sent a flash reflection into the man's eyes making him raise his hand to his face to shield his vision. Danzer brought the axe down on the man's head and face but the blade hit the man's left hand first.

"My God," He shouted. "What the hell are you doing? My hand. You cut my fingers off." He covered his bleeding stumps and ran off the road.

Danzer reflexly reached for his gun but decided against it. A bullet hole is not what he wanted. The axe was on the ground and he picked it up and ran after his victim. The blood had fallen into the dust of the road and looked like dust-covered peas as it balled up. The shed blood looked like dark rain spots as the man went into the woods.

The wine maker looked back at his pursuer. He started to yell but the roar of the falls dulled the sound. When Danzer was twenty-feet away, he stopped and steadied his stance. He turned the axe blade to his rear and threw the weapon spinning toward the man's upper body. An almost palpable contact noise was emitted as the axe blade entered the back of the man's head. He stopped yelling immediately and fell forward like a hanged man being cut down. Generalized convulsions followed.

After the seizures stopped Danzer carried the body toward the cliff overlooking the falls. It looked like a hundred-foot drop with rocks protruding at the water impact point. Danzer had to turn his head as he carried the man. The convulsions had released his bladder and bowel and the odor was noxious. Danzer wiggled the blade free holding a handful of leaves against the wound to contain any brain substance. It had to appear that the skull was crushed after the fall not before.

●

"I must say you're right on schedule Mr. Cotter." Mortimer Pignast had stopped calling Cotter "soon-to-be-doctor" after the prospect of anesthesia training was offered.

"How are you today Dr. Pignast?" Cotter dragged out the "Doctor" title.

"Well as I've said before Mr. Cotter, the word Doctor means teacher. There are Doctors of Music, Doctors of Theology, Doctors of History and I am a Doctor of Phrenology. You will soon be a Doctor of Medicine."

"I have one more year to go, Mortimer."

"So you are officially a fourth-year medical student? I hope you haven't forgotten your offer to sponsor me for anesthesia administration training."

"Actually, I haven't forgotten. How could I? Every time I get a haircut you remind me."

"I'm serous Jacob Cotter. I want to get into the science of medicine."

"So you admit Phrenology lacks a scientific base?"

"No, not at all. Dr. Gall and the Fowler's Society have valid assumptions backing up the tenets of our profession. It is just that I feel it is my calling to do more. I have been reading about anesthesia, Jacob."

"And what have you concluded, may I ask?"

"Certainly. Dr. Morton and Dr. Long have written their observations about some people more easily induced into an obtunded sensorium than others."

"That's true."

"Truly, such an observation validates phrenological aptitudes can detect those that are easily put under the ether and those that are less conducive. Is it not a correct assumption?"

"I don't know whether it's correct or not but it's an astute theory. Mortimer, I'll bring your name to the Chief of the Yale Medical staff. However, in Yale as a senior medical student I'll be referred to as Doctor Cotter but I have to tell you that Yale does not acknowledge Phrenology for the same title. You will not be called Dr. Pignast."

"I can accept that, Doctor Cotter." Pignast trimmed Cotter's sideburns to complete the haircut.

The door to the barbershop opened and closed quickly. Pignast looked up and acknowledged the new customer. "Please be seated, sir. I will take you next."

"Non, Monsieur. I do not wish le haircut. Monsieur Jake, I have found a replacement for our man. It was most good fortune. A man from Hartford was asking about work at Van Haven but they are not hiring. This man has sufficient knowledge and experience for our night shift."

"I heard about your unfortunate employee Jacob Cotter. And who may you be with your French accent?" Pignast brushed the fallen hairs from the drape around Cotter's upper torso.

"I am Fabian Rosicot. I cut my own hair, Monsieur."

"You could do with a professional trim my good man, plus I offer a free reading as a certified member of the Fowler's teachings of Phrenology."

"I do not know of what you speak." Rosicot turned back to Cotter. "This man will start tonight. I will be up with him for most of the evening. Adieu to both of you." He left as quickly as he came.

"That man works for you?"

"Yes, he runs the wine making operation. How did you know about one of my men's death?" Cotter stood up and adjusted his clothes, brushing off any residual hair that Pignast missed. A few clumps of hair had settled on his pistol. He withdrew the silvery weapon from the holster. Cotter blew at the loose hairs and replaced the gun.

"One hears many things as a barber and of course I do readings at the Green Moss."

Cotter stared at Pignast. "Yes, I understand."

"I noticed your Frenchman also wears an identical pistol."

"All of my foremen do Mortimer."

"Yes, well, when may I hear about beginning my apprenticeship Dr. Cotter?"

"I have two more weeks left in August at the medical clinic and surgery officially starts in September. I'll be operating more as a primary surgeon then and that's the best time for you to start. I'll be giving anesthesia for my colleagues and will therefore be training you by my side. If Dr. Hayes gives the okay, you should begin in two-weeks, Mortimer."

Cotter rode his Palomino to the medical building and went directly to Winthrop Noseworthy's office. It was Thursday and another home visit experience awaited him. His thoughts were troubled since his visit with Cyril Bumpkiss, the undertaker, about his night man's death.

"Cyril, we checked the man's horse and there was no evidence he was thrown off the animal."

"The Police Detective found footprints leading to the edge of the cliff. He apparently stopped to look at he falls and lost his footing."

"But the back of his head was cracked so cleanly. Have you ever seen a fall do such a thing?"

"Well, he did fall on wet rocks. However, it is unusual. The only time I saw anything like this was with that Skyler man–Rockland Skyler–he was before your time. A sharp-edged beam caught him in the face and front of the skull. It looked the same. So, yes, it can happen. As to why the poor man fell–it will remain a mystery."

*Rockland Skyler.* Cotter didn't believe in coincidence.

# Chapter 20

## Commitments

Danzer and Mervin Bosch watched first Rosicot and then Cotter leave the barbershop. Bosch was Danzer's height but weighed fifty pounds more and looked bulkier. Bosch's wider brim black hat sprouted a short black crow's feather and was more like Cotter's western style than the shorter Connecticut brim.

"Aren't you to go with the French one?" Danzer stared after Rosicot.

"I'm to meet him at the Green Moss in an hour. I'm checked in at the Holton Inn for the time being. Maybe I can find something closer to the Serenity Winery?"

"There's a cottage five-miles out for rent. It belongs to Mathew Cotter and I'm sure I can get it for you. It needs a little cleaning up, though." Danzer mounted his horse. "One thing I ought to tell you. Jacob Cotter and his foreman are handy with a gun."

"Well, I have these." Bosch reached into his saddlebag after he got on his horse.

"What–gloves?" Danzer laughed.

"Put one on." He handed the brown glove to Danzer.

"My God, they're so heavy?" He put it on his right hand. "What do you have sewn into the leather?"

"Lead birdshot. I can break bones with these gloves." Bosch took back the glove and put it back in the saddlebag.

"No gun?"

"Only a rifle for hunting. I rarely use my pistol and I left both in my room. Are we spoiling for a fight?"

"You sound eager. But, yes, I think the time will come when some test of strength will happen. You may need both the fists and the bullets."

"Good." Bosch smiled and his right upper lip curled up revealing a pinched-in scar on the once-acne ravaged face.

"As soon as you find out what their machines are like, you come to me at the Green Moss. I'm there on Wednesday and Saturday nights." Danzer moved his reins and his horse started a slow gait. He stopped again and looked at Bosch. "The Van Haven people want to know what the smoke-producing machines are and what their production capacity is going to be. I'll see you Saturday."

Bosch left his horse at the livery and went to the Green Moss. He had two beers before Rosicot showed up at the entrance. Bosch motioned him to come in but Rosicot beckoned the burly man to come outside.

"I haven't finished my last beer." Bosch looked at Rosicot's trim frame.

"Monsieur, please finish. I will wait. I have my wagon at the Emporium getting supplies."

"No, it's all right, I'm anxious to get to work. I'll get my horse and meet you at the Emporium."

Bosch sat next to Rosicot on the buckboard with his horse tethered to the rear. They exchanged small talk about France versus Connecticut and then talked about winemaking as Bosch knew it.

"Monsieur, in France the grapes have a history of many hundreds of years. Aging the wine is done in winter as in your America." Rosicot snapped the whip to the horses as they moved along a smoother road well out of New Haven.

"Why do you wear a gun? Are we in danger?"

"The New Haven Valley vineyards have a history of violence, monsieur. Our owner suggests we wear this." Rosicot looked at his new hire. "But don't worry monsieur, I will protect you."

They both laughed. "I can take care of myself, Frenchie."

Rosicot winced at the word. "Please call me Fabian. It is my name."

"Okay Fabian, you can call me Bosch. Everyone does."

•

Cotter waited for Noseworthy in his clinic office. A newspaper lay on a waiting room chair. A photograph of Ulysses S. Grant in military uniform projected the man as a Civil War hero. Cotter agreed with the press article that Grant was a decision maker and was what the country needed, deserved and now had as its new President. Cotter pondered the editor's comment that "Grant was a General and not a Politician and this could mean continued turmoil for the United North and South in the United States". *Time would tell.*

He turned to the other major item on the front page. Something called "barbed wire" was eliciting mixed thoughts but certainly chaos in the western cattle states. The reference to the west reminded him of the letter he found in his mailbox. It was from Charles Garrison. He no longer received any letters from Pamela Skyler. They continued to meet every Tuesday night. He remembered their last Tuesday vividly. After almost an hour of lovemaking she turned on her side and faced him.

"Jacob, we need to talk seriously about us. We've known each other over a year and have been more than friends for the last nine-months." Her eyes began to glaze with potential tears.

Cotter knew this was coming and had mixed emotions. First, he genuinely liked this woman who understood the faults of his brother and sister. However, even though she understood this, she still threw in with them.

"It's just a business partnership." She said over again. "It's just like you and your medical career. You have medicine and a life going on right beside it and that life now includes me. I have the wine business and you." These assertions had not followed with anything beyond statements of her observations–until early last Wednesday morning before he left.

"I agree we're 'more than friends'." He turned sideways to face her.

"It's time to publicly announce our intentions, Jacob Cotter. Nancy and Mathew have openly remarked that we're living in sin."

"Pamela, some of the people I visit at their homes with Dr. Noseworthy have been living together for years, with children I might add. And Mathew, for God's sakes, gets his sex at the Green Moss as does Nancy's husband."

"I apologize. It was a bad attempt at reinforcing what comes next." Now a tear spilled over her right lower eyelid. "Are your intentions with me honorable Jacob Cotter?"

"Of course they are. I'm not seeing any other woman."

"Jacob Cotter, since you're not about to take the next step in our relationship then I am. Have you considered marriage in your overall future?"

"Of course I have."

"Marriage with whom?"

"Well, at the moment with you"

"At the moment? What the hell kind of commitment is that? I'm talking a lifetime situation here, Jacob Cotter."

"Can I think about it?"

"You've had the last nine-months to think about it. I practically mentioned my feelings on the first day we met." Tears were bilateral now.

"Okay."

"Okay, what?"

"I accept your proposal." He laughed and wiped her wet cheeks with the back of his hand.

"It has to be a mutual agreement Jacob."

"That's what I just said."

"You didn't use all the words but if this is the best I can get then consider us engaged." She threw her left arm around him and reached down for his groin.

After a sensational blending of orgasms, they lay facing the ceiling looking at the flickering shadows from the lantern light.

"What do you do on Wednesdays?"

"I can't tell you yet."

"If it's another woman Jacob Cotter, I'll shoot your cock off, so help me."

"It's not another woman, but you're close." He laughed. "When the time is right I'll tell you."

He actually began sleeping better since that night. The quality of his sleep had always been fitful at best ever since the war. Bits and pieces of the vision of his father being shot flitted in almost every night. One of the reasons he started reading the newspaper was anticipation of reading their engagement announcement. Cotter opened the letter from Charlie Garrison.


Dear Jake:

Just when we thought things couldn't get worse, Victor Vlack strung this new fencing around all of his property. It's called "barbed wire". It's heavy gauge wire with double sharpened prongs every ten-to-twelve-inches. The wire is supposed to be used to keep his cattle from straying onto the farms and causing harm to the crops. He is really using it keep the farmers out and deny access to the large lake as well as block the use of the stream on his property. The settlers have had to dig deep wells and are just barely surviving. Anyone caught diverting his water or cutting the barbed wire ends up with a bullet wound. The local law, Vlack's law, is looking the other way.

On the positive side, we added yet another room to our hospital. The advertisements in the newspaper about our practice and the new hospital capacity have doubled our activity–as if we needed it. Please send some more carbolic solution and bicarbonate powder. I've telegraphed payment to your bank. By the time you're ready to come out here, we may be forced to give-up our home-visit practice.

Charlie


This last statement brought him back to reality. He checked his saddlebag's supplies for today's trip to the sick. It will be his first time without Noseworthy.

"Dr. Noseworthy will see you now, Jacob." The receptionist smiled at Cotter. She was single and had been sending him signals at her availability for the past three-months. She stood and went over to him. "I'd like to see you too."

Cotter smiled courteously.

"Jacob, you're more than ready to make the rounds on your own. I want you to write down each patient's complaint, you're assessment of the disease and your treatment. If there's any change to what treatment you began, we'll modify. It might mean another trip out there today."

Cotter frowned. "Even if it interferes with my afternoon clinics?"

"Nothing will interfere with your afternoon clinics. You'll have to go back in the evening. It's how we all learn Jacob."

Cotter had felt confident until Noseworthy threw the last statement at him. He had the use of Noseworthy's horse and buggy today but anything after that would be with his palomino or his own carriage rig. A horseman road rapidly up to him as the road out of town narrowed to a tight two-lane width.

"Jake, I thought it was you. I'm heading out to call on my lady friend. It's her day off today." Mashpit brushed some road dirt from his duster.

"So who gave you the day off, may I ask?"

"If you want a name, it was Bradley Hamer. He's had me working the night shift and day shift to train the new people."

"I was just kidding. This girl, is she the one from the Emporium?"

"Samantha Wigglesworth–my gift from heaven." He smiled and kept his horse apace with Cotter's rig.

"Fabian has a new man to replace the one we lost for the night pasteurizing duty." Cotter said.

"That's good because I had to take up the slack. Oh-oh, here's where I turn off. See you later Jake."

●

They separated and Mashpit sped up his horse leaving a dust trail rising in the hot windless air. This would be the second time this month he had visited Wigglesworth. They had not slept together yet but he hadn't pushed the physical side of their relationship. The small cottage appeared. She lived only four-miles from the Emporium.

Mashpit tied his horse to the front rail beside the carriage stone and jumped to the short wooden porch. The door opened immediately.

"I didn't even get a chance to clean my boots or knock on the door." He reached for her.

"Well if I seem eager Andy, it's because…I'm eager, Andy." She laughed and led him in after he used the boot scraper.

They had a light lunch and began walking through the woods from the side of the cottage.

"Samantha, our conversation seemed strained today. Have I done something wrong?"

"How can you tell it was 'strained'? You can't hear worth a darn."

"I can see your expression. Something's bothering you."

She stopped walking and turned to him. "Oh, I don't know how to say this without sounding like a whiner. It's Mr. Fester."

"Your boss? Is he making advances?" Mashpit put his hands on her shoulders.

"No. Every time he sees you in the store, he makes a comment and last week he implied my job would be on the line if your 'social calls' persist."

"That miserable prick–pardon my language."

"I don't know what to suggest, Andy. I need the job and I want to still go on seeing you but how can we meet in town? I can't get away from the store."

"Let me suggest several things, my dear Sam." He hugged her into him. "I can get a note passed to you from another customer. That'll do for now."

"What other things, Andy?" She pushed away from him so he could read her lips.

"I'll speak to my boss. We need another female presence at the Serenity winery–someone to help manage sales. You are in sales aren't you?"

"Yes, but I sell dry goods not wine."

"Believe me, it's the same thing."

They hugged and went arm-in-arm back into the cottage. Wigglesworth led him into the bedroom. "I'm a virgin, Andy, but I want you to make love to me."

"If I'm going to be your first, then I want to be yours for a lifetime. Will you marry a deaf civil engineer and wine-merchant?"

"Oh Andy."

●

The following Wednesday evening, Mr. Fester was the last person to leave the Emporium. He went through his ritual making sure all the candles and lanterns were extinguished. The sales staff, all three of them, including Samantha Wigglesworth, left at five o'clock. Fester locked the front doors and left by the side door locking it behind him. The Emporium shared a horse stable and barn with an adjacent hardware store. The hardware store closed promptly at four-thirty every weekday and Saturday. Fester saddled his old horse and was leading him from the barn door. Dusk was rapidly getting blacker.

"Fester." It was a harsh penetrating voice.

"What? Who's there?"

Mashpit held the lantern near his face for his identity to be known. "Hold this lantern near your chin." He placed the lantern in Fester's hands.

"What? You're Samantha's friend. What do you want?" Fester let the lantern move away from his face.

"Keep the light on your face Fester." Mashpit produced another lantern and set it between them. The light allowed for Fester to look at Mashpit who opened his jacket.

"Why are you wearing guns downtown?"

"It's Wednesday, Mr. Fester. I always wear my guns on Wednesday. Keep that lantern at your neck Fester."

"What do you want?" His voice raised an octave.

"I want you to be courteous to Miss Wigglesworth from this point on during your earthly existence."

"What? You have your nerve to threaten me. I treat my employees however I want. What are you going to do about it?

"This." Mashpit drew both guns in a split-second and planted each barrel on Fester's crotch. "Don't drop or lower the lantern or the guns may fire." He pressed the gun barrels down hard. "I have one gun for each of your testicles Fester. If I ever hear of you making Wigglesworth unhappy or threaten her with being discharged, I'll shoot your balls off–one-at-a-time."

A wet spot formed beneath the gun barrels and then urine dripped to the hay and the dirt barn floor.

Mashpit re-holstered his guns. "One testicle at-a-time Fester." He took both lanterns and blew out the flame.

That night Fester did not sleep well. His persistent nightmare was of the eerie glow cast by the lit lantern on Mashpit's face. His groin was sore but there was no obvious injury. The word's "one testicle at-a-time" resounded between his ears.

# Chapter 21

## Carleton Strom

It was two weeks before Pamela Skyler formerly announced her engagement to marry Jacob Cotter. She spoke to Nancy and Mathew Cotter first and then sent out written announcements by mail to her relatives in Boston and acquaintances in New Haven and Hartford.

"Good." Nancy Locke actually produced a rare smile. "There should be no secrets between you two now."

"Honestly, Nancy, I can't press him for information about the business just yet. I don't want him to think the business had anything to do with our feelings for each other."

"That's ridiculous. The family business is part of marital life. Didn't you tell him so?" The smile was gone and Mathew handed her a glass of port.

"I think Pamela is correct. We certainly don't want to spook Jacob now. In the meantime, Kelvin Danzer has a plant in the wine press building and we'll soon get the information we want."

Robert Locke cleared his throat to interrupt. "We should get some information now. Serenity Winery filed for a sales license yesterday. They plan to distribute their wine locally as part of their grand opening but their main market is in other states–particularly the west and south."

"What west?" Nancy looked at the group.

"The west. Out west. You know–cowboys and Indians–Texas, Kansas, and Arizona." Robert took her empty glass and refilled it. "And South–the Carolinas, Georgia and the like."

"It may well be that Jacob doesn't plan to offer any New England competition at all." Pamela offered.

"But we don't really know, do we?" Nancy reddened.

"We should have an engagement party. Have you set a date?" Elizabeth Cotter leaned on her husband Mathew and presented her glass for a refill.

"Not yet. Jacob wants to wait until after graduation."

"So that's around June of '70?"

"We can still have an engagement party. It's the announcement we celebrate. We can have it at our place can't we Mathew?" Elizabeth Cotter was already glassy-eyed from too much wine.

"Such a celebration is up to Pamela, my dear." Mathew Cotter guided his tipsy wife to a dining room chair.

"Jacob and I haven't discussed it yet but I'm going to suggest we have it at his place." She smiled. "Of course, you're all invited."

"Perfect. Yes, that's good." Nancy mellowed again. "We're more apt to get a tour of the place. Yes. Brilliant, Pamela."

●

Cotter arrived home early Wednesday morning from Skyler's house. She had talked about having an engagement party to sanctify their relationship in the eyes of the public. Having such an event at Serenity might not be a bad idea. He had to discuss it with the others since some of the attendees would be the Van Haven management.

He saw the familiar buggy and the buckboard with two large wooden crates. Cotter entered the large main house and went directly to the living room where lively conversation was taking place.

"Ah, Jake, here you are." Bradley Hamer motioned Cotter to join them. "Mrs. Colt is pleased we'll be bottling our wine by the end of September."

"Jacob Cotter please sit down and have some coffee. Fabian has been telling me the good news about everything working. We should be ready for a wine-tasting in two more weeks."

"Yes, the grapes came in by boat exactly on time. We got our vines planted for next year's harvest but Fabian told us our crop will only be additive to and not replacing the grapes we get from Charleston." Cotter looked at his staff and saw his guns and holster were in front of Carlton Strom.

"Jacob, in the wine business, if you have a successful vintage you keep it going. Growth is the only measure of ongoing success in any business and especially the wine business. In fact, at Colt Firearms, our factories would shut down if there was no progress." Elizabeth Colt looked to Strom who stood up holding a new double holster rig with two new Colt single-action .45s.

"Thanks for the lead into the conversation Elizabeth. I brought prototypes of our new line of pistols which are destined, we hope, for the Army." Strom placed a double rig in front of Cotter, LaRoque and Mashpit. "The single guns are for Fabian and Bradley and based on your advice Jacob we had the single units made in the bright nickel finish.

Cotter lifted the new holsters. "They seem heavier than our old Colt Pattersons."

"That's because the cartridges are brass and not paper with extra cartridges in the belt itself. You'll get used to it. Now be careful handling the guns. I loaded them with five and not six bullets. I don't want any accidents in the house. The hammer is resting on an empty chamber. Please strap on your holsters, draw the guns and lay them on the table."

They all complied.

"I widened the trigger and angled the hammer back very much like your old pistols. Now pick up one gun and hold it in your hand without touching the trigger. Good. Now with your thumb flick the chamber guard up. Cock the hammer halfway until it clicks. Okay, now the cylinder will rotate at will. Push the spring-loaded ejector rod toward you and a cartridge will pop out into your lap."

They followed Strom's lead as he performed the functions on his own gun as he gave the direction.

"Now put the cartridges back, one-by-one, and ease the trigger back on the empty chamber by holding the hammer with your thumb and squeezing the trigger."

Only Bradley Hamer looked a little awkward.

"Okay let's do it again. We're going to keep repeating loading and unloading until you can do it with your eyes closed."

They practiced for over an hour until they could eject the shells and load new ones in less than 30-seconds. When Strom was satisfied that each one had mastered the task, he put on his duster.

"Okay, let's go practice. I have more than enough ammunition for the whole day."

Elizabeth Colt cleared her throat in complaint.

"But, of course we'll be back here for lunch." Strom met her gaze with a nod.

Strom gave them individual instruction at the shooting range. After an hour he turned control back to Cotter. "Jake please go through your usual routine and then let me know what you think."

At the end of two-hours they had used up considerable ammunition and checked their targets. Cotter and LaRoque had smiles on their faces.

"These guns are phenomenal," Cotter said. "Their pointing characteristics are much better than the Pattersons."

The others agreed and the results spoke for themselves.

"I can't believe I did so good." Bradley Hamer holstered his empty gun.

"After lunch I want to show you how to reload the brass casings. In the meantime I'm leaving you a thousand rounds of loaded cartridges. I want you to shoot these Colts in any weather. I'll come by once a month with Mrs. Colt and we'll evaluate the weapons. I want you to continue to wear your old ones as well."

"Why? These new Colts have spoiled us."

"Your new .45s are most secret. If you go outside of your property, like in town, leave them here and wear your Pattersons. Smith & Wesson and Remington Firearms are vultures when it comes to competitive edge. They'd even shoot one of you to get one of these for testing."

They all agreed to the plan and after cleaning each hand-gun they headed back to the main house.

Mid-way through lunch, Elizabeth Colt stood up to speak at the dining room table. "Everyone. Please everyone." She clinked one of the glasses with a fork.

Only the crackling of the cooking fires could be heard. Colt sipped some water and addressed the group. "After lunch I will be inspecting the winery with Fabian and the rest of you. Mrs. Hamer and I had a few things to talk about when you boys were out with your new toys." She paused to let the laughter dissipate. "I understand we may have two weddings possible by mid-1870."

LaRoque led the applause. Mrs. Hamer brought in the coffee and dessert. "Yes Elizabeth, Andy Mashpit and our own Jacob are engaged."

"I wanted to say this is a wonderful thing and also that we should be extra vigilant about the Van Haven people trying to steal our secrets." She stared at Cotter.

"You mean my family." Cotter frowned.

"Yes. If you open your doors for a celebration, as I understand is planned..." She looked at Cotter and Mrs. Hamer. "...it would be one foot-in-the-door to access our wine production process.

"I've thought about that and we would keep the Pasteur process off limits to scrutiny. Our security process is simple–one of us is with each shift of workers." Cotter nodded to Fabian to continue.

"Oui, Madame, not only do I maintain a watch over the kettles, but so do Monsieurs LaRoque, Mashpit and Hamer."

"I will have to discuss this with the Hunts and the rest of my staff at Hartford. It sounds like a small risk but it is a risk."

Mashpit stood up. "Mrs. Colt, let's consider the worst that could happen. If Van Haven becomes aware of our Pasteur process the only way they could become a rival would be to have a similar heating apparatus. The equipment comes only from France and this in itself is a guarded secret and not for public sale at this time."

"No, Andy that is not what I view as the major risk. The big threat is Van Haven's history of how they handle competition perceived as a serious threat to their income. They burn, pillage and harm the competition." Elizabeth Colt frowned.

"That's why we have Wednesdays, Elizabeth." Cotter stood up and removed his new holster and Colts. "That's why we train with these."

•

The first snow of the fall came the week before Thanksgiving. It was light, cold and blowing. Cotter had not altered his Tuesday night scheduled visits with Skyler. He stamped his feet on the porch to jar the snow from his boots as Skyler opened the door.

"Hurry before the snow blows in." Skyler smiled. She was wearing riding clothes.

"You look fabulous in jacket and pants." Cotter handed her his coat and took his boots off. "I've only seen you in dresses and…nothing."

They laughed, hugged and kissed. Dinner was waiting as usual on the dining room table with its two candle flames becoming motionless again with the front door closed. The snap of the fireplace reminded Skyler to place a few more logs on. She selected large ones to last the night.

Skyler raised her glass of sherry for a toast and reached across the table to meet his glass. "Here's to us." the glasses met with a faint clink.

"Here's to us, graduation and our future."

Just before desert, she sat back with her hands clasped under her chin. "Jacob I'm glad you agreed to have the engagement party at your place. I feel a little awkward. I've never been at your place."

"I know. I told you when things are stable with the winery and school we'd have a proper reception."

"I was beginning to doubt that it wouldn't happen until after our wedding." She got up to serve the desert from the side table.

"It's going to happen a lot sooner Pamela."

"Well, it better. I mean we're engaged, for God's sakes."

"I want you to come to my place next Tuesday evening. We'll have dinner and you can meet the other people in my life."

"You mean it?" She almost dropped the desert dish in his lap.

"Yes. You can stay the night."

"The night? How? I mean we can't share a bed at your place with the others staying there."

"We have a room for you. It will be proper...unless you want us to just keep meeting here?"

"Oh no, I want us to meet here but I want to be more in your life. Oh Jacob, I love you."  She went over to his side of the table and kissed him. "You don't know how much it means to me."

Later at night, after non-stop physical expressions of their affection for each other, Cotter turned to her as he pulled the comforter up to her neck. "You haven't asked about a date for our wedding all night. You usually ask me at least twice."

"Well you always get so vague." She nuzzled up to him.

"Tonight I'm in my 'explicit' mood. Two-weeks before Christmas we can have our engagement party at my estate where we'll announce that one-week after June Graduation, the former Mrs. Pamela Skyler will become Mrs. Jacob Cotter.

# Chapter 22

## Mervin Bosch

Bosch scanned the orderly succession of vats leading to the large storage barrels of wine waiting for bottling. He had been here almost three-weeks. At first, he couldn't fathom how the large copper clad kettle functioned. It was the first receptacle after the wine press. The Frenchman showed him how to keep the stove fire at a constant ember. Rosicot would not offer any information about why they had to "cook" the wine. The other two foremen who rotated staying with the night shift kept their mouths shut too. Last night he gave his report to Nancy Locke.

"They're ready for bottling and distribution. The first batches of wine are going south to Atlanta." Bosch liked this lady. She was aggressive and gave Danzer and him a "no holds barred" release to "bang heads if you have to".

"You still don't know about the heating up the wine before aging and storage?"

"No ma'am." Bosch hated not to have an answer.

"I don't care what you do. I want to know what's going on. If you don't come up with an answer in the next five-days, you can go back to Hartford, understand?"

"I'll find out, ma'am."

●

"Hello Bosch. The fire looks good. Do you need help with opening up the shipment of grapes for the morning crew?" Bradley Hamer counted the thin wooden boxes of grapes that had arrived in the afternoon.

"What kind of grapes are these?" Bosch wanted to maneuver Hamer's position to take his gun away and pummel the answers out of him. Then he could go back to Hartford having done his job.

"Sauterne. They're from France. Our southern states fancy the white wines. We can't grow them this good up here." He turned around with his back facing Bosch.

Bosch acted quickly. He pulled Hamer's Colt from the holster.

"What are you doing, Bosch?"

"I want you to sit down Mr. Hamer. This gun makes me nervous." Bosch tossed the Colt onto a pile of grape crates. I'm going to ask you some more questions." He pushed Hamer down onto an armless chair next to a cluttered desk.

Hamer went to get up. He stared at his gun on one of the grape boxes behind Bosch. Bosch was putting on thick brown gloves.

"Stay in the chair." Bosch backhanded him with his gloved left hand. The blow sent Hamer off the chair to land on his right side.

Bosch pulled him up and slammed him back into the seat. Blood was trickling from Hamer's mouth. He stared up at Bosch with widened eyes.

"I want to know why we're cooking the wine. What does it do for the wine? Look at me, Hamer." Bosch was able to grab the back of Hamer's hair and snap Hamer's face up to look into his. "The second question is, are you going to have all the wine made here pass through the heating kettle?"

"I can only answer your last question. Yes, all of our wine is being made the same way."

"But why, you miserable shitball? Why?" He hit Hamer square on the left chest. Hamer's eyes started to roll up with the pain but Bosch grabbed him by the hair again. "Just tell me what the heating process is for. You don't have to endure this pain." He hit him on the nose and a second after the audible crack, blood poured down Hamer's shirt.

"I told you all I can." The words came through blood bubbles.

Bosch tied Hamer's hands and feet and threw him to the ground. He began hitting him on the head, chest and legs with barrel staves. "Come on Hamer. Tell me what the kettles are for and why did they have to bring Rosicot here from France? Who are Cotter's partners in his wine business?"

Hamer's face was now swollen on both sides. He couldn't breathe through his broken nose and the pain at end of each breath produced flashing lights. His legs were on fire from the ropes holding them to the chair. The ropes were cutting deep as his thighs and calves began to swell from their beating.

"Okay, Hamer you're a tough guy and I respect that. I'm going into your house to get Mrs. Hamer to take care of you. When she gets here, I'll start on her." Bosch punctuated his words with a kick to Hamer's right thigh.

"No. No. I'll tell you what you want to know. Leave my family alone."

Bosch made sure the ropes were tight and left the building. Everyone was sleeping in the houses. He saddled his horse and rode away.

Cotter was studying in his room when he heard the horse gallop away. He ran down to the wine press building. "Oh my God. Bradley!" Cotter untied him and checked him over.

Mrs. Hamer followed Cotter after he banged on her door and shouted for her.

"Oh, no. Is he all right? Bradley can you speak?"

A whisper came out. "I had to tell him Jake–about the Pasteur effect and the Hunts and Colts as our backers. He was going to attack Gertrin and the children if I didn't."

Cotter completed his exam. "You have a cracked rib on the left chest but the lungs sound ok. I can fix the nose in a day or two. You're going to be pretty sore. Gertrin give him a full tablespoon of this." He handed the laudanum narcotic elixir to Gertrin. "So it was Bosch. I wondered why I wasn't pressured before this by my sister. He was their spy. Where does he live Bradley?"

Bradley Hamer whispered the location of Bosch's cottage. "Gertrin, I'll have John stay up with you." He went into the house and told LaRoque what happened.

"Where are you going dressed like that?" LaRoque pulled on his trousers and grabbed his winter coat and boots.

"I'm going after him."

"Won't you need me?"

"Stay with Bradley and Gertrin."

Cotter found the cottage without difficulty. The recent snow and the three-quarter moon gave ample light. Bosch's horse was tied outside the front entrance of the single story cottage. Smoke was billowing from the chimney in bursts, suggesting Bosch was using a bellows on the fireplace. He dismounted his palomino and tied him to a tree a hundred yards away and tread softly to the front door. Cotter leaned his weight against the door and felt resistance by a small hook-and-eye lock. He backed away and then slammed forward with his right shoulder throwing open the door with a loud bang.

"What the fuck?" Bosch was sitting on his bed with his clothes still on minus the hat, coat and gloves. His unbuckled holstered pistol lay on the bed next to him. "I know you." Bosch moved his right hand toward the butt of his pistol.

"You reach for the gun and it's the last time you reach for anything."

The fire began blazing as the fresh logs produced bright yellow tongues of flame reaching up into the flue. The reflection of light on Cotter's hat and leg conchos was like stars dancing in the room. Yellow spots of light bouncing from the bib conchos as Cotter pushed aside his coat diverted Bosch's gaze. "I'm going to beat you like you beat Bradley Hamer."

"You're gonna have to get close to me to do it. I know you–you're Locke's no-good brother. The one she hates." His fingers inched toward his gun.

Cotter turned slightly left. "If you try for the gun you're a dead man."

"A medical student's gonna take me? Fuck you?" Bosch grabbed his gun and pulled it from the holster.

The small cottage was filled with the smoke of three guns discharging. The noise was deafening and Cotter's ears rang. He had forgotten his ear cotton and his mouth wasn't open. Bosch's pistol had fired halfway out of the holster and splintered the wooden beam above the hearth. Cotter's two .45 bullets converged to a large single entry point over the center of Bosch's breastbone.

●

"John, bring the buckboard for the body. Bradley you're going to have to come with me to Yale. I'll keep you there for a day." Cotter turned to Gertrin. "He's okay. I really need for the police to see him and justify being forced to confront Bosch."

Rosicot came up to him with a folder of papers. "Monsieur Jake, I will begin checking the background of the rest of our employees."

"I doubt you'll find anything Fabian but go ahead."

The recent snow had filled in the road ruts and the buckboard was jarring less than usual. Bradley Hamer barely uttered a sound of discomfort. The sun was just rising as Cotter arrived at the clinic. An attendant let him in.

"Get him comfortable in a bed. I'll schedule him for stitching up the lacerations for early morning. I have to make a police report."

The attendant helped Hamer to a soft-mattressed cot and Cotter gave Hamer another dose of laudanum.

"Have the first person who comes in get the Police. I have a dead man in the buckboard."

The attendant looked concerned.

"Don't worry, the man's dead. Just look after Mr. Hamer."

The police inspector arrived with a uniformed officer and wrote down Cotter's statement.

"Would you mind if I talk to Mr. Hamer, now?" The Inspector interviewed Hamer and came back to Cotter. "The poor man is lucky to be alive. I'll have to visit the decedent's home, but clearly this is self-defense. I'll check on Mr. Mervin Bosch with the Hartford Police Department."

Cotter watched the policemen leave as Dr. Timothy Hayes arrived.

"I heard about what happened. Is your man okay?" Hayes looked at the medical notes Cotter had written in the clinic chart.

"I have him scheduled for suturing in an hour. We're cleaning his wounds with carbolic solution with the laudanum in him. I was thinking to watch him here for a day with that possible broken rib. The lung field is good." Cotter held up his stethoscope.

●

Hamer had an uneventful but painful day as Cotter periodically looked in on his patient, friend and business manager. At 4:15 the clinic receptionist summoned him to the patient waiting area.

"Pamela, what are you doing here?" Cotter stared at her as she paced the hardwood floor in front of two patients. "Please step out in the hall."

"Jacob I came as soon as I heard. Thank God you're all right." She hugged him.

Cotter pushed her out of the embrace. "Did you know about him? I mean about Nancy hiring him to spy for her–for your Van Haven group."

"I knew she had asked this be done. I didn't want to know about it. Jacob you know I stopped asking you about your Serenity business a long time ago?"

"Yes, and now I know why. You had someone in our ranks getting the information so you didn't have to ask me. That man almost killed my manager and tried to kill me."

"Oh, Jacob I'm so sorry"

"Sorry? Sorry doesn't get you off the hook Pamela. You had it in your power to tell me about this and get that man out of Serenity. This whole thing could have been prevented and that man Bosch might still be alive or I might have even been killed. Do you understand what I'm saying? I doubt whether you're really in love with me or am I just a pawn in your business life?"

"No, no Jacob, it's not like that at all. Please believe me."

"How can I believe you? I was forced to kill a human being because of Van Haven and their greed. I offer very little competition to them."

"They don't believe it Jacob. That's how they are."

"Is it how you are?"

Skyler stared at Cotter with tears now spilling over her eyelids. "No Jacob, of course not." She turned away from him to wipe her eyes. He turned her back around with both hands on her shoulders.

"We have to rethink our situation Pamela. I don't want any engagement party just yet. Right now I'm grateful to be alive but angry because of your involvement in all of this."

"Jacob, none of this was my idea."

"But you knew about it and didn't tell me."

"I didn't tell you. I realize now that I should have. Jacob there won't be any more secrets between us, I promise."

"Pamela, I have to pay more attention to my business. My schooling is also compromising much of my time."

"When will I see you again, Jacob."

Her sniffling and reddened eyes had no effect on Cotter. "When my foreman Bradley Hamer is back on his feet and I'm confident that Nancy, Mathew and you are not infiltrating my home and business. That's when I'll call on you again." Cotter turned away and went back into the clinic.

●

Saturday night at the Green Moss saloon was always crowded and noisy. The double doorway between the combination bar and lounge section led to the foyer of the rooming part of the building which also had its own entrance from the street. The foyer resembled that of a hotel. There was a main desk with a woman attendant and several lounge chairs, sofas and coffee tables for meeting guests or having after-romance discussions. There were also two small rooms with six-chair dining tables that could be used for conferences. Four men were settling into burgundy brocaded armchairs at one of the tables in the room with a painted green turtle on the door. Robert Locke lit a cigar and sipped brandy from a snifter glass. Kelvin Danzer and Mortimer Pignast each held beer glasses. Mathew Cotter puffed greedily on his fifth cigarette.

"Kelvin, the Bosch debacle was a disaster. Who gave the order to confront Jacob?" Mathew lit his sixth cigarette and drank half his glass of water.

"Facing off with Jacob was not part of the plan. Nancy insisted on leaning on someone at Serenity to find out what edge, if any, their wine would have on our business." Danzer put his beer down and sat back exposing his axe holster.

"We don't have anyone else in their employ and I doubt we could get someone in there again." Robert Locke stared into his brandy. "It's also unfortunate that the incident broke up Pamela's relationship."

"Ah, but it hasn't." Pignast spoke up. "The engagement is not severed but merely put on hold until the fences are mended, so to speak."

"And how do you know this?" Mathew looked from Pignast to the others.

"Over the past several months I have cultivated a professional relationship with Dr. Jacob Cotter."

"Dr. Cotter? He's not 'Dr. Cotter' yet. What are you talking about?"

"Well Mathew, and gentlemen, it was quite natural for Jacob to take me under his wing in the surgery clinic to become trained in the administration of anesthetics."

"How in hell's name did you manage that?" Robert Locke smiled.

"He does frequent my establishment regularly, you know." Pignast paused and continued during the silence. "I am his barber and confidant."

"Barber, yes. Confidant, bullshit." Danzer chugged at his beer mug.

"That's your perception, my good man, but not the truth. Dr. Cotter has informed me the engagement to Pamela Skyler continues."

"Well, that's good, I guess, but Pamela doesn't seem as cheerful as before the Bosch incident."

"If you people would have taken my suggestions, the Serenity winery would not have come into existence." Danzer stood and paced to the wall and back to his chair. "I'm not surprised at the gun play here. I told you what I saw the day the Frenchman arrived with all the winemaking stuff. You have to let me hire some gun hands and just run over there and put them out of business."

Robert Locke held his hand up for Danzer's declaration to end. "We must approach Jacob and his other partners, who we have yet to define by the way. Jacob is near graduation and he's already told us the place is an investment to be sold when he graduates. He's to sell to us. So let's push for that on the one hand."

"And on the other hand?" Mathew Cotter finished his water.

"On the other hand we should be ready to pit force-against-force if we're to terminate Serenity Winery's existence." Locke looked at Mathew and then at Danzer.

"Let me identify my 'assistants' now." Danzer paced again.

"We have two other members who need to agree–the women." Mathew stood up. "Nancy and Pamela have to agree."

"So let's talk to them now and plan to get some hired guns into New Haven by spring. In the meantime, Jacob can go to school and make his wine." Mathew paused. "He's selling the stuff to the southern states and not in New England so he's not hurting us yet."

"That could change," Danzer said.

"Yes, anything can happen. We should explore Kelvin's back-up suggestion. Kelvin, I'm going to assume my sister and Pamela will agree to our proposal. Be prepared to activate your plan upon our confirmation."

The meeting was adjourned. Robert Locke went up to Pignast as the others left. "Mortimer, you have a small share in

Van Haven.  Remember that when you're cutting Jacob's hair or doing what you do in his surgery. Your loyalty is to us."

Pignast looked at his watch. "Right now my loyalty is to the light of my life–Miss Fern Ferndock."

"Ah, yes, we must get to the ladies." Locke slapped Pignast on the shoulder.

Mortimer Pignast knew where his loyalties lay and they were not with Van Haven. He must choose the correct time to talk to Jacob Cotter–perhaps right after Christmas.

# Chapter 23

## Yale

Cotter missed the Tuesday night meetings with Pamela. It was more than their lovemaking he missed. The conversations about life and her interest in their future never touched upon her business with Van Haven or her association with Nancy and Mathew. Innately, he felt his feelings toward her were more than just a biological one. The week after Bosch's death they agreed to meet at the Tea House for their first get together.

Cotter arrived late on that Friday afternoon. The surgery to set a farmer's fractured leg had taken a long time. Pignast had been his anesthesia assistant and did a professional job. He had easily taken to controlling the ether drops for maintenance of a patient's anesthetic state at a safe plane of obtundation. Within two-weeks it became obvious that Pignast was a natural at this science. The patients awoke within a half-hour and other than the usual coughing and occasional vomiting they all recovered well needing only the nurse's postoperative attendance.

Cotter saw Skyler through the window of the small café as he turned the doorknob. Her face was anxious and she kept looking toward the door. When he approached the table she looked up and forced a smile extending her hand to Cotter. He held her hand across the small table for a second and sat down.

"I'm sorry I'm late Pamela. The operation took longer than I expected."

"What is that smell?" She wrinkled her nose.

"It must be the ether. The odor will stay with me until tomorrow but I can't smell it anymore. It always happens that way."

"How come I never noticed it before?"

"I never had surgery on Tuesdays."

"I missed you Tuesday. I couldn't sleep. I kept reaching for you."

"I was taking care of my foreman, Bradley Hamer."

She looked down to her lap. "I wish I had said something before about that man–Bosch?"

"Yes. His name was Mervin Bosch."

"But we agreed not to bring the business into our personal lives. It was what you insisted." She reached across to touch his hand.

"Yes, I know. Pamela, I was wrong about that. But at the time I was suspicious that your initial intentions were to wine-and-dine me to get information about Serenity."

"Jacob we were both wrong. I wanted to do everything you said–and I did. We both have regrets but let's go on from here. Please, Jacob."

The matronly owner placed a tea set and small cakes on the center of their table and left.

"I ordered what we had last time."

Cotter smiled. "You remembered. I'm impressed."

"I always remember things about us, Jacob."

He noticed her eyes glistening. "Pamela what's happened to me right now weighs heavily on my conscience. I had to kill a man or be killed. I'm in training to be a Doctor–someone who saves lives not takes them. I have to make sure my people are protected."

"What about us?" The tears came.

"Give me some time. We can still meet like this. I still consider us engaged. Once my situation at home stabilizes, we have to talk seriously about what comes next." Cotter reached over and squeezed her hand. "I need to have some space right now."

"All right, Jacob. Can we meet on an evening when you don't smell like a chemical?"

Her comment broke the tension. They both laughed.

"Good idea. Mondays are best. Shall we have a standing date for this time every Monday?"

"Oh yes Jacob."

Cotter paid the bill and walked Pamela to her buggy. He would not go back to her house unless he was firmly convinced she was in love with him and would separate from Van Haven after they were married. He had not discussed this thought with her yet. It was number two on his list of "serious things" to discuss.

●

Bradley Hamer healed well. At first, Cotter had a fear the Hamers would quit. Fabian had taken over Bradley's duties but within two-weeks Bradley was back giving the orders. Cotter asked him about his future concerns during an evening supper with the entire group. At least once a week Cotter liked to have LaRoque, Mashpit, Rosicot and the Hamers together during the evening meal. On weekdays they all had supper together except when Cotter used to stay with Skyler. The weekends belonged to the Hamers for family bonding, although occasionally they would still meet as a large group for special occasions like birthdays or holidays. The occasion this evening was to plan the Christmas and New Year holiday celebrations.

"Bradley, I would like to ask you and your family about the effects of the 'incident' on your future plans." Cotter looked around at the others. All eyes were on Bradley Hamer.

"I shouldn't have turned my back on him, Jake. He took my gun. It won't happen again."

LaRoque smiled and began clapping. The answer implied the Hamers were going to stay.

"Monsieur, I can assure you all of the background checks on the current employees are impeccable. Jake you have something to report on the former Monsieur Bosch?"

"Yes Fabian. First let me say that even with good references we must still be vigilant. Unfortunately, my sister Nancy Locke is an unscrupulous woman. I say unfortunately because it is unfortunate we're related."

Cotter raised his hand to quell the laughter. "Bosch did work for several vineyards around Hartford and even in the western Connecticut farm areas. His primary job was not with the winemaking. Bosch was a strong-arm field boss who enforced the company's rules and got rid of any dissenters. In Hartford I found out from a check by Mrs. Colt that Bosch had killed a man at a barroom brawl in 'self-defense'. He did it with his fists." Cotter paused and brought out a pair of gloves which he passed around. "He did it with these. These gloves are the same ones he bashed you with Bradley. The backs of the fingers and hand are filled with lead shot."

Gertrin Hamer changed the subject. "It's behind us now. Let's talk about Christmas. Last year we had a lovely get together. This Christmas am I correct that we have two more guests?" She gestured to Cotter and Mashpit.

"Gertrin I have invited Pamela Skyler and she has accepted."

"Very nice, Jacob. What about you Andy? Don't play deaf, you were looking at my lips."

Mashpit smiled, "Mrs. Hamer I am proud to announce my fiancée, Miss Samantha Wigglesworth, will also be our guest."

●

"Of course I agree. Get them hired now Kelvin. I want to parade them around so there's no misunderstanding. Van Haven rules these lands and with force if necessary." Nancy Locke wagged her index finger at Danzer's chest.

"Wait. I have a say here. Violence has already cost a man his life. My vote is no. No hired assassins. I almost lost my fiancé and I don't want him injured or dead." Skyler stood up facing them.

"I'm inclined to go along with Pamela. As you may know Jacob is training me in a new vocation. Without him as my sponsor I will no longer be on Yale's apprentice anesthesia program." Mortimer Pignast stepped to Skyler's side.

"Pamela you have almost a full-third interest in Van Haven. Your initial investment has doubled. It could go higher. Our intention is to absorb Jacob's Serenity into Van Haven." Mathew Cotter stared at Robert Locke for confirmation.

"Yes, Pamela. Don't sacrifice your feelings for business success with an imagined infatuation with Jacob. Remember, he's not been with a woman since the war. If you left us, you could end up with nothing." Robert Locke was pushed aside by Danzer.

"And remember, 'nothing' means a dead Jacob and no source of livelihood." Danzer leaned his left arm on the chair back allowing his axe holster to be seen just as Nancy Locke lashed out her tongue to Pignast.

"Mortimer Pignast, I will not stand for your attitude. Consider yourself removed from Van Haven. Please leave. You'll receive payment for your shares in the Company next week. Get out." Nancy was red-faced with her jugular veins bulging. She turned on Skyler next. "Pamela, you're a part of us whether you like it or not. Rockland Skyler gave his life for Van Haven. You have a moral obligation to him and us."

"What if Jacob sells Serenity to us?"

"If that happens then all of our back-up preparation will not be needed." Elizabeth Cotter spoke the words from a tongue weakened by four glasses of sherry. "Isn't that right everyone?"

"That's right–except for Mortimer. You're still out. Get out. Get him out of here Kelvin."

Danzer escorted Pignast to the door.

"You couldn't woo Jacob in our direction before. What's so different now?" Mathew Locke went over to Nancy as he spoke to Skyler.

"I'll find out who his partners are. If we get control of Serenity then Jacob is ours. I've been invited for Christmas at Jacob's home. The whole group will be there." Skyler paused. "Jacob implied that one of his stockholders from Hartford would also be there."

"Hartford? We keep going back to Hartford. I tried finding out who in that city would be sponsoring Jacob's little winery but I got nowhere." Nancy reddened again.

"Please give me until the end of January before you bring in your hired guns."

"No, Pamela. They'll be here as soon as Kelvin gets them together. However, I promise we won't use them until the end of January. How's that?"

Skyler looked at the group and found no sympathetic eyes. "Okay. I agree."

"And one other thing, you are not to tell Jacob about our plans or I'll see to it your engagement will break into so many pieces it will never be put back together." Nancy folded her arms against her flattened breasts in triumph.

"If he hears about anything, it won't be from me." Skyler nodded her head in the direction of the door that Pignast left by.

"Kelvin you should have words with our ex-partner, Dr. Pignast." Robert Locke looked from Danzer to his wife Nancy.

"Most definitely. I'll see him Saturday night at the Green Moss," Danzer said. He saw Robert pulling out the ledger books, which would complete the monthly meeting. It was his cue to leave.

"How far do you think Kelvin will go with his persuasion techniques with Mortimer?" Skyler aimed her question at the others in general.

"However far he needs to my dear." Nancy answered between sips of sherry.  "Don't worry about it. Mortimer Pignast will keep his mouth shut because he's been one of us and is equally responsible for our past actions."

Skyler gestured her acceptance of Nancy's comment.

●

Cotter picked up his mail at the Yale box. There was a letter from Charlie Garrison and one from Pamela Skyler. A newspaper wrapped in heavy brown paper was postmarked from Endura, Texas. Cotter spread it open on the long flat counter space beneath the pigeonhole mail slots. A headline was circled in ink.

Barbed Wire Legal–Trespassers Can Be Shot

"Town Marshall, Burr Oliver, told the Endura Clarion that …with barbed wire being legal, ranchers like Victor Vlack are within their rights to shoot trespassers on sight". This editor is sorry to report Mr. Vlack is within his rights. Dr. Charles Garrison and Dr. Stanley Wills have told this paper that over seven people have had to be treated for gunshot wounds and twice the number for lacerations from the barbed wire itself…

Cotter stopped reading the paper and tore open Charlie's envelope.

Dear Jake:

If you haven't read the newspaper article now, please read it and come back to my letter. Vlack is using the barbed wire legality to force the farms neighboring his boundary to be denied water access. He claims he's doing it to prevent his cattle from wandering onto the farmlands. In addition, he's damming the creeks feeding into their property. The violence is creating patients for us on both sides of this growing debacle. Stan and I are too busy with our regular practice to continue to make home visits. In a way, it's a blessing because it's too dangerous to venture outside of town. Vlack's thugs ambush anyone venturing too close to Vlack's barbed wire. Marshall Oliver claims he's not taking sides but he's been on Vlack's payroll forever.

The farmsteads have united and are drilling wells to overcome the water problem. I have to say this is working only partially for most of them. There are a few idealists who feel the water is a God-given right and a few night raids on Vlack's dams resulted in Vlack's gunslingers randomly roughing up farm hands and outright killing suspects. The dead are conveniently found on Vlack's land but some of the patients have told us the victims were killed outside of the barbed wire and the bodies dragged onto Vlack's property.

How is school? Are you still nurturing that "bumpologist" to administer ether? We could use someone like him. Stan and I alternate giving ether for each other's patients but it would be better if we could assist each other in the actual surgery instead.

How's your love life? Are you still engaged after the assault on your foreman? Is she still in the enemy's camp?

It looks like we both have similar problems. Coming down to Texas will be trading one mess for another but life's like that. We still want you, Jake.

Charlie


Cotter pondered Charlie Garrison's last thought. *My whole life has been one hell balanced off against a positive scenario. My mother and siblings hated me but my father loved me. Stress growing up with Nancy and Mathew brought me a love for school and my father's nurturing an academic fulfillment. Medical school was heaven but the Civil War called up both of us. And now I'm almost at my goal to become a physician, a possible successful entrepreneur and a family man. On the other hand, I'm not sure I love Pamela but I do feel something. My brother and sisters are still antagonists poised for physical violence against all I hold dear. My principles as a Doctor are at opposite with the killing of Bosch. In my heart, I was right in confronting Bosch, just as I was right in bringing criminals to justice during my bounty hunter days.*

Pamela was another issue. Cotter had difficulty with personal feelings. Never having developed a sense of true family, except for his father, Cotter now found himself actually desiring such an identity. Perhaps it was seeing the Hamers with their children or his closeness to LaRoque and Mashpit. Certainly his Thursday duties on the home visit circuit taught him a strong sense of the importance of a healthy family unit. Cotter opened Skyler's envelope.


Dear Jacob:

I thoroughly understand your feelings about what happened to Mr. Hamer and the even more unfortunate Mr. Bosch. I wish I could go back in time to have revealed Bosch's infiltration of your winery to you. But I can't. I feel shame, remorse and regret over the whole incident. We must go on, Jacob, as I know you and I are doing. I look forward to the combined Christmas and engagement party at your home.

Love,
Pamela


*The more unfortunate Mr. Bosch.* Cotter was flabbergasted. *The man was a murderer. He was going to torture Bradley's family and maybe even kill them.* Cotter would have to revisit Skyler's true feelings. Right now her credibility was still questionable.

## Chapter 24

### Christmas 1869

Pine branches were braided around the upright poles of the porch and railings of Cotter's main house, Hamer's home and anywhere they could drape such things. Pine cones painted white and red were pinned to the laurel wrappings and wreathes with bright red bows adorned every door on the Serenity Winery estate. The snow was still white and seemingly recent although the last storm was four-days ago. The eaves were frosted with thick white snow and the angles of almost every eave had at least a foot-long icicle. Sleigh bells were nailed to the center of each doorway wreath and announced the arrival and entry of visitors.

"Someone's jingling the bells on the door. Let me get it." Mrs. Hamer opened the door and greeted Samantha Wigglesworth and Andy Mashpit. "Merry Christmas you two, come in and close the door, it's freezing out there."

Mashpit and Wigglesworth removed their boots after banging the snow from them. They both changed into the shoes they carried in. "Merry Christmas to everyone." Wigglesworth gave the greeting since Mashpit hadn't heard it or seen Hamer's lips.

"Yes, Merry Christmas." Mashpit hung up their outerwear. "I don't think we'll see any snow tonight."

"No matter. Everyone is staying the night." Cotter raised a glass of warmed cider in greeting.

A large blue balsam fir decorated with colored pinecones stood off in a corner of the large living room well away from the fireplace. Numerous presents wrapped in red or green paper lay around it. All the gifts had been placed over the past week, including several gifts to Cotter and Skyler from Nancy and Mathew. One large blue-and-white-striped package was also labeled for them with the bold signature of Mortimer Pignast.

"The others should be along directly, I hope," Bradley Hamer said. "I'm getting hungry."

Ten-minutes later the door jingles revealed Fern Ferndock and Pignast. Finally the last guest arrived–Pamela Skyler. She walked into the room with Hamer's oldest daughter and stood by Cotter after a minimal hug and peck on the lips.

"I don't know whether everyone knows everyone else, so I'll go first." Cotter introduced Pamela and in so doing introduced Rosicot, LaRoque, Mashpit, the Hamers and their children.

Pignast and Mashpit introduced Fern and Samantha, respectively. Cotter spoke again. "I would like to propose a Christmas toast with the first bottle of Serenity wine to be consumed in Connecticut."

Gertrin Hamer, Cotter and the Hamer teenager filled the glasses.

Cotter raised his glass. "To peace and tranquility, good health and a prosperous next year. I want to also toast the new women of our family–to Pamela, to Fern and to Samantha."

No invitation had been sent to Nancy and Mathew. Their gifts were for Pamela and Cotter for their engagement. At first Cotter was reluctant to accept them but he succumbed to Pamela's direct pressure about Christmas spirit and family mending. Gertrin Hamer also added that presents for their engagement as well as for Mashpit's would be there and that Elizabeth Colt had sent gifts for both couples as well.

Wigglesworth sidled up to Fern. "Has Mortimer popped the question yet?"

"He's waiting for something called 'stability' to appear." Fern smiled. "I think it will happen when he receives his certificate from Yale to assist surgeons with anesthetics." She smiled a devilish grin. "And if not, then I'll ask him outright about marriage." They both laughed.

"Okay let's eat." LaRoque saw the plates and servings were on the table and couldn't contain his hunger another moment.

After the meal, presents and gifts were opened and general domestic tranquility permeated the pine-scented air. LaRoque threw a few more large logs on the fire which would last the night. Fabian Rosicot had delighted the newcomers with answers to their questions about France and Paris but when questioned about his purpose for being in New Haven and his job at the winery his response was evasive.

"Mademoiselle Fern, I oversee the proper functioning of the equipment which came from France."

"What does the French machine do?" Samantha Wigglesworth looked at Mashpit during her question as well as at Rosicot.

"It helps make the wine." Rosicot's answer was for everyone. "The machine helps the wine with aging." He would offer no more than that.

Pamela Skyler was beside herself with frustration. She wanted to know the nitty gritty about how Serenity winemaking was different than Van Haven wine production. She held her tongue. The risks were too great. She looked at Cotter and their eyes locked in understanding. No business questions or tours or anything to do with the wine business was to issue from her mouth. Skyler also wanted desperately to tell Cotter about Danzer's recruitment of mercenaries. Release of that information would also end her relationship with Cotter. The spirit of the evening, however, was one of personal closeness, Christmas giving, and future family formation.

"Well, happy everything to everyone and now let me tell you all about the sleeping arrangements." Gertrin Hamer had her children help with locating the overnight bags to the rooms rearranged for Fern, Samantha and Pamela. The ladies bid their goodnights with short tender kisses.

Rosicot, Mashpit and LaRoque retired for the night and bid their adieus. Pignast lingered behind and touched Cotter on the shoulder. "Jacob, I have something important you have to know."

"I told everyone that today and tomorrow we do not discuss any business."

"This is about life and death. It's about Kelvin Danzer."

●

On the following Saturday evening with Christmas only two-days away, Danzer sat at a small table in the noisy Green Moss Saloon bar area with Eloise O'Dhik. "I need to know whether Pignast is talking about my recruiting some hired strong-arms for Van Haven."

"It shouldn't be a problem. Fern Ferndock's the only girl he talks to." O'Dhik blew a small steady stream of smoke from pursed lips and put down her gold plated cigarette holder.

"Then tell Fern if she wants Pignast to continue to be alive that he keeps his mouth shut or …." Danzer reached in to his jacket pushing the lever button on his axe holster. The axe handle jumped into his right hand and in one fast arc he buried the axe head into the tabletop. The loud 'thud' penetrated the background prattle and sudden silence brought all eyes to Danzer. He motioned to O'Dhik.

Eloise O'Dhik stood up and signaled the piano player to continue. The noise and chatter resumed. "I'll tell everyone including Mortimer Pignast that no rumors are to be passed around about Van Haven regardless of the source."

"Especially Robert Locke and Mathew Cotter. When Robert gets liquored up, he starts whining about not getting laid at home. If he and Mathew get soused together around here and start taking about Van Haven, they could spill everything."

"I know the girls they favor and I'll try to keep a lid on their booze. I don't think you have to worry about Mortimer but Locke and Mathew Cotter could be your real problem. And what about your hired muscle? What if they spread the word about why they're in town?"

"Just let me know about any of them. I'll make sure my men are closed mouth about their jobs."

"If you ask me, Kelvin darling, you have too many people involved in this for a leak not to occur."

"You're right, Eloise. The best I can hope for is to know who the culprit is. That way I can cover my ass with my bosses and be prepared for any resistance from Jacob Cotter's group."

●

"It was a wonderful party Jacob and I love your friends. How come Fabian and John LaRoque have no romantic ties yet?" Pamela squeezed Cotter's hand under the table of the Tea House.

"Fabian told me he has a lady friend in France. They'll talk future commitment after he completes his job here. As for John, I think he'll start to pursue his hormones with the opposite sex now that his leg is totally healed and the Serenity business becomes stable."

"I'll not ask about the job Jacob, but I want to talk about setting a date–our wedding date. We can't keep saying it's going to be after graduation–when after graduation?"

Cotter smiled. "Okay. One-week after graduation. You can pick the exact day."

"Oh, that's wonderful." Pamela partially stood up to lean over the small table and give Cotter a kiss.

"Will you be coming to my place for New Year's Eve or are you committed to Nancy and Mathew?"

"Jacob, really, I'm committed only to you. I would like you to come to my place. We have privacy. I didn't mind staying with the other women for the Christmas party. I miss having you in my bed, Jacob." Her smile had elements of a pout.

"I just don't think it's appropriate for me yet. Let's get through the New Year. My school assignments are really intense and time-consuming now. I think Serenity will take care of itself with my three foremen in charge. I really need total concentration. I hope you understand."

"Well I don't really understand. I know at least three of your Yale school chums are married. If they can have time for a love life why can't we?"

"Pamela, I haven't forgotten what happened to Bradley Hamer. I don't want you to be caught in the middle of some nasty difficulty. Nancy and Mathew are not about to stop intimidation of my staff." Cotter had set his trap. Here was Skyler's chance to really prove her love for him. *Please tell me what Pignast told me at our Christmas party.*

"Jacob you told me not to discuss the business and I won't. Your rules remember? I don't want to happen again to us what almost happened when Bradley had his injuries."

Cotter sat back and looked at his fiancée. She was a truly attractive woman. He couldn't let his feelings ripen about his affection for her unless she was totally honest. *Come on, Pamela, tell me about Kelvin Danzer.*

"Okay, but if at any time you are aware of something in the works, you must let me know. I don't want any of my people injured again." Their evening was over.

Cotter watched her buggy disappear down the main roadway from his estate. He was disappointed. Pignast had been quite clear about what Danzer's orders from Nancy and Mathew were.

"At least three hired hooligans with guns. The total will be four, counting Danzer." Pignast had whispered the words.

"We can handle anything that comes our way as long as we know in advance." Cotter's voice was also in a whisper.

"Ah, but I have been dismissed. Nancy, Robert and Mathew fired me. They bought out my stock and kicked me out. If they knew I told you, they'd get Danzer after me."

"Was Danzer involved in the killing of my night worker? I know he maneuvered Bosch into the job of replacing him."

"They never spoke of it with me present. My feeling, however, is indeed Danzer was somehow involved."

"Thanks Mortimer, I appreciate you telling me this. I would have hoped Pamela Skyler might have told me the same news."

"I was shooed out the door. I don't know what plans were made after I left or what they told her."

"But she knew about Danzer getting more thugs to target Serenity?"

"Yes, I'm sorry to say. Well, Goodnight now."

*I'll give Skyler some space to sort out her conflict of loyalties and feelings. I'll give her until the hired guns make their appearance in town, which would be in late January or February according to Pignast.*

# Chapter 25

## Discovery

"Sticking a pin through the cork in the ether bottle gives a more uniform drop. You'll conserve the ether and there's less of the stuff for the rest of us to breathe." Cotter had read an article of anesthesia technique in the New England Medical Bulletin and Hayes agreed to try it out at Yale.

"Yes indeed," Pignast shook his head in agreement, "My Fern loses romantic interest when I come in smelling like the anesthetic and some of my barber customers sometimes cancel their haircuts."

Cotter smiled. "My patients will smell it on me for the rest of the day. Okay let's pay attention. The patient is under now. I have to wash my hands and get to the surgery."

Dr. Hayes walked in as Cotter was washing the skin over the operative field. "That's a bad-looking fracture. How'd it happen?"

"I don't know. He came in Sunday morning still drunk and wouldn't let anyone touch him. When he sobered up, he still didn't remember anything but he begged to have it fixed. The last thing he remembered was some big guy pushing him away from Eloise O'Dhik at the Green Moss."

Hayes and Cotter reduced the fracture and aligned the protruding shinbone in place with a small screw. They sewed over the skin after extensive irrigation with the carbolic solution.

Pignast administered two more ether anesthetics for Cotter and Hayes. They were through with surgery by noon and Cotter walked with Pignast outside. He stopped and turned to Pignast. "Mortimer you've become a fine anesthesia administrator. I wish you could come with me to Texas this summer. It's almost March and in three-months I'll be getting ready to move."

"I thank you for the confidence Dr. Cotter and I have yet to make my decision on such a move. It's still possible that Fern and I could be ready for commitment to each other and to a major relocation." Pignast paused. "However, I have to tell you something about the first patient."

"The barroom brawler with the broken leg–what about him?"

"Remember I told you about Danzer hiring some thugs?"

"Yes, although I haven't seen any appear yet."

"They're here and working for Van Haven as wagon loaders for their winery. From what I hear he's hired three just as I advised he would. Well, Danzer wasn't affronted by any perceived advance to Eloise O'Dhik. I mean it happens all the time. He thought the man overheard his conversation about the plot to bring in the ruffians. The man said he'd heard nothing about that and again asked Eloise to drink with him. Unfortunately for him, he pushed Danzer, who fell to the ground. While on the ground Danzer whacked the man's leg with the flat of his axe."

"That certainly explains the severity of the injury. I couldn't understand how the leg could be so bad from a bar fight."

Pignast put his hand on Cotter's shoulder. "Jacob, Danzer is not one to be taken lightly nor to ever turn one's back on. Also, it appears your brother and sister may activate their plan to forcibly absorb or destroy Serenity."

"I've met the likes of men like Danzer before. I appreciate you telling me this, Mortimer."

They separated and Cotter went to the Obstetrics Clinic. His thoughts were troubled by Pignast's news. His feelings for Skyler were troubled by her withholding the information of the new Van Haven muscle from him. They continued meeting twice a week at the teahouse but Cotter still rebuffed her invitation to spend Tuesday nights at her home. This afternoon he would give her another chance at self-disclosure.

●

"Jacob I'm getting the bridal jitters and our wedding day is in June. I think it's because you still haven't come back to my house."

"Pamela, I know it's difficult for you but in my last year at Yale most of my time is taken up with patients. I'm working under minimal supervision now but it means my patient load is increased and my assessments by the staff are intense. Serenity is running pretty well and our wine is selling in Georgia, Virginia and the Carolinas. Our partners are looking at Louisiana for additional marketing and we're importing more grapes each month."

"But what about us? I want to be a part of your life." Skyler squeezed Cotter's hand across the table.

"You can. You can sell your holdings in Van Haven and buy into Serenity."

"But what if Serenity fails? Van Haven is established and it will provide us with financial security."

"Why do you think Serenity will fail?" This was the opportunity Cotter hoped for.

"Any new business can fail, Jacob. Don't you love me? Don't you trust my years of judgment as a businesswoman? As a widow, Van haven was all I had until you came into my life."

"I don't see Serenity failing–just the opposite. And of course I love you. I confide in you and I trust you but I expect the same in return. That's what love is all about to me–complete trust and sharing."

"Love is more, Jacob. Don't you have an inner feeling about us?"

"Pamela I feel you're holding something back. Are you telling me everything about what's going on with Nancy and Mathew and their attitude toward Serenity?"

Skyler grabbed Cotter's hand. Her grip was fierce. Her nails almost broke his skin.

"Ow, Pamela–your hand is digging into me. Please answer my question."

"Jacob I'm sworn to secrecy about Van Haven as you keep total confidence about Serenity. I haven't pushed you, have I? I can tell you though that Nancy and Mathew still ask me about Serenity and I still respond to them there is nothing to tell."

Cotter recoiled. It was not the answer he wanted. Her response was not totally a condemning one as he had posed those ground rules to her himself. The problem now was she was withholding life-and-death information from him. That was the difference. "Some rules have to be broken Pamela."

"Jacob I'll not ask you anything about Serenity and I cannot tell you anything about Nancy and Mathew. Please don't torture me like this."

Cotter looked at his pocket watch. "It's time to go Pamela."

"Jacob, tomorrow is Wednesday. It's your day off. Won't you please spend the day with me?"

"My Wednesday routine is inviolate Pamela. I've told you many times before." He walked her to her buggy and embraced her.

"Please, Jacob, come to my home tomorrow. Please."

"We'll meet here again on Thursday, Pamela." He kissed her tenderly and felt her tears. He hugged her and opened his eyes to see two men in winter coats looking in their direction. They were standing by a Van Haven wagon full of crated supplies. Their presence reinforced the importance of the Wednesday practice.

●

Wednesday's weather was mild. It was the first day of March. Elizabeth Colt and Carlton Strom, Colt Firearms chief engineer, were sitting at the large dining room table with their final cup of coffee for the morning.

"I've made permanent changes to the hammer and trigger of the new Colts based on your performance and suggestions." Strom produced an unloaded .45 revolver. "Fabian, you prefer to fan the hammer rather than rely on your thumb to move through each shot."

Rosicot nodded. "Oui Monsieur, it gives more firepower with my one gun"

"And I like the broad trigger. Will it be part of the new Colt line?" Cotter looked at Strom's pistol and saw the slim trigger. It looked narrower than the original.

"No it will not. The Army is our principal market and they shoot with gloves that are not skin tight like you and your people use. They need a narrower trigger. However, the guns all of you have been using are yours permanently."

Elizabeth Colt smiled at them. "Consider them not only a gift but as payment for being a part of our testing the new weapon. Also, I understand there might be a use for them, hopefully as a deterrent to possible violence by our competition?"

The question evoked silence. Bradley Hamer spoke first. "Yes, Mrs. Colt. You remember about my unfortunate episode with the ruffian who infiltrated our staff under the sponsorship of Van Haven."

"With the five of us and the new Colts, we can pose a formidable reason for any opposition to back down." LaRoque strapped on his double holster rig over his buckskins.

"You know, the way all of you dress the same makes you look like an Army." Elizabeth Colt nodded to Strom after her statement.

"Jacob, your people have reloaded the brass casings many times and they are capable of virtually endless firings if you keep to the proper powder charge. In any event, with the Army scheduled for delivery of the first five-hundred revolvers by July, ammunition will be scarce for almost a year. Mrs. Colt has yet another gift in my wagon. You have six cases of .45 cartridges complete with gunpowder and primers for reloading for the next five-years based on your people shooting every Wednesday."

"I certainly hope we don't need them but we thank you very much." Cotter waved his hand to the others who nodded in agreement.

"Consider it part of the Hunt's and my investment." Elizabeth Colt finished her coffee. "Serenity wines are being accepted down South 'most graciously' as our South Carolina vendors report."

The early morning meeting was over. Cotter and his four staff members mounted their horses. Cotter looked back at them as they followed in a single line. They did look like an army patrol wearing the tan buckskins complete with the shiny conchos on the right side of the hat brim, shirt and pant leg. Mashpit moved to Cotter's side as they all increased their horses' speed to a moderate gallop.

"You sure you only saw two of them?" Mashpit faced Cotter.

Cotter looked at him. "I only saw two but Pignast will keep us posted. According to his last meeting with Van Haven just before Christmas, Danzer planned to hire three men. Fern is keeping a lookout for them at the Green Moss. According to her and the other Green Moss women there are three men who are new to Van Haven and look like hired guns."

The group dismounted at the shooting range and hung the gourds and boards to simulate the enemy. Both types of targets would be fired at–as stationary and moving objects.

"Andy, remember you walk between John and I and shoot at the center targets. John will shoot at the extreme right and I'll take the left." Cotter turned around. "Bradley you and Fabian face rearward behind us and shoot at the same time as we do. Use your pistols first and then swing up your shotguns. You know the routine." Their plan was to form a circle of firepower. It would cover any threat. Fabian and Bradley brandishing and firing their shotguns would give the other three time to reload. "We rotate the positions after each face-off. Andy you must keep to the center at all times."

Mashpit nodded. He was not sensitive about his hearing loss. This was a practical tactic they had practiced for a year-and-a-half now.

They finished stringing the targets and were completely unaware of having been tracked to their private shooting place. The unseen observer was at first overcome with anxiety at seeing a buggy and an unknown female enter and leave Cotter's home. The woman was attractive but looked much older than Jacob.

Still Pamela Skyler felt a pang of jealously. This was her worst fear. However, there was no familiarity of kissing or hugging when the woman boarded her buggy. A wagonload of something heavy had been brought into the winemaking building. The driver of the now empty buckboard followed the unknown lady.

Skyler looked to Cotter and his four foremen. She followed their dust and used it as concealment. She had to leave her buggy and travel by foot when they stopped. She used several large trees still barren from winter but sporting obvious buds to provide cover. Skyler scanned the group with a pair of opera glasses. After only 15-minutes they formed a circle and at Jacob's signal they drew their guns and fired.

She was suddenly aware that the two wearing single guns were shooting at targets facing her. The sound of eight large caliber pistols merged into one deafening roar. Chips of wood flew from two of the trees Skyler was using as cover. She dove for the ground after a piece of pine bark bit through her waistcoat and lodged in her shoulder. She peeked around the tree again. She heard four large booms and a shower of shotgun pellets rained on her location. They were moving around and changing positions. Jacob was looking her way now. There was a look of hostility on his face she had never seen before. He gave a signal and she ducked anticipating another volley of potential wood-chips flying at her.

Before the next firing sequence she ran back to her buggy. It seemed like miles away now. Her breathing was fast and her pulse was pounding in her temples. She released the tether from the tree branch and whacked her horse with the whip. After ten-minutes she slowed the animal to a trot.

At home she gave the reins to Jules, her liveryman and groundskeeper. "Mrs. Skyler are you hurt? Your jacket is torn. Is that blood?"

"A tree branch fell on me. I'll be okay." Inside Skyler removed her jacket and blouse. There was a one-inch ragged tear with a piece of tree bark protruding from the skin of her shoulder.

The pain had been masked by her original anxiety and now was becoming intense. She called out for Nester.

"Oh, my. The first thing is to get that thing out." Nester Smood was calm. "Let me get you some Port to calm your nerves and I have some laudanum from when I burned myself a few months ago." Nester waited until Skyler became sedated from the combination of the alcohol and narcotic. Skyler's eyelids became heavy and her pupils became smaller. Nester knew those signs–the shoulder was ready for getting the piece of wood out. She removed the larger splinter and picked out as much of the remaining fragments as she could.

"No. No. No more. I can't take the pain." Skyler refused any further intervention.

"I've done as much as I can, Mrs. Skyler. We should keep the wound open with a light cover. I've tended to these kinds of things before. In the morning, you can go to the clinic. Maybe Jacob Cotter will be there and take care of you."

With no more wound probing, the severe pain ebbed and she let Nester apply the loose dressing.

"Let me put this oilskin under the towel beneath your shoulder so you don't stain the bedclothes."

Skyler took the second offered laudanum dose and additional glass of port wine. Without the continued manipulation of her wound, the numbing effect of the combination began to overpower her. Pamela Skyler could hear her housekeeper's last words recycling over and over.

"Maybe Jacob Cotter will be there to take care of you." The sentence repeated itself in softer and softer tones. *Yes, Jacob will take care of me tomorrow.*

# Chapter 26

## Andrew Mashpit

"What happened to your shoulder?" Cotter removed the gauze dressing which was saturated with clotted blood.

"Oh, it hurts bad Jacob." The female attendant brought a dressing and debridement tray to the treatment table.

Cotter examined her shoulder. The irregular wound was about an inch in diameter and extremely swollen. An area of redness extended over the entire right shoulder. Cotter put his fingers in her right armpit and felt the swollen lymph nodes.

"Oh, oooo, that hurts too." Skyler moved her shoulder dislodging the sheet covering her bare chest. The attendant immediately covered her up. For a fleeting moment Jacob flashed back to his Tuesday night stays at Skyler's home. Her anguish brought him right back to the current situation.

"A branch of a tree hit me during a windstorm yesterday." Skyler's brow was sweaty.

"That's strange. There was no wind at my place. So Nestor took out the largest fragment but not all of it?"

"Yes, Jacob. I feel sick. My shoulder hurts terrible. I had nightmares last night. I didn't sleep or eat. Oh please help me Jacob."

"I'm going to have to clean the wound out and cut out all the remaining splinters. Once I get it cleaned and put a drain in your fever will go away." Cotter held her hand but reassurance did not occur.

"That's going to hurt. Oh, no, please." Skyler tried to suppress tears but they trickled down her cheeks.

"I'll have Dr. Hayes help. He's the Chief Surgeon and we'll do this under anesthesia."

"I'll be knocked out. Yes. Oh thank you Jacob."

"There will be a scar I'm afraid." Cotter wrote a note for the attendant to have Skyler taken to the surgical clinic within the hour.

In the operating theater, Pignast looked down at Pamela's fearful expression. "Pamela, my dear, this ether has a chemical odor but the deeper you breathe the sooner you will be asleep. When you wake-up everything will be done." He placed the terry cloth cone over her nose and mouth and began dripping the ether. Tiny succinct drops of ether fell in a regular rhythm from the safety pin impaled through the corked bottle. A few pellets of birdshot fell in his lap as Skyler's head went limp.

Cotter cut away the jagged edges and removed the remaining splinters. He washed out the wound with carbolic solution and packed it open with carbolic saturated gauze. Hayes looked at the final result approvingly.

"She's lucky she didn't wait too long to come in. Good job Jacob." Hayes motioned Cotter to follow him to the sink for a final hand washing. "Jacob I've put your name in front of the Board of Staff Physicians at Yale for a position with us after you graduate in June. You'll be a great asset to our staff and we need young talent like yourself."

Cotter dried his hands. "Dr. Hayes I'm genuinely flattered. As you and Dr. Randall know I've made plans to join Dr. Charlie Garrison in Endura Texas."

"I'm not asking for a commitment today, Jacob. Please consider it. You have a few months left until graduation."

"Okay, I'll certainly give it some thought." Cotter offered the words but felt there was no way he would stay. He would take Pamela and head out west. He went back to Skyler as she was waking up. "Let's keep her in the hospital for one day. The dressing should be changed every 12-hours. Give her a double dose of laudanum 30-minutes before and make sure the packing is removed and replaced with a fresh one. Be liberal with the carbolic."

The woman wrote the orders on Skyler's medical chart.

The following day Cotter attended his patients early in the morning and at four o'clock he ended with Skyler. "Pamela the wound is healing well." He felt under her arm. "The swelling in your armpit is almost gone. That's good–there's no more blood poisoning. You can go home."

"Will you take care of me Jacob?" The waxy pallor was also gone from her face.

"I'll show Nester how to change the dressing. The apothecary will give you an ample supply of laudanum for the pain."

The next Thursday Cotter inspected the wound which was healing from the bottom up and was only the size of a thumbnail. "It looks good and so do you."

"Can I resume my full time career, Doctor?" Skyler smiled at him as she dressed.

"And what is your full time career, may I ask." Cotter returned the smile.

"I prepare the accounting sheet for Van Haven and continue the pursuit of the love of my life–you." She squeezed his hand.

"In that case how about a date at the teahouse after four this evening?"

"Anything the doctor orders." She gave him a playful glance.

•

"From what I hear, Serenity will meet expenses this year and maybe even make a small profit." Nancy Locke was pacing up-and-down the long side of the dining room table. "We send some of our Van Haven labels down South but not much. What's worse is those damn Southerners like Serenity wine better than ours." Nancy reached for the bottle of Port.

"Nancy dear, it's not even ten o'clock. Leave the wine alone. Let's discuss the situation." Robert Locke put his arm on his wife's shoulder.

"I knew we should have gotten rid of Jacob's place over a year ago." She shrugged Robert's arm off and poured herself a glass of the Port.

Mathew Cotter saw his wife reach for an empty glass for Nancy to fill. "Look, let's start with talking buy-out or partnership or merger or something like that. Pamela what do you think? You're gonna marry into Serenity."

"I'm totally against any forceful alternative to a merger or financial take-over." She removed her arm from the sling and flexed her fingers several times. Two-weeks had passed and her shoulder was still stiff but getting back to normal. Her relationship with Cotter seemed better although they still met only at the teahouse.

"Have some Port Pamela." Elizabeth poured her a glass. "It takes away all kinds of pain."

Skyler accepted the drink. "I think you should get rid of the criminal element. We could lose everything, you know."

"What do you mean lose everything?"

"Suppose Jacob and his people put up a successful fight. The legal repercussions would ruin us. Just make Serenity a fair offer."

"Fair? This is business and business is like war." Nancy Locke reddened.

"A business solution may be difficult Pamela. You told us Serenity has two partners in Hartford who you have yet to identify. Now that Serenity is an active business unit and registered in Connecticut, I've found a legal means to determine who they are. Yesterday, I received word from my query at the Hartford Business Registration Office that Jacob's two partners are Horatio Hunt and Mrs. Elizabeth Hart Jarvis Colt."

"What?" Nancy Locke dropped her glass of port.

"Yes dear, board members, Hunt is the major wine importer for the upper Atlantic coast and he's now the major distributor for Serenity." Robert Locke flipped a page of the Van Haven ledger. "I don't have to tell you about Mrs. Colt. Her business ventures are legend. She's tenacious and will never give up a good thing or at least what she perceives is a good investment."

"We only have one course of action then. Destroy Serenity. If it doesn't exist, it's not a threat and no competition." Nancy Locke pounded her small fist on the table.

"Wait. How can you perceive Serenity as a threat when they're not? They're not even competition. They created their own market and have stayed out of New England and New York."

"It will only be a matter of time before they became greedy. Look how they're going farther South." Nancy Locke was seething. Her eyes were red from anger and Port. "Let's vote. All in favor of driving out our younger brother's little business raise your glass."

The vote was four to one. "Pamela we have no hard feelings about your vote but the decision is made." Nancy Locke looked over to Kelvin Danzer.

"Kelvin, start with the Serenity farm hands and then get the wine-making employees to quit. Use money and Van Haven jobs as a bribe. If it doesn't work then you know what to do. Burn the place down after you clear them out. That'll keep the casualties down." Nancy Locke looked toward Skyler. "We'll try not to inflict physical harm unless force is absolutely needed."

Danzer grinned. He patted his left chest feeling the comfort of his axe. "We've been ready for weeks now."

●

"Andy, I don't know. Mrs. Colt was very nice and worked with me on the accounting for marketing the Serenity wines, but I'm afraid to leave the Emporium." She walked by his side as they approached the Emporium.

"For God's sakes Samantha. Why?" Mashpit was flustered. They had talked about her getting out of the stressful environment and away from that maggot manager, Farfel Fester.

"Well, for one thing, Mrs. Colt said Serenity was a gamble and she had faith the current good sales would increase but there are no guarantees any new business will be successful. At least I'll still have a job." Wigglesworth looked away from Mashpit.

He touched her chin to move her face back. "Come on Samantha. You have to remember to look at me or I can't hear you. We're going to be married soon. I've put my faith with Jacob Cotter and the others. The whole organization is like a family."

"If you really must know, I'm afraid. That man Strom gave all of you those guns and every Wednesday you go off shooting like you're expecting to go to war."

"I've told you before, Van Haven is known for hostility and we armed ourselves as a deterrent. If they try anything and see us a force going to return fire, they'll just back down."

"Or you'll get killed." Her eyes became glassy.

"I survived the war didn't I?"

"This is different. Two men are already dead and you told me it was because of Van Haven."

"We need you. You're good at marketing and managing the invoices and receipts. The pay is better. We'll be working together."

"Let me have one more week to think about it? Please?"

"Okay. One week." They went into the store.

Fester was pacing outside his tiny office and looking at his watch. He stood by the curtained-off room where employees hung their coats and ate their meals. His right lip was twitching in anticipation of a confrontation with Wigglesworth.

"You're late Miss Wigglesworth. Your tardiness will cost you one hour's pay."

"What kind of rule is that? It's very unfair Fester. Do you dock all of your workers like this or just Miss Wigglesworth?" Mashpit stared at him.

"I am certainly not singling her out. It is my rule and it applies to everyone. Not only that but since you are late you will have to work through your lunch half-hour." He folded his arms on his chest and pushed his chin up in triumph.

Mashpit looked at the anguish on Wigglesworth's face. "Fester, that's unreasonable." Mashpit looked at his own watch and then looked at the pendulum clock on the wall behind Fester. "Wait a minute. My watch and your clock says she's seven-minutes early. I'm afraid you misjudged the time by your slow timepiece Fester and you owe her an apology."

Fester looked at the clock. His face began to twitch more violently. "The clock and your watch are wrong, Mr. Mashpit. I am the boss and I make the rules."

Mashpit put his hands on his hips pushing his long coat back. The sunlight shining through the front window glinted from his nickel-plated Colt. Fester became tremulous.

"You're not supposed to wear guns in public buildings. I can summon the police. If you pull a gun on me, I'll consider it an act of attempted robbery."

"Samantha are you sure you want to wait a week? I'm finding it very difficult to breathe the same air as Fester."

Mashpit could see that Samantha Wigglesworth had been mortified at Fester's attitude and intimidation.

"Mr. Fester, you owe me last week's salary. I want it now. You can consider it my last paycheck."

Mashpit smiled ear-to-ear. "Outstanding. Did you hear the lady, Fester? Pay her now and we'll both leave your sight."

Fester went into his office and came out with a small envelope. "Mr. Mashpit, I want you to take note that I did not fire her. She's quitting on her own." Sweat poured from his brow in the cool store.

"It wasn't so bad was it?" Mashpit hugged her sideways as they walked on the wooden sidewalk.

"No. When do I start at Serenity?" She smiled up at him.

Mashpit looked into her face. "Oops. Excuse me, sir." He walked right into a burly bearded man who stared at both of them.

"You deliberately walked into me." The man pushed Mashpit's right shoulder with his left hand. His open waistcoat showed a holster at his left waist with the pistol butt facing for a right hand draw.

"I didn't walk into you, Mister and I do apologize."

"You too interested in your pretty lady to look where you're going?" He smiled showing his brown, crusty, decayed upper teeth.

"Sometimes that happens to me, yes. We're engaged you see." Mashpit watched the man's eyes and right hand.

"I think you need a lesson in manners."

Mashpit saw the man's eyes jerk to his left holster and the right hand fingers extend. Mashpit had both of his Colts in the man's face within a fraction of a second. "I want you to be thinking about just walking away after you throw your gun down. Take it out with your left hand and drop it."

The man's eyes bulged at the suddenness of the role reversal. His mouth remained open as he dropped the gun.

"Samantha dear, take the gun, break it open and take the cylinder out."

She opened the action of the man's Navy revolver.

"Throw the cylinder far into the street and drop the gun over there."

Wigglesworth threw the cylinder on the moist street and dropped the gun into a mound of fresh horse dung.

"Now get going." Mashpit turned back to her as the man got on his Van Haven wagon. "See, Samantha, the guy's from Van Haven and his aggressive act was neutralized."

"I'm still afraid Andy."

"Any regrets about quitting the Emporium?"

"No, not at all. When I think of the years I cowered before that measly man. But please be careful."

"I'm always careful. Let's go. We can go right to the winery and give Mr. Hamer the good news. Both Bradley Hamer and Jacob have had to keep the books and they'll both be delighted you're finally joining us."

•

"What'd he look like?" Danzer was furious about one of his new thugs being disarmed in public by one of Cotter's hands.

The man described Mashpit and then added, "The bastard didn't even answer me when I told him he owed me a new gun. I yelled after him and told him I knew where he lived and the next time we met he'd be sorry."

"It must have been the deaf guy–Andy Mashpit. Yeah, he's fast with a gun. I seen him at Serenity last year whip both guns out like they were alive." Danzer scratched his head. "I'll get you a new gun."

"You don't have to. I found the cylinder and picked up the rest of the pistol from the horseshit–no harm done."

"Stay away from them until it's our time to make a move."

"When's that going to be?" The man unholstered his gun and smelled it. "I can't get the horseshit smell out of it."

"Don't stick the thing in your face. You'll shoot your brains out." Danzer was concerned about Cotter's people. *This will not be an easy ousting.* "I'll let you know when we go after them. Come on, I'll buy you a beer at the Green Moss."

●

Mortimer Pignast had watched the episode with Mashpit and the Van Haven strong-arm through his barbershop window. He wished he could hear the exchange now and looked pensively as Danzer and his man walked to the saloon. Pignast saw Cotter riding slowly in the opposite direction. He ran outside waving his hands.

"Dr. Cotter. Dr. Cotter." Pignast's voice was out of Danzer's range.

Cotter rode to the barbershop. Pignast told Cotter of the incident. He looked around but no one was looking at the barber-phrenologist talking to the medical student astride his horse.

"It happened this morning?"

"Yes. I don't know what kind of repercussions will result."

"I don't think there'll be any yet. I'm waiting for Nancy and Mathew to contact me about buying out Serenity. We figure it'll be their first move."

Pignast looked around again and motioned for Cotter to lean more in his direction for his modulated whisper. "I can tell you Nancy and the Van Haven clan will speak out at the end of April or early May. At least it was their agenda when I was last with them."

"Well, keep your ears tuned at the barbershop and the Green Moss."

"Certainly, Certainly. I'll keep you informed most conscientiously." Pignast went back into the barbershop.

●

Cotter met with his group on Saturday. They were seated leisurely around the dining room table. The weather was still Spring-like and only a few logs were added to the fireplace. The remaining embers still created pleasant pine fumes. Cotter sat at the head of the long table and pointed to Mashpit to get his attention.

"Andy, did Van Haven's man get a good look at your Colts?"

"I had both barrels against his face. He couldn't see any details of the guns and he had no cause to. His only thoughts were on keeping his bladder and stomach from discharging."

They all laughed. Cotter raised his hand. "Remember, we're sworn to Colt Firearms not to lose a single gun to outsiders. Now, let's consider the consequences of Andy's confrontation."

"I didn't initiate this Jake."

"I know Andy, and I'm glad of the outcome. However, this man will tell his bosses, my relatives, about at least one person able to resist any violence attempted against us."

"Oui Monsieur, he will assume there are others and will think twice about further actions against us."

"No, I don't think so, Fabian. I feel the reverse will happen. They'll try to increase their numbers against us or attack one time in full force."

"I bet it's one time." LaRoque stood up and walked to the gun cabinet. "I think we should wear our Colts at all times now."

"They won't make their move until April or May, but I agree. We should always wear our guns and be prepared for the unexpected."

"Won't the farm hands and the wine-making helpers get suspicious?" Bradley accepted his holstered Colt from LaRoque.

"We've already told them not to reveal the Pasteur kettle process to anyone on threat of losing their job. We pay better than anyone in the whole state. We just reinforce our original agreement with them. In fact, we'll ask them to sign another paper." Cotter looked again at Mashpit.

"You want Samantha to draw them up, Jake?"

"You read my mind. By the way, I'm glad she's on board with us. She's really good with the bookkeeping and has good aptitude for handling the sales. Mrs. Colt will be sending someone out to teach her more about accounting."

"Okay, here are your guns. Hang them on your bedpost at night." LaRoque handed out the weapons.

Cotter went to his room and sat at his large open desk. He pulled out a small box from a right-hand drawer to place Charlie Garrison's latest letter in it. On second thought, he re-read the letter.

Dear Jake:

Time is flying. The fertile population in Endura was extremely active last fall. We're now delivering babies almost every other day and have more scheduled throughout the summer. We're anxious to try out your technique with the low dose ether. Have you talked this Pignast guy into coming to Texas? We really could use him. I have one lady helper who assists with nursing duties in the hospital who's getting good with anesthesia but she can't perform on her own yet.

Victor Vlack is getting worse. His chief hired gun is trigger-happy and provides us with at least one patient a week with a gunshot wound or pistol-whipping injury. He's mean. I wrongly told Vlack that Stan and I'll be increasing our staff when you get here. We'll need another female assistant and hopefully your anesthesia person will join us. He outright told us that increasing the size of our clinic and hospital is a bad reflection on Endura. He claims it'll go against him in his bid to get elected as Representative.

His gunslinger, Ken Boda, stares at us in the street like he wants us dead real bad. I hate to tell you about the bad side of living here but we were always up front with each other.

How is everything at the winery? Have any of the hired badasses shown up yet? I can't help thinking about you and I being in similar situations. You'll be leaving one frying pan to go into another. In the end, I feel we'll prevail.

You don't say much anymore about your future bride. Are you still engaged with a wedding right after graduation? We'll try to get her settled in Endura with our best Texas hospitality.

Keep writing,
Charlie

Cotter sat back in his chair after he put the letter in the box and closed the drawer. *My goal in life is to bring quality medical care to the west.* The thought was always there. Charlie Garrison's letters reminded him of his father's feelings during the war. They were both appalled by the inadequate medical services outside of major cities. *There will be two jobs in Endura for me. One is to help Charlie with the new hospital and the other to help cope with Vlack–and now Ken Boda.*

He walked to the bed and draped his two Colts over the bedpost next to his pillow.

# Chapter 27

## Van Haven's Plan

The mild weather persisted throughout March. Rain was intermittent in April and fed Serenity's new plants and seedlings. May was one week away. The vineyards were green and lush with the grape plantings sending tendrils skyward around the slim support poles. Bradley Hamer had added a new office next to his for Samantha Wigglesworth.

"I have an order from New Orleans for 100 cases of the sauterne, Bradley. We haven't received the grapes yet." Wigglesworth's concern was minimal. The orders for the wine always preceded their inventory update.

"They'll be here next week. I must say, Samantha, that without you we would be behind in our production."

"Thank you Bradley. Oh, here comes Andy."

"Everything in order Samantha?" Mashpit kissed her lightly on the cheek.

"Certainly, except for one thing." She motioned Mashpit into her office for privacy.

"What?"

"I feel funny having you stay over—we're not married yet."

"We can't take any chances. Remember the jerk who tried to rough us up last month? Unless you move in here at Serenity, I have no choice but to guard the future Mrs. Mashpit."

"I just can't up and leave everything."

"You can move everything to this place. We can store your furniture. We have a room for you. Our new home will be ready by the end of June."

"I know and I love the place already. It'll only be a mile from my office and you." She kissed him. There was a knock on the door.

"I hate to interrupt but this is Wednesday." Cotter filled the doorway in his buckskins and two Colts.

"You don't have to remind me. You two have the same clothes on every Wednesday." Wigglesworth placed her hands on her hips. "Honestly you're all like a bunch of boys going fishing."

"Not quite, Samantha. Has Andy told you about moving in here until we get your house built?"

"Yes, why the rush? Do you think we're in danger?"

"I think Van Haven will start to exert pressure on us in the next two-weeks. You really should move in here. Andy and the rest of us will feel more secure about your safety." Cotter moved into the office.

"I have to sell my house first. Honestly, now the both of you are scaring me." She looked at Mashpit.

"You haven't told her?"

"I was about to when you showed up." Mashpit smiled and then looked at Wigglesworth.

"Samantha, Serenity will buy your house and property at top market price. You need to be here–to be protected." Mashpit nodded to Cotter to continue.

"We think Van Haven will be a threat to us within the next few weeks. Please accept our invitation."

Wigglesworth looked at both buckskin-clad men. Her expressions went from concern to stolid. "These Wednesday practices have gone on for almost for two-years now. You were all training for this weren't you." She took her hands from her hips and walked around the room. "I can't say what your doing is wrong. It's actually the only thing to do. I saw what happened seven-years ago when Van Haven drove out and burned-out the other wineries. Up until I met you Andy, I never gave it further thought."

"And now?" Mashpit placed his hands on her shoulders facing her.

"I'll stand by you now and forever as your wife."

They embraced as LaRoque, Bradley Hamer and Fabian entered the outside office area.

"Let's go. We have to be back by noon." LaRoque waved Cotter and Mashpit to leave.

●

"I heard something from two of the girls." Fern Ferndock lay beside Pignast. The piano playing from the saloon's bar could be just faintly distinguished with its tinny music sound.

"About Danzer and his cutthroats?"

"They talked about finally doing the job they're getting paid for. The scraggly one from Tennessee drank too much. He said he was going to miss his regular girl, Daisy, because he'd soon be leaving."

"Did he say something specific about Serenity or Jake Cotter?" Pignast turned on his side to face her.

"They didn't mention Serenity specifically, Mort. The word I got was they couldn't come to the Green Moss after this Saturday. They have a meeting with Danzer at Nancy Locke's place on Sunday."

"I have to tell Jacob right away." Pignast got up and went for his clothes draped over the end of the brass bed.

"No, don't. Mortimer please wait until you see him at surgery on Monday. They might be watching you now and if you look like you're heading out to Jacob's place they'll kill you."

Pignast went back to the bed and lay beside her. "I have to tell him. Maybe you're right. Nothing can happen until after Sunday."

●

Clients were not allowed to remain overnight at the Green Moss even in the case of nearly committed relationships such as Pignast and Ferndock. Mortimer Pignast left the Green Moss at two o'clock in the morning. He buttoned his coat against the chill of the night. The spring days were mild but the night still brought cold temperatures. Pignast used the wooden sidewalks as much as possible to avoid the hard-packed dirt street. The road mainte-nance crews didn't appear until sunrise to remove the dung and fill in the road ruts. The air was crisp with a faint horse odor from the street contents. He looked at the sparkling sky, unaware of the footsteps behind him. The two men were walking on the dirt street.

The wooden sidewalks ended at street intersections separating the rows of stores and office buildings. He stepped up to the last of the wooden sidewalks leading to his barbershop where he lived. There was a small kitchen and living room combination with a fair sized bedroom facing the street. He unlocked the barbershop door and stepped inside. As he moved to close the door and lock it he was suddenly pushed backwards. Pignast tripped and fell on his right side. The barbershop door slammed shut.

"You don't know us, Pignast. We don't get haircuts or have you feel our heads." The scruffy voice belonged to the thug who had accosted Mashpit. Another smelly hulk stood by the door looking out the window.

"What do you want?" Pignast stood back up.

"You're going to take a small trip with us. A friend of yours wants to talk to you."

"What Friend?" Pignast voice quavered.

"A good friend. A friend with an axe."

They grabbed Pignast and moved him toward the door.

"You can't do this to me. I'll yell for help." He tried to struggle but the two men immobilized him with their iron grips.

"If you choose to yell we'll stuff your mouth with this cotton and tie your hands." The talking man slapped Pignast with his callused paw.

"Help. Help. Somebody help me." Pignast shouted as loud as he could and tried to squirm from their clutches. Pignast wriggled free and toppled over one of the barber chairs in his frenzy to escape. The chair fell against the mirrored wall causing a few bottles of bay rum and scented shave lotion to crash on the floor.

Both men grabbed Pignast again and threw him into the other barber chair. They tied his hands and ankles with the rope they had brought in. The silent member grabbed a handful of cotton batting and stuffed it into Pignast's mouth. He removed his sweat-stained smelly neckerchief and tied it around the cotton-stuffed mouth.

Pignast couldn't move and any effort to speak only sounded like a soft murmur. The two men carried him out like a trussed carpet and lay him in the back of a buckboard. The silent man threw a heavy burlap cover over Pignast and they leisurely drove from town in the direction of the Locke estate four-miles away. The moon was full and its light reflected off the "Van Haven" lettering on the sides of the moving buckboard but there was no one to see it.

●

Saturday was bright and mild as Nancy Locke threw open the living room window to let out Robert's cigar smoke. The Van Haven board members plus Kelvin Danzer sat around the dining room table waiting for Pamela Skyler to arrive.

"She should get here on time. She knows how important this meeting is." Nancy Locke and Elizabeth Cotter drained their small-stemmed port glasses.

"It's Saturday morning. We've never met on a Saturday before. Besides, she still has a stiff shoulder from her injury. It takes her longer to get herself ready." Mathew Cotter looked at the door in anticipation as he spoke.

"Here she comes." Kelvin Danzer looked through the door's small rectangular pane.

"I'm sorry I'm late. My liveryman had today off. I forgot and Nester and I had to harness the horse." She hung up her coat and turned her nose up at Robert's cigar. He promptly stubbed it out in a brass ashtray.

"You put that vile thing out for her and not for me. You make me sick even without the cigar sometimes." Nancy berated her husband openly. The comment dissolved in the air and was lost in the milieu of her normal sarcasm.

"Now that we're all here let's get down to business." Mathew Cotter waved to Nancy to take charge.

"Damn right. We're going to make our move on Monday. I want you, Pamela, to make Jacob an offer on our buy-out for Serenity." Nancy poured another glass of port for herself only.

"But we all felt back in March that neither he nor his partners would ever sell out." Skyler stared at Nancy.

"And they still probably won't. I want him to get the message to Hartford. That'll throw him and his Serenity people off balance. They'll not be expecting anything when his place goes up in flames next week. It'll take till the end of the week for Jacob to get a response."

Skyler stiffened in her chair. "He's not just going to let you in through the front door and set his buildings on fire."

"Our plan is to send Kelvin and his men in when they least expect it–a surprise attack when there's hardly any of them there."

"How are you going to know when that is?" Skyler was wide-eyed.

Nancy Locke emitted a snicker. "Kelvin will know, right Kelvin?"

"We have a friend of theirs who is being asked right now in a most persuasive way what day and what time most of them will be absent from the winery." Kelvin smiled and leaned back against the wall opposite Skyler's seat.

"Please don't let any harm come to Jacob." Skyler's plea was to everyone in the room.

"Of course not, he's family, remember. And besides he has to attend school. He won't be there," Mathew Cotter replied.

"He'll come looking for you." Skyler paused. "He'll bring his guns and his men after you."

"After us, Pamela dear–after us." Nancy Locke grinned and sipped her sherry. "But what can he do. He'll have no proof that Van Haven was at fault."

"I know him, Nancy. He'll act without proof. Jacob has a strong sense of justice."

"Pamela, my little brother never won a fight in his life. We used to beat him up for nothing at all. He'll just go on to the doctoring business and sell the Serenity assets to us."

"He has two strong partners remember. They'll rebuild and call in the police." Skyler was persistent.

"We don't think so. Do we, Kelvin?" Mathew Cotter deferred to Danzer again.

"He has to have people to work the winery. After we get done with Serenity, no one will dare to work there, ever." He reached into his left coat pocket. The muted noise of the ejected axe into Danzer's hand was followed by the appearance of the silvery axe head. He held it high in the air.

"I just don't want anyone hurt." Skyler allowed a few seconds of silence. "Who do you have and what are you doing to him?"

"We have someone who works with Jacob and knows the schedule of the workers at the winemaking building." Danzer smiled. "I'm sure he'll be telling us what we want to know."

"If he dies it'll be murder."

"If he dies it'll look like an accident. We've had other accidents before, remember?" Danzer put the axe back in its sheath.

Robert Locke took out another cigar but did not light it. "We'll make sure it's publicly known that Van Haven is seeking a merger with Serenity. I wrote the newspaper article myself. We'll all be together with a member of the press on the day Serenity burns."

●

Skyler whipped the horse. She was angry at Nancy and her partners. She was angry with herself for not being able to do anything. She was angry that her business sense overrode her sense of right-and-wrong. And yet she was afraid. Not for herself but for Jacob and the others who were so different from her partners. *I can't warn Jacob of the threat by the others. If my alarm became known, Jacob will become an immediate target for death.*

These last weeks with Cotter were getting friendlier. They both enjoyed their teahouse meetings and last Thursday Cotter almost made love to her. Their embrace and kissing was intense. She didn't want to lose him. *What poor victim were they torturing?* She slowed her horse as she entered the town limits. Saturday traffic was not heavy but families were shopping, going to restaurants and some going to the Yale Theater. A few people were waiting around the barbershop. She stopped her buggy. *Maybe Mortimer Pignast knows something.*

Skyler eased her rig next to the large carriage stone outside the barbershop. A number of men looked at her. They were mumbling and peering inside the barbershop windows.

"What's the matter here?" *Something is very wrong. The barbershop door was locked. Saturday was Pignast's busiest day. He would never close.*

"The door's locked. I know he lives here. He's not answering and look inside. The place is as mess." The spokesman stepped back for Skyler to look in.

"Oh, my God. They took Mortimer." Skyler spoke to her gloved hand at her mouth.

## Chapter 28

## The Raid

"I think he said Wednesday." Danzer moved back from Pignast's battered face. It was puffy and black and blue.

Blood seeped slowly from his nose and both blackened eyes were swollen shut. His upper body leaned forward stretching the ropes as his head sagged. He was not unconscious. He could hear everything and he hated himself for telling them but he couldn't stand any more pain.

"Yeah, Wednesday morning they leave the buildings and go somewhere for a meeting–every Wednesday he said." The gruff interrogator grinned with satisfaction.

"Good. Wednesday morning we deliver Pignast to his shop and set fire to Serenity." Danzer rubbed his chin. "We round up everyone and get them outside. They'll have to watch what we do."

"What about the ones who resist?"

"We deal with them on an individual basis. If they threaten us with bodily harm, they receive bodily punishment. If they try to kill us, well…" Danzer didn't have to finish the sentence.

"What about Pignast? He can talk."

"Not if he values Fern Ferndock. I think he understands. But just to make sure, let's deliver him directly to her–to the Green Moss–rather than to the barbershop."

"She'll recognize us."

"Not if you wear a bandana over your face."

"Okay. For Wednesday, we have eight men plus you, Danzer. Is that going to be enough?"

"The Serenity men with guns will be gone. It's more than enough."

"Too bad–I would have loved to meet up again with that deaf bastard."

"Forget it. When Pignast comes to, give him a drink. Keep him under guard until Wednesday. Just feed him and walk him to the outhouse. The boss lady doesn't want anyone dying."

"How are we going to make the fire look like an accident?" The stalwart hired gun walked outside with Danzer.

"We don't. We make it look like a robbery. The payroll arrives every Tuesday for payday on Thursday. We go in asking for the money and we steal anything else of value." Danzer paused. "And then we all disappear. Everyone wears a bandana on their face."

●

Pamela Skyler waited anxiously for Cotter at the teahouse. So far nothing had happened at Serenity but she knew it would be this week. She had to tell Jacob something.

Cotter arrived on time and smiled at Skyler as he walked through the door. The owner was already approaching the table with the tea and biscuits. She knew their ritual so well they no longer had to place their order. Cotter lightly kissed Skyler's offered red lips and sat opposite her.

"You look troubled." Cotter reached across the small tabletop and held her left hand.

"Jacob, something terrible is going to happen this week. You have to close down for a while and send your people on a vacation or something like that."

"Your voice is shaky. What's so terrible?"

"I can't say but I do know that Kelvin Danzer has kidnapped Mortimer Pignast. They're trying to force information about you and Serenity from him."

"He hasn't shown up for work in the surgery clinic since Friday morning. His shop is closed. If he were sick he would have come to me, that's for sure." Cotter looked urgently at Skyler. "Pamela, please tell me everything."

"Jacob, I can't. Please trust me. I don't want to see you, your friends or any of your workers hurt."

"What could Pignast possibly tell them that would be important to them?"

"All I know is they want to find out when you and your foremen are away from the buildings." Tears were forming.

"Pignast doesn't know our schedule at the winery and I work with him every day." Cotter immediately stood up. "Every day except Wednesday! Oh, my God it's tomorrow. I have to leave right now."

●

Danzer and eight men rode to the edge of Serenity's borders and stayed in the trees waiting for the sun to come up.

"It's damn freezing." One man complained and threw a blanket around his shoulders.

"We had to come early while it's still dark. They won't be leaving the place until around nine o'clock." Danzer's breath was white in the moonlight.

"That's four-hours from now." Another complainer spoke up.

"Just be quiet. We've been over the plan so many times, I should not be hearing your chicken-shit complaints." Danzer's glare induced silence.

The sun came up and was above the treetops by eight-thirty. The temperature started to warm. The group had tethered their horses to tree branches and were either laying down on pine needles or sitting against trees. Danzer focused with his telescope on the main house and the livery barn.

"Okay. There's activity out there. They're coming out. Look. They're all wearing riding dusters. They must be going a good distance." Danzer was feeling a high with the anticipation of pending action. "Remember, roust out the workers and everyone else from the buildings. We set fire to every single building on the place. Those are the boss's orders and you can bet there'll be hell to pay if she hears otherwise."

"I didn't see any workers go in or go out this morning." A clean shaven gunslinger looked at the others with his statement.

"For God's sakes, it was pitch-black on the road they use. The shift changes at six in the morning. How the hell could we see anything from here?" Danzer held the telescope to his right eye again. "There they go. All five are mounting their horses. One of the women is waving goodbye to them." He looked at his watch. "It's eight-forty. We go in slowly at nine-fifteen."

The eight horsemen covered their faces just above their noses with their bandanas. Kelvin Danzer led them in single file until they reached the main house which was in front of the winery buildings and to the left of the livery and the barn. Danzer signaled them to spread out side-by side on their horses. He dismounted and went onto the porch. The front door was unlocked. Danzer adjusted his bandana, drew his gun and went in.

"Okay in here. Come out to the front door. Everyone." There was silence. Danzer heard a horse galloping from the rear of the house. He ran through the kitchen and scullery. He pushed open the rear door next to the cut wood for the fireplace and saw dust following a rider or riders. Danzer looked through the telescope. The dust cloud could be from more than one horse. He went back in and looked in every room and went upstairs and back to the front door. Outside, he looked at his men. "Go search the buildings and get everyone out. We're going to show them what can happen to their homes if Serenity ever rebuilds and offers them jobs again."

Two of Danzer's men came out of the grape storage building. "There's no one in there," one of them said. "It looks like they were unloading a few wagons and then just stopped."

"What the hell?" Danzer looked at the wine-making building with the smoke still coming from it. "There must be someone there. A stove or something is still burning wood. Get some men in there and post one at the entrance and one at the rear door."

●

"There goes Samantha." Mashpit stood up in the stirrups of his saddle. "It won't take them long to find out the place is empty."

"Okay, I counted a total of nine. Let's go back like we rehearsed last night." Cotter turned his palomino toward Serenity.

The five men had ridden only a mile and hid in a dense wood off the road to their practice range. Cotter had left Pamela at the teahouse without any further interrogation. The sense of urgency precluded any further conversation. She should have told him sooner. He was filled with mixed feelings. She did tell him something but almost too late. *If any of my people get hurt, I'll hold her responsible. But can I really?* Cotter kept thinking back to his dictum to Skyler that he would tell her nothing about Serenity's business and she would tell him nothing about Van Haven.

Two men had died since he had come back in the summer of '68. First was the man from the night shift and the second was Mervin Bosch who almost killed Bradley Hamer. And Hamer's family was a target. No more deaths to his people would occur if he could help it. He had gathered everyone together last night and remembered the planning.

"Van Haven and their hired guns are going to hit us tomorrow morning." He explained the situation with Pignast and his deduction. "They have only one mission–to destroy Serenity and kill anyone who gets in the way. That 'anyone' is us. John and Andy the situation is not different than we had in the Army. It's kill or be killed. We trained for this possibility every Wednesday. I really hoped we would never have to use our new Colts but in the back of my mind I knew my brother and sister would come for us. They want to take away everything. They know we could never negotiate because of our Hartford stockholders. Bradley, you remember what happened to the other wineries in the early '60"s."

"I remember. They burned some of them out and killed those who resisted. They're not going to succeed tomorrow. No, sir."

"Fabian, this is not your fight. You can leave with the other hired help and the women and children." Cotter went over to the gun cabinet.

"Monsieur, what do you mean I am 'hired help'? I am a part of this family. I am a part of you." Rosicot pulled his shotgun from the cabinet.

"Samantha, you're to give everyone who's here tonight their pay and tell them to return on Friday. Tomorrow morning you'll pay all who come to work and turn them away. Tell them we are shutting down for inventory and servicing the equipment. They're also to return on Friday." Cotter turned to Gertrin Hamer and her children.

"Gertrin, you and your children will have to leave. I want you to go to town tonight and stay in the main hotel."

"I'll go. Please be careful Bradley." She hugged him and the children took their turns.

Cotter's thoughts returned to the present as they approached the tree line next to the winemaking building.

"Okay. Remember, if we have to reload we do it from the defensive circle. Only shoot to kill if there is no other alternative. You can all shoot their gun arms. You're all marksmen equal to or better than I am. Let's go."

●

"Someone must have warned them." Danzer scowled at his appointed leader of the hired guns. Danzer pulled his bandana from his face. The others took this as a signal to do the same and they all unmasked.

"We can still torch the place. Only instead of just burning down the winery building we're going to raze the whole place. Burn every building. Get any livestock out of the barn and set fire to it. Go get the wagon with the torches." Danzer was furious. Nancy Locke had instructed him to burn down just the winemaking structure and intimidate all the employees. He removed his coat as the May temperature moved well above the nighttime freeze.

One man rode back to get the wagon. He tied his reins to a tree branch and went to board the wagon with the incendiary supplies.

"Stay where you are." John LaRoque faced the man who immediately turned around going for his gun.

The man had his gun cleared from the holster with the barrel still pointing toward the ground when he saw the buckskin clad man with the conchos reflecting the sun in intermittent sparkles as the tree branches moved with the wind.

"Raise that gun another inch and you're dead." LaRoque had both his guns aimed at the man's chest only six-feet away.

"Fuck you." The man's gun had moved up to find an aim point. LaRoque moved his left wrist slightly and fired his left hand Colt. "Owww, Dammit. You cocksucker. Jesus Christ, that hurts." The man's gun went flying laterally as LaRoque's .45 caliber round went through the man's right forearm.

"Now move to that tree and get away from the wagon or my next shot finds your right leg."

"You prick." The man moved to the tree where his horse was tied. He rested his good arm on the saddle, faking a need for support. "I'm bleeding all over the place. Oh, God it hurts." As he moaned aloud he pulled his rifle from the saddle scabbard and swung it toward LaRoque.

Another shot rang out and the man fell to the ground releasing the rifle to hold his right leg. "You bastard." He tried to get up but fell down again grimacing in pain.

"Use your rope to cut down the bleeding." He threw the man the saddle rope. LaRoque took the man's rifle and pistol and walked back to the Serenity buildings.

LaRoque moved quickly. The shots would put the Van Haven mob on alert.

"What the hell was that?" Danzer looked toward the tree line where their wagon had been left.

"I would say that you're now one man short." Cotter stared at Danzer who immediately looked at the voice's owner. Cotter positioned himself and the others so the sun would reflect off their conchos.

Cotter, Mashpit, Fabian and Bradley Hamer were twenty-five yards apart in a semi-circle facing Danzer and five of his men. Two of the Van Haven men were still at the winery and the grape storage building.

"Tell your men to drop their gun belts or go for their iron now." Cotter kept eye contact with Danzer.

"You're outnumbered, you stupid fucker. Cut them down!" Danzer shouted. He went for his gun and snapped it to his front just as Cotter's two guns appeared and spurt fire and smoke from both barrels. One shot got Danzer's gun hand and the other hit him in the chest sending him flying backward and to the ground.

The other Van Haven men reacted to Danzer's order and drew their guns.

Fabian shot one in the arm and the one on his right got a load of buckshot to his right side which spun him around before he fell to the ground.

Bradley Hamer drew his Colt before Danzer finished his call to arms sentence. He hit his target in the shoulder. Hamer immediately dropped to his knees and fired his shotgun at the second man who was brandishing a rifle. The load of buckshot hit the rifle and splattered the man's neck and face producing multiple red spots. The man's right hand and the rifle butt were blown away.

Mashpit was in the middle and faced his man squarely. It was the same man who confronted him and Samantha outside the Emporium.

The man smiled before Danzer shouted the command to shoot. "I'll shoot your balls off first and then just wound the rest of you. Your lady friend will have nothing of yours to play with after that." As soon as Danzer shouted he pulled his gun from his holster.

Mashpit couldn't hear the conversation between Cotter and Danzer. He watched his man's eyes. As soon as the man's facial expression changed with a full blink of both eyes, Mashpit had both guns drawn and fired. His opponent never fully cleared his holster. Both rounds caught the man to left of the sternum. He was dead before he hit the ground. Mashpit felt a rush of intense heat pass his right temple and looked to his left. The man from the barn was running toward him and firing. Mashpit adjusted his position to have the conchos glinting at his second opponent. He felt the wind tracks from two bullets pass by his right side and fired from each Colt. The man crumpled to the ground holding onto both thighs as claret color emerged between the fingers of each hand.

"Form the circle," Cotter shouted as LaRoque came to join them. They kept their Colts out as they complied.

"There's one left, Monsieurs." Rosicot looked from his arc in the circle. They were still almost twenty-yards apart. Some groans and curses could be heard from the fallen enemy.

"Come on out. There are five of us and only one of you left." Cotter shouted and looked for movement. No one appeared.

"Does anyone need to reload?" LaRoque asked.

"I just reloaded my shotgun." Bradley Hamer looked at Rosicot.

"Oui, and I also."

"Wait. I see something." Mashpit pointed with his shiny Colt.

"He has his hands up but don't trust him." Bradley Hamer brought his shotgun up with his left arm. The man's gun was holstered. "Take out the gun with your other hand and drop it."

The man complied.

"Okay tie everyone's wrists. I'll look at the wounds." Cotter broke from the ranks first. He examined each casualty and for now assessed that only pressure dressings and tourniquets were needed. He hadn't bothered with Danzer since he knew the chest wound was fatal. He walked over to Rosicot stepping over Danzer's body.

"I left word with the police that we had been warned about an action against us. They couldn't do anything unless something actually took place. Our ride into town will not be a surprise."

"Monsieur, I have asked three of them about where their orders did come from and they say only of Monsieur Danzer."

"I guess Van Haven planned it that way. Danzer and not Van Haven will be held responsible for this." Cotter watched as LaRoque and the others organized their round up of the prisoners for the move to New Haven. His back was still turned on Danzer.

Danzer's gun arm was on fire. His left chest hurt like hell but he was alive. He felt where the chest wound should be and there was no blood–only soreness. Cotter's bullet had struck the axe. Danzer twisted his left hand to press the release tab and the axe leaped into the waiting palm. Danzer could throw the axe accurately with either arm. Cotter's back was an easy target. He forced a sitting position and extended his left arm back in launch position.

Cotter felt the pain like multiple bee stings on his right shoulder blade before the loud boom of the shotgun made both he and Rosicot dive for the ground.

Bradley Hamer came running up. "I'm sorry Jake, I had to use the shotgun. I couldn't trust my accuracy with the Colt from that angle."

Cotter got up and looked at Danzer. Half of Danzer's right shoulder and face was a maroon maceration of torn tissue. The axe was still in his outstretched extended left hand. Frothy red bubbles came from his mouth. He was still alive.

"Did you kill my night man? Did Nancy give the order for this?" Cotter pulled Danzer to a sitting position.

"You'll never know." The juicy reply came through bursting red bubbles from his lips

"What about Rockland Skyler? Did you kill him, Danzer? Did you."

"That fucking wimp." Danzer's last words were followed by a long wheezy exhalation and he went limp.

# Chapter 29

## Aftermath

"The ones who survived all got jail sentences but never implicated my sister or brother." Cotter sipped his tea across from Skyler. Nester brought in some light biscuits.

"I'm glad you agreed to come to my home for this talk, Jacob." Skyler wore a clinging dress reminiscent of their former evening soirees. "When I heard about the raid on Serenity by those thugs, I held my breath hoping you were not hurt."

"What about the others being hurt? Some of Danzer's men were killed and Danzer died trying to kill me with his damn axe." He let out a long breath. "Pamela, if it wasn't for you telling me about Mortimer Pignast, I never would have concluded what day they had planned their attack on Serenity. Did you know about this?"

"Jacob, I can tell you now that I did. I can also tell you now that if I revealed their plan, they promised to have you killed outright."

"How could they have done that?"

"I don't know. You told me that someone confronted Andy Mashpit. It could've happened to you."

Cotter poured himself some more tea. A long ten seconds of silence passed. "I can't live in 'what if' scenarios, Pamela. I can't help thinking about how our church going has influenced my opinion about the outcome of what happened two-weeks ago."

"What do you mean?"

"I mean I don't think there are such things as coincidence. God was looking out for us. There were bullets flying everywhere and none of us got hurt. And we had a chance to get the women and children away before Danzer and his cutthroats came."

Nester Smood came in wearing her light jacket. "Good night folks. I'll see you in the morning."

"Was she talking to just you or the both of us?" Cotter relaxed a little.

"She remembers old times. The last time you came it was because of my shoulder wound but you didn't stay."

"I have to ask a few more questions, Pamela." He paused and placed his hands on the edge of the table. "Do you still want us to be married?"

"Don't you?" She brushed a nearly formed tear from her right eye.

"Yes, I do." Cotter stood up and went around to her chair. He placed his hands on her shoulders, bent down and kissed her on the neck.

Skyler shivered at his touch. "I'm being honest when I say that Nester was talking to both of us. Will you stay tonight? Our wedding is two-weeks after graduation." She stood up and fell into his arms.

"I thought you'd never ask." Cotter held her close and then kissed Skyler. They cleared the table and went into the bedroom after the dishes were set soaking.

Cotter couldn't get to sleep after their vigorous love-making. Skyler woke up nestled in his left arm.

"What's wrong?"

"I have another question. Will you be selling your interest in Van Haven after our wedding? It might be best. After all we aren't even going to be living in Connecticut."

She pushed herself up abruptly with the sheet only covering her from the waist down. "You aren't still thinking of going to Texas?"

"I never said otherwise. I'm going to sell my part of serenity to John, Andy and the Hamers. I never intended to make a career bottling wine."

"Texas? I'm a well-bred New Englander. I can't survive in Texas. Tell me you're not serious."

"If you're a well-bred proper Bostonian woman, then you know that a wife goes with her man."

"Not at all, Jacob..." She lay on her side pulling the covers to her shoulder. "...a farm woman or a wife with children maybe, but not me. I want my family to be started in Connecticut."

"I want you to think about it some more. Calm down now." He cuddled next to her and they both fell asleep.

●

Cotter smiled at the receptionist. "Good morning Mrs. Roth. Dr. Randall wanted to see me before my final surgery today."

"Yes, graduation is only a few days away. Congratulations 'Dr.' Cotter." Just go right in, he's expecting you.

Cotter knocked politely on the door and entered. Dr. Wainright Randall and Dr. Timothy Hayes were standing facing him as he came in.

"Oh-Oh, am I in trouble? I didn't expect both of you to be in the same room this morning."

"Quite the contrary Jacob, I wanted Tim to be here to hear the final decision of the Dean's committee—my committee. Jacob, it gives us great pleasure to name you as valedictorian of your class. You will be graduating Summa Cum Lauda." Randall extended his hand to Cotter followed by Hayes.

"I have something else, Jacob. It's something I asked you several months ago." Hayes folded his arms. "You're one of the best surgeons and all-around physicians ever to graduate Yale. I, that is, we..." Hayes stumbled a little with the words. "...or rather Yale would like to have you continue on the staff at the University Medical School."

"I'm honored on both fronts, I really am. I'm committed to bringing the high quality of Yale medicine to Endura, Texas. It's already off to a small but significant start with Charles Garrison's efforts."

"I think we understand. Yale wanted one last chance to entice you to remain. In a way, I envy you because you're fulfilling the mission of Yale's credo. Our goal is to train quality physicians to do just what you're doing." Randall put his left hand on Cotter's right shoulder and shook his hand again.

"You've set a great example, Jacob." Hayes shook Cotter's hand one more time. "I'm sure your address to the class will project patriotism from the war and your amazing academic accomplishment after such a long time away from the formal university setting."

They walked him to the door. As Cotter was leaving, Randall put his hand on his shoulder and spoke softly. "That was quite a good bit of soldiering you did at your place with those hooligans. I'm sure your father is looking down on us and is proud on all fronts, Jacob."

"I think so too, sir."

Cotter walked to the surgical clinic building with mixed emotions. He was going to miss Yale. He had hopes Pamela Skyler would overcome her ingrained notion of society and loyalty to class stratifications. He was also looking forward to teaming up with Charles Garrison and Stanley Wills in Endura. The thought reminded him of the unopened letter from Garrison. He stopped in the hallway leading to the doctor's entrance to the surgery and opened the envelope.

Dear Jake:

I had your shingle already posted. I arranged our names in alphabetical order–Dr. Jacob Cotter, Dr. Charles Garrison, and Dr. Stanley Wills. They were hung outside the gate and walkway to the clinic. Yesterday, we were shocked to see the sign was shot down. The only placard that was destroyed was yours. It was riddled with bullets. Stan and I think it was Vlack's gunslinger, Ken Boda. After he got drunk at the Nellie's Leggs Saloon, he boasted about how the Doctors at the Doctors Clinic should be shot just to show them what it felt like.

We don't want Victor Vlack as our Congressman, Jake. Several of the people at the Mayor's office have put the bug in

Stan's head that he should run for the position. Stan said he would do it if he didn't have his obligation to the clinic and the hospital. Vlack went berserk when he heard the rumor about another physician joining us, and that's when the sign went down. He hates us, Jake. It could get rough down here.

I was glad you came out of your situation with all your people intact. Is your man Mortimer Pignast coming down to give ether for us? We need him as bad as we need you. More than half of our practice is surgery, and that doesn't count the baby business. How'd your work with the ether in the delivery room come out? Are you still coming out right after your wedding?

We're all looking forward to your starting. We haven't told anyone when you'd arrive because Ken Boda also slurred around the saloon that you'd never get here if he could help it. He's such a bad man, Jake. He dresses all in black and always wears his black hat tied at the chin. The mail is safe for you to answer my letter. It'll probably be the last letter you write since you'll be here soon. Whatever you do don't send any information about your arrival by telegraph. Vlack monitors every message coming in by wire. The telegraph office and the town marshal are on his payroll.

Congratulations on graduating and best to your new bride.


Charlie


*One hurdle after another. That's what life's all about.* Cotter's thoughts next turned to the surgical theater. He had three operations today. Pignast had recuperated completely but he still had more bumps on his head than even his phrenology training could cope with. He could still recall how bad he looked when they brought Danzer's cronies to town that Wednesday. Fern Ferndock was waiting at the emergency medical clinic.

"Oh, Dr. Cotter, Mort is hurt bad. I had him brought here." Tears streamed down her face.

"What did the clinic doctor say?"

"They wouldn't say how bad it was. Oh, please, Dr. Cotter, go see him. Make him better. Please don't let him die."

Cotter, LaRoque and Mashpit brought in the wounded Serenity marauders and Cotter went right to Pignast. He read the staff doctor's evaluation and then examined Pignast. The man's face was swollen to melon-size. His eyes were so puffy the lids were indiscernible. Cotter examined Pignast from the shoulders down. There were no broken bones. His head was another matter. Pignast's ears were black and blue with irregular cauliflower-like swellings. He palpated every inch of the skull eliciting moans.

"Mort, I don't find any fractures in your skull. Can you move your jaw? Open your mouth."

"Jahhkke. Yourrrr...'live." Bloody drool came from the slit-like opening. The jaw wasn't broken but the swollen tissues inside his mouth almost occluded his airway.

"So are you, Mort. You're going to make it." Cotter pried open one of the eyelids. The whites of the eyes were replaced with smooth crimson infiltration. "Can you see me?"

"Yethhhh." A spasm of cough followed the word as some drool caught in his windpipe.

"We'll get you something for the pain and keep you here a few days. Then you can stay with us. I'll tell Fern the good news."

Pignast let out a long sigh of relief and promptly went to sleep.

"I think he was waiting for you to arrive. He refused any medication. He didn't want to sleep until he knew you were okay." Fern was still tearful. "Thank you for taking care of him. I have to tell you something Dr. Cotter."

"Come on Fern. Mortimer will be okay. He'll look bruised and battle scarred for a few weeks but he'll be okay."

"No. I have to tell you that I was against Mort going with you to Texas. He wanted us to get married and go out west with you but I refused. After this, I changed my mind. We...I...need a new start and a new life. We'll be going with you." She grabbed his hand with both of hers.

"It's great news, Fern. But let me tell you that Texas can be as violent as here."

"Mort wants it and I want to be with him without any regrets. He'll be happy and that'll make me happy."

"It's great you feel this way, Fern." Cotter walked back toward LaRoque and Mashpit. *Why can't Pamela feel like Fern? Why can't I feel the same love for Pamela that Fern Ferndock has for Pignast.*

●

Cotter woke up in a sweat. His father had been bleeding from the two bullet wounds in his chest. His father's last words resounded in his head.

"Remember the plan, Jacob. Finish Yale and bring your education and experience out west–work with Charles Garrison."

Cotter looked out the window at the starry night sky. "Yes, dad, I remember the plan."

# Chapter 30

## Graduation

"The graduation ceremony was wonderful, Jacob." Pamela walked arm-in-arm with Cotter. "I do wish you'd invited Nancy and Mathew."

Cotter stopped and stared at Skyler. "How can you even consider it? They tried to kill us and destroy Serenity."

"They did make me Chairman of the Board after that. I think we can consider Van Haven no longer having a carnivorous attitude, don't you?"

"No, I don't. Remember, their change in attitude happened only to satisfy the police. They originally refused to lay all the blame on Kelvin Danzer."

"But the minutes of our board meetings are to be reviewed by the Superintendent of Business's office. It will be a controlled situation, really Jacob."

"And that office is run by Robert Locke. No, Pamela I don't see any meaningful change."

"You underestimate my power. Nancy has handed over all authority for being the spokesperson and major policy maker for Van Haven."

"I don't believe it'll be effective." Cotter held both of her hands. "Especially since you'll be leaving Connecticut after we're married. You'll have to hand over the reins back to Nancy."

"Jacob, we agreed I would take some time to consider your accepting the Texas job with your friends."

"No, that's not what we agreed on. I've accepted the partnership with Garrison and Wills. The decision is whether you or I will be married and we both relocate to Endura." He paused and gazed into her eyes. "My wife will be by my side."

"Jacob, you're squeezing my hands too tightly." She shook his hands away. "I can't possibly leave my social status and my business situation. It's only appropriate that you change your plans."

Cotter thought of Pignast and Fern Ferndock. "A man's wife goes with her man if she loves him."

"I do love you Jacob, but such an attitude doesn't apply to people of our station. You must stay on at Yale or at least maintain your practice in New Haven."

"You haven't heard a word I've said." Cotter's look of frustration was noticed by Pignast who was coming toward them. "There will be no marriage if you don't come with me."

"I'll give you until Friday to change your mind, Jacob Cotter–three days. I can't marry a man who doesn't love me enough to support my career and financial obligations."

"I don't need three days. I'm really sorry. Goodbye, Pamela." Cotter turned and immediately was confronted with Pignast and Fern.

"Congratulations to you Dr. Cotter–from both of us." Pignast beamed as he waved Fern's nod of congratulations to Cotter. "Our departure date is in two-weeks, correct?"

"You're departure date is in two-weeks. Mine is in one-week. I'll meet you both in Endura."

"That won't allow you much of a honeymoon Dr. Cotter." Fern's face was a question mark.

"I'm afraid there'll be no wedding. Mrs. Skyler cannot extricate herself from New Haven for any man, object or ideal."

"Oh, dear. We're sorry Dr. Cotter." Fern touched his forearm.

"Don't be sorry. I've prepared myself for this outcome over the past month. She could never be happy in a non-New England setting. We both see that now." Cotter placed his hand on Pignast's shoulder. "But congratulations are in order for you two, Mortimer. You have your certificate as a credentialed anesthesia assistant to surgery."

"I owe it to you Dr. Cotter."

"Now hold on, you're a talented scientist in that area of medicine...and in private my name is Jake." Cotter held his hand up to prevent a response from Pignast. "I still do not consider Phrenology a science but, whatever it is, I'm sure you are an expert purveyor of its practice."

They all laughed.

Cotter excused himself. "I have to send a telegram to Endura about my change of plans. We'll meet at my home on Friday and discuss the move."

Cotter walked briskly to the telegraph office. He stopped when he suddenly remembered Charlie Garrison's warning about using the telegraph. *"Victor Vlack monitors the telegraph wires. Keep your arrival a surprise."*

The telegraph operator came to the glass window and spoke to Cotter through the circle cutout. "We charge one cent a space for out-of-state wires. The 'stops' are free. Write your message on this form and the address just above it."

Cotter took the paper and wrote Charlie Garrison's address on it. He thought carefully about the wording and then read the message aloud.

"Change of plan. No wedlock. Will arrive alone next Tuesday. I'll take the stage from Forge City."

The train did stop at Endura but Cotter wanted to leave the train 20-miles away and advertise his leisurely arrival by stagecoach. He knew Vlack would intercept the message. He paid the wire operator the fee and stayed while the message was sent and receipt was acknowledged.

●

Cotter assembled his "family" for one last late Sunday breakfast. Mrs. Hamer was obviously regretful at his leaving. "I know you've been telling us about going to Endura for two-years now. I do wish you'd stay but I know a man has to do what he has to do."

"I want you all to understand that I'm going to my dream. My new partners will be as good as all of you." Cotter pulled some papers from a saddlebag. "I have legally turned my one-third interest in Serenity over to John LaRoque, Andy Mashpit and you Bradley Hamer.

"I'm not doing it for free. Each of you will pay an equal amount over a two-year period to assume your part ownership." He faced Rosicot. "Fabian, I know you'll be working as part owner for Mrs. Colt."

"Monsieur, why do you do this?"

"It was my plan from the beginning. I'm getting every penny I put into Serenity plus a profit. And you all deserve to become partners."

"We'll miss you on Wednesdays." Mashpit smiled.

"I'm glad you're keeping the tradition. Things may look good on the outside with Pamela Skyler running Van Haven but take my word, it may not last. I know my brother and sister."

After breakfast, which spilled over until early afternoon, Cotter packed his last piece of luggage. He folded his two buckskin outfits neatly on top of his buckskin boots. His Colts went on top of them. *Ten boxes of .45caliber ammunition should be enough.* He added his reloading dies. *I could send for more if I need it.* He placed his conchoed hat in a hat box. *I know I'll need the Colts, hopefully just as a deterrent.* As he cleaned out his drawer he found Mervin Bosch's birdshot-loaded gloves. *Why not? A surgeon's hands must be protected.*

# ENDURA, TEXAS

# 1870

## TO

# 1871

# Chapter 31

## Stagecoach

Victor Vlack looked at the telegrams. They were sent to him at the end of each day by the telegraph station manager. It cost Vlack only five dollars a week for this service. He could get them for nothing but paying off the telegraph operator linked the man to involvement in a federal criminal act. Vlack enjoyed the intimidation and it bought a sort of loyalty.

"Jonah, here's an extra five for this batch. I've been waiting for news of this new doctor's arrival. I thought it was going to be next week." He rubbed his smooth shaven chin. "Sneaky bastard, comin' a week early." Vlack dismissed the telegraph man.

Vlack opened the door to the ranch bunkhouse. It was well after sunset. He shouted into the open section containing a dozen single bunks. "Boda, we have something to discuss." He waved the telegraph in the air. "Come into the house, right now."

The tall Ken Boda grabbed his single holster rig from its place around the bedpost at the head of his bunk. The holster had silver studs placed every inch at the top and bottom of the belt, outlining the holster down to the tie-down thong. He entered the main house buckling the rig but left the tie free. "Yeah, what's up?"

"Read this."

Boda handed it back after a quick scan. "This 'Jake'… he's the new doc from the East we been lookin' for?"

"That's him. He's comin' in early but he's gettin' off the train at the Forge City station and takin' the stage to Endura. I don't want him to get here."

"I can make it look like a stage robbery." Boda rested his right palm on the butt of his black Navy Model Colt revolver.

"Good. Wear a duster to cover up your outfit. You wear that black shirt and pants like a uniform. Have the others cover up too."

"Do you want me to say anything to this doctor…before I shoot him?"

"I don't want you to shoot him. Just cover him and let one of the boys do it. Otherwise the focus will be on you and not the shooter. The witnesses won't be able to give a good account of what happened. Just take two of the men. That should be enough."

"Anything you say boss." Boda walked back to the bunkhouse. Four hands were still awake. He signaled one and kicked the feet of another hanging over the edge of a bunk bed.

"Ooo…Wha..?" The startled man sat up.

"The three of us are meeting the stage out of Forge City on Thursday about noon." He gave them the simple hold-up plan.

●

The train stopped too many times for Cotter to count. He boarded the railroad car just before eight o'clock on Tuesday. He stayed over in Daytonville, Ohio at a station-side hotel to make the connection for the train that would get to Endura on its way to Texas. The station liveried his palomino and Cotter had his luggage brought to his room.

He lay on his bed thinking about his final departure from Pamela Skyler. She begged him to come to her home after the graduation day scene. Cotter couldn't comprehend how one-sided her attitude had been. She'd paced the floor on one side of her dining room table.

"I can't believe you don't love me enough to stay with me. You could join us–be with your brother and sister, finally. The four of us could make for a stronger and more stable company. With you at my side, we could keep Nancy and Mathew under our thumbs. You wouldn't have to dirty yourself with being a doctor."

This was the final statement dissolving their relationship. "I am a doctor. I'm through with the wine business."

"If you want to play doctor out west with the gamblers, the hoodlums and the Indians, then go without me. Our engagement is done–it's over."

Cotter stared at her. There were no tears and no sense of regret or remorse. Seeing her like this made the separation easier. He had made the right decision. With that closure his thoughts returned to the present.

*Once I board the train I must be wary. Vlack and his henchman–Ken Boda–will be intercepting me.* He went over his plan one more time and fell asleep.

Early morning brought a hearty breakfast. Cotter supervised his luggage being loaded. "Make sure my bags continue on to Endura. I'll be getting off the train with my horse at Forge City." He watched as the tags were placed securely around his bags. "This one I'm carrying with me." He kept the bag that once contained his Colts. It was still heavy with the boxes of ammunition. The weather was cool and he hoped it would remain that way. It was cool enough for his duster, which he put on but left unbuttoned. He walked to the passenger car and found a seat with a clean window at the back. There would be no one sitting behind him and he had a good view of anyone coming onto his car from either direction.

There didn't seem to be that many stops after they left the Mississippi Border States. Cotter slept between stations and bought some snacks from some vendors who jumped on the train at the longer stops replenishing coal and water. He noticed more men wearing their firearms as they picked up passengers from the west central states. He removed his duster and no one seemed to notice his two Colts. He had decided to stay on the train rather than stop another night before they reached Louisiana and headed true west into Texas. Cotter went to visit his horse twice and talked to him comfortingly as he fed him.

"Forge City Station in two hours, sir. You wanted me to give you an alert." The conductor tapped Cotter gently on the shoulder.

At Forge City, Cotter tied his small carry-on case over the left saddlebag. He would not be taking the stagecoach. The sun was shining with about an hour before high noon. He put on his duster and waited for the stagecoach to depart with its five passengers. Cotter watched the shotgun guard next to the stagecoach driver check his weapon and he reflexly touched his Colts. He had checked them several times and they were oiled and loaded. He waited for the stage to go about a mile before he fell in behind the coach's tracks. The dust from the stage's wheels fell to the ground well before Cotter and his horse. He should have plenty of time to catch up with it should something happen.

Forty-minutes passed and Cotter removed his duster. The air was hot and humid with a slight breeze blowing in his direction. His palomino's steady lope made little noise and he could hear the rhythmic thumps of the stagecoach horses and the bumpy mechanical sounds from its metal-rimmed wheels. He noticed the palomino's ears turn out at the same time he detected a new sound. More horses–probably three or four and they were slowing down.

The three mounts headed toward the stage on a dead-on course. One of the men fired his .44 twice to signal the stage of their presence as it rounded a gradual curve. As the coach came to them, they turned their horses to ride alongside while motioning with their guns for the stage to stop. The stagecoach guard signaled the driver to ignore the warning and reached for his shotgun. The second highwayman fired a shot into the guard's chest which caused the man to pull the trigger of the shotgun firing both barrels. The stage driver held onto to the man's body with his right arm while he pulled on the reins to stop the coach.

"Whoa. Whoa." The driver shouted at the horses and pulled on the large wooden lever to slow the coach's wheels. He turned to the trio. "You killed my man. What do you want? This stage ain't carryin' any money."

The large man in the duster with the bandana over his lower face motioned for the driver to get down. He turned to his two henchmen.

"Leave the dead man and get the bags outta the back. Get the passengers outta the stage."

They complied and prodded the riders to assemble on the right side of the stagecoach.

"Go to your bags and open 'em for us." The bandana outlaw had his now dismounted duo push the passengers forward to the littered luggage. They had not donned dusters or bandanas as Vlack had ordered.

There was one middle-aged woman with a scarf around her hair and four men. The oldest was about sixty.

Boda tightened his bandana to alter his voice. "Which one of you is the doctor?"

No one responded.

"Which one of you is from the East–Connecticut?"

More silence.

"I don't want to have to kill alla you to get the one I want. I mean what I say." Boda motioned his sidekick to shoot the man closest to him. "Shoot him in the leg to start."

The shot rang out and within seconds the man had fallen holding onto his bleeding leg with a loud shriek.

Cotter had ridden to the arc of the curve in the road just as he heard the two pistol shots followed by the shotgun. He looked at the sun and moved to position it at his back. Cotter quickly rubbed his silver conchos free of dust, pulled his bandana to cover his lower face, and moved forward just as the lethal shot to the guard was fired. The stage came into view at the moment the passenger was shot. Cotter was only 50-yards away and adjusted his position to avoid any firing at the passengers. One of the passengers saw him and looked his way.

Boda looked down at the fallen man. "Okay, which one is the doctor?"

There was only silence and palpable fear.

"Okay. No doctor, then this man on the ground will now die." He motioned the gunman to shoot.

The shot was louder than expected. The man on the ground looked up in surprise as his executioner fell over dead after the simultaneous explosions from Cotter's Colts.

The second man turned abruptly pointing his .44 at Cotter. The loud thunder claps from Cotter's Colts sent the man on top of his colleague with the same expanding crimson stain on his chest.

Cotter looked at Boda. "Drop your gun or go down with your friends."

It was ironic that both men had bandanas to hide their faces. They looked like bandits out for the same booty. Boda holstered his gun.

"I said throw it on the ground or you're dead." The timbre from Cotter's words brought an immediate response.

Boda dropped his .44 and grabbed the woman passenger, pressing a knife blade to her neck. "I'm riding outta here with her or she gets her throat slit from ear-to-ear."

Cotter sensed the lack of fear in Boda's voice. "I'll give you five-minutes on your horse and then I'm coming after the woman. Leave her unharmed or the next time we meet I'll shoot you on sight."

The woman's eyes bulged in terror as Boda got her on his horse and rode away. Cotter went to the passengers and driver. "Your guard is dead." He knelt beside the passenger with the wounded leg and applied a tourniquet with a length of rope from around a piece of luggage. "You've lost some blood. The bullet went through the muscle without hitting bone." He looked at the stage driver and then spoke to a passenger. "When you get to town, go right to Dr. Garrison's clinic. Release the rope two turns every ten minutes and bind it up as soon as you see bleeding. There will be less damage to the leg."

Cotter rode his horse hard for a mile when he came upon the woman. "Are you all right, Miss."

"Yes. I think so. He didn't hurt me."

"Did he say anything to you?"

"No. I guess I should thank you."

"Don't thank me, thank God. Here comes the stage. Goodbye."

"Aren't you going to finish robbing us?"

"I wasn't after you, Miss. I was after them."

Cotter rode off away from the oncoming stage. *That must have been Ken Boda. I'll remember his holster with all those silver studs.* He looked at the map Garrison had sent months before showing the roads on the outskirts of Endura. About three-miles from Garrison's house, he stopped and changed clothes in a thicket well off the road. He changed hats and secured the Colts in the carry-on bag. He looked at his pocket watch. Charlie Garrison was still working at the clinic. He would be surprised to see him at his home. Cotter watered his horse at a creek on the way and gingerly sauntered to the ample, comfortable-looking house. Garrison had told him about the gingerbread ornamentation over the porch.

# Chapter 32

## Reunion

"What do you mean another man robbed the stage? How'd the hell did one man get the drop on you." Vlack's face was purple with anger. "What about the bodies of the other two?"

"I imagine the stagecoach brought them into Endura." Boda was looking at Vlack's gun cabinet.

"That's just great. Someone will recognize they work for me." He slammed his fist on top of a dresser.

"No, I don't think so. I picked two that never went into town–two of the new boys." Boda walked to the gun cabinet. "I need a new gun."

"Are you sure there was no Dr. Cotter on that stage?"

"Believe me there was no Dr. Anyone on that stage."

"What did this guy look like?"

"He wore a bandanna like me. He wore a buckskin outfit and carried two guns. I've never seen guns like them before. They didn't blow a lot of black powder smoke like ours. He had shiny conchos on one side of his outfit and one on his hat. Come to think of it, he had one nickel-plated gun and one dark gray gun."

"He should be easy to recognize with that outfit." Vlack walked in a small circle. "Get yourself another gun from my cabinet. Go into town every night and poke around. Ask about the arrival of Dr. Cotter at the clinic."

●

Garrison rode his horse and buggy directly into the barn as was his new daily routine at the end of his workday. He had given up his occasional walks to his office. His only hired hand–Logan Pipps–removed the horse from the rigging and walked the animal to its stall.

"Logan, whose horse is that?" Garrison pointed to the palomino.

"He belongs to your guest, Dr. Jacob Cotter. He arrived earlier."

"Jake's here already?" Garrison brightened and hastened to the house. He walked in and saw his wife and Cotter talking with two children.

Cotter stopped his conversation and stood up. The two men shook hands and hugged.

"Charlie, you don't know how much I looked forward to today."

The two men looked each other up-and-down.

"Jake you look very fit."

"I don't see any fat on you either, Charlie."

"I see you've met Josh and Mary. They're Sadie Rand's kids–both very bright."

"Yes. Deirdre introduced me. I didn't know your wife was such a beauty. You didn't prepare me in your letters." Cotter looked at Deirdre who blushed slightly.

"Dear, I've told him all about Sadie." Deirdre's redness faded.

"Yes, Jake, wait until you meet her. She got most of her nursing training during the war. Sadie was also responsible for getting our other nurse and we're looking for a third–especially now that you're here."

"Okay, Josh and Mary it's time to do your school lessons before your mother picks you up." She motioned for the children to adjourn to another room. "The school is about two-miles from here and Sadie lives a few miles from us. They stay with us until Sadie finishes work. Now that the clinic is getting its third Doctor, and I understand obstetrics is your strong point Jake, maybe Charlie and I can have time for starting our own family."

Garrison laughed. "It's all she's been talking about since you sent the telegram about coming here. Why on earth did you send the telegram, I told you it might be dangerous."

"I just wanted to throw them off the track. I didn't actually take the stage. I got off at Forge City and rode my horse here. There was no problem. My bags should be at the train station by now. I can get them in the morning. I have enough to change into for another day."

"Well you're really lucky. I heard the stage was held up by two different bandits. The shotgun guard was killed by the first group. Two of the crooks were killed by the second highwayman and one passenger was roughed up a bit."

"Any suggestion they were Vlack's men?" Cotter sat down with the Garrisons in the dining area.

"The two bodies weren't known to anyone."

"What about the second robber who shot them?"

"No one knows about him either. The strange thing was, in that entire fracas no robbery was actually committed."

"That is strange." *They had to be Vlack's men. They were asking about a 'Doctor'. They were looking for me.*

"When do you want to begin work? You're a week early. You could get a head start on getting a place to live while you're staying with us. We've already looked around and there are a few places I can show you."

"That'd suit me fine. I also have to check out a place for our anesthesia person and his wife. They got married the day before I left."

Garrison looked at his wife's face. She pointed to her wedding ring.

"Oh…er, Jake, if I don't ask you this now it would make for awkward social situations. I take it Pamela Skyler didn't have Endura in her plans?"

"I was going to tell you up front anyway. I'm glad you brought it up." Cotter told them the story starting from the Civil War, his brother and sister, the Serenity-Van Haven altercation and Skyler's "business" over "family" decision. He left out the part about Skyler sequestering the information about the Van Haven raid and their confrontation.

"You know Jake, Texas is still a rough place and I've told you how bad Vlack is."

"Charlie we'll take each day as it comes." Cotter pointed to a rifle and a shotgun over the mantle. "Have you ever used those?"

"I've hunted and can hit anything I aim at. Pistols aren't my big forte, Jake. I know you were in the war and had to kill a few people but I never have."

"Could you? If you had to?"

"To defend myself, Deirdre, the Rands and all of us at the clinic? Yes, I believe I could."

"Sometimes we have to perform preventive action–just like preventive medicine, Charlie?"

"What do you mean Jake?"

Deirdre stared at both men.

"During the war, if we heard the rebels were on the way, we didn't wait around. We set up an ambush. When I heard about Van Haven coming to burn me out and inflict mortal harm, I let them come to an empty scene."

"What kind of talk is this?" Deirdre asked.

"Endura is a lot like New Haven, Deirdre. It's a garden with occasional weeds growing in it. I don't wait for the weeds to kill the plants. I do the weeding as an ongoing process."

"So if we see a bad apple about to hurt us we act rather than react?" Garrison leaned forward."

"Sometimes we do both Charlie."

"Well Endura is full of weeds of the Vlack variety."

Cotter stood up with the Garrison's. "I can hardly wait to meet Stanley Wills and Mrs. Rand. What happened to Mr. Rand?"

Deirdre stopped on their way to the living room. "He was killed by one of Vlack's men almost eight-years ago. Vlack claimed self-defense but Daniel Rand was no gunfighter. Dan Rand was a lawyer in town. He confronted Vlack several times about his usurping the law with his illegal land grabbing."

"The Rand children always stay with you after school?"

"Yes. It's safer that way and Charlie projects a needed father image."

"I can hardly wait to meet this Victor Vlack. I'd like to see the extent of Vlack's empire. How can I get an introduction to this man?"

"I'm putting an announcement in the Endura newspaper with your picture in it. That'll be attraction enough. He'll come to you–most probably at the clinic." Charlie smiled.

"As a patient?"

"Probably not. He claims to hate doctors with nothing specific against us other than our political beliefs about congressional representation. He'll invent some social reason to meet you. Wills saw him once two-years ago in the clinic. He had a severe fungal infection on both feet. Vlack was slightly overweight but was in otherwise top condition."

"How far away is Vlack's spread?"

"Five miles. He keeps to himself mostly but does come to town two-or-three times a month. Sooner or later you'll meet him."

*Sooner not later, I'll see to that*. Cotter's thoughts gelled into a plan. "We'll see. I bet it'll be sooner."

# Chapter 33

## The Visit

Cotter waited for Garrison to leave for work. "I'll be scouting out some of those housing possibilities you mentioned. This map of Endura will be a help." He watched Garrison disappear into the thin woods on the road into town. Deirdre was cleaning up the kitchen.

"Your horse is ready Dr. Cotter." Pipps had tied the palomino outside the front door trough.

"Thank you Pipps. You can call me Jake when I'm not working." Cotter tied his carry-on bag to the left saddlebag. About a mile from the house he went into a dense thicket and changed his clothes. The day would be bright. He oiled the conchos and his Colts.

The side road branching off toward Vlack's domain was as large as the main road and could let two wagons pass each other. Jake halted the palomino at the top of the hill looking down at the large main house, the barn and the long bunkhouse. He waited until no more hands left the bunkhouse to ride out to their jobs somewhere on the range. There was no further activity and no one from Vlack's house had left which meant Victor Vlack was still there. The temperature was rising and he saw a single window open from the center of the house. Cotter rode along a tree line out of any line of vision from the house and left the palomino behind a supply shed next to the kitchen. His buckskin boots made no sound as he entered the kitchen softly closing the Dutch door.

Cotter waited five-minutes before progressing further. The cook was outside washing the kitchen dishes from both the bunkhouse and the main house. He moved silently through the house following the scent of a fresh cigar. Directly off a fireplace living room he could see the smoke rising from Vlack. The man was at a large desk with a ledger of some sort capturing his attention. Cotter had his bandana pulled up and moved to within five-feet of the seated Vlack. Still the man continued to puff on his cigar and write in the ledger. When he was right behind Vlack he resumed his normal breathing which became audible.

Vlack stopped writing. He was about to turn around when the nickeled Colt quickly went from its holster to Vlack's head.

"Don't move Vlack."

"Who are you? What do you want?" The bass voice was raspy.

Vlack moved his right hand slowly toward a recessed pigeon hole in the desk.

"I said don't move." Cotter cocked the Colt's hammer. The "click" of the ratchet mechanism filled the room.

"Do you want money? I can get it for you but it's not at this desk." Vlack's upper lip began to perspire.

"Your boys interfered with me yesterday. Two of them are dead. This is a warning. If you or any of your men cause any Endura citizen harm they will answer to me. Put your hands solidly on your desk and don't move or one of my bullets will pierce your body."

Cotter moved back and drew the other Colt. He rapidly fired three shots from each gun to either side of Vlack's frozen position. Splinters and smoke surrounded the now shaking Vlack. Cotter knew Vlack's hearing would be impaired from the shots. He withdrew from the living room and went rapidly out the kitchen door.

Outside he whistled for his palomino and saw the cook walking to the house. He fired two shots from the left hand Colt directly in front of the man. "Lay on the ground until I leave."

The man hit the ground and looked up at the bandana-masked buckskin figure.

"Head down." Cotter mounted his horse and rode into the woods. When he felt safe he took the cotton from his ears and let the palomino move at a slow pace while he pocketed the warm spent cartridges and reloaded his Colts.

"So much for introductions." Cotter spoke to the humid air. He headed back for the thicket to change his clothes and went back to the Garrisons.

"Back so soon?" Pipps received Cotter and his mount.

"Yes. I just rode around to exercise my horse and now I need to borrow a horse and buggy to go to town. I have to pick up some luggage at the train station."

"Need any help?"

"No, thank you Pipps."

●

Vlack's ears were still ringing when Rhumy, the cook, ran into the study. "That man shot at me. Are you all right Mr. Vlack?"

"I never even got a look at him. What did he look like? Speak up loud–my ears are ringing."

"Tall…he was dressed in buckskin and fired two shots at me."

"I mean his face. What did his face look like?"

"I don't know. He had it covered with a buckskin bandana."

"Look at this mess. He destroyed my desk." The only thing still intact was the ledger Vlack had clung onto during the gunfire. "How come he didn't shoot you?"

Rhumy patted himself down confirming lack of bullet wounds. "I don't know. I don't think he meant to shoot me–just keep me down."

"Go out to the north pasture and get Ken Boda. Right now." Vlack brushed himself off.

In a half-hour, Boda arrived with Rhumy. Boda looked at the desk. The odor of recently fired guns was still in the air.

"Rhumy told me who did this. It was the same guy at the stage. What does he want?" Boda stood before Vlack who was now in the living room sipping whiskey.

"He told me there'd be consequences if we lean on anybody in town."

"Well, fuck him." Boda patted his gun handle.

"He's fuckin' us right now. We don't know who he is. I want you to find him and kill him on sight. Goad him into a gun-fight with plenty of witnesses." Vlack took a large gulp.

"I agree with the plan but where to start?"

"He's your problem. I don't ever want to see this man again–alive." Vlack walked over to the study and pointed to the desk. "There were six shots that destroyed my desk. I want him riddled with six bullets."

"I'll go to town every night until I find him and believe me I'll find him." Boda looked longingly at the bottle of bour-bon.

"No liquor for you with him on the prowl around here. Go back to the pasture and pass the word.  You know what he looks like. He kept my back to him. I just know from what you and Rhumy told me that he's the same guy as at the stage."

Boda left. He didn't know where to start. Until yesterday there was no such person to worry about.

●

Cotter rode the wagon in with a roan borrowed from Gar-rison's stable. He kept to the main street where he knew the clin-ic would be. The air was hot and humid and filled with horse manure and urine scents. New Haven never got this bad. He wondered about road maintenance. Cotter spotted the clinic. It was painted white and was nestled between the dry goods store and a vacant storefront. A signpost shaped like an upside down letter "L" held three names. The first one was Jacob Cotter MD.

He walked into the waiting area and was met immediately by a comely woman about his own age.

"May I help you sir."

"Are you Sadie Rand?" Cotter looked at the four people seated in the waiting room. "I'm Jacob Cotter."

"Oh, dear. Dr. Cotter. I'm so embarrassed I didn't know you. Now that I look at you, I should have recognized you right away. And my children talked about meeting you yesterday."

Cotter could see some of her features in Joshua and Mary. "They're wonderful children."

"Dr. Wills and Garrison are with patients. Our other nurse, Minna Lord, will manage the reception area and stand by for their call. Let me show you to your office and explain some of our procedure.

"The other Doctors' offices are the same–desk, chairs, examining table and movable curtain. You can tell me where you want to hang your diploma and any pictures." She waved her hand around the 8-by-12-foot room. "Next, I'll show you the operating room. We're set up to do small procedures in your office and we have a separate room for emergency things like large lacerations and broken bones needing to be set. The emergency room is in the hospital building attached to the back of the Doctors Clinic."

They entered the hospital section which extended twice the length of their office area to the back with its separate entrance for women in labor or patients scheduled for surgery.

"How many women per week come in for delivery?"

"Not many now–about one each week. We still have to go to the homes for most of them. Dr. Wills alternates with Dr. Garrison and takes one of us with him."

"Are there patients in the hospital rooms?"

"Yes, we have two. Dr. Garrison has already seen them and they're resting comfortably with their medication, I think. At least they were earlier this morning."

They went from the labor room into the main floor of the five-bed hospital. The layout was "L" shaped with the short foot being the labor and delivery room with two beds for post-partum care.

"This sleeping gentleman had a gunshot wound to his side. The bullet didn't enter his abdomen but he needs carbolic dressing changes three-times-a-day for two more days or infection will set in. His visitor sneaked in a bottle of whisky which put him to sleep after he took his laudanum for pain."

She went around the wheeled curtain to the second patient. "This is George. He had an abscess on his bottom that had to be opened up yesterday. Once his drain is removed this afternoon he can go home." The man opened one eye. "George, this is the new doctor, Dr. Cotter."

"Hello George, how are you doing today?"

"My ass still hurts, doc. It's better than yesterday and it doesn't stink anymore." He shifted his weight favoring the good side of his behind.

The room with the patients had three beds and led into an adjacent room with a similar set up. Rand took him into the second room. "Our original plan was to have one ward for males and one for females. Most of our patients are men. As you can guess most of the women are here for delivering babies or need a surgical procedure."

"Tell me about the gunshot patient."

"It's a typical story. Most of our bullet wounds come from the saloons. Endura has four of them. That poor man just bumped into Ken Boda who is bad tempered on a good day and yesterday wasn't a good day. He just took out his gun and shot him."

"Why isn't this Ken Boda in jail?"

"Boda works for Victor Vlack. The marshal works for Victor Vlack. Dr. Garrison can tell you more."

"Charlie…Dr. Garrison wrote about some things happening here. Vlack apparently doesn't like the Doctor's Clinic." Cotter walked slowly on the return path to his office.

"Vlack doesn't like anyone or anything that could represent more power than he has–or thinks he has." She stopped at the intersection of the hospital building and the office section.

"What kind of power does the Clinic have?"

"Trust, Dr. Cotter. The people trust the doctors. They're educated to listen and trust the doctors. Dr. Wills and Dr. Garrison have spoken out against Vlack." She stared into his eyes. "You'll be hated by him even though he doesn't know you."

"Dr. Garrison told me last year about Vlack threatening the Clinic if his public donation was refused." Cotter saw strength in her eyes.

"Dr. Wills and Garrison didn't go public with that but everyone in town knew about it. Vlack had his men spread it by rumor. He thrives on intimidation. I hope no harm comes to you or your friends." Her face suddenly brightened. "Your friends? When are they coming?"

"Mortimer and Fern Pignast are due to arrive the middle of next week. They're moving into the building next door."

"Mr. Pignast is going to be our ether administrator. It will help us out so much. Why does he need a storefront building?" They continued their walk toward the offices.

"Well, Fern is an accomplished hairdresser and Mortimer is also a barber and a phrenologist."

"She will be most welcomed. We have only one real hairdresser but we have many barbers." She laughed. "I know what a phrenologist is but I don't know if Endura needs one."

Cotter returned the laughter. "I guarantee Dr. Mortimer Pignast will make Endura wonder how they ever got along without a phrenologist."

They arrived again in his new office. "I have some things to bring in from the wagon. Thanks for the tour and don't worry."

"Worry. Worry about what?"

"Worry about harm coming to me or my friends. There are now three more friends who are part of the Doctor's Clinic."

"You haven't met Ken Boda or Victor Vlack. They're pure evil."

"Speaking of good and evil, is there a church you go to. I've gotten into the habit of going to church every Sunday back east."

"Oh yes. My children and I go to the church at the north end of Endura. It's next to the schoolhouse and the cemetery. We'd love to have you join us."

"I accept the offer." Cotter thanked her again and walked to the entrance of the reception area. He went to the wagon parked at the side of the clinic building. Cotter pulled back the canvas tarpaulin and grabbed one of his small trunks. He sensed his actions were being observed and put his saddlebag on top of the case of ether cans.

Cotter brought the trunk into his office and strapped on his two Colts and put his suit coat on. He went back out to resume his unloading. A tall man in gray pants, dark shirt and soiled wide-brimmed hat was leaning on the end of the wagon. Cotter surveyed the wagon bed. Nothing was missing.

"You the new Doctor?"

"Yes. I'm Dr. Jacob Cotter. I've just been added to the Doctors Clinic staff today. What can I do for you?" The man had a sour breath. It was a breath from morning drinking.

"I don't like doctors, new or old. My boss don't like doctors. What my boss likes is for doctors to mind their own business and not ask questions about their patients, see?"

Cotter unbuttoned his suit coat and smiled at the man. "Well you and your boss aren't going to like me because I ask lots of questions."

The man rested his right palm on his holstered gun. Cotter picked up a suitcase and moved to step up to the clinic entrance. The man blocked him. "It looks like you need some learnin'. I'm tellin' yer to just tend to doctorin' and keep your trap shut."

"Are you going to get out of my way or do I have to ask you a serious question?"

"An' what question is yer goin' to ask, Mr. Northern Doctor?"

"How did you get that cut on the side of your head?"

"I don't have a cut on the side of…"

Cotter drew his right Colt and slammed it against the man's left temple. The man crumpled in a heap. Cotter bent over him and went into the office.

"Sadie, I need a pressure dressing. A man was drunk and stumbled against my wagon. His scalp is bleeding. I think we can handle it in the clinic treatment room."

"Okay, I'll get Dr. Garrison."

Garrison and Cotter brought the sour breath man into the outpatient treatment room. "He fell against the wagon? He does smell a little boozy."

"We can stitch it up without any ether. Let's do it while he's still out cold." Cotter cleaned the wound and closed it with five stitches. When they were through Cotter asked, "What do we do with him? He's waking up. Who does he work for?"

"He works for Boda." Rand looked at them. "I can send a message to the saloon a few streets down. They'll take him away."

# Chapter 34

## Ken Boda

An unshaven cowhand hefted the unconscious man with the bandaged head over the second horse's saddle and went to the Nellie Leggs saloon. Ken Boda came out and looked at his cowhand.

"What happened to him?"

"The new doctor at the clinic said he fell into his wagon parked at the side of the doctor's place. Said Al must have been drinkin'."

"Al doesn't drink so much. Let's get 'im into a room upstairs and wait until he comes to. Somethin's not right with this."

There was a knock on the door.

"Boda, what's going on in there?" Mona Herring knocked first and then went in. She managed Nellie' Leggs–Vlack owned it.

"One of my boys, Al is comin' to. He fell or somethin' outside the Doctors Clinic. The new doc had to put some stitches in his head."

"What was he doing there in the first place?" Mona shifted here flouncey dress to kneel down beside Al.

Boda stared at her. She was loyal to Vlack. He decided to bring her into the plan. "I sent him there to harass the new doc. Let 'im know his place right off."

"Looks like it happened the other way around, Ken." She went to the washbasin, soaked a small towel and placed it behind Al's neck as he moaned and attempted some movement. He stirred some more.

"Whadya mean?" Boda didn't like being told anything negative and especially by any woman–and more especially by Mona Herring.

"Al usually has his wits about him. Something happened out there. He lost control."

"Well, he's comin'to." Boda slapped him on both cheeks. "Al. Al. Wake up." He continued his facial stimulation until Al tried to sit up.

"Oh, my fuckin' head. What happened?" Al immediately fell back onto the pillow and the wet towel.

"Take it easy, Al. You were at the doctor's place, remember?"

"Wha'—oh yeah, I remember goin' there. I met the new doc. He was unloadin' his things. I started buggin' him—you know like you said."

"All right, all right, so what happened? The doc had to sew up your head. You fell against the edge of the wagon's gate."

"I don' remember nothin' except blockin' his way. I was going to start a fight and then everthin' went black."

"Word we got wuz you wuz drinkin' and staggerin'". Boda was accusatory and slightly angry.

"I didn't have more'n my usual two before noon." Al put his hand to his head again."

"Wuz there anyone else there?"

"No. Just me and the new doc. I did like you said. I hassled him when he was takin' his stuff from the wagon into the doctor's place."

"How much did you hassle him?"

"He didn't scare much, I can tell ya. So I just blocked him goin' inta the place." Al closed his eyes tight in pain. "That's the last thing I rememba. God, my fuckin' head is killin' me."

"Maybe it's time for me to call on the new doc." Boda headed for the door.

"Before you do that, I need help fixin' up the stage. It's why you and your guys came in early. Did you forget?" Mona Herring grabbed at his shirtsleeve.

"Okay." He shrugged her off and motioned for his two ambulatory men to follow.

"I need those two poles to lift up the sagging beam holdin' up the stage curtains." Herring pointed to the long shiny brass tubes lying on the stage floor.

"They look like the brass rails from the bar." Boda motioned his two cronies to comply.

"They're the same kind of tubing cut to the right height. Put them on the right and left of the stage with seven footsteps between them."

They put up the poles and aligned them shoring up the bend in the central ceiling beam. One of the sweating men stepped back and commented. "Them poles are goin' to block the view of the dancin' girls ain't they?"

"No. And I have a new routine for the girls to swing on the poles while they take off a few clothes–one swing at a time."

"Did you clear it with Vlack" Boda jumped at the chance to challenge the pushy bitch.

"This isn't your business, Boda. I told the boss this gimmick would take business away from the other saloons. Why don't you go hassle the new doctor like you're supposed to?"

Boda glared at her and then looked at his two men. "Come on we're through here." Boda had to leave and cool off. He didn't want to push Herring too far. Vlack had talked to him several times about leaving her alone. They had some kind of relationship but it wasn't romantic or sexual. He didn't understand.

●

Boda longed for the days during the war when he was more in charge. He could remember those days well.

Sergeant Kenneth Boda led his men on the right flank charge as part of the second wave of the non-mounted assault. He waved his pistol in the air as the march turned into a running charge. It was the seventh-hour of battle. The battle lines were going back and forth. Grey and blue uniformed bodies mingled and blood slicks were patterned like the spots on Holstein cows. "Nashville will be remembered as a milestone of Southern victory", General Lee had projected to all of his generals. Boda was caught up in the hype and fervor. He wielded his pistol and his troops followed with the rebel yell.

Boda's unit overran a Union position complete with its field hospital. Half the Union hospital personnel retreated and half remained with the bed-ridden combat casualties. Boda and one patrol went into one of the medical tents. The moans and wails of the wounded were music to his ears. "Line up the orderlies and get the doctors out front," Boda ordered.

The medical staff stood outside the large tent. An older doctor with blood on his once white apron was the Union spokesperson. "Please let us tend to the wounded–yours as well."

"Why, so you can kill off our men and save yours?" Boda and his men mounted their horses. He pointed his Colt revolver at the elder physician and fired point blank into his chest. "You all are prisoners of the South and will leave this area." One of the medicals knelt over the elder Dr. Cotter. "You, get away from him or you'll join him." Boda pointed his pistol at him. The man retreated.

*Yes, as Sergeant Boda I had power then and I have power now.* Today Victor Vlack was his commander and he was Vlack's senior officer. He didn't know much about the new doctor. The other two, Garrison and Wills, never served in the military during the war but he hated doctors anyway. *I'll get those doctors to do what we want.* Boda and his two men rode to the Doctor's Clinic.

●

"That's certainly a strange way to be introduced to your first patient." Dr. Stanley Wills listened to Cotter's story about the man requiring treatment for a scalp laceration.

"One of Vlack's men. What happened to him after you sewed him up?" Garrison joined his partner's query.

"I sent his horse with him draped over it with a passerby to deliver him to the saloon where he apparently hangs out." Cotter acted unconcerned.

"We'll have to see how this plays out. Vlack and his chief foreman, Ken Boda, may come calling." Garrison frowned.

"Why the concern? I'm hoping someone responsible will show up. Someone has to pay for the man's medical expenses." Cotter smiled.

"Vlack already hates us for more reasons than just being doctors." Garrison stood up from his chair in Cotter's new office.

"Like what–the political thing?"

"Yes, Jake–the political thing. Stan here once voiced he would run as State Representative against Vlack but backed down when he threatened to destroy us. Now we're both open advocates to back his opposition."

"Who's the opposition?"

"No one yet but we're actively looking. We have a little over a year for the elections." Garrison paced in the small office.

A loud knock on the closed door drew their attention. Sadie Rand walked in looking worried. "Ken Boda is in the waiting area. He wants to talk to Dr. Cotter."

"Did he ask for me by name?"

"No. He wants to see the doctor who took care of his hired cowboy. What shall I tell him?" She looked at all three.

"I'll see him. No. Wait. Send him in. We'll all be present. Keep his cronies in the waiting room."

Boda strutted forth into the room with Cotter seated and his two colleagues abreast of him. Boda stared at Cotter. "You must be the new doctor."

"Brilliant deduction, as you already know my colleagues." Cotter moved his chair to be able to get at his saddlebags beside him for his two Colts.

"Don't get smart with me. What did you do to my man?"

"I saved his life. He could have bled to death. Don't you think he's worth saving?"

"Don't mix words with me. What happened to him?"

"He came around to my wagon while I was bringing my things into my new office. Apparently he slipped while trying to allow me passage and hit his head against the metal railhead of my rig. He reeked of alcohol. Didn't he tell you what happened?"

"He can't remember."

"Well then, he also has a concussion. He may never remember, but that's what brought about his need for medical care. So you've come to pay his bill?"

"What?" The red-faced Boda looked from doctor-to-doctor.

"You owe the clinic ten-dollars for stitching him up and examining him. The fee also includes a follow-up visit and removal of the stitches." Cotter put his hand on top of his desk grabbing a small bottle of carbolic and several cotton balls while his other hand flipped open the saddlebag beside him.

Silence filled the room. Boda placed his hands on his hips. Cotter had his right hand on the grip of his Colt within the saddlebag. Cotter stared at Boda's silver-studded holster.

"Have someone wipe this carbolic solution twice a day over his stitches to prevent infection and then have him come in seven-days from now."

"I'll have the ten dollars from Mr. Vlack in seven days." Boda picked up the cup of carbolic and the cotton balls and left stomping loudly on the floorboards.

"That was close, Jake." Garrison wiped his brow with a few cotton balls from the surgical tray.

"Why? What did you expect?"

"Boda has shot men for just looking the wrong way at him."

"I don't think this was the time or place for Boda to make such a move." Cotter released his hand on the Colt and eased his hand from the saddlebag.

"Just the same, I think you have to tread softly with that one. He's Vlack's emissary. What if his man tells a different story?"

"Don't worry he won't."

"How can you be so sure?" Stanley Wills looked to Garrison.

"The blow was to the temporal part of his skull. The concussion will be permanent. Believe me I saw hundreds like him during the war."

Sadie Rand came in as the others left. "Boda looked angry. Did everything go all right?"

"Angry people make mistakes and get off balance, Sadie. Yes, everything went the way it should."

"Just watch yourself Dr. Cotter–especially with the likes of him."

"Please, Sadie, when we're alone or with Stan and Charlie please call me Jake." His smile was infectious and Sadie Rand smiled a dimpled smile.

# Chapter 35

## Mortimer Pignast

Logan Pipps helped Pignast load their bags into Garrison's wagon. Cotter was there to greet them.

"Welcome to Endura, Mortimer and Fern. You'll be living above your shop until you find better quarters."

"It's was really fortuitous that the place was available for rental and right next to the Doctor's Clinic, Jacob." Pignast helped with their last trunk. "I brought the signs from my former structure." Pipps placed the "Barber Shop and Phrenology Readings" sign on top of everything and they drove the mile to the vacant building.

"It's bigger than the New Haven shop Mort." Fern stepped down onto the wooden walkway. "No carriage stones here, I see. Be careful with that long board wrapped in the carpet. Let me take it." Fern removed the three-foot white board with the large green letters. "I think it should be bigger but it'll do for now." She read it aloud, "Fern's Place–Ladies Hair Dressing."

"We debated on calling the side-by-side offices as 'Pignast and Pignast' but decided on keeping things as they are." Pignast looked at the building. Two offices with identical large window frontage were bisected by a central entryway leading up to the ample living quarters above.

"There's a back door at the rear of each office leading into a common stairway so you can also go up that way." Sadie Rand arrived and hooked her arm into Fern's after introductions were over. "Come, I'll show you around. I used to live here when my husband had his law office practice. He actually used both sides. We were really busy until..." she paused "...I had to join the workforce myself."

"We understand and sympathize with your loss." Fern gave her a quick hug.

"How is it you never rented or sold the place?" Pignast grunted as he bore two large suitcases up the stairs.

"The only person who wanted to buy it was Victor Vlack. He was the man responsible for my husband's murder. I'd rather keep it vacant than sell to him. He blocked any other offers and even tried to get a few people to buy it under the guise of being private buyers."

They continued the conversation as Fern and Rand supervised placement of the luggage. "I had experience as a volunteer nurse here in Endura during the war and Dr. Wills and Garrison offered me the job in their hospital and clinic. Between being a nurse and caring for my two children, my days are pretty full." Rand stared at Pignast.

"Is there something wrong, my dear?" Pignast returned the gaze.

"You have some scars that are still healing. Forgive me, its just my work doesn't stop my medical thinking once I leave the clinic."

"Mort was involved with New Haven's equivalent of Ken Boda and survived." Cotter answered for them. He looked at the quizzical look on Rand's face. "We understand we traded one frying pan for another."

"Wait until you meet Vlack and his major henchman, Ken Boda." Rand looked at the Pignasts.

"We had one like him who carried a gun and an axe." Pignast looked at Cotter.

"And he's history, so let's focus on today. We'll overcome our hurdles if we stick together. Come on you Pignasts, let's get settled. Mort, I want you ready to give anesthesia by Monday of next week."

●

"Boda, I need a few more fast guns. Get them." Victor Vlack rubbed his sore left elbow. A splinter from the shooting up of his desk took up residence there. Now it was infected. "If you need more men to ride the barbed wire, get them too. I want the cattle vote to win the election next year. I need a good number of the farm vote too. I want to start a protection plan with them. First we scare the shit out of them and then offer protection from our own men. The price is a vote for me."

"How many fast guns?" Boda stared at the beads of sweat on his boss's brow. The temperature in the room was cool.

"One top gun with three more as good but with no brains. You ride honcho as usual." Vlack experienced a sudden chill. "Christ my arm is killing and under my arm too."

"You need to see a doctor."

"Fuck. I hate to go to them–especially Garrison or Wills."

"You said you wanted to go anyway to the see the new doc. He wants payment for taking care of Al–ten dollars."

"Al still doesn't remember how he fell? He wasn't drunk?"

"Can't remember shit and swears he only had two drinks. You know Al, he does what we tell him."

"Something doesn't set right. Christ my elbow's killin' me. All right, it's time I meet this Dr. Cotter. What's he like?"

"Stands his own ground. He's like Wills and Garrison. Maybe all docs are like them. Oh, there's something else."

"What now?"

"Cotter brought two people with him. They do hair."

"What? This is getting confusing."

"A man and a woman–married. Rand rented her place to them."

"Shit. I feel like we're being invaded. What's his name?"

"Pigshit, or something like that. You can probably find out from Cotter when you see him."

●

"Jake, I don't understand why you left a solved problem for a new one." Rand looked at Cotter as they walked next door to the clinic.

"I'm fulfilling my life's plan Sadie. Charlie Garrison and I have talked about bringing modern medicine to the west since before the war. Endura needs a hospital. It will be a county facility in the near future."

"I've seen how fast it's already grown and with you here and Mortimer our capacity will increase."

"And you're a part of it, Sadie." Cotter looked at her with a smile. He wondered what she would look like with her hair down from the tight bun. *Stop it. I can't let another Pamela Skyler happen.*

"I do feel a sense of purpose with my life and my husband gone these past years. The children plus Dr. Wills and Dr. Garrison have really pulled me through some despairing times." She returned his smile.

Their smiles disappeared when they saw Victor Vlack's buggy pull up to the clinic with Boda driving.

"Here comes trouble," she said.

Cotter and Rand went in the back entrance. Rand went directly into the waiting area to meet them.

"Hello, Sadie. You're looking nice and fit as always." Vlack rubbed his elbow.

"It's Mrs. Rand in this office Mr. Vlack. Why are you here?"

"I need to see Dr. Cotter. I have an infection in my elbow."

"Dr. Cotter hasn't really officially started yet. He's just getting settled in his new office."

"Nonsense. He treated one of my men a few days ago. I want Dr. Cotter."

Boda stood beside Vlack with his hands on his hips. Boda stared at the door to Cotter's office.

"I'll talk to him." She disappeared for a minute and explained the situation to Cotter.

"Send him in to the treatment area and have him strip to the waist. I'll check his arm." Cotter debated on bringing his saddle bag into the treatment room and opted to leave it on the table behind his desk.

Cotter walked into the room with Vlack seated bare-chested, on the examining table. He could see the reddened lump on the left elbow and the arm slightly extended out from his left side. Boda was in the room.

"I only see one patient at a time. Mrs. Rand, please escort Mr. Boda to the waiting room."

"I stay with Mr. Vlack at all times. I'm his bodyguard." Boda folded his arms and stood fast.

"Who was guarding him three-days ago when you came inquiring about your man with the concussion?" Cotter stared at the silver-studded holster.

Vlack intervened. "Ken, go outside. I see no threat to my body from the new doctor."

Boda left.

"You're Dr. Cotter I understand. I'm Victor Vlack. I have a splinter in my elbow here and it even hurts under my arm."

"Mrs. Rand, wash the entire arm with soap and water. Include the armpit and then paint it with the carbolic solution." Cotter began washing his hands and then felt the knobby red, inflamed elbow.

"Ow." Vlack followed this with another louder "Ow" when Cotter felt under his arm.

"You're developing an abscess on the elbow which will have to be lanced. Blood poisoning is setting in. That's why your armpit is swollen and sore. Mrs. Rand get me a scalpel from the carbolic tray. Give Mr. Vlack a tablespoon of laudanum."

"I don't need any drugs. Just do what you have to without it." Vlack began perspiring.

"Suit yourself." Cotter quickly and deftly made a one-inch incision over the area of splinter entry. Green-yellow pus exuded followed by bright-red blood. Cotter inserted a forceps to extend the wound and extract the splinter fragment.

Vlack's eyes rolled back; he passed out and wet himself.

"This happens most of the time to the ones who put up a hard front." Rand straightened him out and provided a pillow for his head.

"It's okay, I can do a better job now." Cotter flushed out the abscess with the carbolic solution and put a gauze drain in. Vlack began to wake up.

"What happened?" Vlack looked around the room.

"You lost consciousness. Intense pain does that to most people. I warned you to take the pain killer." Cotter finished bandaging the elbow. "Keep your elbow on your chest with the sling and beginning tomorrow soak it in water that's been boiled and allowed to stand for a half-hour. Come back in a week."

"What do I owe you?" Vlack sat up and saw the wet spot in his crotch.

"That happens when a person faints. It's nothing to be ashamed of. Please pay Mrs. Rand fifteen-dollars for the surgery and you owe us ten-dollars for sewing up your hired man's head."

Vlack used his good arm to retrieve his purse and pay the fees.

"Is there anything else you need from the Doctors Clinic, Mr. Vlack?" Cotter kept eye contact.

"No. Thank you Dr. Cotter. I was hoping our first visit would be more of a social greeting." Vlack rose slowly and walked to the door.

"Watch out for flying splinters," Cotter said as the door closed.

Vlack stopped outside the door. "Flying splinters? I said nothing about flying splinters." He turned to the waiting Ken Boda. "Did you tell him how I got the splinters?"

"Of course not. By the way, no one but the barber and his wife came to town. I haven't found anyone who looked like the guy at the stagecoach or the one who shot up your desk."

"Quiet. I don't want anyone to know about that." Vlack looked at Rand recording the payment. She didn't appear to hear anything.

After Vlack and Boda left, Sadie Rand looked out the window and watched their buggy pull away. *Know about what?*

# Chapter 36

## Victor Vlack

Victor Vlack winced as his housekeeper, and only female on his ranch, washed and dressed his elbow per Dr. Cotter's instructions. "Ow, easy Carmelita." *Better her seeing me react to pain than my men.* Vlack had no use for women in his world. Some men ruled, some men worked and some men did what they were told. His father had given him this advice when he was five. His father was a rancher who had acquired his property and position with his gun. Vlack knew little of his father's pre-parenthood life other than what his father told him.

"Might is right," the senior Vlack had said. "It says so in the bible, I think. Anyway this is a world of takers. The man who built this ranch owed me and paid me with the deed as he died." No other details were offered. His father died when Victor was eighteen. The transition from teenage manager of the beef ranch was easy and natural. The elder Vlack had hired a live-in teacher for him. Lessons were in the evening. Victor rode with his father and at sixteen became the foreman. A hired gunslinger taught him to shoot fast and straight. The man was also his dad's bodyguard. "Pay someone to protect you, son. Loyalty is something obtained for a price and leadership will always provide the money."

Vlack never saw his father with a woman. "Your mother was a necessity to provide an heir–you. She would have been a good housekeeper had she not died when you were born. There'll come a time in your life when you'll need an heir. Find someone strong-willed, intelligent and teach her to obey."

There were several times before his father died when he was schooled in sexual activity. "You should get rid of your urges and continue to pay attention to the family business. Dominate even in bed–especially in bed." After his father died, Vlack had only been intimate with five women, each of which was promptly discarded after the sexual act. That was how Vlack thought of it–"a sexual act." In the past three-years Vlack had projected to the future for a "Mrs. Victor Vlack". His political advisors had told him he should have a family in place for election purposes and for when he assumed political office.

During Vlack's travels he never found a woman or a ready-made family to qualify. He was growing concerned. His encounters with the Doctors Clinic, however, had stimulated a possibility. The head nurse, Sadie Rand, fulfilled the qualifications laid down by his father and by his future aspiration needs. She was attractive, assertive, and intelligent but obeyed Garrison and Wills one hundred percent. She had two children, one of whom could be his heir. *I'll use my new status as a patient to gain her attention. I'll have to work on the death of her husband as being by one of my rogue hired hands and not at my bidding. Her damn meddling husband. His designs on becoming politically active were overshadowing my front-runner edge. At the Austin rallies, he was being seen as a more viable candidate than me. Now there's no opposition and with Stanley Wills no longer outspoken, I've been able to buy favored status at the Capital.*

"Carmelita, please that hurts." His reverie was snapped. He pushed the matronly Mexican aside. "Tend to my lunch and send for Boda." Carmelita's husband was the cook for the ranch hands. He was the one who first helped him after the masked stage robber shot up his desk.

*The stage robber–who the fuck was he? Boda and his men had combed the countryside looking for him. That dimwit town marshal sent out telegrams to find out if such a person was wanted. No information came of it. It had to be someone hired by the dirt farmers. Ever since the barbed wire, some of them had become vocal about the barriers to their grazing cows and blocking the water supply. Usually it was the farmers who put up the wire. They should be grateful. Cows, screw them, it was steer beef that Texas was all about. Farmers should have stayed in the Midwest.*

Boda knocked and then entered.

"You had almost a week. Any word yet." Vlack placed his left arm back in the sling.

"Parkland Rhodes–ever hear of him. He's a bounty hunter but he's also the fastest gun in Texas."

"No. Why a fucking bounty hunter. I want a killer, like you."

"Because he's legal. During the war my men and I could get away with a lot because in war everything's legal. We have a range war and enforcement of boundaries is legal. Rhodes can pressure the farmers with his gun."

"I want incidents. How can he produce incidents?" Vlack stood up.

"Don't worry. It's his specialty. I also got three other gun-slingers that aren't so legal but there's no one to challenge them." Boda smiled.

"No one? What about the fuckin' buckskin freak who shot up my place and killed our men at the stage a few weeks ago."

"I'm countin' on them flushin' the asshole out."

Now Vlack smiled. "Good. Very good. Sometimes you come through and rightly so for all the money I pay you."

"Thanks boss."

They walked outside to the stable.

"Ride with me along the barbed wire after lunch. Get a few more of the men. I want a regular patrol set up every day about noon."

"Anything you say, boss."

"I love that kind of answer. Help me strap on my gun. Tomorrow we go back to the doctors' place. Bring Al along for his appointment, too."

"Okay. He still doesn't remember shit about fallin' against the friggin' wagon."

●

"It's good you got the windows covered with the dark blankets. It's so hot in Endura, I wouldn't be able to control the ether." Pignast dripped the ether slowly on the patient's conical gauze.

"This one's going to have to be quick." Cotter washed his hands with soap and water.

"Fortunately we can work with his head to the side Mort. When he's deep enough hold his face away from us." Garrison had already used the soap wash and was shaking his hands from his carbolic soak.

"How'd he get this abscess on his jaw, anyway?" Pignast asked as he finished his final ether drop.

"From a fight at Nellie's Leggs."

"This isn't a new casualty from Ken Boda?" Cotter joined his colleague.

"No, it's some new guy. They say he looks like a gun-fighter but he's more articulate than Boda or the usual Vlack scum." Garrison asked for the scalpel.

"You know, I've only been in Endura for five-weeks and it seems we get too many patients from the saloons." Cotter blotted the bleeding points with a square of cloth bandage.

"More surgical patients, you mean." Garrison dissected around the one-inch submandibular abscess trying not to break it.

"No. I've seen pneumonia from vomiting, cuts, bruises, broken ribs and other things we can fix without the operating room. And many stem from people frequenting the saloons."

Garrison laughed. "We've been sending you all those to break you in. Stan and I have been seeing most of the general medical family things. Next week you can take your share of the deliveries and the new pregnancies."

The abscess was shelled out and placed on a glass tray for examination later. Garrison and Cotter irrigated the wound with carbolic and sewed the layers back together. The patient started to stir with the last skin stitch.

"Perfect timing." Pignast straightened out the man's head while the bandage was wound from under the chin and over the head like a winter scarf.

"So that's the story is it?" Cotter walked with Garrison to the wash basin to clean their hands again.

"You know how it is, Jake. The new guy in town gets the crap until he learns the routine."

"I shouldn't complain. Most of my patients paid their bills up front." Cotter went with Garrison and stopped at his office.

"Most of our revenue comes from the other patients who pay us a little every week. By the way, part of the pregnancy management is going out to the patient's home when they're in their last month. The roads are so bad they'd go into early labor if they came by wagon every week."

"I can hardly wait." Cotter watched his colleague retire to his office and sat behind his desk as Sadie Rand came in.

"Dr. Cotter, I want to say something to you before you see your next patient." Rand smiled and was a little awkward.

"Have I done something wrong?"

"No. It's just that I didn't expect an unmarried man to attend church on Sundays."

"Why not? I believe in God."

"Well out here–in the West–it's usual for a person with family to have faith but unattached men tend to hang out in the saloons unless they're farmers." She gazed into Cotter's eyes. "My children think you're wonderful. They look forward to you picking us up on Sunday."

"I look forward to seeing all of you."

They stared at each other for a long moment. Sadie Rand looked away and broke the silence. "Your next patient is quite ill and may have to enter the hospital."

Rand brought in the bloated woman who was in extremis with gasping inspirations. Cotter had the woman sit in an examining wheelchair.

"She's not to lie down." Cotter completed his examination of the elderly woman. "Her legs are swollen from the ankles to the knees and her lungs are filled with fluid. The pulse is rapid." He placed his stethoscope ear pieces around his neck. "She has a failing heart. Ma'am you have 'dropsy'".

"I'll get her son. He's outside."

A man in his mid-thirties came in. "Is she all right."

"No, she isn't. She has too much fluid in her circulation. At this stage the medications may not work. I have to keep her in the hospital for around-the-clock care."

The worried son gave his mother a kiss on the forehead. "You do everything the Doctor says. I'll be close by."

They wheeled her into the hospital unit beside the bed and had her sit on the large chair with its self-contained chamber pot. The other nurse came in as Rand left to go back into the busy office area.

"Zenia, start her on the digitalis right now and have her drink the mercury salt. If she can start to urinate, we may be able to help her."

Boda beckoned the old woman's son to come out of the office.

"I saw your rig out front. Whaddya doin' in there?"

"My ma's sick–she's pretty bad."

"You get the new doc?"

"Yeah, he seems to know what he's doin'."

"Maybe. He's takin' care of Al and the boss. See if ya can find out anything about him. He came from back east–Connecticut. He doesn't seem to be a dude though."

"I'm really concerned about my ma."

"Do what I tell ya."

"Okay, ya don't have ta get testy."

Boda walked away. The worried son went back into the waiting room. Five more patients came and went and two-hours later, Cotter asked to have him come into his office.

"Mr. Mumford, please sit down. Your mother is responding to the medication. What she has is a fluid overload plus being overweight. Our nurse tells me this has happened before but not as severe. From our record she's was supposed to be taking the digitalis preparation and watching her diet closely."

"Ya know how old people are, Dr. Cotter. Once she felt better, she stopped taking her pills and she still eats what she wants."

"Her heart can't take another episode like this. Once she gets more coherent I want to talk to her in your presence. We're keeping her here overnight. Our other nurse, Zenia Lord, will be tending to our inpatients tonight. Come back at ten in the morning."

"I hope she takes a likin' to ya, Dr. Cotter. She yells at Dr. Wills."

"I'll try my Connecticut charm on her. Do you have any children?"

"Not yet but we're tryin'."

"Okay that'll give me something to start a friendly dialogue with her–give a few reasons to go on living. I'll see you tomorrow." Cotter shook his hand as Rand knocked and entered.

"You said you're from out east–Connecticut? You seem accustomed to Texas life." Mumford needed a few crumbs of information to satisfy Boda.

"I met a lot of people in the army during the war from out west. When they were sick they liked to talk about home."

"It may not be as friendly as you heard about, Dr. Cotter. Almost everyone out here has to wear a gun for protection against bandits and critters."

"Maybe I'll get one if I have time or really see the need. I'm a Doctor, remember. This is my weapon." Cotter held up his stethoscope. He stood up and acknowledged Rand's presence as Mumford left.

"I heard what he said. Do you know how to use a gun? Dr. Garrison and Dr. Wills carry them when they go to home visits and when they go to and from home."

"Do you have a firearm Sadie?"

"Yes and no. My deceased husband had a gun and a rifle which I have at home. He taught me to shoot but I don't carry a gun. Who would hurt a woman?"

"Well I heard people say the day I arrived, some stage robber held a lady passenger hostage and threatened to kill her."

"Yes, I remember. But I don't think ladies are in danger."

"No one has presented me with the need for a pistol and until that happens, I'll just be a tenderfoot doctor doing my job caring for the citizens of Endura." Cotter paused. "To change the subject, I have to start in earnest to find a house to live in. I'd appreciate it if you and your children show me around after church on Sunday."

"We'd love to."

# Chapter 37

## Parkland Rhodes

Boda grunted a few times to get Vlack's attention. "Boss, this is tha man I wuz tellin' ya about. Rhodes, meet Mr. Victor Vlack."

The tall man stepped forward as Vlack stood to shake his hand. "Parkland Rhodes at your service, sir." His holstered nickel-plated and pearl handled .44 pistol reflected sunlight coming in from the study window. It was a bright contrast to his dark brown pants, shirt and leather vest. His heavy duster was draped over his left arm. Despite the travel dust on his lower legs beneath the duster, his steel-tipped-toe boots and steel spurs flashed a glint to Vlack's eyes.

"I understand Boda has told you of our needs. We have to harass the farmers and enforce our barbed-wire boundaries. I'm told one of your acquisitions will put a dent in the farmers' incentive to remain in Endura?"

"Yes." Rhodes rested his right hand on the handle of his .44. "The man is called 'Knuckles Newly'. He's a professional prize fighter and has never lost a fight. Many of his opponents are permanently disabled or dead."

"You realize everything must be done according to the law. The barbed wire thing is straight forward. What about this Knuckles?"

"His manager, a man named Todd, offers five-hundred dollars for any man who can stay in the ring for five rounds. They fight with light-padded gloves. The rules are pure sporting regulations and no dirty-fighting is allowed."

"Five-hundred, huh. That'll certainly lure them to their slaughter. What happens if he loses? There are a few stalwart men who push the plows around here. Strength and bulk are no match for your Knuckles."

"I told you, sir. He's never lost a fight." Rhodes rubbed his chin.

"It sounds good. Remember to be firm and above all within the law for the barbed-wire violators."

"I've done this before, sir. May I leave to get settled and tend to my horse?"

"By all means. Boda I need to talk to you about Dr. Cotter."

After Rhodes left, Vlack sipped his wine and offered Boda a seat.

"This Dr. Cotter is getting a start at being in good opinion with the townspeople. He even goes to church." Vlack had followed Rand one Sunday and was stunned to find Cotter already in a favorable relationship with her.

"Doctor-wise, ya have to admit he's bin good with us. He even saved Mumford's mother from near death."

"I heard about that. Everyone thought she'd bought it this time. Did Mumford find anything out?"

"Yeah. The guy's apparently a real dude. He was doctorin' in the war and doesn't believe in guns."

"What about political aspirations?"

"Aspir…what?"

"Ambitions. Is he likely to oppose my running next year?"

"Not likely. Cotter just wants to keep doctorin' and build up the clinic with those other two."

"All right. Who's this 'nasty guy' that came with Cotter? I don't understand. He's a barber, fortune teller and helps knock out the patients so the three of them can operate? I've been keeping Rand's place from being rented ever since her husband got himself killed."

"Word is that Garrison got Sadie to offer the rental. His name is Pignast. His wife does women's hair and he's a barber. He claims he had schoolin' on how to tell the future about people by feelin' tha bumps on their heads. He learned to knock out people at tha medical school Cotter came from. Cotter brought him with him."

"Does he carry a gun?"

"I don't think so. He's a bald guy, a little overweight but his wife's a knockout."

"How're you doin' about the guy in buckskin who robbed the stage? Who is he?"

Boda swallowed. "I still don't have anything yet. He didn't end up robbing the stage. The woman I grabbed told the marshal the guy said he never intended to rob the stage."

"So why did he wear the mask?"

"Damned if I know."

"Ask some of the new people about him. Maybe Rhodes. The man's outfit seems distinctive."

"Distin…what?"

"Distinctive–unique, memorable." Vlack dismissed Boda.

●

"Ladies and gentlemen, I say again–five-hundred dollars cash goes to any man who can stay in the ring with Knuckles Newly." Todd held up a sign that bolded the dollar amount.

"Where's the cash?" A member of the saloon clientele spoke up.

"It's in the Endura bank my good man. Ya want a crack at it?"

The man sat down silent as Knuckles Newly in skin colored tights and bare-chested strutted around the ten-by-ten ring.

"C'mon, now. Five-hundred dollars goes to anyone playing by the rules-of-the-ring who can knock out Knuckles or just go five three-minute rounds with him. We're going to make a circuit at all the Endura saloons–a week at each."

The Cactus Spine Saloon was mostly a watering hole for the farmers. Very few went to Nellie's Leggs where cattlemen would verbally abuse and, with enough alcohol, sometimes physically assault, one or two singled out for being anti-barbed wire. A large Irishman, robust and burly from daily fieldwork finished off his fourth beer, slammed down the glass and stood up.

"I can take you in less than five rounds." The Irisher nicknamed Sully looked around as his peers cheered him on.

"Okay, gents. We have a contestant. Come on up." Todd waved Sully to the ring amidst more cheers.

Todd explained the rules to both fighters and in a voice loud enough to be heard by all Cactus Spine's patrons. "Ladies and Gentlemen," Todd continued. The ladies present were the saloon's prostitutes. "Ladies and Gentlemen, I repeat–five-hundred dollars will be awarded to Mr. Sully if he knocks out or lasts five rounds with the light glove champion of the west, Knuckles Newly." The applause was thunderous.

"I bet he doesn't last the first round–five dollars," Rhodes said to the members of his five-man card-playing circle. He slammed the five-dollar note on the table. Several farmer card players took him up on the bet with smiles on their faces.

"When I hit the bell with my hammer the first round will begin." Todd raised the hammer over his head and clanged the signal to start the fight.

Both men wore snug lightweight black leather gloves with minimal padding. They circled each other with Newly poised in a professional fist-fighter stance, hands in front and arms bent at the elbows. Sully moved clumsily in the circle with his right arm bent up at his shoulder and his left arm straight down. Both men were bare-chested. Sully was thickset and diffusely muscular compared to the trim, well-toned Knuckles Newly whose physique defined every muscle group.

"Stand still. Ya tryin' to get me dizzy walkin' in circles?" Sully suddenly moved forward releasing his poised right arm at Newly's head.

Newly ducked and hit Sully twice at belly button level knocking the wind from his opponent. Sully doubled over and grabbed the boundary rope. The referee kept Newly from following up with more punches.

"Are you done Mr. Sully?" the ref asked.

"Get…outta…my…way." Sully recovered but labored to restore his respiratory reserve. He charged Newly now at the center ring. Newly turned sideways and slammed a firm fist into Sully's left chest. The patron's closest to the ring could hear several ribs crack as the man screamed in pain. Sully was now an enraged bull. Newly was still at his pugilistic stance and now making small circles with his fists. Sully launched a frontal attack which was met with Newly's straight left arm jab to his jaw followed by a quick blow to Sully's temple and down he went.

"One, two, three…" The referee counted Sully out as he lay with labored breathing and blood coming from his mouth, nose and left ear.

"Take him to the Doctors Clinic emergency," someone yelled.

"We'll have a thirty-minute recess before we ask for the next volunteer. Five-hundred dollars gentlemen–five-hundred dollars."

"Fastest twenty-five bucks I ever made." Rhodes collected his money. Other men on Todd's payroll did the same.

The next opponent almost completed round one but ended up with a broken nose before he went down on the canvas-covered wooden floor.

The third man ended up with a fractured left forearm trying to protect his face while the fourth man had cracked ribs and a fractured right collarbone. There were no more volunteers after that. All four farmers with visions of winning the five-hundred dollars were taken to the Doctors Clinic emergency entrance. Dr. Stanley Wills had the physician duty.

●

A red-eyed Stanley Wills greeted his two colleagues the next morning. "We had four victims from the Cactus Spine last night. They were all from some prizefighting contest." Will explained the situation and the high cash award as the bait. "From what I can fathom, the fighter and his manager made a bundle on side bets just before each fight began." He continued to check off the condition of the fallen challengers. "I had to keep Sully. I thought he had a stroke from internal brain bleeding but he just came to an hour ago."

"Can we go to the marshal to shut him down?" Cotter had recall about his nemesis from New Haven. He didn't want a Kelvin Danzer in his new hometown.

"No. We've had sideshows like this before, but not fighters. The marshal was told by Vlack that these things bring a lot of money into town." Garrison looked at his partners. "I really don't know what we can do about it except be available for the casualties."

"Oh come on Charlie. By doing that, we're giving Vlack permission to lure and intimidate the farmers."

"You're right of course," Garrison agreed, "But short of going to the Mayor's safety committee what else can we do?"

"Well for starters, let's get a petition going to get rid of Todd and Knuckles Newly. This is just another way for Vlack to get rid of the voting agriculture people. The wife of one of the disabled victims–and they are victims–told me they're leaving Endura when her husband get's well. They'll sell their place and acreage to Vlack." Stanley Wills waved his hands and slapped them on his thighs.

Cotter stood up. "I didn't come here to see the same intimidation I left back in New Haven."

"We didn't have Newly until a week ago." Garrison was not apologetic.

"Then we should give him notice to leave." Cotter looked to his colleagues for agreement.

"The town council will do that." Wills offered.

●

The church bells stopped as the preacher motioned his parish to stand. Cotter stood beside Sadie Rand. Josh Rand was next to him and Mary was next to her mother. After several hymns and prayers the preacher's sermon was coming to a conclusion.

"My good friends, we recognize hard times are mixed in with the good times. The good book tells us many things on how to deal with life on life's terms. When an enemy threatens, we can turn the other cheek or pray for them that they will change their ways. When the enemy smites us we can lie down awhile but rise again to show the Lord's will that we all shall coexist. Only when our backs are to the walls shall we form an army of God-fearing folk to oppose those who would physically harm us. I see the forces of evil around Endura and I see the good in front of me today. We are a mighty force to present against evil. Endura can use the might of the political system to emerge victorious. The day of David and Goliath will not likely happen again. One person cannot do what we as a united mass can. Go forth with faith. Amen."

A resounding "Amen" concluded the days worship. Eight-year-old Josh looked up at Cotter. "Was there really a David and Goliath, Dr. Jake?"

"I believe in the bible and I say yes, there truly was David who struck down Goliath."

"But why can't someone beat up the boxer mom says is almost killing our friends?"

Rand and Mary looked at Josh's hopeful face.

"If he doesn't stop or go away, maybe someone will." Cotter stared at Rand.

"You two kids go and talk with the other children while I talk with Dr. Jake." Rand dismissed the children and turned to Cotter.

"I wish it were as simple as Josh's mind wants it to be. Sometimes the good book doesn't seem to apply to our specific needs. How many has Newly hurt since he's been here?"

"We've been getting at least two a night. Most are still the farm people. We had one last night who was a cattle ranch hand from a spread that wasn't on Vlack's payroll, but it doesn't matter. This has got to be stopped. The Mayor and the town council's petition was laughed at by Newly's manager."

"What do you think will happen, Jake?"

"One of several things has to happen. Either Todd will go somewhere else or people will stop volunteering to get their brains beat upon." He paused. "Or a David will come and smite Knuckles Newly."

Rand smiled. "Now you're sounding like Josh." She put her arm into his as they walked toward their wagon. It was a natural action that seemed to happen only when they went to church.

Cotter felt a warmth cover over him when Sadie Rand got close to him. At the Doctors Clinic their relationship was purely professional. After hours when he would accompany her to Garrison's place they would talk about the children and about what kind of house Cotter should live in. Occasionally the Pignasts would come into their conversation but Vlack's aura always seemed to be hanging over them like a black cloud. Cotter had trouble sorting everything out.

"I've decided to build a house since I can't find one I like or that fits what I think my future should need." Cotter looked at Rand as they climbed onto the wagon.

"What kind of home are you looking for, Jake?"

"A home for my future family." It seemed like a normal thing to say but Cotter found himself looking at Josh and Mary running toward them and thought–*a family like us.*

Almost four-months had gone by since he arrived and more and more each day, Cotter looked forward to the ride with Rand to the Garrison's to pick up her children and see the three of them go off to her home alone. Lately he found himself wanting to go along. However, gnawing inside him was the feeling that a "David" wanted to get out first. Something had to be done about Knuckles Newly.

# Chapter 38

## David and Goliath

Cotter could not overcome his feeling of déjà Vue with church and being with Sadie Rand and her family. Caught up again in an atmosphere electric with violence, he remembered the Hamers and the importance of church and a sense of God. The combination of a feeling of family and a higher power added to his innate idealism within his chosen medical profession. A further feeling of tragedy overcome with purpose paralleled but did not equate with Pamela Skyler's husband being killed and her obvious pursuit of another man in her life. Rand did not thrust herself into his life. On the contrary, something was happening naturally and he was letting it happen. It had started quite subtly when he volunteered to escort her to the Garrison's to pick up her children. It became a routine. Then he found himself looking forward to the end of the day when they would be sitting side-by-side on the wagon and talking of life's values and the forecast of good and evil. The conversation always came down to establishing the hospital and clinic versus Victor Vlack and his aura of blackness. In his mind, he reflected on the forces of Van Haven verses his own home base of the Serenity vineyard. Cotter found it easy to relate to this attractive, homespun and idealistic woman.

Eight-year-old Josh and ten-year-old Mary bolstered this feeling of continuum from his Connecticut life and yet it was new. Josh was too young to remember his father and seemed to plug Cotter into this role. Mary had a sense of fatherhood as someone who was with her mother when she was very young and now there was "Dr. Jake". He loved talking to them using the simple language of childhood. The bible, church and school were easy communication pathways. There were times, especially recently, when he asked himself whether he looked forward to being with the children more than with Rand.

Cotter let Rand talk about her late husband. He had been a lawyer championing the rights of the people of Endura and had fallen into the role of political representative. This brought him in confrontation with Vlack and, according to his colleagues and Rand herself, was a lethal challenge. No one could prove Vlack's sponsorship of the gunslinger who goaded Rand into a one-on-one face off with firearms but logic could not deny what had happened. Rand told of this the first week he was in Endura and it had acted as a closure of the subject and a starting point for them to get to know each other.

Last month Cotter began in earnest to look for a place other than the Garrison's to live. In his mind he wanted another Serenity estate. Cotter remembered his conversation with Rand and her children when he realized there were no suitable sites for his permanent living situation.

"The town is getting too big to exist on its own. My husband saw the growth coming and the need to approach the state capital just before he was killed." Rand's conversation was a factual statement.

"How big does Endura have to be to become a city?"

"Over five thousand people with a petition signed by half the population. We have at least that number now."

"No wonder we're overworked. Back in New Haven we estimated that there should be one doctor for every thousand people."

"And it's why there's no extra housing Jake." She looked at him with raised eyebrows. "What kind of place do you want and what kind of place do you need? You told me of your winery in Connecticut. Do you want or need such a huge place again?"

"I don't know and maybe that's my problem. I don't know what I want or need in Endura. Texas is so different from the northeast."

They had arrived at her house. The house was a large two-story structure on four acres of land. There was a large barn for the two horses and the buckboard. The house itself was nestled in a wooded area of thin pines. There was no dense forest like on the Atlantic coast. The trees in this part of Texas were slender but the firs were green year round. The winters were mild except for February and March when it did get cold and one could expect a snowstorm or two but not more. The October air was mild and Cotter was at a loss to define the place he wanted to establish as a home base.

There was no such place to be had in the emerging city of Endura. He had forgotten the benefits of such a transition from village-to-town-to-city. Endura was growing fast and the agriculture community was edging out the cattle ranchers in sheer numbers. Garrison and Wills and the town council wanted Endura to become a city and as such to qualify for more state-directed benefits. One of these benefits was the use of the Texas Rangers, a new and upcoming statewide law enforcement group which could check on corrupt law officials like the town marshal. City establishment would also put the brakes on Vlack and his barbed wire empire.

At that instant, Cotter felt that what he was looking for was what Charlie and Deirdre Garrison had–a loving family. It was not just shelter and privacy. He found himself imagining living with Rand and her children. The trigger was the woman herself. He felt some warmth from within and some aura emanating from her. And yet they had not moved in any intimate direction. But he had a feeling and they had exchanged sensitive looks and extended gazes of unspoken feelings at the clinic. These also occurred during the drives to-and-from the Garrison's place in the evenings. A feeling of bonding with Rand was fortified at church. And now he felt a sense of guilt or was it distance. The preacher had defined the bipolar atmosphere in Endura. Good and evil–David and Goliath. His alter ego was a David and he didn't know if it would negate any future possibilities with the Rands.

Cotter read the bible story about David and Goliath and put the book away. Newly would have to be dealt with but Vlack was behind Newly. He had also found out that Todd and Newly were brought into town by this newcomer, Parkland Rhodes. Rhodes seemed familiar but he couldn't place him. *First things first.* David used a stone against a sword, what should he use against Newly. Cotter opened one of the luggage bags which had remained closed for months. It held his cache of .45 Long Colt cartridges and his re-loading equipment. As he moved things around he found what he was looking for and remembered Marvin Bosch.

●

Garrison was covering the clinic tonight. Cotter left his palomino behind the hospital and watched as the last casualty from Newly's lethal pugilism was brought in for treatment. There was a full moon against a sky dotted with jeweled stars. The light from the moon was bright and cast shadows from the buildings which Cotter used as concealment. One of the victims died on his coverage night. That was the night he made his decision. He rode his horse to the back entrance of the Cactus Spine saloon where the manager and fighter were living. Except for the shiny conchos, his tan buckskins were almost invisible in the moonlight. Todd and Newly had to come out back to go up to their rear quarters in the saloon. He could hear them coming.

"It amazes me, every night these settlers think they have a champion. The betting is as good as ever. We got fifty-dollars tonight clear profit." Todd counted the money as they closed the rear saloon door.

"When do we move on?" A sweaty Knuckles Newly rubbed his shoulders with crossed arms.

"Not until Vlack tells us. Rhodes told me to keep on going. We managed to get six families uprooted and leave their spreads." Todd patted the pocket of money for reassurance. "The marshal and that town council thing weren't worth shit about gettin' us outta here."

"I'm not the marshal or the town council." Cotter's deep voice behind the tan bandana stopped them cold.

"What? Who the hell are you?" Newly was on guard and put up his fists.

Todd had his left hand on his single strapped-on .44 and went for it. Cotter's two Colts came up like lightning and stopped Todd with his hand still on the handle of his holstered pistol. Todd swallowed hard.

"What do you want?"

"Take your gun out with your right hand and drop it on the ground." Cotter motioned with the shiny Colt and holstered his second gun. He threw a length of rope to Newly. He pointed to Newly with his gun. "You, tie him up to the stair rail."

Newly tied Todd's hands to each other and then ran the rope around the middle of the hand truss and tied him to the rail next to the post of the first step.

"My argument is with you Knuckles." Cotter kept his gun aimed at Newly and pulled out the pair of lead shot gloves from his saddle bag. "You and I are going to fight with our hands. If I win I get the money and you leave town."

"What do I get if I win?" Newly strutted back and forth between Todd and Cotter. The air was cool but Newly took his shirt off.

"You get to live."

"That means we fight to the death." Newly smiled.

"That's what it means." Cotter took off his hat and draped his holstered Colts over his saddle and put on Bosch's gloves.

"Hah. I don't need gloves to finish you. Are you gonna take off the mask."

Cotter remained silent. Newly brought his fists up and closed on Cotter. He went forward and straight-armed a left to Cotter's head. Cotter ducked and moved around Newly.

"Kill the bastard." Todd strained at his tethers watching the combat unfold.

Newly turned to face Cotter again but turned right into a side punch to his jaw. He moved back. He had rarely been hit in the face before by any of his non-professional adversaries. The blow hurt. The man had power even with gloves on.

"Break his neck. You know how to do it. Just like the asshole from the other night. You remember the guy Rhodes told us to eliminate."

Cotter took in the words. They were what he needed to justify what he perceived to be his duty. Todd and Knuckles Newly were one of Vlack's tools. Newly came at him again in his fists-up stance.

"Okay my masked friend, your time has come." He swung his left and missed, staggered a bit but recovered and swung a roundhouse right at Cotter's head.

Cotter ducked and moved sideways ramming his right-gloved fist hard into Newly's right rib cage. Cotter could feel the give as several ribs cracked.

"Ahhh, fuck, I'm gonna kill you, you pig fucker." Newly leaned to his right with severe chest pain and ran at Cotter. He faked a roundhouse right and kicked Cotter's right calf, sending Cotter to the ground.

Cotter rolled as his right side met the cold earth and he sprang up to face Newly who came at him swinging. Newly's left fist hit Cotter's right shoulder at the margin of the collarbone. Cotter felt a searing pain as the juncture separated. He ducked Newly's right hand aimed at his jaw and slammed his left hand into Newly's right temple with all the strength of his arm and the momentum of his body. Cotter concentrated his total body weight behind this one punch. Newly hit the ground immediately. Cotter backed away but Newly didn't get up. Cotter nudged the immobile torso with his leg.

"Get up Newly."

There was no response.

"C'mon Knuckles. Get up for Christ's sakes. Kill the bastard. You've done it before. Smash his brains. Break his neck like you did the guy the other night." Todd was sweating. His eyes widened as he digested the scene.

Cotter knelt down. He looked at Newly's face and turned it into the moonlight. Newly's right pupil was larger than the left. The legs and arms began to twitch and generalized seizure activity made his body flap up-and-down. The dark stain of a released bladder appeared between Newly's legs and the odor of feces reached the observers. Cotter knew the right side of the man's brain had hemorrhaged and his neck was broken. Newly's head was fixed at an unnatural angle even during the generalized seizure.

"You killed him. You'll hang for this."

Cotter leaned against his saddle and saw stars as he relocated his collar bone using the saddle's hard surface for leverage. It popped back into place. He removed Bosch's leaded gloves, put on his hat and strapped on his guns. Cotter was amazed that his bandanna was still covering his lower face.

"Let's go up to your place. You can give me the thousand-dollars you owe me."

"You're crazy. I'll give you nothing. Rhodes will kill you for this. Vlack will hear about this."

Cotter placed the barrel of his nickeled Colt against Todd's temple.

"I'll kill you right here."

"Ok. Ok."

Cotter removed the tether to the stair rail. After Todd gave him the money he pushed Todd to his bed. "This money goes to the dead man's widow–the man that Newly killed the other night. You can tell Rhodes, Boda and Vlack these are the consequences if more citizens in Endura are hurt or killed."

"Who are you?"

"Just tell Vlack what I looked like–he'll know who I am."

# Chapter 39

## Home Visits

Cotter told Rand, Garrison and Wills he had hurt his shoulder making a repair on his wagon. It was his rotation to make home visits and Cotter took this as a welcome diversion away from further questions about his injury. Only Rand persisted.

"I don't think we ever saw anyone injure their shoulder fixing a wagon wheel?"

"Back east I had others do livery work for me. I guess I'm still just a tenderfoot about these things. I'll learn."

"You need someone to look after you Jacob Cotter."

"I know." He looked tenderly into her eyes. "Well, I have to go. I have two pregnant women to see and a bunch of other post-op patients and who knows what else from this list you gave me."

"Well, take care of yourself and watch out for snakes. Do you have a gun?"

"I don't use firearms much. I have this shotgun." He raised his double barrel 10-guage shotgun but winced as his right shoulder twinged with pain.

"See, you're still hurt."

"I'll be okay. This shotgun will hit anything I point it at."

"Your treatment case has everything you should need. Dr. Wills and Dr. Garrison have me keep it supplied for the weekly home visits." She paused with her hands on her hips. "I know you all have to do the house calls as part of the clinic's mission. When we get a third nurse, one of us will go with you."

"But until then it's just one of us and a shotgun." Cotter smiled and lightly touched the whip to the horse's rump. "I'll be back in time to take you to the Garrison's and pick up the kids." He looked back at her. *She worries about me more like a wife than a nurse caring about her employer. I don't know why I can't talk to her about my feelings for her. They're definitely different than they were for Pamela.*

The first homestead was the Conner's' place. He hadn't been there before. The area Endura serviced was huge when the total acreage was measured. This was his sixth time at rotation for the home visits. The weather was getting colder and many of the people who became patients stayed away from excursions into town. Word was left with friends who were traveling to Endura proper that someone was sick and Rand or the other nurse, Zenia Lord, would put the list together for the weekly sojourn. Cotter took the time on the trails to read, and sometimes re-read, his mail.

Since arriving in Endura in the summer, he had received letters from Mashpit, the Hamers, or LaRoque. When any one of them wrote, the content was a collective summary of the happenings at Serenity. So far it was all good news. He had written two letters to Dr. Hayes describing the medical practice and thanking him and Yale for keeping him on the medical journal newsletter list for the latest in medical and surgical advances. Cotter read the last paragraph of Hayes's letter from earlier in the week.

Dear Jacob:

…. There has been some experimentation with using two solutions for preventing and treating infections. Carbolic solutions followed by alcohol works better than either one alone. I'm taking the liberty of sending you supplies of both with the usual reimbursement expectation. The ether inhalation for deliveries is catching on and our publication of the technique will be sent to you for your review. Your name will be entered as a co-author. We're all glad of your updating the quality of medical care way down there in Texas. Dr. Randall has asked Yale Admissions to broaden acceptances of applicants from west of the Mississippi to Yale Medical School. If you ever need anything of an urgent nature please use the telegraph.

Best wishes from me and your colleagues at Yale,
Timothy Hayes

Cotter folded the letter which he had already shared with Wills and Garrison. He picked up the unopened latter with Pamela Skyler's return address. It arrived last month but he had built up a wall to opening it. *What am I afraid of? I have no feelings of guilt or regret for what had happened. According to Hamer, Mashpit and LaRoque the wine industry is still stable and without any conflicts. So open it.*

Cotter held the reins with the fingers of each hand after he had opened Skyler's envelope. He unfolded the paper and read her brief words.

Dear Jacob:

I surely miss you and have the deepest regrets we had to part. I've been able to maintain an assertive and aggressive position within the Van Haven Vineyard operation. Your brother and sister are well-contained as long as the business is successful, which it indeed is.

Jacob, there is an emptiness within me now that you're not with me. If you are likewise unhappy please come back if only for a visit. Perhaps we can rethink the decisions we've made.

I still love you,

Pamela

*How can I answer her? There is no rethinking to be done.* Cotter tore up the letter and let the breeze scatter the pieces. The Conner's place was 30-minutes away.

●

Rhodes and two henchmen rode fast down the grade to the Conner's farm. Rhodes dismounted quickly and tied the reins around the hitching post in front of the three-bedroom log-walled ranch. Smoke was rising from the chimney. He pounded on the front door.

"Open up Conner. Open up or I'll break the door down and set fire to the place."

The door opened and Rhodes faced a shotgun at his face from Mrs. Joe Conner and a rifle from Joe.

"Who are you to come barging on my property with threats?" Conner was as large as Rhodes and just as assertive.

"I just came from the fence line on your property. The barbed wire is torn down and the dam on the creek is destroyed. The water is flowing onto your land. Do you know what the penalty for trespass and destruction of private property is? Victor Vlack has the full power from the marshal to retaliate."

"You have to prove it first, whoever you are." He signaled his wife to cock the two hammers of the shotgun.

"Today is a warning. If there is any more violation of the barbed wire barrier or the dam on your property line, my job is to protect Vlack's interest and livelihood. My name is Parkland Rhodes, Conner. You've been warned."

Several of Conner's farmhands were also pointing rifles at Rhodes and his two men. They mounted their horses and rode away. About a mile away, Rhodes stopped and turned around to look at Conner's spread. He spotted a man behind a plow horse and motioned his men to follow.

Rhodes and his men rode hard to the plowman. One of Rhodes hands stopped the plow horse.

"Who are you? What are you doing?"

"I'm a messenger and I'm delivering a message." Rhodes drew his .44 pistol and shot the horse.

"You can't do this." The plowman reached for his pistol but halted with the gun just clearing his holster as Rhodes pointed his .44 at him.

"I just did it and you just made a mistake drawing your gun." Rhodes shot him in the head.

"Let's get out of here."

The trio rode fast on the main roadway. After about ten-minutes Rhodes saw a slight rise of dust two-miles ahead.

"Looks like we have another one to give a message to. Let's see who we have." They rode to the direction of the dust cloud.

Cotter thought he heard a shot in the distance. From the minimal echo it had to be a pistol. He moved the shotgun onto his lap and speeded up the buggy. In a short time he saw a dust cloud coming toward him and slowed down. Rhodes and his two cronies were coming fast and fired their pistols in the air for Cotter to stop.

Cotter pointed the shotgun at Rhodes. "I want you to know there are people who are aware of my trip out here. I'm not carrying any money if this is a holdup."

"Put your guns away boys. I know this man." Rhodes smiled. "You're one of the docs that took care of the jerks who fought Knuckles a week or two back."

"That's right. Who the hell are you and you're blocking my path. I have patients to visit."

"You can put the shotgun down. We're after some tres-passers to Vlack's land. They tore down a section of barbwire fencing and destroyed a dam on Mr. Vlack's creek."

"A natural water shed is no man's property. The water goes where God wants it to go."

"A doctor and a God-fearing man–that's good, doc." Rhodes stared at Cotter. "Go ahead and pass. I understand you took care of Vlack and some of his men."

"Like the creek, as a doctor I treat all men as equals when they need medical attention."

"Good. I like that. You never know when a person is go-ing to need a doctor. And it looks like you needed one yourself with that sling on your arm."

"I can still pull the trigger on this shotgun."

"Goodbye Doctor…?"

"Dr. Cotter…Jacob Cotter."

Rhodes and his men rode around Cotter's rig and disappeared.

Cotter kept the shotgun on his lap for another five minutes and then speeded up the horse. He arrived at Conner's place to find a wagon being readied and a body placed in the back.

"Hello Joe, what happened to your man? Let me take a look."

"You needn't bother. He's dead. That guy Rhodes shot him."

"He just passed me. Did you see him do it?"

"No. He threatened us and then left. A few minutes later we heard the shots and found poor Gunter here and the plow horse shot dead."

Cotter verified "poor Gunter" was beyond medical help. "If you didn't see him do it then we can't legally confront him." Cotter saw Joe Conner favoring his right leg. "I'm here to take care of your injury Joe. Let's go inside."

Joe Conner, with the help of his wife, removed his trousers.

"That's a nasty rip in your skin. It's infected. I'm going to have to open it up a little. It may hurt." Cotter recognized it as a barbed wire tear. A five-inch tear in the skin went deep to the fascia overlying the quadriceps muscle. Conner winced and gave a low moan as Cotter allowed the foul gray pus to drain. He placed a loose saturated carbolic dressing over it.

"Mrs. Conner you have to change this three times a day." He turned back to Joe Conner. "Joe stay away from Vlack's barbed wire."

"We need the water for our corn, doc."

"You're going to have to drill some wells. As bad and as wrong as Vlack is, he's still within his legal right to do whatever he wants with the resources on his property."

"Even murder?"

"No. If it could be proven, we could remove him from this situation but I'm not sure about the barbed wire. One of my colleagues is looking into the 'natural privilege' aspect of water sequestration."

Conner looked at his wet dressing getting a little red tinge to it. "What's the name of your colleague? It's not Dr. Wills again?"

"No. Stan Wills is not political anymore. We're focusing on getting our hospital to meet the needs of our growing city. His name is Mortimer Pignast. He's our anesthesia specialist. Pignast also has a shop for barbering and phrenology readings."

"Phrenology? Yes. I've heard about him. He's well liked so far. Well, if he gets popular and survives being an antagonist to Vlack's political ambitions then I'm for him. Does he really think it's against the law to deprive natural water from personal boundaries?"

"If the town becomes a city, the water comes under state jurisdiction. Pignast is for Endura becoming a city. Vlack, of course, opposes it."

"Vlack. We should get rid of Vlack." It was Mrs. Conner speaking. "He's killed or is responsible for some of us getting killed just because we're not cattle ranchers. We heard about the boxer brought in by him. Over ten homesteads are closed down because of the maiming caused by the temptation of Vlack's money in that fisticuff game. Five-hundred dollars was just too much to ignore by the desperate ones."

Conner looked at Cotter again. "Who killed that Newly guy? We heard it was the same man who tried to rob the stage."

"As I understand it, that man never intended to rob the stage. One of the abducted ladies from the stage gave testimony." Cotter gave a bundle of gauze dressings and a bottle of carbolic solution to Mrs. Conner.

"How can you believe a woman who dances around a pole at the Nellie's Leggs saloon?" She looked at her husband.

"Don't look at me. I've never been to the place." Conner avoided her gaze.

"I have to go now. I have some maternity calls to make. Joe, you watch yourself. Just let fate take care of Vlack." Cotter boarded his wagon and waved goodbye to the Conners.

"Fate, he says. Fate is what ripped my leg open. We have to make our own fate." Conner watched as the wagon with his dead plowman went to town for burial and registration.

# Chapter 40

## Nellie's Leggs

Mona Herring yelled to be heard above the piano player. "Slow the music down, Georgie. Christine, I want you to take off one item of clothing after each verse of 'Home on the Range'."

Christine "Christie" Wooly was hired as a dancer and stripper. She had some renown back in Kansas. Adapting her strut to swinging around the shiny brass poles was new but exciting. She could remove a garter or one of her three small shirts and swing an arc while she threw the item to the audience.

"I think it would be more suggestive if I bumped my way to the opposite pole each time I take something off. Let's try it." Christie worked well with Mona.

"Let's see how it looks. We're getting more customers since the boxer died and I know some of the Cactus Spine regulars are coming to Nellie's now."

"Why do we have to be in competition if Victor Vlack owns both saloons?" The buxom Christie moved gracefully as she removed her flouncy skirt and now only donned one shirt, a break-away bodice vest and frilly pantaloons.

"The Cactus Spine is for the farmers. We take the smelly cow-punchers in here." Mona grinned. "But some of our God-fearin' farm boys like to see the girls dance down to their undies."

"Yeah, it'll get them horny for the other girls." Boda puffed on a thin cigar as he watched Christie. He liked the woman and wondered what she would think of him if she knew he was her kidnapper four-months ago at the stage incident. They had been getting along well and he felt he could bed her down without paying if their relationship developed further. His thoughts turned to the buckskin marauder who had thwarted their efforts on that day. "Mona has anyone seen this guy Todd said killed Knuckles?"

"Tall, dressed in buckskin and wears two guns?" Mona raised her eyebrows at Boda.

"Yeah, that's him." Boda moved forward from leaning against the bar.

"No. No one's seen anyone looking like that." She laughed.

"Well if anyone sees him, get the word to Victor or me right away. There's a hundred-dollars goes to the person who fingers him." Boda left Nellie's Leggs.

Mona Herring signaled two other dancers to come over. "I think we ought to work on a finale dance with the three of you stripping at the same time. Christie, can you come up with a routine?"

"I can work the two brass poles with one of us in the middle. I have an idea that should go over really well where we can take something off at the pole, move to the center and throw it to the crowd just as we move to the other pole. We can keep moving in time to a faster song–'Riverboat Shimmy Shinin'–going from one pole to the other."

"Sounds good, Christie, What should we call the act?"

"Oh. 'Pole Dancin's' catchy enough."

"I like it. We'll make a banner for the front of the saloon."

●

The wind was brisk but typical for December at six in the morning. Cotter wore his duster over the buckskins. His collarbone was healed and his range of motion was back to normal. Occasionally he felt a little "click" at the junction of the clavicle to the shoulder in the front but it didn't hurt. He faced the bottles he had set up as targets. Three were swinging from ropes tied overhead to a tree limb. It reminded him of the Wednesday practices at Serenity but today was Saturday.

Cotter looked at the targets and turned his back to them. The images remained and he turned rapidly shooting two stationary targets in front and two to the side. He quickly knelt down and fired at the moving bottles which were swinging in opposite arcs. Cotter holstered the Colts and viewed the results. All the bottles were gone. A small pall of smoke was rapidly being diluted by the breeze. His shoulder didn't hurt. Cotter put his duster back on and rode the palomino back to the Garrison's barn.

He occupied a large room on the first floor of Garrison's four-bedroom spacious house. In his room he took off the duster and put the buckskins in the small duffle bag and strapped it shut. The Colts went into his saddlebags. A knock on his door was followed by Deirdre Garrison's musical voice.

"Lunch is ready."

Cotter sat at the kitchen table with Charlie. "I read your notes from your home visits Jake."

"I wish these people could come into the clinic. At the most, they're only an hour away."

"C'mon, you saw how busy their homesteads are, especially the pregnant ones. We're lucky to get them in when they're in early labor." Garrison put down his water glass. "I read between the lines about Joe Conner. He tore the barbed wire down and diverted the stream. He could get himself killed."

"I told him to be careful. He'll be coming in the end of next week. His skin was torn by the wire and infected down to the fascia, but everything should drain and be okay with the carbolic dressings."

"What about this Rhodes character? You think he killed Conner's plowman."

"There's no doubt in my mind. Rhodes stopped me just before I got to Joe's place. He threw an implied but definite threat my way." Cotter finished his cold boiled chicken and stood up. The air was blended with the slight fireplace fumes and the moist chicken aroma.

"We can't get in their way Jake. You don't have the back-up you had in New Haven. The police aren't our friends."

"Mortimer Pignast says the Texas Rangers would help us if Endura becomes a city."

"Pignast just better watch out too. He's getting too political. Vlack may take issue with him."

"I'll talk to him." Cotter looked out the window. Rand and her kids were pulling up to the house.

"Oh, good. Jake go back and sit down for desert. I invited Sadie for lunch." Deirdre Garrison went to open the door.

The children looked at the apple pie and reached for it.

"No you don't Josh. Eat the chicken and potato first and drink the milk–you too Mary."

Cotter lingered with his pie and coffee as the children went out to play.

"You look fit Jake," Rand said. "No sling for over a week."

"Yes, I took a ride this morning and exercised it. I'm back to normal and can do my own surgery again." Cotter smiled and Rand returned the smile.

"I heard from a patient yesterday that Vlack is offering a reward for information on the buckskin stage robber. Apparently the man also killed the boxer." She looked at each of them.

"Newly killed one of the farmers and caused a bunch of them to pack up and leave. He needed to be dealt with." Cotter panned the kitchen audience.

"An eye-for-an-eye, is that your feeling, Jake?" Rand was serious.

"I see it as David and Goliath. Remember the sermon the other week?"

"But who is he? He sounds like one of Vlack's hired guns." Deirdre looked at her husband.

"Except–he's done no harm. He apparently killed two of the stage bandits who were going to kill him and, according to Todd, he picked a fight with Knuckles Newly where he could have outright shot him."

"So where is this Robin Hood?" Garrison said.

"Who knows? I'm just glad we have someone who knows how to use a gun and his fists against Vlack," Cotter added.

"Jacob Cotter you just remember not to provoke the likes of Parkland Rhodes or Ken Boda." Deirdre flashed a look to Rand.

"That's right Jake. Don't even wear a gun. Those men will kill you and say you drew down on them. They did it with my husband." Rand placed a hand on Cotter's shoulder.

"Don't worry." Cotter placed his hand over Rand's. "I know my limitations."

•

"Watch yourself Jake. Fern and I know it's you. We knew from the day we heard about the stage hold-up it was you. Those clothes and the guns are memorable. You do have style Dr. Cotter." Pignast did the final trimming on Cotter's hair. They were alone in the barbershop.

"Style wasn't exactly what I had in mind. People fear the unknown. Vlack doesn't know who he's up against and that means he'll be off guard and not quite sure of himself." Cotter smiled. "I know I don't have to tell you to keep the secret. The only thing Kelvin Danzer got out of you was the Wednesday practice but you didn't tell him what we looked like."

"My barbering will keep a watchful eye and ear for what's going on around town—Fern too, with her hairdressing ladies. Her business is better than mine."

"That's because she has pictures of all the possible hair styles they can get."

"But I offer free phrenological consultation with every haircut."

Cotter laughed. "In Texas phrenology means nothing. Why don't you advertise what phrenology is in the newspaper."

"By God, you have a point well taken. I'll do it. I'll talk to the editor and write a few articles on the science of Phrenology."

"Bull crap science." Cotter laughed again.

The dangling bell at the top of the door tinkled as the next customer came in.

"Hello Mr. Pignast. I'm relatively new in town and I'm overdue for a haircut. My name is Rhodes, Parkland Rhodes." Rhodes removed his winter coat revealing his tied down six-shooter. Rhodes looked at Cotter who was just getting out of the barber chair.

"Hello again Rhodes." Cotter looked at the man's holster. It wasn't visible two-weeks ago when he visited the Conner place. There was a silver coiled rattlesnake with a gaping mouth in the center cross-strap of the holster.

"Ah, the good Doctor–Dr. Cotter. I see by your haircut that this man does fine work. Good." Rhodes sat in the chair and Pignast threw a half sheet around his upper body and pinned it at the neck.

*Where have I seen that holster before?* Cotter's déjà Vue was intense. "Did you say you were from Arizona?"

Rhodes raised his eyebrows. "I don't think we talked about my origin when we met on the road. I know you're from Connecticut–not exactly the 'wild west' is it?"

"Certainly not." *I know that coiled snake but from where?*

"And you Pignast or Mortimer, what shall I call you? Rumor has it that you and your wife are from the same town as the good doctor."

"New Haven, Connecticut, yes. You can call me Mortimer as do all of my clientele." Pignast palpated the back and sides of Rhodes' head.

"Am I getting a massage?"

"No sir, I am merely getting my first vibrations about the protuberances from your skull. I'm a phrenologist you see."

"What the Christ is a 'frenagiligist' or whatever you call yourself."

"A phrenologist my dear sir can detect the aptitude or potential skills and disposition of a man or woman by merely palpating the shapes on a person's head."

"And what do my lumps reveal, Mortimer?"

Pignast closed his eyes and ran his fingertips and thumbs over Rhodes's head. "I detect a most assertive or outright aggressive man with a superior intelligence."

"Good, very good. I like it and as I consider your words I tend to agree." Rhodes looked at Cotter as he was about to leave the barbershop.

"Dr. Cotter, do you believe in this 'frenigily' something'?"

"Not at all. I believe more can be obtained about a person by how he dresses. That snake on your holster sends clear messages to me." Cotter left and shut the door.

Rhodes was startled by the affront and sat up straight in the chair. "What did he imply by that?"

"I would interpret that in light of my first impression–a snake can be assertive or aggressive."

"What about the intelligence part?"

"I don't know about a snake's intelligence. They try to stay out of people's way. That implies intelligence, I suppose."

"Let me ask you another question, Mortimer." Rhodes sat back again and allowed Pignast to begin trimming his hair. "Has a man dressed in buckskin and wearing two guns ever come in for a haircut and a head-lump reading?"

Pignast recoiled slightly and then resumed the hair cutting. "No."

"I have one more question and then you can finish your job uninterrupted, "Are your politics with the farmers or with the ranchers?"

●

There were gunshots everywhere–in front of his tent, behind him and at his right side. Horses were snorting and some were in pain, obviously wounded. He looked at the litters which were the standard field hospital beds. The men on them were groaning with pain, some delirious and some unconscious. Blood was on every dressing and the room smelled of cordite from the rifle fire outside and mixed in with the fatty scent of the smoky candles. A tinge of fecal smell was present from the recently dead as their sphincters relaxed for one last time. More casualties were brought in. Cotter went among them for triage.

"Send these two directly into the operating room. I'll be right in. Father, we have to close this abdominal wound and amputate the foot on this one." Dr. Cotter and his son Jake went into the surgical tent. The sweet, pungent odor of chloroform mixed in with the other smells.

Cotter assisted his father as they operated on first one patient and then moved to the next table where a casualty had been put to sleep. And then another and another–back-and-forth. Both Cotters hated this war. The mortality and morbidity was endless and seemed senseless. A torch landed on top of their tent and a bearded man mounting his horse pulled back the tent flap. He let out a rebel yell and fired his pistol at the patient on the table killing him instantly.

"Get all of them out front." The voice was gruff and somehow familiar.

The man pointed his pistol at Cotter and his father. Another horseman came next to him. Smoke was everywhere. He couldn't see very well. Both gray uniformed men had the surgical staff line up side-by-side.

"Which ones are the doctors? Step forward, right now." The bearded gunman seemed like a giant on his horse.

Cotter watched as his dad and two others stepped forward.

The second horseman pulled on his reins and the horse reared up on its haunches. "The only thing worse than a blue-coat Yankee is a doctor blue-coat Yankee." He pointed his pistol at the doctor next to his father and shot him in the chest."

The bearded one shot his father. The second horseman came up to Cotter and fired but missed. A bugle sounded and the two killers turned their horses to leave. Cotter stared at the man who had shot at him as the rider returned his pistol to his holster. The holster–it had a coiled silver snake on it. Cotter ran trying to find a gun to shoot the man. It was too late. He went over to his fallen father. His father was mortally wounded.

Cotter bolted upright in his bed. Beads of sweat coalesced into tiny streams and drenched his pillow. *Rhodes. Parkland*

*Rhodes. Was my nightmare true? Had my memory banks been stirred to recall the reason Rhodes' holster was familiar. The voice of the man in the dream was Rhodes' voice. But did I insert it into the dream? I need to find out about Parkland Rhodes. And who was the other man? His voice was familiar and there was something else the dream conveyed about the first man but the focus was not complete.*

Cotter opened the window to let in the cold winter air. He closed it again. The sun was coming up and he couldn't get back to sleep. He cleaned himself up and went into the kitchen to wait for Deirdre Garrison to awaken and make breakfast.

●

The next day was Friday. Cotter walked into his office and washed his hands for the first time prior to examining patients. He estimated he washed his hands over a dozen times a day. A soft knock was followed by Sadie Rand's appearance.

"Hello, Jake."

Cotter sat back in his chair and looked at her. Rand wore a fresh apron-fronted cover, now becoming traditional for all nurses. Her sandy hair was piled up nice and tight. "Hello to you too. You look a little nervous. What do I have out in the waiting room–Victor Vlack with bad hemorrhoids?"

She laughed. "No. I just wanted to ask you something before we got started. All of you have a full schedule today. The children were wondering if you could have dinner with us tonight."

"The children were wondering? Well I certainly wouldn't mind coming if it's their invitation but if you had anything to do with it, I would definitely show up–even early."

"Jake. You know I suggested it to the children first. Around six o'clock would be fine." She blushed.

Cotter felt butterflies in his stomach. "You've really given me a reason to rush through the day." He stared at the door for a minute after she left. *What's happened to me? I never had such feelings with Pamela Skyler. And the children? I look forward to seeing them almost as much as seeing her.*

Another rap on the door–this one much harder. Pignast came in, closed the door and stood in front of Cotter.

"What's the matter Mort? We don't have any surgery scheduled for today."

"It's the man from the other day. You know, the one who got into the chair after I did your haircut. He called himself Rhodes?"

Cotter leaned forward, his pulse quickening. "What about him?"

"He started asking me about politics. He wanted to know who I would vote for in the election next year and what my feelings were about Endura becoming a city."

"So, what did you say?"

"I told him I was from a city and Endura as a city would benefit greatly than being a local township under the thumbs of a few privileged and moneyed self-interests. Rhodes almost leapt from the chair and then he asked who I would vote for–and this was when I got scared."

"Scared?"

"I told him I would probably vote for myself. He went silent until I finished his haircut but I could tell he was tense. When I was done and he paid me, he smiled and said. 'You can't vote for a dead man.' Then he left."

"Don't worry about Rhodes. By the time the election campaigning gets under way he'll be long gone."

"Oh, and another thing. He asked me if I had ever seen a tall gunslinger in buckskin who wears one silver gun and one gray one."

"I know your answer to that one."

"I denied any knowledge but I was practically shaking when he hit me with that question."

"You had a lot of reasons to be shaky. Rhodes wouldn't know which one of the things he brought up triggered the fear. I checked up on this man, Mort. He's a bounty hunter and during the war I think he rode with a Confederate marauder outfit, but I have to be sure. Maybe you can help me."

"How?" Pignast kneaded both his hands.

"Get some of your customers talking about the war. If you get Vlack's people in, hammer them with questions in your suave, devious style."

Pignast at last smiled. "I'll do better than that. If we get one of them in for surgery, I can talk to them as they wake up from the ether. It's amazing how uninhibited people are as they emerge from the stupor of anesthesia."

"It sounds like a solid plan. We have an edge against them, Mort." Cotter rose and gave his friend a pat on the back as the now slightly more confident phrenologist left the office.

Cotter let the day's patient load absorb his main focus. It seemed more women were coming in than male patients. Many brought their children which was a change in their practice. Usually the children were the predominant part of their home visit patients. Before he knew it, the time had come to accompany Rand to the Garrison's to pick up her children.

The routine for the past months evolved into a pleasant ride, although the weather was getting colder. Rand would drop her children at school and come to work in her buckboard. After the clinic closed, Cotter would tie the roan horse to the back of her rig and drive the twenty-minutes to the Garrison's house and talk most of the way there. The conversation always started the same with a mini-review of the day's outstanding patients.

"Where did you learn that technique of getting rid of jiggers, Jake?" Rand hated the little mites that burrowed under the skin just at the hairlines on people's bodies.

"During the war I noticed some of the men with jigger infestations would be cured if they didn't clean off the combination of gunpowder residue, smoke and sweat on their faces. My dad and I mixed up a concoction of grease, carbon from the fires and gunpowder and lo-and-behold we had a treatment for jiggers. At Yale, we refined it into a coal tar and oil base."

"What about Mortimer Pignast? He looked so ill this morning and when he left he was his usual chipper self."

Cotter explained about Rhodes, the preoccupation with Endura politics and the threat to Pignast's life.

"That's how it started with my husband. Oh, God, Jake, tell Mortimer to drop the whole thing."

Cotter laughed. "You can't talk that way with Mort. Once he has a plan for advancement in his head, nothing will change it. It's how he became our anesthesia partner."

"But no one can stop Vlack and his cutthroats."

"You're forgetting about church."

"Church?"

"David and Goliath, remember? Endura has a David lurking in the shadows."

# Chapter 41

## A Touch of Family

Cotter watched Sadie Rand and her children head for her house two-miles away. He was excited and nervous about seeing them again in a more domestic setting. His thoughts went back to Serenity and the Hamers, LaRoque and Mashpit. The visions of his friends reminded him he hadn't opened the letter from Mashpit. He retrieved it from his saddlebag after he got the roan horse settled for the night. Logan Pipps, the hired man had today off.

Cotter went to his palomino and stroked the mare's nose and shoulders. "The weekend is almost here and we'll be out and about the whole day." He leaned against the large horse and opened the envelope. Mashpit's precise printing was the most legible of any letter from New Haven. Andy Mashpit had developed the style in the army as part of his mapmaking-surveyor training.

Dear Jake:

It's my turn to write. We are somewhat anxious about the situation you continue to describe with the man called Victor Vlack. Just to let you know, we still practice on Wednesdays and last week the Frenchman showed up from his company down south. He's been practicing on his own and is as good as ever. Needless to say defensive training keeps our confidence up even though we don't need to. Your brother and sister are no longer any threats with Skyler running the show. Elizabeth Colt keeps checking up on the Van Haven vineyard through her Hartford connections.

By the way, Pamela Skyler always asks about you whenever we meet. She claims you don't return her letters. God knows you have reason. We just tell her you're absorbed in your medical practice and your new life is going well. From your last letter, Gertrin Hamer sensed that something is developing between you and your head nurse–the one with the two kids. I hope things work out if she's right.

We've sent you some things to remind you of us. In your next crate of medical supplies from Yale and Dr. Hayes you'll find some baked goods from Gertrin and two boxes of some new gunpowder from Colt. It's actually made by a company called Dupont and is less smoky.

Always remember that we're here for you, as I know you are there for us. By the way, Samantha is pregnant. In seven-months time there will be another Mashpit in the world.

Your grateful friend (s),

Andy

Cotter felt a pang of sentiment as he remembered their good times. Good times will always be cherished, he felt. He patted the palomino again and went into the house to wash and get ready to leave for the Rands.

"Have fun at Sadie's." Deirdre Garrison smiled at him. "Be careful coming back. It'll be pretty dark."

"The roan knows the rode better than I do."

"Charlie tells me you're thinking of building your own place rather than rent a room. That's fine with us and you're still welcome as long as you need a place."

"We couldn't find a place that suited me. Sadie showed me all the possibilities and nothing's workable."

Deirdre didn't comment on the word "we". Charlie Garrison came into the entryway. "How come you don't use the palomino more, Jake? He's a fine animal and he looks like he wants to run around."

"I give him a good workout every weekend. He's okay. See you all later but if it's too late, don't wait up."

●

Cotter arrived at six o'clock. The few miles seemed as long to him as they did to the observer who tracked Cotter a half mile back. Cotter tied his horse to a rail at the side of the house entrance. He smiled as he saw the two small heads peeking out the window. He raised his fist to knock on the door when it suddenly opened.

Josh and Mary were all smiles and giggles. Mary ran into the house shouting, "Mommy, Mommy, Jake's here. Jake's here."

Josh just looked up at him. "Hi Jake."

"Hi Josh."

From within came Rand's melodious, "Come on in Jake."

Cotter had never felt more welcome in any place than just now. He followed Josh into the dining room where dishes and bowls of steaming food sent out their own olfactory invitations. The children began an argument of who was to sit next to Jake.

"Jake will sit opposite me and next to Josh. Mary, sit next to me over here, please." She pointed to the seat next to her.

"Chicken, eggs, greens and bread–I'm starved." Cotter said as he looked at Josh. "Aren't you?"

"Jake, mom said we can call you 'Jake' but we have to call you 'Dr. Jake' at work. How come?" Josh passed the bread after taking a sizable piece.

"Because it's just the way we do things, that's how come." Rand scanned them all with her response.

"The food is terrific and the company's even better," Cotter said midway through the meal. Cotter had talked about school and their lessons between mouthfuls at the start of the meal but now was the time to focus on their relationship. "When I was a child, my mom was sick and we never did anything but my dad would take me fishing and hunting or just go out riding. What do you kids do when you're done with chores and schoolwork?" It was a risky question designed to address their absent father figure.

"Sometimes we play with other kids, mostly at church or at school. We never knew our dad." Mary said.

Cotter nodded. There was no remorse. It was a true statement. They were both too young when their father was alive.

Rand knew what he was doing and kept silent.

"So, I think we should organize a day to go riding and have a picnic and when the spring comes we can go fishing. First, let's hear what mom has to say about this."

"Does that mean I'm invited?" It was a question for all.

"Yes," Jake and Josh responded.

"No." Mary said.

"Mary, I'm talking about family things. Aren't you a member of this family?" Rand raised a concerned parental eyebrow.

"Yes. I guess so. Okay mom, you can come."

"Well, thank you everyone." Rand bowed to the consensus.

Desert was a huge apple pie with coffee for Jake and Rand and milk for the children.

"Anyone have homework to look at?" Rand looked at Jake.

"No. It's the weekend. We never get homework on the weekend."

"Then go sit by the fire and Jake will tell us a story about New Haven, Connecticut after we clear the dishes."

"How'd I get roped into this job?" Jake dried the dishes after Rand washed.

"It seemed like a natural part of the evening to me." Rand flashed a warm smile.

"This whole evening seems natural but it's the first time I've ever done this."

"So, what's with the fishing and riding thing?"

"It's better than reading medical journals and, for me, it's certainly better than doing those things by myself."

"I agree with your answer, Jacob Cotter." They were done and she pulled the bow on his apron and pointed to the living room. "It's story time."

"Tell us about New Heaven, Kunnettykit," Mary shouted. Josh and Mary were sitting on cushions near the fireplace facing the sofa.

"It's New Haven, Connecticut. Well for one, it's a bigger city and we have many buildings made of stone and brick and some have four floors. We also have factories." Cotter went on to explain what a factory was, how the streets were maintained and told about the police department.

Rand sighed. "A police department for Endura would be nice but it wouldn't happen even with becoming a city."

"No, but the state would have to take an interest and stop the likes of Vlack and his hired guns."

"We need a David and Goliath." Mary shouted.

"We have Goliath. We need someone like David from the Bible." Rand said.

"Maybe Mortimer Pignast is our David." Cotter looked at them.

"Who's a nasty pig?" Josh looked at his sister.

"It's Pig-nast, Mr. Mortimer Pignast works at our clinic and hospital. He's also a very wise man who might become a Representative from Endura to the Governor of Texas and maybe even Washington." Cotter hoped this would help. It didn't.

"Let me try to explain it. Mr. Pignast wants to be elected by the people in Endura so the leaders in the capital of Texas can help us fight against bad and evil." Rand saw some comprehension seep in.

"Doesn't he need a sling or a gun?"

"No, just words. In school they teach you how to use the right words to say the right thing. We need someone like Mr. Pignast to tell the right people in the capital that Mr. Vlack is evil." Cotter saw he was gaining credence. "And then the capital people send in good guys who may have to use guns–like the Texas Rangers."

"Yay." Both children clapped.

Cotter talked of the Serenity Winery and his friends back in New Haven. He talked about medical school and the importance of schooling. Rand picked up on this.

"Now, I know there's no school tomorrow but you still need sleep, so get to bed. Jake and I will talk about going for a ride soon."

Josh and Mary scurried to their rooms. Rand turned to Cotter. "You go with Josh and I'll go with Mary. We have to hear their prayers."

Cotter went with Josh and listened to the boy bless everything from the horses to the man called "nasty pig". Finally Josh ended with, "Please God let Jake be my daddy." He turned, flung his arms around Cotter and hugged him. When he was tucked in, Cotter kissed him on the forehead. "Josh, sometimes a town like Endura needs two Davids to fight all the Goliaths. I wouldn't be surprised if Mr. Pignast has help. Good night." Josh went to sleep immediately.

Rand listened to a similar listing of blessings unaware of Cotter's silent presence in the doorway. Mary ended with, "Please God let mommy and Jake love each other and maybe even make him into a daddy."

Rand smiled and kissed her 10-year-old on the cheek. "Good night." She stood up and went to the doorway and bumped right into Cotter.

She almost fell and Cotter held her up, facing her with his arms under her shoulders. Cotter felt his legs turn to wet straw. His pulse was racing. Rand locked her eyes on his. He pulled her closer. The embrace was fused with a soft touching of lips. Cotter had never felt lips so warm or so soft. The pressure of their kiss increased as they adjusted their breathing with closed eyes. Rand's essence of lavender added to the mellow moment. For a second he wondered if his odor was any more than the plain soap he washed with at the Garrisons. They finished the kiss and Rand laid her head on his shoulder.

"Josh asked God for me to be his daddy."

Rand looked up into Cotter's eyes again. "Mary asked for the same thing."

"I know what Mary asked for. I was standing here."

Rand stared glassy-eyed. "Did you hear her last prayer?"

"Right now, Mary has the first part of that prayer answered–from my side anyway."

They hadn't let go of each other. "Are you sure Jake? Are you really sure, because I am. I've known for the last two-months."

"I'm sure."

They walked arm-in-arm to the front door entryway. "I'll come by tomorrow and we can talk. Maybe we can all take a ride if it's not too cold." Cotter put on his coat and opened the door. The full moon outlined them as dark silhouettes. They embraced and finished with another long kiss.

●

"Well, well, well," Boda said to his horse. "Our boss is gonna love this." Boda headed back to Vlack's ranch. "It was worth the long wait in the cold."

# Chapter 42

## Pole Dancing

The only activity open to the public on Friday night in town were the saloons with their gambling, drinking and paid womanizing. Joe Conner had to go to town and get two of his men back to the ranch for an early morning hay baling. It would be the last hay harvest for the year. Christmas was only three-weeks away. Two of Conner's farmhands were due back from town. Clement Downs, his muscular baler and foreman of his six hired men, always liked to stop in one of the saloons, usually the Cactus Spine, for a beer or two. It was almost midnight and he and the other man hadn't returned. Joe made a decision to go to town to get them.

"Clem talked about going to Nellie's Leggs to see that new pole dancin' goin' on down there. I wish we'd hired married men so they'd stay away from those dancin' girl places." Conner's wife had her hands on her hips.

"Nellie's Leggs, huh. I warned the men about going there. It's where the cow punchers go. There could be trouble–his being late."

"Maybe you should stay home. Remember the Rhodes man. I'm sure he goes there and we still think he killed our plowman."

"Clem probably got too much beer. I'll just collect him and the other one and bring them home, that's all."

●

With Cotter on board, the rotation to cover the hospital patients was easier. Garrison, Wills and Cotter worked every third night. The need to stay in the hospital was mandated by someone required to tend to the patients. When they first opened the clinic and hospital, they often went days without anyone needing hospitalization. In the past year, however, there was always at least one patient and lately it seemed like two was the rule. According to their current list, Wills estimated five women were due to go into labor this December and hence arrive at the hospital at any time. The nurses did not have to stay at night and never alone, of course. They worked an on-call schedule. If a nurse was needed and she was on-call, the doctor would send a runner, usually the deputy marshal, to summon and accompany her. For Sadie Rand, it meant waking up the children and bringing them to the Garrisons. The other two nurses, Zenia Lord and Hessie Blinger, were single and lived closer to the center of town.

Wills looked at his watch and decided after his ten o'clock check on the man with the fractured hip and the boy recovering from asthma and bronchitis, he would turn in. *Thank God that boxer is no longer with us. I should get some sleep tonight.*

As he rested his head on the pillow of the hospital bed, he thought he could hear the piano music, laughter and applause coming from Nellie's Leggs. He remembered when the saloon was first opened. Ten-years ago it was just called the "Leggs Saloon" after its owner, Daniel Leggs. Then Daniel Leggs married Nellie Juggnutz. Daniel's first thought was to add Nellie's last name to the Saloon but the "Juggnutz Leggs Saloon" might not sound much like an attractant to the local patrons. He opted for "Nellie" instead which his bride agreed with, and her name was added. Victor Vlack bought the place after Leggs died from tuberculosis and his wife Nellie moved back to Arizona. The sounds of the night brought him back from his reverie. He could definitely hear cheers. One of these days he was going to check out what this 'pole dancing' was–if his wife Miranda let him.

The cheers were, of course, for the ladies as they removed an article of clothing and swung a leg-extended-arc around one of the poles. Christie Wooly's routine was a hit and the boozy patrons climbed over each other to catch the tossed garments. The man who caught a shirt, garter, stocking or skirt would get a free drink upon its surrender. The burley bouncer would then retrieve the clothes. A knuckled fist to the head of any reluctant patron guaranteed the strippers' garments return for the next show. There were three shows a night beginning at seven o'clock. Boda and Rhodes were regular patrons but their main mission was to help keep the peace and perhaps intimidate the occasional farmhand.

Rhodes was eyeing Clement Downs who had imbibed too many beers by ten o'clock. His friend was urging Clem to leave with him but Downs was immovable. Rhodes decided to push their buttons. They were from the Conner spread and he remembered them pointing rifles at him and his men a few weeks back. He turned to Boda.

"Back me up. Watch the second guy. I'm goin' after Clem. They're both wearin' guns so we might get lucky and get them to draw on us."

"Whooeee!" Clem Downs raised his beer glass in salute to Christie as she threw her vest to the audience. The piano player watched her intently to time his music to her moves.

Rhodes moved next to him and then rammed his shoulder into Clem's back. "Watch where ya goin' fat boy." Rhodes watched Clem's beer glass shatter on the floor splattering the pant legs of two seated card players.

"Hey. You made me drop my beer." Clem staggered a little from his alcoholic instability. "You owe me a beer. And who you callin' fat. You're as big as me." Clem made an attempt at pushing Rhodes but stumbled and bounced against the bar.

"You insultin' me? Look at you. You're a drunkin' slob." Rhodes knocked Clem's hat to the floor and stepped on it.

"Pick up my hat." Clem was shouting to be heard over the dance audience and the piano.

"Clem, stay calm. Easy does it. Let's go home." Conner's second man tried to coax Clem away.

"I say pick up my hat. Don't let me force ya."

"How ya goin'ta force me you pig farmer." Rhodes pushed him on the chest with his palm.

The piano player stopped. Ten card players and the men at the nearby three tables got up and headed out the door.

"Clem. Don't. Let me take you outta here. C'mon...."
The second man hit the floor unconscious from Boda's pistol whack to the head.

"Whaddya do that fer. He's my friend. You're packin' a gun and you better go fer it." Clem reached for his pistol but Rhodes was faster–much faster.

The entire saloon was silent. Rhodes had his gun pointed at Clem. Clem still had his hand on the grip of his weapon which still hadn't cleared the holster. The few seconds seemed like minutes and then Rhodes pulled the trigger. A red starburst the size of a dollar-piece blossomed on Clem's chest and a larger one came out two-inches from near his spine. Clem went down to the floor like a boulder dropped from a cliff. He fell beside his fallen farmhand friend. Blood began pouring from the entry and exit wounds. Finally, Clem's mouth trickled blood, his body twitched twice and he was dead.

Mona Herring ran over and knelt down. "Get this one to the Doctor's Clinic. The other one's dead. You..." She pointed to a patron "...go get the deputy marshal."

●

Wills examined the farmhand. The pupils were okay and no blood was coming from the ears. He opened a spirits-of-ammonia vial and the man emerged to consciousness coughing and sputtering.

"What happened? Oh, my head hurts real bad." He lay back down on the stretcher.

"You got hit on the head with a gun butt. I want you to stay the rest of the night. Where are you from?"

"The Conner's' place. Oh my head." The man turned his head to the side and vomited on the floor.

The door to the emergency entrance burst open and Joe Conner ran in. "What happened? Mell, are you all right?"

"Oh, my achin' head." He looked at his boss. "I'm sorry about this Joe. Is Clem okay."

"Clement Downs is dead, I'm afraid. I was told he drew on Parkland Rhodes." Wills placed a towel over the vomitus.

"Rhodes?" Joe Conner reddened. "That man threatened me a week or so ago. I think he killed my plow boy."

"I was told it was a fair fight with Clem even though Rhodes provoked it." Wills picked up the soiled towel and threw it in a dirty linen bucket.

"A fight about what?" Conner looked at the man called Mell.

"He bumped against Clem, knocked his beer glass to the floor and called him a fat slob." Mell held a cold towel to his head.

"That's why he was killed?"

"Clem was drunk."

Conner sat down and put his head in his hands. "Two of my hands killed within two-weeks. And by Rhodes. What can we do Dr. Wills?"

"If witnesses say Clem drew first then there's nothing we can do Joe. Come back tomorrow afternoon. Mell should be okay by then."

Wills left Mell with Garrison who replaced him for the Saturday hospital coverage. "Stan, can you go by my house and tell Jake what happened. I think Victor Vlack is getting more aggressive and he should know about it."

# Chapter 43

## Parkland Rhodes

"Rhodes." Cotter paced once and looked at Wills. "What do we know about this man Rhodes?"

"I asked around when he first came to town. He's apparently a bounty hunter and hired gun who Boda knew from the war."

"From the war?"

"Yes, Jake. They rode together in a marauder outfit. Nothing but pillagers and looters from what I heard."

Cotter sat down staring at the ground.

"Is there something wrong?"

"No. No. It's terrible that men are dying at Vlack's initiative." Cotter looked up at his colleague. "Thanks for the information. Tell Charlie I'll relieve him tomorrow morning."

Cotter watched Wills go out the door and then had a thought. He ran after him.

"Stan. Do me a big favor. Can you drop by the Rands and tell Sadie I won't be by to go riding until just before noon.

Cotter remembered that most of Vlack's men who frequented Nellie's Leggs stayed in town over night in the upstairs rooms. Rhodes would roust them out in the morning and send them back to the Vlack ranch for breakfast. Rhodes always ate his breakfast in town and came back around midmorning. Cotter went into the kitchen for a second cup of coffee.

"Deirdre, I'm going to exercise my palomino before going on a picnic with the Rands. I'll be back in about two-hours."

"Picnic, huh." She smiled a knowing smile. "How'd dinner with the Rands go last night?"

Cotter blushed. "Very well, thank you. I mean… we had a good visit. I…er… told the kids some stories and …er… today we're going on a picnic. I mean… before the weather gets too… cold."

"Too cold, huh. Let me ask you this. Did you help with the dishes?"

"Er...so what. Doesn't Charlie help you with the dishes?"

"Not since we got married. Watch out Jake." She laughed. "Actually Jake, she's a wonderful woman and you already know her children are jewels."

"I'll be back in two-hours." He stumbled over the door stoop. *God, what's happened to me? I have to concentrate on Rhodes.*

Cotter dressed in his buckskins and belted on the Colts. He wiped the excess oil from both guns. They were smooth and he drew them effortlessly returning them into the holster with a circular spin with his trigger fingers. He put on his duster and saddled the palomino.

He started with a casual lope and then picked up the gait to a fast gallop finally slowing down as he came to a small bunch of trees interspersed with thickets of inter-looping bush. He had scoped out possible places of ambush during his weekly home visit excursions the past few weeks. This spot provided good concealment as the bushes still had dense green leaves and many were taller than a man mounted on a horse.

Forty-minutes went by before he spotted a telltale dust ball in the distance. He pulled the monocular telescope from his saddlebag. It was a single rider at a casual gallop in no particular hurry. Cotter took off his duster and tied his horse to the copse of brush about a 100-foot from the road. He walked behind the cover of the trees a good distance from the horse.

Rhodes always felt refreshed after a confrontation in which he used his fists or especially, his gun. He scanned the sides of the road and the horizon as he always did ever since his army days. His company Sergeant had given the same advice daily. "First look to the right and then the left side of the road. Look at the wind and see if there is movement going against the expected wind flow or if there is wind resistance. Take in the horizon for human shapes or moving objects like wagons or animals."

"Whoa." Rhodes slowed his horse. There was something about a mile ahead. A horse, a tan horse was tied to the bushes to his left. He approached cautiously. It was a palomino. Boda had told everyone the masked buckskin bastard rode a palomino. Obviously this wasn't an ambush since the horse was in plain sight. He looked for its rider.

Cotter watched as Rhodes slowed his mount. The sun had warmed up the previously cold morning air and he felt comfortable.

Rhodes stopped at the side of the road and stared at Cotter's palomino. He dismounted and walked his horse over to Cotter's and tied his animal next to him. He patted the palomino's haunches.

"Easy there, fella. That's a good boy. Where's your rider?" He looked at the saddle bags and brought his hands up to open the one on the left when he froze at the sound of the penetrating voice.

"Parkland Rhodes." Cotter shot the words at him like arrows. "Keep your hands in the air and turn around slow."

Rhodes kept his gloved palms in plain view as he turned clockwise to the voice's owner. Rhodes smiled when he saw the tall masked buckskin form. Cotter was 20-yards away.

"Keep moving to your left away from the horses." Cotter had both guns pointed at Rhodes. He kept Rhodes moving until the sun was slightly to his right. The conchos would catch the light.

"What do ya want with me? I don't have much money. You want my horse? Are you a horse thief as well as a coward who shoots up furniture?"

"You and Boda killed my father."

"Your….I don't even know you or your father, but if you give me a chance for a fair fight, I guarantee you a better challenge than a desk."

"I'll play by your rules but first you should know who my father was."

"I don't care who your father was. I've been hired to deliver you to Victor Vlack–dead."

"I think you should know who I am."

"Oh I think I know who you are. I remember after the war there was a bounty hunter like you going around plyin' his trade in Texas, Arizona and even up in Wyoming. Am I right?"

"Maybe." Cotter held both guns aimed at the man's chest.

"Except, I never heard you had to wear a mask. There's only the two of us here, you can uncover now or after I kill you– that is, if you give me a chance at a fair fight."

Cotter spun his Colts back into the holsters. He reached up to his face and pulled his bandanna down.

"You." Rhodes was stunned.

"I was a surgical assistant in the war with my father. You and Boda killed him and two other doctors."

Rhodes tried to recover his shock. He forced a grin. "Yeah, we killed a lot of the hospital bluecoats. And now you're goin' to give me a chance to kill another Yankee doctor. Well, that's what I do best." Rhodes lowered his hands to his side and flexed the fingers of right gun hand. "Ya want to call a count or just go for it?"

"If you don't go for your gun, I'll shoot you down where you stand." Cotter's piercing tone was felt as well as heard.

Rhodes recoiled and shifted his shoulders. "Okay, anytime you're ready." Rhodes slapped his hand to his pistol and drew two-seconds after his last word.

Cotter's two guns exploded at the same time sending a .45 caliber bullet into each of Rhodes's shoulders. Rhodes was thrown back against a tree preventing him from falling. Cotter walked toward him. Rhode's gun fell to the ground.

"There's something more you should know before you die. I know you murdered Conner's farmhands and I would have come after you just for that."

Rhodes dropped to the ground and grabbed his pistol wincing with the pain from his bleeding shoulder muscles. He tried to aim his gun.

Cotter shot him in both legs. "I want you to know, I would have come for you just for bringing in that killer boxer."

Rhodes grimaced. His pain experience was excruciating. He spoke in short gasps. "I got something for you.... Boda and Vlack are going to take...your woman away... from you. Boda told me he saw you two...last night. Vlack wants her and the kids...for 'political...window dressing'... he says. Just so you know... if I had it to do over again, I would still kill...all you fuckin' Yankee doctors."

Cotter's Colts roared again and two bullets entered Rhodes breastbone side-by-side. Cotter dragged Rhodes' carcass and draped him over Rhodes' saddle. He mounted his palomino and rode to Vlack's ranch, stopping on a rise one-mile away. The smoke from the fireplaces of the main house and the bunkhouse rose straight up in the absence of any wind. He tore off a concho from his shirt and wedged it into the right glove still on Rhode's hand and slapped Rhode's horse sending him away on a fast gallop. Cotter turned and rode his palomino back to the Garrison's

●

Boda delighted in telling Vlack about the confrontation and the outcome with Conner's farmhands.

"Good. Good." Vlack blew cigar smoke toward the ceiling. "What about the barber who tells fortunes and works at the Doctor's Clinic? Rhodes tells me he aspires to political office."

"He's some of kind of a head doctor that can tell about people by feeling their skull. I can't pronounce the name of what he does. In the doctors' place, he puts the ether on your face to knock you out for the surgery." Boda lit the cigar that Vlack had given him. "About running for office–I only know the rumors from around town. The guy talks good, like you, about the town and what he can do for it."

"Rhodes had his hair cut by him and pushed him for information. Apparently he could be my opponent next year. Maybe I should change barbers and see what he's like."

"I don't know about that. I do know something about that nurse, the one with the kids you talked about."

"Sadie Rand and the little ones? Yes. What's going on with her?"

"I followed the new doctor, Cotter, on Friday. He had dinner with them."

"Dinner? He's the one that drives her to the Garrisons and goes to church with them?"

"Yeah, the one who fixed you up with the splinter thing."

"So, what about Friday night?"

"He gave her a passionate kiss when he left."

Vlack stood up. "What? Are you telling me she's soft on him?"

"Looked like they both didn't want to let go."

Vlack walked around the room once, puffing on his black cigar. Blue-white smoke swirled around him as he returned to his chair at his new desk. "This town got along fine with two doctors and it can do so again. Rhodes told me Cotter carried a shotgun when he went out to visit a few homes."

"Word is he's shy about guns and violence." Boda tapped some cigar ash into a small tray.

"And he goes to church with the Rands." Vlack rubbed his stubbled chin. "Maybe this Cotter can meet with an accident and I can come to the rescue of the Rand family. What do you think?"

"Anything you say boss."

"Good." Vlack pushed himself away from the desk and tilted his chair back. "You and Rhodes engineer an accident for Dr. Jacob Cotter."

A sudden loud pounding on the front door accompanied by loud shouts from his male cook, Rhumy, almost caused Vlack to fall over in his chair.

"What the Christ?" Vlack sat upright and then he and Boda went to the door.

"Mister Vlack, Mister Boda, the horse he come running with Mr. Rhodes laying over the saddle.

"Goddamn," Vlack said. He looked at the body with blood dripping to the ground from the upper and lower torso. "Get some men to lay him out on a buckboard."

When the body was laid out with Rhodes blink-less stare to the sky, Rhumy vomited as Boda examined the wounds. "He was shot six times." Boda probed the entry wounds. "He got it in the shoulders and legs first–see how much blood clotted there. If he got shot in the chest first the other holes wouldn't have bled much."

"Do we know who did this?" Vlack had a terrible feeling that he knew Rhodes' executioner.

Boda continued to examine the body and then stood up on back of the buckboard. He held up the shiny silver concho. "The man who did this jammed this concho inside Rhodes' glove." Boda checked Rhodes' boots. "Wait there's a note."

Cotter had written his previous prophetic words for Vlack. "If you or any of your men harm any Endura citizen they will answer to me."

## Chapter 44

## December 1870

Cotter changed and washed off the sweat of mortal combat using the pitcher and basin in his room. He had to hand wash and dry his buckskins himself but that could wait for another day. He was on his way with his buckboard heading to the Rands' home. Living with the Garrison's had some drawbacks. His personal space only consisted of his room. Fortunately, Charlie Garrison had a huge barn which accommodated the buggy and buckboard he bought in Endura and his horse he had brought from New Haven. Cotter had since purchased the roan horse from Garrison. He paid for the care and feeding of his horses and offered to pay rent for his room but the Garrisons refused. They did accept him paying something for his breakfast and dinner on a monthly basis.

"Jake, your being here has given me my husband back every third night. We're even planning to start a family." Deirdre's words were full of sincere gratitude.

For someone self-sufficient like Cotter, living like this was difficult but currently necessary. Endura wasn't like New Haven and its suburbs with available housing and even available farms to be bought like the Clark's old winery.

It was a few minutes past eleven when Cotter arrived at the Rands. The children must have been waiting because they were outside waving to him.

"C'mon in. They saw your dust from the trail." Rand was dressed in denim pants and a heavy wool shirt. She stared at him for a few seconds remembering Friday night.

Cotter didn't hesitate. He gently held both her shoulders and kissed her quickly and lightly on the lips.

The children stared with opened mouths. "Yay." Mary went up to Cotter and hugged his leg.

"Okay. Let's go on the picnic." Josh was eager to leave.

They packed Cotter's buckboard and climbed in. Josh and Mary were sitting with the food basket and blanket and immediately began nudging each other for the best position.

"You kids behave." Her feet felt the shotgun. "Have you ever fired this shotgun?"

"Of course, I tested it out in Connecticut when I first bought it. I wanted to make sure it worked. I pointed it to the sky, closed my eyes and pulled the trigger. It works." He smiled at her.

"Did you ever shoot a gun during the war?"

"No, I helped my dad–he was a surgeon and I assisted him. He was killed right in front of me at Nashville." The overhead sun blinded him for a second. A sudden picture came into his head–a smoky vision of a rider shooting his father and then holstering his gun. For a second, noise, smoke and silhouettes flashed against a brightly moonlit night. The holster, there was something about the holster that was different than Rhodes's snake-adorned one. He shook his head back to the present.

"That's sad. My father died from a stroke a few years before I married. The children never knew a grandfather."

"Let's talk about the present and the future." Cotter flipped the reins and increased the speed of the wagon.

"Okay. What's next with us, Jake?" She looped her left arm around his.

Cotter had both hands on the reins and accepted her touch and warmth by slightly leaning against her.

"Well, Christmas is coming?"

"Yes, it is."

"We should talk about what the kids want."

"They want what I want."

"Which is what?"

"You."

●

The death of Parkland Rhodes caused two of Vlack's men to quit. The morale was one of less confidence. Everyone, including Victor Vlack, felt a new sense of their own mortality.

Two-weeks went by and the aura of gloom was still prevalent. Vlack paced around his study. Rhumy walked in.

"Do you want anything before I go into town for cooking supplies, Mr. Vlack?"

"No, your wife can get me lunch as usual." Vlack had to do something about the buckskin gunfighter–that Vigilante. He walked to the fireplace and placed two more log halves on the already blazing fire. The weather had gotten colder. Boda knocked on the front door and came in.

"Another one of the men Rhodes brought with him quit this morning. What are we gonna do boss?"

"Timing's important." Vlack rubbed his chin and sat at his desk. "After Christmas, we step up our barbed wire policing. I also have to increase my presence for my campaign for the Representative spot in Austin."

"What's the plan?"

"I need to find out more about this Pignast person." He paused and tapped the back of his pen on the desktop. "And I need the Rand family with me. We have to get Doctor Cotter out of the way by April."

"I'll need to replace the men that Rhodes signed on."

"Do it. And find that prick Vigilante. I made a list of everything he's done to us. Listen up." Vlack read from the sheet of paper. "He interfered with the stage hold-up; he shot up my desk and threatened to kill me; he killed the boxer, and he killed Rhodes." Vlack stood up and threw the paper onto his desk. "Who the fuck does he think he is? Who the hell is he?"

●

It was a sunny, crisp Christmas day at the Rands. The Pignasts, Garrisons and the Wills had gone home after the fulfilling evening exchanging presents. Cotter had given everyone a case of Serenity wine courtesy of his friends in Connecticut. All had delighted at seeing the two children with their new game, books and toys. Cotter mildly objected at Josh's toy rifle but the boy went around claiming he was David looking for Goliath.

Cotter was ambivalent about his own duality. He was above all else in his mind, a Doctor–a person who healed and saved lives. And yet he was a ruthless avenger. A police force was not the answer in society as everyone knew it. New Haven was a good example of that. He and his own people had to take charge to exact justice and defend themselves.

The house was quiet after the children went to bed. Rand and Cotter sat on the sofa watching the fire. A residue aroma of cooked chicken, baked cake and apple pie added to the secure pine odor of the fireplace's glowing logs.

"Thanks for being here Jake. You were the best present for me and the children."

"Where else would I be on Christmas Day?" He placed his arm around her shoulder, turned and kissed her. "Oh, I forgot, I have a special present for you?"

Rand looked at him. "We agreed there would be no gifts between us this Christmas."

Cotter ignored her. He produced a small box wrapped in gold-toned paper with a narrow red ribbon around it. "Open it."

Rand undid the ribbon slowly from the tiny box. She removed the lid and fell back against his shoulder. "Oh, Jake." She held the diamond engagement ring up against the light.

"I had it sent from New Haven." Jake remembered Mrs. Hamer's words when he told her about bringing Pamela Skyler's engagement ring back to the store. *Wait, Jake, someone more disserving will surely come along.* She was right.

Their embrace and kiss seemed to go on forever. Finally, Rand stopped and stood up. "Jake, you don't have to go home tonight."

"What would Deirdre and Miranda say or think?"

"Nothing, when they see this." She smiled like a teenager and did a turn around spin falling in his arms.

Jake made love to her tenderly and slowly. They lay comfortably in each other's arms. Rand traced the outline of Cotter's right shoulder with her fingertips.

"What's this?" She pressed the jagged scar. "And this?" She found the scar on his right side.

"Just scars from a previous life–the trauma of growing up."

They laughed and made love again.

# Chapter 45

## Mortimer Pignast

Fern Pignast, as well as her husband, distributed the circulars touting Mortimer Pignast as the people of Endura's best choice for elected Representative for their town. The only other candidate was Victor Vlack. Vlack advertised in the newspaper and presented his slate of ideas which were pro-cattlemen, barbed wire and against Endura becoming "too big". Vlack wrote about the bad effects of becoming a city such as having the state tell Endura citizens what to do. Pignast's document extolled the opposite–that cattlemen and agriculture citizens have equal rights which includes letting water go where God had intended. "Let there be no dams on God's streams," Pignast's flyer proclaimed. The election in the fall would decide the winner.

Fern handed a circular to each of her customers, as did Mortimer to his barbershop patrons. Pignast also brought the paper sheets to the Doctors Clinic where they were handed out in the waiting room.

With the holidays behind them, the surgical schedule became active again. Cuts, bruises and abscesses were the main pathologies but fractures, hernias and deliveries added to the three mornings-a-week operating agenda. Wills, Garrison and Cotter alternated in manning the office on surgery days. The person on call became the primary surgeon for emergencies. One worked the office practice while the other two assisted each other in the operating room. The only person working extra hours was Mortimer Pignast. He became the ether anesthesia administrator for all procedures, including labor and delivery. Plus he was on call every day, a fact that didn't bother him too much since he lived next door over the barbershop and hair salon.

Pignast was washing his hands, followed by a carbolic solution rinse. He did this between every patient. He even did this in his barbershop. Running his hands through soiled hair for his Phrenology readings gave him visions of invisible bugs swarming over his hands.

"Mort, how do you feel now that Rhodes is no longer a threat?" Cotter dried his hands on a clean towel.

"The threat has always been Victor Vlack. Rhodes will be replaced, I'm sure, by another gunslinger." Pignast picked up a bottle of ether. "Be careful Jake. Boda has everyone looking for the 'man in buckskin with the two guns and palomino horse'."

"Just let me know what's going on around town. You're the one to be careful being Vlack's direct opposition in the election."

"Fern and I are taking our campaign outdoors. I'll be speaking on the new bandstand next month."

"Be careful."

"We're going to go in the saloons too, Jake."

"Mort! You're inviting disaster."

"Fern and I are planting our roots in this town. We're doing well and it's only under a year. The people like us. The Doctors Clinic is thriving. Life is all about risks, Jake."

"Promise me you'll keep me informed about what you're doing?"

"Certainly. By the way, congratulations with Sadie. I don't think there's much risk with that decision. You're a lucky man Jake."

Cotter smiled. He really liked this man. "Get in there and get the patient ready. He has a hunk of wood wedged in his thigh and it's infected. I need him deep enough to cut out some muscle around the whole area."

"I know my job, Doctor."

"You certainly do."

●

The first week of February brought the first snow. There were many cold days but snow didn't come to Endura until now. The tiny bell on the door of the barbershop tinkled as the two tall men entered. They stamped their feet on the burlap doormat to get most of the snow and mud off and finished the job on the bristled bootjack.

"Good afternoon, Mr. Pignast. We finally meet. I'm here today both as a customer and as a worthy opponent."

Pignast accepted Vlack's handshake but ignored Boda's offered greeting.

"Haircut and shave, Mr. Vlack?"

"Of course."

Pignast seated and draped the half-sheet around Vlack and began cutting his hair. "I also offer a phrenology analysis at no extra charge."

"What exactly is this 'phrenology'?" Vlack shifted slightly in the seat. He looked in the mirror to make sure Boda was vigilant as his bodyguard.

"It is the science of relating the rounded protuberances on the skull to the brain segments underneath. There are direct correlations between the geography of a person's skull to their personality characteristics and aptitudes for success and failure." Pignast began trimming the beard.

"Do you tell the future with this phrenology?"

"No, sir. This is not a Gypsy ruse. One can only imply outcomes by virtue of a man's aptitude. For example, a person with prominent frontal lobes will always be uncaring, indifferent and without many friends."

"How are my 'frontal lobes'?"

"Slightly protuberant, sir."

Vlack shifted uneasily. "I have many friends and look at how much I care about this town. I've even contributed to the expansion of your Doctor's Clinic."

"That comes under the category of buying favors and purchasing public opinion, my good man." Pignast finished his trimming.

"What have you done to further the public notion that you could succeed in politics, Mr. Pignast?"

"I happen to excel in positive public relations. You will get a chance to see me later when I take my platform to the people." He handed Vlack a "Pignast for State Representative" circular.

"Who printed these for you?"

"I paid for these myself at the newspaper office."

"Do you think public speaking is going to make a difference? I've made personal contributions for the betterment of this town. You have done nothing."

"It is what I can do as Representative that will count. I have no financial self-interests which is what the public will vote for."

Pignast removed the sheet after brushing the fallen hair and opened the cash box. "That will be fifty-cents, please."

"What about my phrenology reading?"

Pignast accepted the money and faced Vlack and Boda. "Your cranial anatomy demonstrates that you are a self-centered individual who puts himself ahead of the welfare of others."

"What the hell does that mean?" Boda spoke for the first time.

"It means that Mr. Vlack is for Mr. Vlack and for no one else."

Vlack put on his coat and gloves. "Are those going to be your words to the public, Mr. Pignast?"

"Yes but not as a result of your phrenological anatomy, Mr. Vlack. It's a result of your actions with barbed wire, depriving people of water and lying about the benefits of being a city with state-guaranteed law enforcement, road development and establishing a civil court with a circuit judge."

"We shall see, Mr. Pignast." Vlack and Boda left slamming the door as they went out.

Pignast sat down in the barber chair and let out a sigh of relief. His pulse was racing. He had faced his enemy and laid his cards on the table. He had to tell Fern of the possible dangers. He had to tell Jake.

Outside Vlack and Boda climbed aboard the canopied buggy. The snow was blowing up from the ground with the wind adding to the bite of the cold.

"What do ya want us to do with him, boss?"

"First, go talk to the newspaper. There will be no more printing jobs for Pignast. Next thing you have to do is hire more people and get a mob together every time Pignast speaks."

"Why not just arrange another accident or just set him up to get shot like we did with the Rand lawyer way back when?"

"Let's see how we make out without arranging an 'accident'. You're forgetting the Vigilante. If we could get rid of his concho-hero image, it would make me look like the better candidate."

"It would be easier to just kill Pignast, boss."

"It may just come to that Ken. It may just come to that."

# Chapter 46

# Campaign

"We can't keep the people from going to the town hall to hear him." Boda sat in a chair watching Vlack light another cigar at his desk.

"Don't tell me what we can't do. We can do several things. We can stop Pignast from speaking or we can muddle his speech and deal with him right after everyone leaves." Vlack was red-faced partially from anger and partially from his fourth glass of wine for the afternoon.

"I have five new hires ready to shout and boo at the mere mention of anything that don't go along with your plans." Boda stood up after his rebuke from Vlack.

"I've written down what I want shouted when Pignast talks about the benefits of the state. And here are the ones they yell when he talks against barbed wire." Vlack handed the sheets of paper to Boda. He knew Boda had trouble reading but he could do it albeit slow. "Can your men read?"

"Some can. I'll go over it with 'em." Boda read each page slowly out loud.

"Good. Now, about after the meeting, I want Pignast to get hurt and preferably in front of some of the people. Make it happen after most of them leave. Does Pignast wear a gun?"

"He carries a small pistol in a shoulder holster."

"Good. Make him use it, but don't kill him. I've told Marshall Oliver to be the first one out the door before the incident happens. I don't want him in an awkward position to have to work against us. He can come back in later, after Pignast takes a bullet."

"What about the Vigilante?" Boda rested his hand on his holster.

"You think that buckskin asshole is going to show up in public with his bandana covering his face and be part of the crowd? I doubt it." Vlack sipped his wine. "But that's a good thought, Ken. I wouldn't put it past him to be waiting outside somewhere. Make sure you have extra men around."

"Okay, boss."

•

"You really have the right words, Mort." Cotter commented as Pignast delivered some key statements to his medical colleagues.

"Do you want us to be up front with you?" Wills had helped Pignast prepare his primary points. "I was going to run for election on many of the same issues. The people will add our presence as an endorsement. I would be honored to introduce you."

"Good idea. I appreciate it Stan. You all can be up front."

"Well, I'd like to kinda be in back since I have the clinic coverage. It would look funny if I had to leave and everyone saw me run out during one of your key points," Cotter added.

"Yes, you're right Jake. Fern will be seated near the podium. It'll be good for the women to push their men into action. I actually have a small part for her to say."

"Good thinking, Mortimer." Rand spoke up. "I've already talked to some of the women who'll be there and we'll give a shout in agreement when she speaks."

"I didn't know that women will be attending." Cotter looked at Rand.

"I'm bringing the children too. I want them to see what they learn in school actually happens–Democracy in action."

"Good idea." Cotter smiled at her.

"I've even sent a copy of my speech to President Grant and I so note in my address." Pignast puffed himself up.

"Okay, well we have two-hours until the meeting. I have to tend to our three patients in the hospital. The new mother and baby are doing well and they'll be going home just before I leave for the town hall." Cotter turned to Rand. "Sadie, can you go home with Charlie?"

"I planned to do just that and I'll be coming back for Mort's speech with Deirdre, Charles and the children."

•

The evening was dark and although the February air was cold, the town hall was filled to capacity. There was no central heating in the hall and everyone had their winter coats and gloves on. Fern, Wills and Pignast were seated on the stage-like platform waiting for the stragglers to be seated.

Two chandeliers provided enough light for the audience and the clean smell of melted wax overcame the cold musty odor of the little-used town hall. Pignast went to the podium and waved. A few people clapped which started the rest of the room to applaud. Pignast waved his hands downward to begin the proceedings.

"Many of you know me but all of you know Dr. Stanley Wills who will open our meeting tonight." Pignast stepped down and new applause welcomed Wills to the podium.

"Thank you all for coming to this important meeting of the Endura Township. Many of you know that as a responsible group in Endura, the Doctors Clinic has been for, and is a champion of, progress in our town. Twenty-years ago I was the only doctor in a small office where now we have three doctors, three nurses, an emergency room, a delivery room and our hospital. Twenty-years ago Endura became a town from its status as a small village. My duties here at the clinic preclude my availability to continue to represent Endura at the county and state level. However, my esteemed colleague, a very learned man, who works in many capacities, is my choice for leading Endura forward to becoming a full-fledged city…"

"We aren't ready to become a city–ask Victor Vlack," an unidentified cowhand shouted waving his hat.

Wills banged a mallet against an oak block on the podium to continue. "…Mortimer Pignast knows the people because he's 'of' the people. His scientific expertise gives him insight into people's behavior and his work at our clinic has acquainted him with the physical needs of the community. I give you Endura's best and only choice for Representative to the great state of Texas–Mortimer Pignast."

The thunderous applause did not allow the few hisses and boos from Boda's five dispersed men in the hall to be heard.

"Thank you Dr. Wills. As many of you know, a man can't really move ahead unless the home front is behind him. My wife Fern has spoken to a lot of the women in town, and I'm glad to see they are represented here tonight. Before I go any further, let me introduce my wife–Mrs. Fern Pignast."

Fern walked up to the podium and gave her husband a hug. As the applause died down, two hecklers shouted, "Women don't vote. She has nothing to say."

A volley of boos and hisses shut the two men up. Most were female voices.

"Well, I guess that proves you wrong whoever you are. I hope your wives aren't here–that could go bad for you." Fern smiled and her statement brought on laughs followed by applause. "Women stand by their men. Becoming a city is all about family. Families need security, the security of state-endorsed law enforcement, the security of nature's resources and the security of free expression. We…"

"We have a town marshal and deputies. We don't need outsiders running our town," another Vlack infiltrator shouted and tried to get others to shout with him. No one else responded.

Fern continued. "…We don't need our boundaries marked by barbed wire." Fern looked at her husband amidst the applause and returned to her seat.

A heckler shouted as the applause died down. "We need the fences to keep the farm animals away from the cattle." The man drew his pistol and fired in the air.

Immediate silence was followed by Marshal Burr Oliver running up onto the stage. "I'll arrest anyone else who draws his pistol and fires. Let's get that understood." Vlack had rehearsed this scene with Oliver just this morning. Murmurs of agreement followed.

Pignast resumed as primary speaker. "I'm glad Dr. Wills and Mrs. Pignast got right to the point." Pignast then slowly and deliberately traced Endura's history as a town in which animal husbandry and farming have coexisted without fixed boundaries, the blocking of God's resources and the death and destruction that had now emerged in Endura. Vlack's scattered hired voices tried in vain to disrupt Pignasts masterful oratory. In fact, Pignast used each interruption as an example of opposition to freedom of speech as well as the kind of thought and action in Endura by the Vlack "movement".

The audience of men, women and children were caught up in the excitement of the evening. No one noticed the tall man hidden in the shadows of the square pillar at the back of the hall. Cotter's unbuttoned duster concealed his Colts and his pulled down hat hid his bandana pulled up to the bridge of his nose. Cotter scoped out the position of Vlack's men. There were six including Boda. Boda was in the rear to the far left of the hall— almost opposite himself. Three men were close together about fifteen-yards in front of him. The other two were up front. Cotter felt the two in the front row were the greatest threat to Pignast, Wills and Fern. He looked around to find Rand, Josh and Mary were also near the front.

"In conclusion, ladies and gentlemen, my voice is your voice. Upon my election we will have monthly meetings right here to discuss your needs and the needs of Endura." There were loud shouts of approval amidst the staccato applause.

People began filing out. Boda stayed put while the three men in front of Cotter moved outside with the crowd. Cotter saw Rand and the children start to move down the aisle but they stopped halfway, apparently waiting for Wills and the Pignasts who were still up front shaking hands with the more enthusiastic constituents. Finally, only a dozen or so people remained scattered in the hall. The two Vlack hired guns separated but stayed aligned in the front row. One of them opened his coat, uncovering his right holster.

"I take offense to your calling my boss a crook." The stubbled-face spat a wad of tobacco spittle onto the floor.

Pignast gazed at the man and looked for Marshal Oliver. Oliver was gone. "Who, pray tell, is your boss."

"Victor Vlack and when you insult him you insult me."

"Insults are perceived only by those with a guilt-ridden mind, my good man."

"You callin' me a crook too? I know you're carryin' a gun. You better use it to back up your talkin', Pigman." The second man also became poised to reach for his gun. Boda had his hand on the handle of his holstered .44.

"I fight with words and offer your boss to a challenge of words. It's called a 'debate'. You may tell him that."

"That's not getting' you outta this. You betta reach for ya gun."

Rand drew the children to her and ducked behind several chairs. Boda moved to cover the front door. He knew one of his men would be at the rear in case Pignast ran that way.

"I back up Mortimer Pignast's words with bullets. Turn around if you want to challenge words with guns—both of you." Cotter stepped from the shadow. The light from the chandeliers reflected on his conchos and the nickeled Colt. Cotter's duster was wide apart with both Colts visible.

Boda turned immediately but too late to add to the decision of his two men who drew down on Cotter. Cotter fired at the right and left gunslingers just as their pistols cleared their holsters and in a single turning-action was now pointing his Colts at Boda. The two hired guns were dead before they hit the ground. The noise left the remaining attendees with ringing ears.

"Go tell your Victor Vlack that his assassination plan didn't work. Get out now, or I'll consider your presence reason enough to kill you." Cotter's voice penetrated the tinny resonance from the gunshots left reverberating in everyone's head.

Boda left with Cotter's guns trained on him until the door closed with a bang. "Everyone get out front with the rest of the crowd. No harm will come to you." They filed by rapidly with

Rand and the children lingering. Josh looked up at the man in the duster and tan buckskins.

"It's David and Goliath. Wait till we tell Jake."

Rand stared at the eyes above the bandana and then moved the children along.

Cotter opened the window when the hall was empty and ran down an alley and behind several buildings until he came to the clinic. He quickly changed his clothes and put his buckskins and guns in his "on call bag". He went outside heading toward the town hall where the crowd was still assembled.

"What happened in there?" Marshal Burr Oliver knew of the plan to induce Pignast to draw his pistol on Vlack's men. He spied Boda talking to his remaining three gunslingers.

"The Vigilante got two of my men just as Pignast was going to draw on them." Boda's words were loud.

"No. That's not the way it happened." One of the attendees spoke "Those two men drew on a man who was protecting Mr. Pignast."

Several other townspeople reaffirmed the story.

"Bullshit," one of the gunslingers said, "My friends were murdered."

"You keep quiet. You were outside when it happened." Boda glared at the man.

Rand and the children went up to Oliver. "Two of the hecklers tried to intimidate Mortimer Pignast to draw his pistol but he wouldn't meet their challenge. There was a man who faced them and they drew their guns to kill this man."

"Who was he?" Oliver looked at the crowd of townsfolk around him.

"I don't know. It was dark. His bandana was over his face." Rand moved toward the buckboard as the Garrisons rode up.

"Guess I missed it." Charlie looked at the marshal and Rand.

"Missed what." Cotter walked up to the group.

"Oh Jake, some of Vlack's people tried to push Mortimer into a gunfight right after the town meeting was over." Rand reiterated the story.

"I'd better get in there and tend to the victims."

"They weren't victims. They tried to kill me." Pignast stared knowingly at Cotter. He touched Cotter on the shoulder. "No need to rush. They're both dead."

Cotter went over to Rand and put his arm around her. "Did the children see the shooting?"

"They saw the confrontation but not the actual shooting. I had them crouched behind the chairs."

"The preacher is right, Jake. It is David and Goliath." Josh hugged Cotter's leg.

Cotter looked down at Josh. "I hope it was 'good against evil' Josh."

"I don't know whether I'm glad I wasn't there or not. Charlie do you think you'll be okay taking them home?" Cotter looked from Garrison to Rand.

"Sure. Mortimer was the target, remember?" Garrison shot a glance at Pignast.

"Oh, thank you for reminding me. Now, I won't stop shaking until morning."

Rand lifted her head from Cotter's shoulder and looked up at him. "I don't know what to tell them about this, Jake." Her eyes stayed with his and a sudden vision of the man with the two guns flashed back for a second.

# Chapter 47

## Aftermath

A month later, the town's people were still talking about the Vigilante hero of the town meeting. Who was this man? The Endura newspaper advertised a reward of five-hundred dollars for information leading to the capture of the buckskinned gun-fighter now officially known as the Vigilante.

"Why should he be captured? He's done nothing wrong. Why is Vlack condemning this man?" These were the words all over town and added to Pignast's campaign questions against Vlack.

April brought comfortable weather and the mild winter of only three moderate snowfalls was history. Winter clothing was relegated to the nighttime chill. Rand set the table for supper and Cotter's twice-weekly attendance was settling into a routine.

"No Mary, Spain is next to France." Cotter loved helping the children with their studies. He had wished his parents had made time to help him. Only when he was in college and medical school did his father interact on this level.

Rand smiled as the two of them looked at the map in the book.

"Jake, which do you like better, France or Spain?" Mary placed her index fingers on each country.

"I like France."

"Why?"

Cotter was ready for this one. "Because Dr. Louis Pasteur is from France and he discovered how to prevent and treat infect-ed wounds." Cotter next launched into the germ theory about un-seen organisms all over the human body just waiting to cause trouble. Josh got caught up in the dialogue as well.

When they were asleep, Rand and Cotter nestled in front of the fire.

"They sure didn't argue about taking a bath tonight." Rand laid her head on Cotter's shoulder.

"They used the soap like a weapon against the germs they couldn't see. I just hope they don't have nightmares tonight." Cotter kissed her on the forehead which transitioned onto her lips.

"Oh, Jake. We should set a wedding date."

"How about November, after the election. Hopefully Vlack will back off once he's defeated."

"November? That's too far away. How about July? The kids will be out of school."

"I had hoped to start building us a home. If we start now, we could be done by November."

"I have a home. We have a home. This is plenty big enough for us right now."

"Let me think about it."

"Okay, I'll give you ten-seconds." She started counting. "Time's up."

"I've decided."

"All right, what have you decided?"

"July it is and we'll stay here. We need a bigger barn though."

"That's a decent compromise."

They kissed. Cotter got up and moved the logs around the fireplace to create a pile of embers and eliminate any large tongues of flame or spitting sparks.

"Are you staying the night?"

"I thought you'd never ask."

●

"So what if they're engaged." Vlack paced an oval in front of the fireplace, "She was married once and I could have won her over if I wanted to."

"Are you sure? I was the one who had her husband killed by the gunslinger from Nevada. I bet she still thinks it was you who was behind it." Boda removed his boots with the boot jack.

"That was over seven-years ago." Vlack tugged on his beard. "The memory of his loss will be rekindled with Cotter's accidental death."

"Why accidental? Why not stage a robbery? Cotter gets shot but you arrive and rescue the rest of the family."

Vlack remained silent. "And from then on I'm seen with the family in public. I become a hero instead of the Vigilante. Vigilante? What about the Vigilante bastard? Pignast is using him to contrast against me."

"The Vigilante only appears after something happens to an Endura citizen, right? Well, you appear on the scene and there is nothing for this asshole to do. You've grabbed the glory already."

"How do I 'grab the glory?'"

"You shoot the Vigilante who's holding them up. But it's our man dressed up like him. We use blanks. I have a guy who's the same build. We dress him up in buckskin, bandana–conchos and all."

"Ken, I like it. You've obviously thought this out." Vlack smiled for the first time since the conversation began.

"They go on picnics every Saturday. Cotter likes to fish with the kids on Palutra Pond. We ambush them on their way back."

●

The Saturday sun stretched slightly beyond its highest noon overhead position. Cotter looked at his pocket watch–one-thirty. Cotter, Rand and the children had finished their picnic lunch. The children had each caught a good-sized bass.

"If you two can catch some more fish we can have them for supper–one for each of us. A half-hour left for fishing then we have to head home."

Josh caught two more and Mary caught one. One was a trout and they had two more bass. After the arguments about who caught the biggest fish grew tired, they packed up their stuff, climbed on the buckboard and found the road to head home.

In less than a half hour, Josh got restless. "I want to drive the wagon, Jake. I'm big enough."

Cotter and Rand exchanged affirmative glances. "Okay, sit on my lap."

"It's not fair. I'm stuck here with the stinky fish." Mary scowled at her younger brother.

After five-minutes they rounded a wooded turn in the road and Cotter and Josh had to pull hard on the reins. A horseman with a tan bandana covering his mouth and nose blocked their path. He had his gun drawn. The man in buckskin fired a shot in the air causing the horse to rear slightly up and to the left. Cotter and Josh held him in place.

Cotter couldn't reach the shotgun with Josh in his lap. "What do you want?"

"You're Dr. Cotter?" The gun pointed at Cotter and Josh.

Cotter gave an affirmative nod.

"Doctors make more money than I do. Let me have your wallet."

"I can't get it with the boy in my lap. It's in my inside jacket pocket."

"Let the lady get it." He motioned to Rand with his gun.

Cotter absorbed the image. The man had dull conchos erratically sewn on his outfit. He had one gun with a dull matte gray finish. Someone was trying to discredit the so-called Vigilante.

"You can't rob us. I thought you were David. You're supposed be a good guy." Josh tried to stand but Cotter held him tight.

"I'll show you how good I am. He fired point blank at Cotter but didn't want to hit the boy. The shot caught Cotter on the side of his head and he collapsed in place immediately. Blood oozed from the wound flowing over the left side of his face.

Rand immediately grabbed a napkin from the picnic basket and pressed it to cotter's head. "Oh, no." She checked Josh and found he was okay.

Mary screamed. "You killed Jake."

A second shot was heard to their left. Victor Vlack and Ken Boda came riding up. Vlack took in the scene and drew his pistol. The man in buckskin fired two shots at Vlack. Vlack pulled his horse to the right, turned in a complete circle and fired point blank at the counterfeit Vigilante. The buckskinned villain grabbed his chest and fell from his horse. Boda jumped from his horse with his gun drawn and ran to the fallen rider. He knelt down and pulled down the bandana.

"I don't know who he is but he's dead." Boda took the wallet and tossed it to Vlack.

"Here's the wallet back. Let me check Dr. Cotter." Vlack dismounted and started to climb aboard the wagon.

"Just get him in the back of the wagon and drive us to the hospital." Rand told Josh to get into the back with her and Mary.

"Okay. Let me drive the rig into town." Vlack turned to Boda. "Ken, you take this Vigilante's body out of here."

Vlack took the reins after tying his horse to the rear of the wagon. Rand blotted the blood on Cotter's forehead. *He isn't dead, but a head wound–Oh, my god.* She had tears in her eyes as the buckboard lurched forward.

●

Garrison was covering the hospital and emergencies at the Doctors Clinic. He had just finished a delivery with Zenia Lord, the on-call nurse. Vlack helped Garrison load Cotter onto a stretcher and then onto an examining table in the emergency room.

"Thanks for your help Mr. Vlack." Garrison's remark was a dismissal. "Sadie, can you stay and help with Jake? Zenia is tied up with the new mother and baby."

"Of course." She had the children stay in the waiting room.

Garrison washed the wound on the left side of the scalp which began at the hair line and went to a level just behind the right ear. Cotter did not respond to the stimulation during manipulation of the linear laceration. "The bleeding will stop when I bring the wound edges together."

"Did the bullet go into his brain?" Rand could see an entry-exit wound but she had to ask.

"No, and there's no blood coming out of the ear now that I have everything cleaned up. So there's no skull fracture. His pupils are equal and that means there's no increased brain pressure."

"But he's unconscious. Isn't that bad?"

"Not necessarily. His breathing and pulse are regular. He hasn't had a release of his bladder or bowel. It may be a severe concussion. If it is he may be out for as long as two-days or he could wake up today. Tell me again what happened."

Rand related the story of the Vigilante.

"The Vigilante? That's certainly a change from his past behavior. I had hoped he was on our side. And Jake didn't provoke him?"

"Not at all, the man just shot him. I think he aimed for the head because Josh was sitting in his lap."

Garrison finished rubbing the wound with carbolic solution. "And Vlack just appeared out of nowhere?"

"Victor Vlack shot and killed the Vigilante."

"Did they bring in the body? I'd like to see what he looked like."

"Boda took it away. The man had a face like a drifter and his voice was different than the Vigilante from Pignast's election rally."

"This is going to take a lot of stitches." Garrison began his suturing. Cotter seemed to stir and move his legs a little with each stick of the sewing needle. Rand steadied the head which moved a little with the procedure. "Any movement is a good sign. There's no lateralization of his arm and leg motions so, for now, both sides of the brain are intact. I'd like to hear some moans and groans, though."

Cotter remained unconscious as nighttime developed. Zenia and Rand tended to the children with food. The waiting room began to smell of the fish they brought in to get them out of the sun's heat.

"Please let me know when he wakes up?" Rand received a positive nod from Garrison.

Garrison monitored his colleague throughout the night. In the morning, just before sunrise, Cotter moaned. Garrison rose quickly and found Cotter moving his head from side-to-side. The mumblings were mostly incoherent but he thought he heard Cotter complain about his head and bladder.

"Ohhh…head…have…to…pee.' Cotter tried to sit up but fell right back down with his hands on his head.

"Jake. Jake. You're okay." Garrison noticed Cotter's body's movements were symmetrical. He examined Cotter and found that his bladder was indeed distended. "I'm going to slide a urinal down there for you. Just let it come out."

Cotter gradually stopped thrashing and focused on the ceiling. "Josh…and…Sadie…Mary… are they okay?"

"Yeah, they're all right, Jake. Just rest. If your head hurts real bad, I'll give you some laudanum. So far your brain has been spared any damage."

By mid-afternoon, Cotter was moved from the emergency section to one of the hospital beds "I'm going to keep you here until Monday at the least."

"That man…he…wasn't the Vigilante." Cotter shielded his eyes form the few rays of sunlight coming onto his face.

"What do you mean?"

"The clothes weren't right. He only had one gun and it wasn't nickel-plated like the Vigilante. Did Vlack or Marshal Oliver come by?"

"Several times, why?"

"I have a bad feeling about this. Don't tell anyone I woke up."

"Not even Sadie?"

"No. She'll see me when she comes to work but let the word be that I'm in a coma and can't have any visitors. I think somehow Vlack was behind this…maybe for political reasons. Ask Pignast to come by."

Pignast had been there twice already before Cotter woke up. The phrenologist's grim face lit up when he saw his bandaged friend alive and speaking. "Mort, what's the word around town about me?"

"Vlack's talking like he saved Sadie and the kids from certain death. He claims the Vigilante is a murderer."

"Did they bring in the body?"

"Boda said he buried it. What should we do Jake? I just about had a heart seizure when I was told you…the Vigilante… was killed."

"I think he's going to make his final move. He wants everyone opposing him to be dead and that includes you, Fern and Wills."

"What are we to do? This reminds me of New Haven all over again."

"We need to send a telegram but Vlack can't know about it. Ride to the next town and send it. Write it down. I'm having trouble focusing."

## Chapter 48

## The Plan

The train was hot, stuffy and sticky on its final leg. The passenger wished there was a place to change clothes. The night journey was too noisy to sleep as were the other two nights. It was so cold at night mandating winter clothes but during the day the climate reversed. There was a whole day's trip ahead in probable hot, humid coal-fumed air.

The passenger tugged at the conductor's sleeve. "What's the weather in Endura like?"

"Just like Atlanta–warm in the day, hot if there's sun and freezin' at night."

"Can't I change my clothes anywhere on this train?" *Arriving in a sweat-stained outfit wouldn't do. First impressions mattered.*

"Well, we do stop for a half-hour in Forge City. You could run into the hotel and ask for a place to change. Do you have a change of clothes in that bag?"

"Yes."

"It's the only way I know to do it."

"Will you let me know when we get to this Forge City?" A dollar passed into the conductor's hand.

"Why sure enough. I'll come get you directly when where there and I'll make sure you don't miss the train when we start up again."

The passenger was satisfied. *Money talks no matter where you go in this country.*

●

"Being in a coma is not dead." Vlack was furious. "We have to make sure he's dead. I gave the Endura newspaper a story that said both he and the Vigilante were killed."

"We can't just go into the Doctors Clinic and finish him off." Boda stared at his irate boss.

"Today's Tuesday–he's been unconscious since he was shot on Saturday. That 's a good sign he may never wake up." Vlack thought a few seconds. "But it's not good enough."

"What do want to do Mr. Vlack?"

"How many men do we have?"

"Five good gun hands." Boda raised his hand with the count. "And me is six."

"The first thing is to repair all the barbed wire boundaries. Dam up all the creeks and streams. Shoot any trespassers on sight. I'll have a bulletin come out in the paper today."

"What next?"

"I want Pignast and that asshole wife of his killed. Burn his place down with both of them in it." Vlack was breathing heavy. "And while the place is burning, I want the hospital to catch fire and have Cotter overcome with smoke."

"When do you want this plan started?"

"Wait until tomorrow's newspaper warning before you do the dams. We'll need a week before we do the fire–next Monday. In the meantime, I have to pay a visit to Mrs. Sadie Rand to remind her she owes me her life."

●

Rand didn't understand Cotter. "Why do you have to keep it a secret? Why let everyone think you're still unconscious?"

"Because I think Vlack has a hidden agenda." Cotter winced as Rand removed his bulky head bandage.

"Your scalp is healing fast. What does he have to hide? Vlack was always up front with his conniving ways."

"I think he was trying to kill me. That Vigilante was a fake. I mean he was not the real guy."

"What? How do you know that? And the man's dead."

"Show me the body. I think the whole thing was faked but I don't know why." Cotter touched her shoulder to steady himself while she put on a less bulky firm bandage. "And if Josh wasn't sitting in my lap he would have shot me in the chest and not risk a glancing head wound."

"Why would he want to kill you, Jake? I think your head is a little scrambled because of last Saturday." She smiled. "How do you know the Vigilante wasn't the guy from the town meeting? You've never seen him."

"I just know" *Damn.* "Anyway, you have to go along with the ruse that I'm still in a coma and may die at any moment. Just trust me."

"Okay, but the kids are practically in mourning."

"I feel bad about not telling them, I really do."

She kissed him and handed him the newspaper. "I don't know how Victor Vlack is going to win himself votes with this story in the paper."

"You're right. This is insane. He's declaring war on the farmers. How's that going to get him votes?" Cotter held his head with one hand.

•

The passenger just made it as the train began to pull out.

"That was pretty close. You do look like a different person though." The conductor hefted the carry-on suitcase and lifted it to the overhead rack.

"How well do you know Endura? I have to check into a good hotel."

"Well, there are several places to stay but the best is the Viceroy Manse. Everyone just calls it 'The Manse'. You can get a ride to the hotel from one of the buckboards for hire. There are usually a few of them waiting to meet each train. We have a 20-minute stop at Endura. I'll be glad to be of further assistance."

"You certainly can and I thank you very much." Another dollar crossed the conductor's palm.

The former passenger watched as the buckboard driver brought in the three luggage bags. A twenty-five cent tip was much appreciated. The lobby of the Manse was clean and spacious with a large fireplace against a central wall. A large chandelier produced ample light with minimal shadows. The check-in desk was attended by a man in a vested suit and string tie.

"I'd like a room with a view of the street please."

"Let me see. Yes, we have one available. How long will you be staying with us?"

"At least a week, maybe longer."

"We can arrange a weekly rate." The manager quoted an acceptable price. "Please sign the register." The manager turned the ledger book around and read the entry. "So nice to have you stay at the Manse. May I get someone to take your bags to your room?"

"Yes, please. And can you tell me how far away the Doctors Clinic is from here?"

"Of course, Miss…" he looked at the ledger for the name "…Mrs. Skyler. It's about two-blocks away. You'll be able to see it from your window."

"Thank you very much. I'd like to rent a horse and buggy for the week also. Will you see to having one at about ten in the morning?"

"Yes indeed, ma'am." He motioned for a young man to carry her bags up the stairs.

From her room Pamela Skyler looked out at the street. She was a little hungry but didn't feel like going out tonight. Her crisp appearance had the desired effect on the hotel manager and she knew that a report of a sophisticated-looking lady being in town would be the morning rumor. She opened her carry-on bag, which held some bread, cheese and fruit bought at Forge City. She raised the window about an inch to let some air in. The noise of a piano playing and some background merriment came from a building diagonally across the street. The light poles were far apart but she could make out the sign–Nellie's Leggs."

●

The appreciative Friday night audience applauded Christie Wooly and her girls as they swung around the poles stripping down to their brief above-the-knee pantaloons and flimsy lace vests. After the act, she and the girls mingled with the patrons seeking offered drinks and considering more intimate relations in one of the ever ready upstairs rooms. Christy was in one of the rooms with a cattle buyer. He had the least offensive body odor of the men who hit on her so far tonight. The man had been drinking all evening and his performance in bed was at best, pathetic.

"I like tha' man Mr. Victor Vlack. Do you know him?" The words were a little slurred. "He's a man like me. Gonna burn out some of tha farms ya know." He drank some liquor from a glass.

"What do you mean burn some farms?" Christy didn't like Vlack, Boda or any of the grabby, grubby hired guns that came from Vlack's ranch.

"He's gonna burn the hospital too. I don' like doctors much either." His head fell back onto his pillow and he closed his eyes.

"What? Our hospital?" She shook him but he didn't stir. "Oh, no." Christy was shocked. She had to do something. The hospital was almost across the street. She put on her clothes, boots and her coat and left the saloon by the rear door.

Stan Wills had the call tonight. Cotter had just nodded off to sleep when the door at the emergency entrance shook from the urgent rapping.

"Yes. How can I help you?"

Christy pushed her way inside and shut the door. "Dr. Wills I have to warn you. Vlack and his crowd are planning to set fire to the hospital building."

"What? Are you sure?"

"Yes. I heard from a reliable source. He's still up in my room if you want to find out for yourself."

"Thank you, Christy. Go back before you're missed. I'll tend to it."

Wills watched her run around to the back entrance of the saloon. He turned to go back to the hospital wing when he bumped into Cotter.

"Stan, I overheard. Let me go. You have to stay with the other patients."

"But everyone thinks you're dead. Didn't you want it that way?"

"I have some old clothes I had Charlie bring. I won't be recognized."

"Are you sure you're up to it?"

"I'll be okay." Cotter disappeared to his bed area and pulled out his buckskins from the bag he had asked Garrison to bring him. His scalp dressing was now a thin bandage and was hidden with his hat. He strapped on his Colts and pulled up his bandana.

"You. You, Jake. All this time."

"I know I can trust you. Not a word, understand?" Cotter checked his Colts. They slipped in and out of the holsters easily.

He left the rear of the hospital and entered the back door of the saloon via the steps leading upstairs to the rooms. He knocked lightly on the door.

"Dr. Wills is that you?"

"Dr. Wills sent me." Cotter opened the unlocked door.

"Oh my god. It's you." She stared at Cotter.

"Don't worry. I won't hurt you."

"I know. You saved me a long time ago at the stage, re-member."

Cotter's eyes adjusted to the dim light. "Yes, I remember. Help me wake up this man."

It didn't take long for Cotter to extract and confirm the details of what the cattle buyer had told Christy. Cotter left and kept to the shadows. The only light disclosing his presence was a brief five seconds in front of the hospital.

Pamela Skyler went to the window to close out the now cold air. She looked out the window and saw the buckskinned form.

"Oh my God." She gasped and backed away from the window and leaned on the wall. She poured herself a glass of port from her luggage. She remembered the Wednesday when she saw Cotter and his men dressed that way. She spoke to her wine glass. "What is happening? What have I walked into?"

# Chapter 49

## Two Women

It was a comfortable Saturday. Vlack had Boda stay a distance behind and out of sight. He wanted his meeting with Sadie Rand to be without any external pressure–real or imagined. He rode his buggy to the front porch. His pocket watch said 9:15. *Maybe it's too early for the children to be out. That might be good. My hero image would be enhanced by the kids.*

Rand heard the knock and went to the door a little disturbed she had not heard someone ride up to the house. She told Josh and Mary to be quiet while she answered the door.

"Mr. Vlack. I'm surprised. I never expected to see you at my house."

"My dear Mrs. Rand, may I call you Sadie?" Vlack removed his hat even though he was still outside.

"Mrs. Rand is still appropriate." She looked around him to see if any of his men were with him.

"Okay. Mrs. Rand, I'm here merely to see if everything is all right. I still shudder to think about the Vigilante almost shooting your family."

"Yes, we're all grateful." Josh and Mary were right behind her peeking at Vlack.

"Might I come in? I'm here also to offer condolences about Dr. Cotter." Vlack noticed she was still wearing the engagement ring.

"Okay. For a little while, we have to go to the hospital to check on Dr. Cotter."

Vlack moved into the fireplace living room. "Yes. How is Dr. Cotter doing? It's been a week since the shooting. It's a long time to be in a coma."

"His head is healing but he's still unconscious." She looked remorsefully at the floor. Josh began to sob.

"Such an evil man, the Vigilante. Is there anything I can do for you or your family? I mean, with the stress of the shooting. If I hadn't happened by, I shudder to think of the consequences."

"Thank you for your concern Mr. Vlack"

"Victor…please call me Victor."

"All right…Victor". She avoided his face. "Victor, I have to head into town now and tend to Dr. Cotter. I have to get the children ready. I promised them they could see that Dr. Cotter was still alive."

"Of course, of course."

"Thank you for stopping by. Josh and Mary get your coats on. Hurry up."

Vlack left after a further refusal for his help to hitch up their buckboard. He drove his rig to the cover where Boda was waiting.

"How'd it go?"

"Not good. As long as Cotter is still alive, I have no chance to distract that woman. Are your men ready to start with the homesteaders?" Vlack watched the dust trail following Rand's buckboard.

"Yeah. By the way we found some fencing torn down again by the Conner's' place. That's the second time."

"Was the dam released?"

"Yeah, we probably will have more diversion on some of the other sections with the planting season on them farmers. They'll need the water."

"Then we'll start with Conner. Try not to kill anyone. Just burn their barn for starters."

"What if they resist?"

"Just wound them."

"We'll try." Boda rode beside the wagon as Vlack flicked the reins to get the horse moving.

●

"What are we going to do about Vlack?" Wills checked Cotter's dressing. It was dry and the wound was clean. "Your stitches are ready to come out."

"I have a plan. It depends on what Mort has to tell me—he's part of it." Cotter felt good today. The brief exercise last night helped bring his mind away from the isolation and convalescence at the hospital.

"What about the Vigilante? Why the ruse?"

"I had hoped the 'Vigilante' would help contain Vlack's hand, but obviously not."

"Do you think he knows about you?  Do you think it's why he tried to kill you?"

No. No one but you and Pignast knows about the Vigilante. I don't know why he wants me dead."

The door opened and Charlie Garrison came in. "Good morning. How was the night?"

Cotter explained the events of the previous evening.

"What? Burn the hospital? Why? When?"

"We don't know but that's only part of it." Wills told about the plan to attack the farms and get rid of Pignast's place.

"What are we going to do about it?" Garrison watched as Wills started to remove Cotter's stitches.

"We have to wait for Pignast to come back today. I sent him on an errand. One thing's for sure—we have to prepare some kind of defense. Everything will happen within the next week."

There was a knock on the door.

●

Pamela Skyler had breakfast at the Manse. A horse and small canopied buggy was delivered to the hotel. She drove to the Doctors Clinic and secured the horse and buggy at the patient entrance. The main door was locked and a small card with printed instructions directed the reader to the emergency entrance on weekends. Skyler walked around the covered porch and rapped on the emergency door and walked in.

Wills and Garrison looked at the apparently healthy attractive woman and were about to question her emergency need for the clinic services when Cotter's voice cut them off.

"Pamela? Pamela, are you okay?" Cotter was aghast.

Skyler noticed the small dressing on Cotters head. "I'm in good health, Jacob but what about you?"

Wills and Garrison looked from Skyler-to-Cotter and back again.

"Excuse me. Pamela Skyler, these are my colleagues Dr. Wills and Dr. Garrison. Gentlemen…Pamela Skyler. She was a colleague and friend back in New Haven."

"Colleague? Oh yes, I remember from Jake's letters about the wine venture."

"Jacob, I was concerned because you never answered my letters. John LaRoque and Andrew Mashpit only conveyed you were alive and flourishing here in this town. They offered no more information than that." Her voice softened from a terse tone. "I see you've been injured."

Cotter looked at his friends. "Stan, Charlie, I believe Mrs. Skyler would like some words with me in private." They left the hospital area and went into the office section of the connected adjacent building.

Cotter and Skyler stood staring at each other, enduring a long minute of silence and appraisal.

"Pamela, why are you here?"

"Oh, Jacob my life is incomplete without you. I looked around this town earlier and this is no place for you. Please come back. We can start over."

"You're wrong, Pamela. This is where I belong and this is where I'll stay the rest of my life. There's nothing left of our relationship. You terminated everything right after graduation almost a year ago."

"But I need you. I realize my mistake. I do love you Jacob." Skyler moved toward him to hold both hands.

Cotter withdrew. "No, Pamela. You walked out of my life forever."

"But look at you. You're injured. What happened? And I saw you running around last night in that outfit you used to wear when you went shooting."

His heart skipped a beat. "What do you mean, I was running around last night?"

"I saw you from my hotel window. You wore the same clothes and those guns when you used to go shooting with LaRoque and the others. On Wednesdays, remember?"

"How did you know about that?"

"I have to admit Jacob, I followed you one night. I thought you were seeing another woman. You always denied us any time together on Wednesdays. I saw you and the others together." She smiled. "You all looked so silly wearing the same clothes and shooting at vegetables."

"Pamela, no one is to know about what you saw last night." He grabbed her by the wrists.

"Jacob, you're hurting me. What is the problem?"

"I've had to use my guns and disguise to provide justice at certain times in this town. That part of my identity is secret."

"I don't understand but you know I'll respect your confidence." She paused. "Jacob don't you see, this kind of stress doesn't exist in New Haven anymore. I truly love you. Please come back with me."

"No, Pamela. Our relationship never really developed toward a lifetime commitment. Please go back to Connecticut. It's dangerous here right now."

"I know my arrival is a shock to you. We have to talk more. Will you be here tomorrow?"

"Yes. And that's another matter. No one must know I've fully recovered from my coma." Cotter almost regretted the words but they had to be said.

"Coma! My God! This is too much. If you stay here you'll be killed."

Cotter had to grab her again. He took her by the shoulders and stared into her eyes. "Pamela, please go home."

"Let me think about all of this today. We…we'll talk tomorrow."

Cotter released her. Skyler put her coat on and turned to the door just as it opened. Sadie Rand entered and put her fingers to her lips.

"Jake, be quiet, I have the children here. They still don't know about your recovery." Rand noticed Skyler. "Oh, I beg your pardon. I didn't see you behind the door."

"Sadie, this is Pamela Skyler, a former patient of mine. She was just leaving."

"I don't remember you as a patient." Rand eyed the trim, expensive coat.

"I was passing through Endura. I was a patient of Dr. Cotter in Connecticut." Skyler looked at the eye contact between Rand and Cotter. "I have to go now."

"What kind of patient?"

"A piece of tree bark got lodged in her shoulder and I had to do surgery. It was over a year ago."

Rand accepted and dismissed the situation. "Well, how shall we prepare you for Josh and Mary?"

●

Skyler was confused and upset. *How can he want to remain in this violent world? There must be some way I can get him back.* She started to signal the horse to move when her recall of the parting scene with Cotter and the woman came back in a flash.

"The ring! That was my ring. Oh, my God. She's the reason he's staying." The horse moved his ears backward at the suddenness of the foreign words. Tears welled up in Skyler's eyes. She drove the buggy to the hotel after patting her face dry. *Another woman. I can handle another woman. Jacob Cotter, tomorrow we face reality. You are mine.*

# Chapter 50

## Smoke and Fire

"The sentiment in this town is in favor of the cattle ranchers. We were responsible for the railroad and own or underwrite more than half of the businesses. We have to show these voters we are the power and I'm the best candidate for state representation." Victor Vlack spoke to the outdoor gathering at his ranch. The applause was spontaneous. He concluded his remarks with a caustic barb against the farmers. "These homestead farmers are a threat to our dominance. They want absolute ties to Austin and state rule rather than town rule. And town rule, ladies and gentlemen is our rule. State rule is farmer rule. What do we want?"

"We want cattlemen representation," Someone shouted. Unanimous agreement followed.

"All right then. We must unite against them." More shouts of agreement. "Let's all adjourn to the barbecue pits."

While the cattle ranchers and their families intermingled at the outdoor festivity, Vlack motioned Boda and two of his chief gunhands to follow him into the house.

"Are your men ready?" Vlack lit a cigar from his desk's humidor.

"Yes. We tore the wire and pulled the posts at the Conner boundary. I had the dams broken. It'll look like we were provoked. The law will be on our side, as you said."

"I'm sure Joe Conner will fire the first shot if there's to be any opposition. Marshal Oliver will be with us to verify their initial use of arms." Vlack blew the blue smoke to the ceiling.

"What about Sadie Rand?" Boda folded his arms on his chest staring at his boss's cigar.

Vlack took the hint and offered him a cigar. "You can dismiss these two."

Boda motioned his two men to go outside.

"Sadie Rand will come around after we get rid of Dr. Cotter."

"When will that be?"

"In two days. We wait a day for the smoke to settle on the Conner raid. I'll be conducting a rally at Nellie's Leggs while you burn the hospital down with Cotter in it."

"I can give you five men for the saloon. I'll use four for the hospital."

"Why do you need four men for the job?" Vlack offered the humidor to Boda.

"Well there'll be three of them and I always like better odds."

"Three?"

"Cotter, one of the other Doctors and Pignast."

"Cotter? Yes. I almost forgot about him. I think you can count him out–he's still unconscious."

"Aren't we going to get rid of him at the same time?"

"Yes. Burn them out with the hospital and get rid of Pignast and his wife. Good, very good."

"Just one other thing boss." Boda lit up his cigar. He puffed until an orange ember became the cigar's tip. "What about the Vigilante?"

"He's just one man. You have ten."

They both smiled and blew blue smoke at the ceiling.

●

"You look a little shaken today, Jake." Rand touched his bandage tenderly. "Are you okay?"

"Yes, yes. I'm okay. I'm trying to get back to full activity and my body is telling me I'm not quite ready."

"Are you ready for the kids?"

"Yes. How shall I act?"

"Don't act. Kids can tell. Just tell them you woke up and you're still getting better." She turned to open the door when she stopped. "Oh Jake, Victor Vlack paid me a visit this morning."

"What did he want?"

"I don't really know. He seemed to be implying I owed him something for saving my life and the kids."

"What about my life?"

"That's another thing. He seems upset because you didn't die."

"I'm beginning to think the whole robbery scene was a set-up to kill me–a set-up by Vlack. But I don't know why."

There was a knock on the door.

"It must be the children. They're impatient."

Rand opened the door and Pignast walked in.

"Oh, good morning Sadie. How is our favorite MD?"

"See for yourself Mortimer. Excuse me. I have to prepare the children for Jake's miraculous recovery."

Pignast waited until the door was closed to talk with Cotter.

"Mort, did you send the telegram?"

"Yes. The reason I'm so late in getting back is that I had to wait for the answer. You wanted confirmation about them acknowledging the message?"

"Yes, I did. What did they say?"

"Here. Read it for yourself." Pignast handed Cotter the return telegram.

"Well, that's good news. Now I have some bad news." Cotter motioned Pignast to sit down. He related about the events on Friday night.

"Burn our place? Kill us? Burn the hospital and kill you?" Pignast's face flushed a dark red.

"I don't know when, but he has to make his move soon."

"What are Fern and I to do in the meantime? I don't like being a target."

"Don't panic. I think he'll do both things together–burn your place and the hospital. But he'll need a distraction to do it. Is there anything going on that would draw a lot of the townspeople away?"

Pignast rubbed his chin. "I don't think so. Only a rally for Vlack's campaign at Nellie's Leggs on Monday night."

"Rally?"

"Yes. Like the one I had at the town hall only he's using the saloon. He's also hosting free drinks and free food. The place will be mobbed with people. Mostly with cattlemen but the drinks and food I'm sure will attract a lot of the townsfolk. He's even inviting wives but no children."

"That's got to be it. On Monday, he'll have his men make their move." Cotter looked at his telegram again. "God, I hope this telegram was in time."

"I have some good news, I was saving for last. I received this letter the day I left to send your message." Pignast handed Cotter the elegant stationary.

"From President Grant?" Cotter read the text. "Wow, Mort. Grant endorses your 'live and let live' policy. What are you going to do with this? The newspaper is owned by Vlack. They'll never print it. This letter alone could get you elected."

"That's another reason I was late getting back. I had a lot of copies made at Forge City. I'm going to post them all over town."

"Great idea, but get some school kids to post them. You don't want to force Vlack's hand before Monday night."

The door opened and the Rand children shrieked with delight when they saw Cotter standing and talking to Pignast.

"Yay, Jake you're awake." Mary grabbed onto his leg and hugged him.

"I knew you wouldn't die." Josh let Cotter pick him up and give him a kiss and a hug.

"All right you guys, you don't won't to tire Jake out, do you? I'm going to have some food sent over for lunch for all of us." Rand looked at the children. "It'll be like an indoor picnic."

"Can Jake come home with us?" Josh was still in Cotter's arms.

"It's up to Jake."

"I think I'm still better staying here, Sadie. Wait until after Monday." Cotter saw the disappointed look in the children's faces.

"Why Monday?" Rand looked confused.

"Vlack's having an election rally with free alcohol and food. There's bound to be a need for the clinic. I'll be here with Charlie. I'll leave after Monday. I promise." Cotter did not feel the timing was right to tell her about the pending confrontations.

"Okay. Let me go get lunch. You kids can keep Jake company until I get back."

"I have to go too, Jake. I have the posters to tend to." Pignast waved goodbye.

●

The six men rode hard and fast, sending up a cloud of dust behind them. The sun was moving from high noon in the mild April day. Ken Boda was in the lead. The group stopped at the tree line overlooking the Conner place. There were four buildings—a barn, bunkhouse, storage house and the main home.

"They're probably all in the bunkhouse eating lunch." Boda surveyed the area. "Pull the bandanas over your faces." He watched as his men complied. "Light up your torches. We'll go in a file of two's. I'll take the main house. You two fire-up the barn and you other two throw your torches into the bunkhouse with two more torches on the roof."

"Shouldn't we get them out of the buildings first?" One man asked.

"Just do as I tell ya. The fires will get them all running out and then we can face 'em. Cover them with your guns when they come out but don't shoot unless someone looks like they're goin' to shoot at us. I want to deliver the message to Joe Conner myself."

The men rode down to the housing area. Boda threw one of his torches through the living room window and the other on the porch of the main house. The rest of his men tended their own missions. Marshal Oliver observed and said nothing.

Conner and his family came running out of the smoke-filled house. Joe Conner gathered his wife and three children close to him. Boda and his gunslinger pointed their pistols at the family.

"Just so's we're clear on this. You destroy a cattleman's property means you get it back in spades."

"What…" Conner coughed and wiped his eyes with the backs of his hands. "…what do you mean?"

"The wire fence is down at your boundary line and the dam is broke. You think you're going to keep on gettin' away with it?"

"None of my men did anything to Vlack's fence." Conner hugged his wife to him. He wore no gun. He coughed again. "You all wear masks but I know Vlack sent you."

"You don't know nothin'." Boda fired a shot a foot in front of Conner.

The rest of Boda's men rode to his side.

"The hands are all out tryin' ta put out the fire. Whaddya want us ta do?" His masked henchman pointed his gun at the Conners.

"We did to them what they did to us." Boda turned to Conner again. "Let this be a lessin' to you farmers."

The farmhands had let the livestock including about a dozen horses out of the barn and the animals ran close by, frightened by the flames.

"Tell Vlack he'll pay for this–all of it." He looked at the marshal. "Aren't you going to do anything? Boda's men have masks on, for God's sake."

"The law is on their side with this Joe." Oliver turned his horse and rode away from the scene.

"The bandanas are for the smoke from the fires. I'm not hiding where we came from." Boda glared at the Conners.

Joe Conner and his family moved to let the fleeing horses come between them and Boda's men.

"Look. You're lucky no one got hurt today. Next time we won't be so nice. Why don't ya just sell your land and get out?" Boda turned to his horsemen. "Let's go." They left shooting their pistols into the air.

●

Cotter, the Rands and Charlie Garrison finished the plentiful lunch. There were two patients left in the hospital area. The one man with a leg laceration allowed Rand to apply the dressing over the stitches Garrison had put in using only laudanum medication. The man had groaned a little with each prick of the sewing needle and gave a louder shout when the carbolic and alcohol mixture was applied at the end. Cotter and the children were in the front office section.

"Looks like all's well now. The children act like you were never hurt." Rand held Cotter's hand. "So why are you staying until after Monday?"

"Well, you're going to hear about it anyway. Rumor has it that Vlack is going to try to set fire to the place next door with the Pignasts in it and do the same to the hospital." He then told her how the information came to them.

"Oh damn that evil man." She wrung her shawl with tightened fists.

"You can come to work as usual but make sure the kids are at Charlie's like always."

"What kind of protection do we have?"

"There'll be Charlie, Stan and Mort plus me. We may need all three nurses by the end of the day. We'll try to prevent them from torching the place. They don't know we know, so that should be to our advantage."

"Shall I come by tomorrow?"

Cotter smiled and looked at the children playing with the stethoscope. "Sure. It'll keep me from going nuts." Cotter became aware of several horses pulling up to the emergency entrance. A buckboard followed. "I wonder what that is."

"Jake, Sadie, come on to the emergency room. We have some people with burns. There's been a fire."

Several of Conner's farmhands had burns from putting out the fire. Joe Conner came up to Cotter."

"Dr. Cotter? I thought you were still in a coma." He had soot blotches on his clothes, hands and face as did the rest of his casualties.

"What happened?" Cotter helped Garrison get the men onto examining tables. Rand moved the washing basins beside each one.

Conner talked as Cotter and Garrison examined, cleaned and dressed the burns. Fortunately none of the burns were greater than second degree.

"Are you sure they were Vlack's men?" Garrison looked from Conner to the man he was bandaging.

"The lead man spoke of nothing but Vlack's fence down on our border and the dam opening up the stream to my place. And Marshal Oliver was there claiming it was all legal. It was ridiculous. I mean, except for Boda, they had their faces covered. If it was legal why would they hide their identity?"

"Did you tear down the wire and release the water?"

"No. I wondered why the stream started to flow again. It happened first thing this morning." Conner accepted a small dressing on his burned hand.

"Did you report this to Marshal Oliver?" Garrison asked.

"Yes. He told us he'd already been to Vlack's to check their fences and verify the story. But honest-to-God, no one from my spread did anything to Vlack's border."

After they left, Cotter and Garrison helped Rand clean the emergency room and replace the linens.

"This is the start of it, isn't it, Jake?" Rand walked with Cotter to the reception area where the children had been sent to play.

"Yes. Why don't you and the children go on home now? Charlie and I have to go over some details about tomorrow. Zenia is on call tomorrow and right now we'll make a show of business as usual for Monday morning. Don't take the kids to school. Leave them with Deirdre Garrison. "

"When do you think they'll make their move on the clinic?"

"I don't know but tomorrow Stan Wills and Mort will be here to work out a few things about Fern and their place next door."

"I'm scared Jake." She hugged him.

"Don't worry. We aren't going to be caught off guard like Joe Conner."

# Chapter 51

## Preparation

Wills relieved Garrison for the day's coverage on Sunday. A woman and her baby from a Saturday's delivery had been picked up by her husband and another patient who was brought in drunk and with a fractured forearm was released to his friends. Wills and Cotter were looking out Cotter's office window at the sunny morning.

"Let's hope we have a quiet day today." Wills examined Cotter's dressing. "One of the bar flies from Nellie's asked me about you a little while ago. I told him you were still in a coma."

"Good. If we can keep them thinking that there'll only be two of you plus the two nurses tomorrow, they'll really be off center. You didn't tell Charlie about Friday night, I hope?"

"You mean about you being the Vigilante?"

"Yes. That'll be another surprise when they make their attack."

"So that's what you call yourself, Jacob–Vigilante." Pamela's Skyler's voice startled them.

"Pamela. What are you doing here?" Cotter stood up and went over to her.

"Doctor Wills, I'd like some private words with Jacob, if I may?"

Wills went to the emergency room looking over his shoulder at the closing door to Cotter's office.

"I knocked on the emergency door and when there was no answer I came in. The door was unlocked."

"It's never locked. There's always one of us here." Cotter stared at her.

"Jacob, I heard you two talking about Friday night. Why the secrecy about your 'Vigilante' identity?"

"This is no affair of yours. You should leave now, Pamela."

"You shouldn't have to live in the shadow of such violence, Jacob."

"Why did you come back again, Pamela?"

"I'm here to tell you that you're coming back with me. It was easy to figure out why you're hesitating with me, once I saw my engagement ring on her finger. Don't let the attraction of a ready-made family get to you Jacob. We're both still young enough to have our own children. I told you I've changed." Skyler put her hands around Cotter's waist.

"No Pamela, I truly love her and the children. My future is here and they're worth fighting for." He removed her arms and moved away from her.

"Jacob, look at yourself. You got shot in the head and have to play dead. I heard the rumors about you being unconscious. You don't know what's really good for you." She moved toward him again and placed her hands on his shoulders.

"No. Don't do this. You're only torturing yourself."

"Jacob Cotter, I'm giving you just one more day to think about us. After tomorrow I'm going to have some words with your nurse. She'll find out about her Vigilante fiancé."

"Pamela, please, it's important that no one knows about that. I've had to administer some justice in this town as the Vigilante. Some people have died and the law official in Endura is as crooked as the man behind the evil here. You could place us all in danger."

"And what about your coma? What would disclosure of that mean?"

"You can't tell anyone about that either. If you care anything for me, you have to be silent about these things." Cotter put his hand on her shoulder.

Skyler put her hand on his. "I want your decision after tomorrow or everyone will know about this sham. One more day, Jacob dear. Please," she pleaded. "Things have changed back in New Haven."

"Please leave, Pamela." Cotter turned his back on her.

●

"Will she be a threat to us?" Wills motioned for Cotter to sit on the treatment table.

"She won't say anything until after Monday and then it won't make any difference."

Pignast came in through the emergency room door. "Well, I spread copies of my letter from the President all over town."

"I don't think it's going to be safe for you out on the streets once Vlack gets hold of one of those." Wills removed Cotter's bandage.

The wound was now a reddened linear scar. Wills put only a superficial dressing over it.

"I'm sure he's already seen it. I stuck one on the front of Nellie's Leggs."

"Mort, for God's sake. Why take chances like that?" Cotter stood up.

"Vlack won't do anything until tomorrow." Pignast surveyed Cotter's head. "Looks good, Jake. What's Monday's agenda looking like?"

"I want everyone here tomorrow. Have Fern go to Charlie Garrison's the first thing in the morning. You come here for work, as usual."

"Okay. Say, wasn't that Pamela Skyler I saw leaving the Clinic?"

"Yes." Cotter told him of her threat of disclosure.

"She's still a calculating woman, Jake."

"Yes. Nothing's really changed about her."

"Well, church is still safe." Wills looked at his watch.

Cotter looked out the side window. He could barely make out the church steeple. "That's one thing I've really missed. Going to church with Sadie and the kids is a part of me. God was an important part of my life back in New Haven too, Stan."

"Well Mort, how about Fern and you joining me this morning. Jake, you better lock the door and put the 'gone to church' sign up."

"Good idea Stan. Fern and I could use all the Godliness available."

"Me too. Talk to God for me, guys." Cotter watched his friends leave and took his Colts from the saddle bags.

There was ample ammunition for his Colts. He cleaned and oiled all surfaces of the weapons. Cotter practiced his draw and dry-firing from different positions. His head didn't bother him and his confidence level with his performance was high. Wills came back from church with lunch.

"Are you going to be wearing those guns around the Clinic?"

Cotter smiled. "Yes. I want them within easy reach."

"Since it's quiet today, why don't you take a nap. I'm going home for awhile. I'll be back with supper and keep you company for the night."

"A snooze is definitely in order. Put a sign on the emergency door. I don't think we'll have trouble today but if any of Vlack's men try to get in, I'll be ready."

Cotter felt fatigued. *Is it the stress of waiting for tomorrow or is it the summation of everything hitting me at once? Pamela Skyler, Sadie at risk tomorrow, anticipation of the face-to-face action with Vlack's men and no news from Pignast's telegram. It's enough pressure to tire out anyone.* Cotter slept on his hospital bed and was immediately transported to Nashville and that fateful night.

"Killing you Yankee Doctors is like killing a regiment of blue-coats." The horseman shot the doctor next to his father and then took aim as his horse reared up with its forelegs clawing at the smoke-filled night.

"No. Don't." Cotter cried out in his sleep.

The horseman in the confederate gray uniform laughed as he pointed his .44 at his father. "Take out the others," he called to his henchman.

A sudden hot breeze created by the flames from the burning tents cleared the smoke from the killer's position. Cotter couldn't see the man's face. His hat was pulled down too low. The pistol fired twice into his father's chest and the rebel re-holstered his gun. The single holster rig was not army issue. It was a gunfighter's fast draw holster which was adorned with silver studs at half-inch intervals throughout the belt and holster perimeters. The image flashed immediately to the stage robber when he first came to Endura and then to the man who questioned him about the ruffian he pistol-whipped at his first day at work.

"Boda. It was Boda." Cotter sat up in the hospital bed, his face sweating and his hands on the handles of the Colts.

# Chapter 52

## Confrontation

The Monday morning sun was a repeat of the pleasant weather that started on Sunday. Shortly after Wills and Cotter tended to their morning grooming rituals, Pignast, Rand and Garrison came in. Rand carried breakfast from the diner across from Nellie's Leggs. Zenia Lord, the second nurse, arrived 15-minutes later.

"We shouldn't have any clinic patients today. I was lucky to get the word out Saturday to cancel everyone." Rand poured hot coffee for everyone.

"Good. We don't need any one here when Vlack's marauders come calling." Pignast opened one of the bags Charlie Garrison brought in.

Cotter helped unload the bag. "Three rifles, two shotguns and plenty of ammunition–it should be enough." Cotter's brow furrowed. "Mort have you heard anything about the train station."

"What about the train station?" Rand asked.

"We're expecting visitors–friendly ones. I asked Mort to send a telegram from Forge asking for help. I had hoped they would have arrived yesterday."

"There are two trains coming in today–one at noon and one at five." Pignast hefted a shotgun.

"What if your help doesn't come, Jake?" Rand faced Cotter and then turned to the group. "Are we all alone in this?"

"Well, we couldn't very well ask Marshal Oliver. He's in Vlack's pocket." Cotter paused. "There are four of us and we have plenty of guns."

"Won't they just roll right over us? You said they want to burn the hospital." Zenia picked up a rifle.

"We have the element of surprise. They think I'm unconscious or dying and we'll be waiting for them. As soon as they come at us, we shoot them before they can release their torches. This won't be like Joe Conner's attack."

"And there aren't four of us there are six of us. I can shoot straighter than most men and I know Sadie can fire a rifle too." Zenia picked up a box of rifle cartridges.

"We should be okay until later in the day. When I passed out my posters yesterday, I heard about the rally not getting started until three in the afternoon." Pignast smiled. "They're starting with free drinks and a free dinner to follow."

"The liquor might make them edgy sooner or at the least make them sloppy." Wills said. "I suggest we get our lunch ordered now. We shouldn't leave the clinic after noon. Vlack's men may be looking at us even now because of the posters."

They busied themselves checking the guns and planning their positions. Cotter assigned himself to the front of the office building and Garrison to the rear hospital windows. Wills was staying lookout at the emergency entrance and Pignast was overseeing the view of his building next door."

Lunch passed quietly. Cotter walked from position-to-position reassuring each one. "Did the children adapt to not going to school today and staying with Deirdre?"

"Oh, they were happy to forego school." Rand gave Cotter a kiss and a hug. "Will we be okay, Jake?"

"I have a strong feeling we will, dear." He gave her another hug. *But we could all be killed. Maybe Pamela Skyler is right.*

He walked to Pignast's post. "Did Fern get to Charlie's okay, Mort?"

"I took her there myself. She'll be all right."

"What do you think about the train and our friends?" Cotter unholstered his nickel-plated colt and twirled it back into the holster.

"We tried Jake. A lot of things could have happened along the way."

More time passed with the tension rising to a palpable level. At four o'clock Cotter made rounds again.

"Get ready. They have to make their move now. There's only a little more than two-hours daylight left." Cotter went back to Pignast. "Remember Mort, shoot first–don't let them throw their torches." He touched his flat dressing and looked at Pignast. "The trains have come and gone."

"Like you say Jake, 'we'll be okay'."

At four-thirty Jake saw four riders coming from behind Nellie's Leggs. They were riding fast and held their torches to the side above saddle level.

"Here they come," Cotter yelled. "Open your windows."

The riders wore bandanas to beneath their eyes and broke off into pairs. One pair was heading for the hospital and the other to Pignast's place. They slowed their horses as they neared the buildings. One man circled in front of the Doctors Clinic building and the other rode around back. The second pair did the same at Pignast's building.

"Shoot them just before they throw their torches. Don't give them any chance–they don't plan to give us any." Cotter shouted and drew his Colts.

Wills and Garrison had their pistols out and the women shouldered their rifles ready to back up the men.

Cotter, Garrison, Wills and Pignast took aim. The horseman in front of Cotter swirled the torch in the air to increase the flame. Suddenly, he flew back off his horse as two bullets hit him square in the chest. The man in front of Pignast's house took a bullet to the head and chest and fell to the ground with his torch smoldering in the dirt. Wills aimed at the torso of his target and watched him propelled by the force of two bullets each to the chest and abdomen. Garrison was sweating as he positioned his man in his sights. The gunslinger was thrown sideways as bullets tore into his neck, chest and shoulders. The barrage of shots into all of the riders coalesced into a prolonged several-second boom.

Cotter and the others stared in disbelief. Cotter looked at his two Colts. The others were similarly confounded. Cotter, Wills, Garrison and Pignast had not fired a shot.

Rand and Zenia shouted. "Look–around the back of the hospital."

Four men with bandanas wearing 'Vigilante' clothes formed their palominos in a semi-circle. They pulled their bandanas down after they holstered their Colts.

LaRoque, Mashpit, Hamer and Rosicot smiled as they waved a greeting.

•

The free food and liquor-induced background prattle and conversation rendered the noise of the torch attack inaudible. The pole dancers were not dancing but were serving drinks and food to the masses seated at every table, standing around the saloon wall space and crowding the bar. Marshal Burr Oliver pounded the podium lectern with his gun butt. The noisy crowd could not hear him. He pointed his gun into the air and fired. Oliver didn't notice that his bullet hit the left brass pole support at the lintel junction breaking off the two securing bolts. The loud discharge of his .44 produced the desired silence.

"Ladies and gentlemen, let me have your attention. We are here today to support our candidate for State Representative, Victor Vlack." Oliver's words induced applause and shouts of delight. He waved his palms up and down to regain quiet. "Your host and I want to remind everyone that the right person for Endura will make sure we gain state benefits and not state meddling." He had to wait again for the noise of approval to die down. "I give you Endura's first and next congressman, Victor Vlack."

Vlack walked onto the stage to the podium and shook hands with Marshal Oliver who took a seat to the left of the central podium. Vlack wore a light gray vested suit, highly polished brown spurred-boots and waved high in acknowledgement and then motioned the audience to silence.

"Welcome all you voting men and to your ladies who give support, I want to say that you are just as important to me and Endura as they are. I say to you all, please carry my message to those who could not come tonight." Vlack moved to the side of the lectern. "As Marshal Oliver has said, some things from the Capital are good for Endura and some are not needed. We do not need a police department or the Texas Rangers." Loud applause erupted. "We do need our rights to stop the farmers from draining the water supply needed for our cattle." The applause was accompanied by loud shouts keyed by the five men Boda had positioned around the saloon hall. Vlack continued a tirade against the agriculture citizens of Endura as threats to the cattle ranchers and all they employ. "It was the cattle trade money that started this town. Endura and I go back over twenty-years. We all go back twenty-years. There are more cattle tax dollars supporting this town than any money from the farmers."

"And it'll always be like that." One of Boda's men yelled. This triggered a volume of expletive agreements.

Vlack continued. "Votes. Votes are what will carry us to power in Endura. We need your votes."

Four men had infiltrated the audience at corner positions front and back of the saloon. They wore tan dusters and their hats were pulled low over their faces and marked each of Boda's men for possible targets. The crowd, including Boda's hooligans, paid no notice.

"And who else is trying to steal our votes? Pignast. Mortimer Pignast. And who is this Pignast. He's neither a cattleman nor a farmer. He represents only himself." Vlack paused to allow more triggered comments. Vlack looked to Boda and received the nod that his arsonist-killers had already been dispatched and assumed to have completed their jobs. "The man is a barber. He is a gypsy fortuneteller. He works with the Doctors to render us unconscious with ether. Let me tell you, Mortimer Pignast is trying to put us all to sleep with his strange ways." More incited remarks. "The man fabricates a letter from that northern general who calls himself President. I have a copy here." Vlack waved the circular in the air. "Pignast is himself a Yankee and has only lived in the great southern state of Texas for less than a year. This letter says he'll represent both cattlemen and farmer. Well, let me tell you right up front, Mortimer Pignast does not represent me."

The applause was deafening. Vlack allowed a longer pause to permit refilling of drinks and serving more food.

"I accept your agreement. Remember, barbed wire is a right to set our boundaries to guarantee our livelihood. The election in six-months will protect our rights only if you vote for me. I even invited my gypsy opponent up to the stage tonight to speak in debate to my declarations. Is Mr. Mortimer Pignast willing to do that? I gave him a personal invitation." He paused and feigned looking for Pignast in the audience. "Of course not. He's not going to show his face here tonight."

"Of course I am, Mr. Victor Vlack." Pignast's resonant voice projected from the rear of the saloon. He walked to the stage with Cotter at his side.

Cotter was dressed in black and had his black suit jacket unbuttoned and nearly covering his Colts.

Vlack's mouth opened without the egress of any words.

Cotter and Pignast came onto the stage. Pignast turned to the people. "I am only too glad to explain to you all just exactly what a State Congressman does for the people in Endura."

The four men unbuttoned their dusters over their buckskin outfits to free access to their Colts. They each eyed their unsuspecting targets.

Vlack was purple with rage. "Cotter alive? Pignast alive?"

Marshal Oliver looked to Vlack for direction.

"They want to assassinate me." Vlack motioned to Boda and Marshal Oliver to cut them down. Vlack pushed aside his suit coat and went for his gun.

Cotter drew his guns with lightening speed. His left Colt caught Oliver in his right shoulder causing his gun to discharge toward the ceiling shattering the wooden base connecting the left brass pole. A second shot from Cotter sent Oliver's gun flying to the back of the stage. Cotter's right-hand gun, drawn at the same speed, faced Vlack's chest. Vlack had his gun out of the holster but was far short of any aiming point. He turned to the stunned audience and stared at Boda.

Vlack ducked behind the podium and fired at Cotter and Pignast who had dropped to the floor for lack of cover. Vlack's two shots hit the right brass pole moving it three inches off the overhead lintel and ricocheting around the salon. Panic ensued and people were now leaving. Men were shouting and women were screaming as they went out the front, side and rear doors to escape the gunfire.

"Get up on the stage and get them." Boda had his gun drawn and waved it toward the stage for his men to gun down Cotter and Pignast. More than half of the rally attendees had left and the rest were continuing their flight from Nellie's Leggs.

Mashpit stayed at his right rear position. He saw the action and smoke and even without his hearing, his input of the situation was unimpaired. Mashpit called to the man with the drawn gun who was running toward the stage. "Stop and put down your gun."

The man turned. "The Vigilante." He tried to focus his gun on Mashpit but Mashpit's speed and accuracy pushed the man backwards with two .45 bullets to the chest.

At the word "Vigilante", LaRoque's man turned only to confront a second man dressed in buckskin. "No, he's over here," the man said. The gunslinger drew on LaRoque who shot him in both arms.

Fabian Rosicot was at the right front corner near the stage. "I think you are wrong, Monsieurs, I am right here." The gunman near him turned and fired in one motioned only to be hit in the abdomen by both barrels of the 10-guage shotgun. The man who had been on the last step of the stage stairs was blown back against the already weakened right brass pole which now fell backward against the rear stage wall. The lintel detached and hung precariously dropping fragments of wood and ceiling plaster onto Cotter and Pignast.

"Mort, we have to get off the stage." Cotter motioned for both of them to crawl over the shot-gunned corpse to drop off the stage edge.

Vlack was experiencing a total mental detachment. "Vigilantes? Three Vigilantes. I'm seeing things." He saw Cotter and Pignast crawling from the stage and fired two shots at them. Both bullets thudded into the dead man.

Bradley Hamer was closest to Vlack on the left front corner of the saloon hall. He fired two shots into the podium to prevent Vlack from shooting further at Cotter and Pignast. The overhead support of the ceiling was creaking and over nine-feet of the supporting lintel and beam started to hang down. The left brass pole supporting the wooden base, which had been fragmented by Oliver's shot shifted slightly with a scraping sound. Hamer looked up and then looked back at Vlack. Vlack now turned to engage Hamer.

"Four? Four Vigilantes?" Vlack stood up behind the lectern to shoot at Hamer who was behind an upturned table.

"Jake and Mort. Get off the stage quick." Hamer heard the noise of falling plaster and wood and pointed his shotgun at the base of the remaining brass pole. The double blast knocked out the final support and the last brass pole flew to the side of the stage. The unfettered ceiling, including the saloon's stage section of the roof, came crashing down on Vlack who screamed as the tonnage buried him.

"Four of these men? How was that possible?" Boda surveyed the scene with horror. He backed out of the saloon front entrance and ran for his horse just as the stage ceiling disintegrated throwing out a cloud of dust and debris.

# Chapter 53

## Ken Boda

Miraculously the rally attendees escaped injury from the Nellie's Leggs disaster. Marshal Burr Oliver remained the sole Doctors Clinic emergency casualty.

"I'll have to take the bullet from your shoulder, marshal. Mort, he'll need ether for that. Sadie, prepare him for the operating room." Cotter and Pignast washed their hands and changed into surgical gowns from their dust-covered shrouds.

"After you recover, you'll have to answer to your dealings with Vlack. Corruption is no more in Endura, marshal or ex-marshal." Pignast helped the two nurses remove Oliver's bloody shirt.

"We'll stay as long as you want us, Jake." LaRoque spoke for the buckskin quartet.

"You guys came in like the cavalry." Garrison smiled at them.

"We took the cue from Jake. When he came to Endura, he stopped at Forge City and rode in. We did the same. We actually arrived in town at sunup. Mort's telegrams indicated today was the day you expected the attack." Mashpit washed the dirt from his hands and face as did the others.

"Monsieurs and Madams, we were hopeful the bad man Vlack would not change his plans." Rosicot piled his duster with his friends' garments.

"Why are you all dressed alike and if this is the first time in Endura for you, who is the other Vigilante?" Rand stared wide-eyed at them.

"God provided for you Mrs. Rand." Bradley Hamer turned up the lantern near him.

"Come on Sadie. We need you to help with Oliver." Cotter routed her away from asking more questions.

•

"I'm going to see my friends off. Stan and Charlie will take care of the clinic. You nurses have a full day. The patients we cancelled yesterday are coming in today." Cotter kissed Rand and went to the hotel where LaRoque and the rest were staying.

They gathered in the lobby to say goodbye.

"You know I'm more grateful than I can ever say." Cotter shook hands and embraced each of them.

"Well, it's over. You can now lead a less troublesome existence down here." Mashpit said.

"Aren't you supposed to have a baby by now?" Cotter smiled at his friend.

"Samantha and I had a baby boy last week. We named him Sam. If it was a girl she was going to another Samantha."

"Jake, I talked to your Sadie. She's a fine God-fearing woman and she told me about your going to church with the family. Gertrin will be happy to hear that." Bradley Hamer beamed.

"I want you all to come back for my wedding." Cotter shook hands again with his friends and went outside to see them off at the train station. He went back to the hotel to settle their bill.

"Four Vigilantes?"

The alto voice caught him off guard. Cotter turned around at the hotel desk.

"Pamela." He looked at the luggage at her side. "Are you leaving?"

"Yes, Jacob. After what happened yesterday, I realize I can't have you back." She moved close to him. "I hope you understand and bear me no ill-will. I had to try once more. I just hope I find someone like you did."

"It'll happen if it's supposed to."

"I overheard Bradley Hamer talk about church. I remember you went to church in New Haven."

"God will provide for those who seek him. You ought to try it Pamela."

"Maybe I will Jacob." She moved closer and kissed him on the cheek. "Good luck." She signaled the man to take her luggage to the buggy for the train departure.

•

Boda rode hard to Vlack's ranch. He changed his horse and had Rhumy prepare a packhorse with enough supplies to get him to the Mexican border in three-or-four days.

•

"Jake, are you sure you have to do this?" Charlie Garrison was leaving his house for the Clinic.

"The man killed my father. I could never rest until I confronted him."

"The man's a killer. You're no match for him."

"I can't let him kill again. Don't worry about me. I'll be back within a week." Cotter took out a sheet of paper from his saddlebag. "I had Marshal Oliver draw up this poster."

"A thousand dollars reward for Ken Boda? Who's posting the reward?"

"I am. When I meet up with him, I'll make sure the locals see the poster before I confront Boda. In the meantime have Mort telegraph the reward notice to all the Texas towns south of here. I'm counting on Boda heading for the Mexican border."

"If you want, I'll go with you." Garrison put his hand on Cotter's shoulder.

"No. Thank you anyway. This is something I have to do alone." Cotter watched his friend ride away. Cotter changed into his buckskins and oiled his Colts. The conchos were polished and he reached for his duster. There was a light knock on his opened door and he turned around surprised.

"Jake...oh my God." Rand put her hand to her face.

"Sadie. What are you doing here?"

"Stan and Mort said you were going after Boda and I wanted to talk to you." She took a deep breath. "Are you the Vigilante? I had thought after Monday it was one of your friends from New Haven."

"I didn't want you or the children to know." He hugged her and kept talking. Cotter told her of his nightmares and Boda's murdering his father.

"Can't you just let it go? Boda will meet his fate by someone else. I need you alive. The children look to you as their father."

"We both believe in God. Don't you think it's more than just coincidence Boda and I ended up in Endura?" He still held her and looked down longingly. They kissed. "I have to go."

She watched as Logan Pipps brought the palomino and helped Cotter cinch down the blanket roll and his supplies. Cotter put his duster on and mounted his magnificent horse. He rode to her and looked down. "I'll be back, Sadie. It's a promise."

●

"I remember you from last year. Your name is Rhumy."

Cotter had both gloved hands on Rhumy's collars lifting the tremulous man to his toes. He fixed his threatening gaze over the bandana. "Tell me where Ken Boda is."

"Don't hurt me, please. Ken Boda, he took a fresh horse and a pack mount to go south." Sweat and tears of fear drained over his eyelids and both nostrils.

"South where? How much food did you pack for him?"

"I packed enough food for him and the horses for four days. Boda said Mexico."

Cotter released his hold on Rhumy and drew both Colts. "Where on the border does he plan to cross into Mexico? Tell me now or take your thoughts to the grave."

Rhumy's bladder released. "I don't know. He's from a gang near Laredo but I don't know. He didn't say."

Cotter picked up Boda's trail 8-hours later at a small town a hundred miles from the border. *Boda had stayed there overnight. Good. He doesn't think he's being followed or he would have kept going. He didn't change his horse either.* Cotter watered and fed his palomino regularly with appropriate rests. He gave himself and the horse only five-hours of sleep and covered three more towns the next day. The sheriff of the last town wasn't informative until Cotter showed him Boda's wanted poster. The lawman told him Boda was talking about staying in Laredo for a few days. *So Rhumy was right.*

The sun was going down in Laredo when Cotter arrived. He and his palomino had ridden for over two-days. Cotter checked in with the town sheriff.

"I'm looking for this man–Ken Boda."

"You're a bounty hunter not a lawman." The sheriff was a robust thirty-year-old man exuding confidence.

"You take him and the reward is yours." Cotter touched the poster with his gloved hand.

"Boda has a reputation that exceeds my abilities." The sheriff looked at the poster again.

"All you have to do is get a deputy and grab him."

"It's not the way the law works. My jurisdiction is in Laredo. Boda has done nothing in this town that warrants my confronting him. He's yours. He hangs out at the La Penta Cantina and has a room upstairs."

Cotter rode to a livery but didn't like the quarters for his horse. He was directed to the small mission a quarter mile from the La Penta. The mission was in need of repairs with the stone and brickwork exposed from fallen segments of beige stucco. Cotter gave his horse to the attendant.

"Perhaps you would like a word with God?"

Cotter smiled at the monastery's friar. "Yes, I think you're right. It might be my last contact and maybe He'll listen." Cotter went into the Spartan church sanctuary and removed his hat as he sat on an unvarnished pew.

*Your will not mine. Let my arms be your guide this night.* Cotter felt unburdened as he offered his two-sentence prayer even though no thoughts of redemption came to mind. He walked the short walk to the La Penta Cantina.

The cantina was small by Endura saloon standards. The air was humid and reeked of wine, beer and sweat. A guitar player strummed a low lament and hummed mournful sounds. Cotter stopped just inside the two full-length swinging louvered doors.

A few patrons at the rustic uncovered tables stared at him. When the guitar player stopped abruptly, the evening bar crowd glared at the musician and then followed his stare to Cotter. Cotter walked forward a few steps. The chandeliers were two large suspended wagon wheels with oil lanterns on their circumferences. He moved to have the flickering lights reflect off the conchos. Cotter's bandana was down and he had pulled his hat low to shade his face. He saw Boda at the bar.

Boda turned to face the direction of the cantina men who began to move away from Cotter's line of sight to the bar. He dropped his wine glass spilling the dark claret and sending the glass to roll and clink next to another empty glass.

"You." Boda's eyes widened. "What do you want?"

Cotter reached into his buckskin bib blouse and pulled out the poster. "There's a thousand-dollar reward for you dead or alive for murder in Endura Texas."

"You can't touch me down here." Boda moved a foot away from the bar facing Cotter.

"You're also wanted for crimes committed in Nashville during the war." Cotter pushed up his hat slightly to reveal his face.

"Dr. Cotter. Hah. I saw four men in Endura dressed like the Vigilante and you weren't one of them. You think you can fool me?" Boda's right hand touched the outside of his silver-studded holster.

"You killed my father and some other doctors during the war—in cold blood. They didn't even have weapons."

Chairs moved and people began running from the cantina. The guitar player moved along the wall until he could join the exodus. A few remained and one man seated at a table to Boda's right had his hand on his holstered gun. The barman stared at Cotter.

"Bartender, put your hands on top of the bar now." Cotter didn't take his gaze from Boda.

"You think the clothes you're wearing make you good enough to take me down, Cotter? I'll drop you like I dropped those Yankee doctors." Boda wiped his moist lips with the back of his hand.

"I wore the same clothes at the stagecoach when I first came to Texas. I talked to the sheriff. He'll jail you if I take you in alive." Cotter moved his hands to the sides of his Colts. The right hand Colt gleamed with the reflected light. He turned slightly to his left.

Boda began to sweat. He wiped both hands across his black shirt front and dropped them to his side again. "Okay, then, make your play."

"You first. I don't want to take advantage of someone who's been drinking."

"Hah. I can take you drunk or sober." Boda went for his pistol. His draw was quick and he fired a fraction of a second after Cotter.

Cotter's two Colt's boomed. One .45 bullet passed into Boda's chest and the dull finish Colt caught the man at the table in the right shoulder as the man attempted to draw his gun. Boda fell forward. Cotter panned the cantina with both guns drawn. There were no more apparent enemies but he couldn't take any chances. Boda's bullet had whizzed by his right ear. It had been close.

"The rest of you take your guns and place them on the floor." There was a moment's hesitation followed by a new voice.

"You heard him." The sheriff's words brought action. Five guns were dropped to the floor. "Now get out–all of you."

Cotter looked back at the sheriff. He and a deputy had guns drawn. The cantina emptied. "Thanks for your help."

"We got here just as he drew down on you. We came when the music stopped." The sheriff bent down to Boda's body. "He'll not be needin' my jail. How do you want to handle the reward?"

"I'm sending half to the monastery. They need it."

"And the other five hundred dollars?"

"The rest goes to this town. The livery services are a shambles."

•

Cotter sent a telegram to Pignast to inform his friends of Boda's death and his survival. He arrived back at the Garrison's four-days later.

"Good to have you back Dr. Cotter." Logan Pipps took the palomino's reins.

"I need a bath. Can you heat up some water?" Cotter patted his duster producing a cloud of amber dirt.

Deirdre Garrison waited until Cotter presented himself in his fresh clothes. "What do you want me to do with those?" She pointed to the bundled buckskins.

"They need to be cleaned and put away–for a long time, I hope."

"Where are you going now? The clinic's closing for the day."

"Are the children done with their schoolwork?" Cotter didn't realize how much he wanted to see them again.

"Yes, they're dying to see you. I told them you came back but had to get cleaned up. Sadie should be on the way to pick them up."

Cotter went quietly into the room where Josh and Mary did their schoolwork. Josh was drawing on a chalk board and Mary seemed to be criticizing him.

"What are you two fighting about now?" His baritone stopped their antics.

"Jake." They both shouted and ran to him.

Rand's wagon pulled up and she came inside to gather the children. Josh and Mary appeared and said hello to their mother.

"Why are you two so quiet?" Rand turned to Deirdre. "Have they been bad?

"No. They have a surprise for you." Deirdre smiled.

"A surprise? What could you possibly have to surprise me with?" She stared at the devilish gleam in their eyes.

The children disappeared into their study and playroom and pushed Cotter to the doorway. "Surprise." They shouted.

"Jake. Oh my God." Rand ran into his arms. Tears gushed as she hugged and kissed him.

"Wow. I should go away more often." Cotter cradled her tearful face in his hands.

"No, never. I never want you to go away again."

# Chapter 54

## May 2006

"Are you and your family enjoying alumnae weekend, Dr. Cotter?" The librarian read his name from his identity tag. Cotter's son was one of the graduates of the Class of 2006.

"Yes, we love the Yale campus and I love to come to the library." Dr. Joshua Cotter, his wife, son, daughter-in-law and new grandson walked to the lobby halls with the large oil portraits of honored past Yale physicians.

"Dad, there's Edward Cotter. He was one of Yale's most famous surgeons. I looked up his biography as part of my address to my graduating class. He was killed in the Civil War–at Nashville."

"It seems we always had a Cotter as a battlefield doctor, Jake. Most of our lineage trained at Yale but came back to Texas." The elder Joshua looked accusingly at his son.

"I'm still undecided, dad. My internship and residency is in Boston but Nora and I are keeping an open mind. I have a list of places that'll need cardiac surgeons in six-years. There are two places in Texas, but let's wait and see. Six-years is a long way off."

"World War I and II, Korea, Vietnam and Desert Storm all had a Cotter physician." Joshua Cotter stopped at another old portrait.

"Yeah, dad, you did your stint in Desert Storm. I put all the Cotters in my speech. I hope there aren't any more wars when I'm ready for practice." Jacob Cotter looked at the nameplate on the portrait.

"Jake, look, this one has your namesake." Jacob's wife read the nameplate. "In memory of Dr. Jacob Cotter, who brought the best of Yale's teachings to Endura, Texas."

"I bet old Jacob Cotter would have been happy about this, although Endura Medical Center has a huge bronze statue of him on a horse at the main hospital green," Joshua said.

"It's an unusual portrait, Josh. See, he's holding a stethoscope in his right hand and there is a holster with two guns draped over the chair on his left." Jacob's wife continued.

"When I was doing my research for my speech, I tried to find out the story behind the guns but I drew a blank." Jacob Cotter looked up at the large oil painting of his ancestor.

"Well what's the story about this necklace?" Jacob's wife addressed her mother-in-law, Marion Cotter. She touched Marion's necklace. It was a string of shiny, silver, oval conchos.

"I do know about the history of the concho necklace. Jacob's wife Sadie had it made when her husband died. She asked that it be passed on to the succeeding generation of Cotter wives. When I die, the necklace goes to you, Nora."

"It's beautiful. So what's the story?" Nora stared at the necklace.

"As Josh's father and mother told it to me, these conchos were once a part of a famous gunfighter's outfit during the time of the first Jacob Cotter's practice in Endura." Marion paused.

"Gunfighter–a bad guy?" Jacob and Nora's seven-year old son perked up.

"No, Stanley, he was a good guy," Marion continued. "He was a sort of Zorro character but without a sword. In Endura's archives you can read about it. There was a man who wore a buckskin outfit who appeared whenever some evil doer needed to be put down."

"What about the Texas Rangers?" Young Stanley asked.

"I guess he helped out until they got there. Anyway, these conchos were used like buttons on his clothes and when he died old Grandma Sadie had the necklace made."

"So it's kind of symbolic of triumph over hard times." Jacob looked at his son.

"That's a nice story but what about the guns in the portrait?" Nora persisted.

"No one knows. Maybe they're symbols of the hard life but I have another option." Joshua Cotter looked at his expectant family. "I think the stethoscope represents the power of healing and guns stand for enforcement of good over evil."

"Zorro, wow." Stanley stared in awe at Cotter's portrait. "Did he use those guns himself, daddy."

"I don't know. I don't think so. He was a doctor, after all."

## Author's Note

When I started to write Cotter, my family asked why I chose a western theme. My answer came easier than the fifth generation Jacob Cotter's explanation for the guns in Cotter's portrait.

After a facilitation meeting with a group of patients at a Connecticut drug and alcohol treatment center, I was called to the television room by a middle-aged housewife who was one of the patients recovering from alcohol addiction. I remember her words as she pointed to the TV.

"Dr. Glassman, see the man in the stagecoach drinking the booze?"

"Yes. What of it?"

"He's an alcoholic."

"So aren't you and some of the others here." I didn't know where this was going.

"Well, he's a doctor. Why do all the western movies portray doctors who went out west as alcoholics? Is that how doctors with alcoholism were treated back then?"

"No, of course not. Many of the doctors who trained here at Yale and Boston set up their practice in the developing west at great self-sacrifice. They brought modern medicine to settlers who otherwise would have had poor quality medical care."

"Well, why doesn't someone write about them, instead of having everyone think of early western doctors as drunks?"

And so I did.

Peter Glassman MD, San Antonio, Texas March 2013

**Novels by Peter Glassman**:

**THE HAPPY HAT**- A deadly U.S. cartel imports heroin from Vietnam in the plaster casts of orthopedic patients. http:// www.amazon.com/Happy-Hat-Peter-Glassman/dp/150875621X/ ref=sr_1_2?ie=UTF8&qid=1427416904&sr=8-2&keywords=peter+glassman

**MY NAME IS KEVIN**–Kevin kills a member of an alcoholic recovery group and becomes involved in a Middle East attack on the US banking industry. http://www.amazon.com/MY-NAME-KEVIN-Peter-Glassman-ebook/dp/B00IN8J0F2/ ref=sr_1_1?ie=UTF8&qid=1394300665&sr=8-1&keywords=my+name+is+kevin

**THE DRUID STONE**–The power of Stonehenge reaches 2013 to combat the last earthly holocaust. Can anyone survive? http://www.amazon.com/THE-DRUID-STONE-Peter-Glassman-ebook/dp/B00FWYY0R8/ref=sr_1_4?s=digital-text&ie=UTF8&qid=1381944451&sr=1-4&keywords=peter+glassman

**WHO WILL WEEP FOR ME**–A group of college students and a mob-connected friend maintain their bond from high school when one is murdered by the Boston Strangler. http:// www.amazon.com/WHO-WILL-WEEP-ME-ebook/dp/B00DC8GNWG/ref=sr_1_10?s=books&ie=UTF8&qid=1371049827&sr=1-10&keywords=peter+glassman

**THE ADJUSTMENT CLINIC**–A murderous vigilante organization, the FDA and the DEA are after corrupt evil drug company staff who place profits above patients' lives. http:// www.amazon.com/THE-ADJUSTMENT-CLINIC-ebook/dp/

B 0 0 C A 5 K F I U / r e f = s r _ 1 _ 2 1 ? ie=UTF8&qid=1366129075&sr=8-21&keywords=peter+glass-man

**THE HELIOS RAIN**–An American soldier returns from Afghanistan to San Antonio with unusual powers. http://www.a-mazon.com/THE-HELIOS-RAIN-ebook/dp/B007X4L2QW/ref=sr_1_7?ie=UTF8&qid=1361911732&sr=8-7&keywords=pe-ter+glassman

**COTTER**–Historical novel of a dedicated doctor bring-ing modern medicine to 1870s Texas from Yale Medical Center. http://www.amazon.com/COTTER-ebook/dp/B00A3MHLU2/ref=sr_1_1?ie=UTF8&qid=1361911732&sr=8-1&keywords=pe-ter+glassman

**THE MYOSIN FACTOR**–The treatment for Muscular Dystrophy could enhance the powers of an Army. http://www.a-mazon.com/THE-MYOSIN-FACTOR-ebook/dp/B00AVA5720/ref=sr_1_5?ie=UTF8&qid=1361911732&sr=8-5&keywords=pe-ter+glassman

**THE DUTY CREW**–The last Christmas of the Vietnam War in Queens Naval Hospital http://www.amazon.com/THE-DUTY-CREW-ebook/dp/B0092QUNCI/ref=sr_1_10?s=books&ie=UTF8&qid=1365525577&sr=1-10&keywords=pe-ter+glassman

**THE EYEMAN**–A marine can't turn off the Vietnam War and targets Asians for 15 years after the war ends. http://www.amazon.com/THE-EYEMAN-ebook/dp/B0096UVRJI/ref=sr_1_2?ie=UTF8&qid=1361911732&sr=8-2&keywords=pe-ter+glassman

**Facebook**: http://www.facebook.com/pages/Peter-Glass-man/327031907361357

**Website**: http://sbpra.com/peterglassman/
Peter Glassman San Antonio, Texas. February 2015